Alysaun cried.
"'Tis little enough I own."

"You have me, dear wife, and with nothing else, are rich. If you can find any solace in a title, you are now the lady of the Count de Chevercé, a title older than any in England." Brand knew a moment's pleasure in the surprised widening of Alysaun's eyes. "I remember another time you most willingly offered yourself to me. Then, I knew only your name, no more." His fingers curled over the edge of the sheet that covered her. "Now," he said, tugging at the linen, "I have a mind to see what treasures were purchased by granting you my name."

"Please, Brand, don't or you will have me hating you! We must part. We both agreed. Please do nothing that will make the annulment impossible."

Brand pulled, and as the sheet came free and flew back, his glance swept from the enchantment of gently rounded breasts to the shock of Alysaun's expression. He had meant to tease her, to make her aware of how she'd played into his hands because of that one, simple lie she'd told; but when he gazed at her slender trembling body, desire flared deep within him, banishing all other thoughts.

Books by
Donna Comeaux Zide

Above the Wind and Fire
Caress and Conquer
Lost Splendor
Savage In Silk

Published by
WARNER BOOKS

Above the Wind and Fire

Donna Comeaux Zide

WARNER BOOKS

A Warner Communications Company

This book is dedicated, with love, to
Wendy and Alan

WARNER BOOKS EDITION

Copyright © 1983 by Donna Comeaux Zide
All rights reserved.

Warner Books, Inc.,
666 Fifth Avenue,
New York, N.Y. 10103

 A Warner Communications Company

Printed in the United States of America

First Warner Printing: July, 1983

10 9 8 7 6 5 4 3 2 1

Above the Wind and Fire

PROLOGUE

Hanley Manor, Gloucestershire
February 1068

To the privacy and solitude of a greenwood bower perched on a hill overlooking the honor of Hanley, to this sheltered set of willows that had been her secret retreat since childhood, Alysaun Meau had slipped away for a moment's relief from her duties. In the vale that stretched below, her father's land as far as she could see in any direction, Hanley spread in a neat, orderly group of timbered buildings, its imposing two-storied manor house overshadowed to-day by the elegance of their new chapel.

She felt a bit guilty at leaving her mother the full responsibilities of playing hostess to so great a gathering, but she longed for a few minutes' relief from the pressing throng of well-wishers and guests who had come from as far as London and Worcester to join the family for the chapel dedication. No one would miss her presence for so short a time, and she would return refreshed, better able to aid her lady mother through the activities and entertainments that would last well into the night.

The pavilion Lord Brihtric had erected to shelter his guests stretched more than half a mile across the green fronting his manor. Its red silk awning, hemmed in cloth of gold, had cost a fortune; but since the advent of the Bastard, there were few occasions for Saxon celebration, and Hanley's lord had meant this day to be remembered as a fine and enjoyable event.

Gazing down upon the milling crowds, Alysaun took note of the air of forced gaiety, the almost nervous revelry. The sigh that whispered past her lips was for herself as much as for the celebrants and for times now lost—those days when merriment was unshadowed by the gloom of a conquered England. Some of those passing amongst the heavily laden trestle tables must even be bitter at the show of bounty, for they had lost all to the encroaching greed of the foreign sovereign known to all Englishmen by the derisive title *Mamzer*, Bastard.

In these lean days Englishmen were outcasts in their native land, and those who still retained their holdings lived in daily apprehension about their own uncertain lot. The Mamzer's army of ravenous wolves had done more than rape England's women and pillage its wealth; they had ravaged the peaceful land, murdering for no more cause than a resentful look, treading upon the pride of its menfolk, leaving them dispossessed, remnants of a race settled far before William's ancestor, the Viking Rollo, was a thought in the scheme of God's creation.

It was wrong to dwell upon such melancholy thoughts. Alysaun's father warned against such pessimism, but Brihtric Meau was a trusting man, a kind and just soul who had consigned his fate to God's grace. Another sigh escaped her, and Alysaun leaned back against a willow trunk, long-lashed eyelids closing to shutter irises that rivaled the color of the clear, sun-bright heavens.

Although the snowfall that had brightened the festivities of Christmastide had vanished with the week's warm, west winds, the air was still chilly enough to frost the breath, and Alysaun drew her fur-lined mantle closer. It would be months before the coming of spring would touch the trees with buds and green the land; still, in this brief respite from hoarfrost and the onslaught of heavy snows, it did seem that God's blessing had been laid upon the day of celebration.

As the sound of laughter and soft music drifted up the hillside, Alysaun's delicate mouth curved into a smile. In addition to the entertainment and feasting, the success of her father's fete was enhanced by the Mamzer's recent departure from the town of Gloucester. It had been the custom of the Confessor to hold a great meeting of worthies at the palace of Kingsholm, north of the city, so William had followed suit and celebrated the feast of Christmas there. His presence darkened the joy of Christ's birthday; the feeding and quartering of his army of chevaliers, attendants and serving people strained winter-depleted food storage as well as the sensitive temperament of the populace. Now that he and his scavengers were gone from Gloucestershire, everyone could breathe more easily.

Eyes shuttered, expression bemused and dreamy, Alysaun was unaware that her solitude was broken by a young man who lounged against a tree some three or four yards from her hidden bower. Kyrre Magnusson had watched her leave the gathering and, curious over her destination, had followed her confident climb through thicket and dense, winter-dry bracken to the stand of willows. Their long, weeping branches, denuded by autumnal frost, surrounded the girl, half shadowing her oval face with a lacework play of sun and shade.

Pleased to observe her without calling attention to himself, the tall, broad-shouldered Saxon crossed his arms over his chest and relaxed. His gray eyes warmed with a hint of desire as they surveyed her face and figure. His father's lands adjoined those of Lord Brihtric and for over a year now, Kyrre's interest in Lady Alysaun had been growing. He had exchanged visits and hunted with the girl's sire, always hoping to catch a glimpse of Alysaun herself.

If at the beginning of that year he had thought her a pretty child, he judged her now ten times as lovely. Her golden tresses were hidden by veil and wimple but for a tantalizing sweep of heavy, silken braids that hung like burnished ropes to the swell of her breasts. Kyrre envisioned her hair free of the jeweled clasps that secured it, free to tumble in gossamer waves around ivory shoulders and caress the high, proud breasts that had flowered from last year's buds. An uneasy stir of lust tugged at his groin, an impatience he restrained with difficulty.

Weeks past, his father, Einar, had noted the ardent glances his son cast upon the maiden, and, with a mind to melding the boundries of Hanley and his own manor of Meltonsham, approached Brihtric with an offer to secure his daughter's hand. At first the lord of Hanley was reluctant, unwilling to engage his favorite child in a loveless match, but Einar's assertion that a consolidation of neighboring lands would ensure Alysaun's future security and her inheritance made too much sense for him to refuse outright.

With their invitation to today's dedication ceremony and festivities, Brihtric had sent a bluntly worded message to the effect that if a just settlement could be agreed upon, he would bestow his daughter's hand in marriage on Sir Kyrre. That was the first Kyrre had heard of any negotiations; as yet, Alysaun's father had not spoken of it to her.

Kyrre found it difficult to believe. The marriage was certainly advantageous to his father, and ultimately to himself, but that mattered little in comparison to the acquisition of Alysaun for his bride. Confident in battle, bold and sure in the company of other young women of his rank, he was made awkward and stumble-tongued at one look from the only girl he truly wanted.

Alysaun was a just-emerging butterfly, an exquisite creation barely aware of her power to dazzle and charm, a girl so sheltered by a doting father that she had had only the small world of Hanley in which to test her wings. Kyrre continued to study her, brooding on the possibility that she would resent the match that bound her to one man before she had been given the chance to choose someone for herself.

Suddenly he was stiff with anger, silently cursing the timidity he felt. His family ranked with Alysaun's and their holdings were nearly as large; he had no reason to be ashamed of his personal honor or of a rugged visage that had made more than a few female hearts flutter. His diffidence was unbecoming in a man who had bravely fought the invading Normans and established his valor on the field of combat. Lady Alysaun was beautiful and gently bred, an untouched gem of Saxon maidenhood, but not a goddess to be worshiped. She was flesh and blood, no matter how perfectly sculpted by the Creator; and if she cared little for him on their wedding day, he would in time earn her affection, the more to make his possession of her complete.

A warbling nightingale drew Alysaun from her daydreams, stirring her to open her eyes and search the surrounding trees for the winged creature whose song had interrupted her brief reverie. Expecting to glimpse a flutter of dark wings, Alysaun spied instead a two-legged animal whose fair-skinned features reddened with a flush of embarrassment before he ducked beneath a low-hanging oak branch and stepped forward.

"You followed me," Alysaun declared angrily. "Why?" Unsettled, Kyrre could hardly deny the truth. The twisting maze of path that led to this hidden spot was too mired in bracken for him to have happened here by accident.

"I . . . I found your departure curious," he stuttered in defense, then frowned at the nervous timbre of his voice. If he allowed the girl her head now, how he would suffer her tongue-lashings once they were man and wife. "My regard for your father's honor caused me to follow you, m'lady," he insisted righteously, voice strengthening now with the conviction that he would win out in any battle of words. "Have you no more care for Lord Brihtric's reputation than to traipse away without a companion? I know you innocently sought to find a moment's respite from the gathering, but how many saw you slip away and judged you guilty of trysting with a lover?"

Angry at first over the intrusion upon her privacy, Alysaun was now afire, indignation coloring her high cheekbones crimson. "Until you chose to act the watchdog, sir, I doubt a single soul took note of my flight." Alysaun didn't care for Sir Kyrre's tone, his manner, or the impertinent suggestion that she had somehow besmirched her father's good name. "Now by your presence here it is you who have ruined me," she went on in a scathing tone of rebuke. "I'm sure by

13

now the wags have me deflowered and breeding. By the robe of the Blessed Virgin, Kyrre Magnusson, what possessed you to follow me?''

Even in anger, Kyrre thought, she is a sight to make angels blush. ''In truth, m'lady, I desired to know who . . . or what had made you leave attendance on your father's guests. I've my reasons, Alysaun.'' Kyrre was hesitant to speak of his offer of marriage, fearing she would fling the proposal in his face and destroy an already shaky confidence.

''You came after me not out of concern for my father's honor,'' she asserted. ''Tell me why, honestly. I must have some explanation to give my parents for your company in so secluded a spot.''

''Your father will believe we met in innocence, I swear.'' He approached her hesitantly—the short walk across the faded winter-brown grass requiring more courage than a charge against the enemy. A few steps in front of her he paused, sensing her wariness. ''Even as we speak, our fathers meet in counsel, discussing the terms of our betrothal and marriage. So you can see that even if rumors fly, the speaking of our holy vows will still them.''

The color drained from Alysaun's face and she pressed for support against the sturdy tree trunk at her back. ''You *lie*, sir,'' she declared, yet her voice revealed her awakening doubt, for Kyrre had no reason to lie. Could it be true? Would her father have allowed such a serious proposal to reach this stage without telling her, without asking her feelings? ''I have in all ways been courteous to you, Sir Kyrre,'' Alysaun added in a bewildered tone that shook the young knight. ''I cannot think . . . why you, who seemed so kind of heart, would utter such a falsehood. Say only that you jested and I'll forgive you the fancy of such thoughts.''

Kyrre stared at her, somewhat bewildered himself, stunned that she would consider his offer for her a mockery. ''If I say I jested with a matter so dear to my heart, m'lady Alysaun, that admission would be a lie. Your father feels''—Kyrre straightened his shoulders, pride stiffening his back—''in his great love for you, Lord Brihtric has done me the honor of accepting my offer to take you to wife.

14

Your welfare is to be entrusted to my keeping, a privilege I will defend until breath departs my body." Kyrre dropped down on one knee, seized her hand with chilled, clammy fingers, and bowed his head to press a kiss on her captive hand. When he raised his head, the beseeching sincerity of his features stilled the giggle rising in Alysaun's throat and transformed it into a choked whimper. Truly, this was more than she could bear—to have this tall, usually dignified warrior kneeling so humbly before her. Embarrassed, she pleaded with him to rise.

Kyrre obeyed but his eyes never left her face as he brushed away the soil from the hem of his tunic. If not overjoyed by the news, the lady at least had lost the furious look of outrage that had hardened her blue eyes into chips of ice. "You *do* believe me, then?"

"I believe you've made an offer for me," Alysaun sighed, glancing down at the knot of her tightly clenched fingers. "What I find impossible to believe is that my father has decided my future without confiding a hint of his intentions."

Alysaun glanced up at Kyrre, for the first time viewing him as a prospective husband. If not handsome, his features were a landscape of strength, all rises and valleys, from the jutting, eagle's beak of a nose to the lean hollows that emphasized the prominence of his cheekbones and the deep clefts that framed his full lips. He was not what she had dreamed of, but, then, few women were allowed to choose their spouses. She closed her eyes for a second, resentful of and hurt by her father's insensitivity to her feelings.

"We shouldn't tarry here any longer," Kyrre said, and Alysaun, startled by the presumption of command in his voice, looked up at him first with rebellion, then with resignation. "If you are to be my wife, m'lady, I'll not add to any gossip about your good name."

Alysaun felt suddenly very alone and vulnerable. "It matters not how long I am away, sir . . . the damage is done. And I have not said I would be your wife. *You* say so and my father and yours, but 'tis my life, and I'll wed no one unless I choose."

It hadn't occurred to Kyrre that she might refuse to obey her father. Such independence of mind was unseemly for a girl. She owed her father more respect than to flout his wishes. "I . . . I think the matter is out of your hands, Alysaun," he said, injured by what seemed a rejection of himself. "All maidens look upon their wedding day with apprehension. 'Tis only natural that you fear the unknown. I vow to you, upon my honor, that I will treat you gently. Love and affection follow—"

"Nay, not for *me*," Alysaun exclaimed, turning before he could see the bitter tears that had sprung to her eyes. "I do not even *know* you, Kyrre Magnusson . . . and I will *not* wed a stranger, a man who has barely spoken in passing." A tear slipped down her cheek, and she brushed at it before it betrayed her weakness. "If you planned this, if you profess some feeling for me, why am I so taken by surprise at your suit?"

He understood a little of her confusion and blamed himself for being such a laggard in the ways of courtship. How could he tell her that the sight of her had left him dull-witted and speechless, that he'd revered her from afar, too shy in her presence to speak the praise that stirred in his mind? "I have wanted you for over a year now, Alysaun," he said at last, his cheeks coloring with a ruddy flush even at that mild admission. "Each passing week enhanced your beauty until I could not look upon your comeliness and not be blinded, struck dumb by its brightness. Only when I feared you would be given to another did my desires find a voice."

Alysaun turned her head, surprised to hear him speak so eloquently. His large, calloused hands reached out to grasp her shoulders and for moments Alysaun allowed him to hold her, too fascinated by the flare of passion in his gaze to protest. His head lowered to kiss her, his hands releasing her to slide around her back and press her to him. With a languor born more of curiosity than desire, Alysaun lifted her head to meet his lips.

Emboldened by Alysaun's pliancy, Kyrre unleashed his long-checked passion and the tenderness of his first, tentative kiss was swept away, replaced by a powerful surge of need that crushed her mouth beneath his. In his delight at sampling what would soon be his, he ignored the sudden stiffening of her body, the tension in the muscles that strained to pull away.

Alysaun's mind, as chaste as her young body, recoiled in horror at the abrupt change in Kyrre's attitude. If this . . . domination by a man who praised her with so awed a tone was love, then she would never let a man love her. To sate his own lust, Kyrre had no thought of gentleness, no mind for her pitiful attempts to escape him. One hand cradled her head, the other banded her chest so tightly she could not breathe. His tongue darted out to probe at her mouth, and a shiver of revulsion rippled across her skin as he succeeded in thrusting past her bruised lips in an invasion that mingled his hot, panting breath with hers.

She struggled against him with the strength of a wild, panicked animal yet with as little effect as if she were a sparrow he had captured. The degrading assault on her senses brought a flood of tears cascading down her cheeks. The salt stung Kyrre's taste buds, bringing him back to reality, and he released her so suddenly she would have stumbled had he not thrust out a hand to steady her.

Alysaun glared at him for a minute before she struck at his hand and stepped back from him, one hand clutching the support of a tree behind her. Neither was aware of anything save what had passed between them. Kyrre couldn't take his eyes from her face, from the trembling mouth bruised by the pressure of his kisses, the soft lips crushed the color of wild spring roses, from the narrowed, wary eyes that condemned the roughness of his mauling. She said nothing; there was no need to voice her disgust. It met his own rising shame and choked off any attempt at an apology.

Kyrre turned away, defeated by his longing for her, and stared out across the valley below. What he saw banished all thought of the furious girl behind him. The flat expanse of the manor green was covered by a sea of mounted Normans, still in formation except for a small detachment that circled Lord Brihtric, his lady, and Wulfstan, bishop of Worcester, who had traveled so many miles to bless and hallow the new chapel.

Swallowing hard, he cast a glance over his shoulder, relieved to find Alysaun seated where he had originally found her, the delicate pouting of her mouth assuring him her thoughts were still upon the indignities of his kisses. 'Twas just as well that she did not see what was taking place on the manor green. Soon enough, she would know the pain.

He faced the green again, shoulders stiff with anger and compassion for Brihtric's family. Although he was too far away to hear the voices, Kyrre could discern the changing expressions on Lord Brihtric's face: disbelief, a brief thought of resistance, followed by a numbing resignation as his wide shoulders slumped in defeat. His wife clutched at him, weeping unashamedly, and the good bishop pounded the earth with his staff of office, arguing in useless defense. The Norman leader turned his back on the red-faced, gesticulating clergyman and signaled to his men to dismount.

Four of them—tall, faceless figures clad in stiff, glistening armor and mail—surrounded Alysaun's father, two of them seizing his arms, two wrenching Lady Edana away from her husband. Many of the guests had departed, fearing for their safety in the midst of a possible melee. Others, stunned by the abrupt incursion of enemy soldiers on private land, froze where they stood, helpless to do more than watch.

There must have been no warning, no chance for the armed retainers or knights present to repel the force of the Norman troop. Spotting his own father and younger sister among the crowd, Kyrre wondered that his father had made no move to interfere when Brihtric was seized. Even as he watched, Einar bent his grizzled head to whisper to Kyrre's sister. Her shrug and puzzled look seemed to enrage him, and, roughly seizing her by the forearm, he dragged the girl through the crowd, shoving others aside in his haste. A long, heartrending scream jerked Kyrre's gaze back to Edana. That poor, gentle lady, who had never uttered a harsh word or raised her sweet voice above a moderate tone, stared up at her husband, mounted now with his hands tied behind his back like a common criminal, her face a twisted mask of pain before all expression faded and she collapsed into the arms of the bishop.

Behind him, Alysaun had raised her head at the anguished echo of her mother's scream, recognizing only a feminine cry and puzzled by so strange a call in the midst of a celebration. She cocked her head, listening. No longer did the laughter and merriment of the crowd drift up to her bower; there was nothing but an unearthly silence, even more frightening than the scream. Recovered from her tussle with Kyrre, she stood and in a haughty tone announced that she was leaving.

When Kyrre did not respond, she moved forward and looked down into the valley. For a moment she paused in confusion, then she grasped the meaning of the scene before her. The company of hated chevaliers, their double-leopard pennon unfurled from its standard and rippling in the breeze, struck such absolute terror in her heart that all else was blotted out.

The sound of Kyrre's voice, full of pity and sympathy, urging her to turn away, murmuring that there was nothing anyone could do, sobered her dazed mind. With startling clarity, her narrowed view expanded to take in the limp form of her mother's body, cradled in the arms of Bishop Wulfstan. Alysaun's fine, arched brows furrowed in bewilderment. Mother never fainted; her nature was strong and calm. And if she had, where was her father? Why was it the bishop who held her? A thousand queries clamored in Alysaun's head, drowning out the reasoning that might have produced answers. She turned to look at Kyrre and found him moved to tears, swallowing hard to hide the unmanly show of emotion.

The question "Where is my father?" died upon her lips, and in its place an anguished, incredulous whimper tore from her throat as she located him at last. The proud and noble lord of Hanley, the generous and beloved lord of holdings in Devon, Cornwall, and Worcester, a man guilty only of loving peace and family, Brihtric Meau sat bound upon the saddle of a Norman horse, his head bowed. Alysaun turned to run down to the vale and her father, but Kyrre's strong hands seized her once more and pulled her back.

She struggled, sobbing in frustration, and the knight shook her, forced to shout to penetrate her hysteria. Finally she heard him, and her sobbing ebbed to silent weeping. She turned back to look once more and ceased even her weeping. Brihtric's shoulders had straightened in unvanquished pride, and his golden head turned to search among the crowd of people. He was looking for her, Alysaun knew, for one last glimpse of her. Every muscle in her body tensed, every fiber of her being, every nerve keened to will him to look for her on the hill. He knew of her haven; it was his strong hand grasping hers that had brought her here as a child, to a place of uncommon peace that was his secret in boyhood.

Alysaun saw his head rise, following the slope of hill to its crest. There was too much wood and bracken covering the peak for him to see her, but the slow smile that spread across his handsome face told Alysaun he knew she was there. The silent message of love was all too brief, cut off by the shouted commands of the Norman captain directing some thirty of his men to escort the prisoner away. Alysaun buried her head against the russet silk of Kyrre's tunic, hysterical again at the sight of her father being led away.

Kyrre gathered her in his arms, silently cursing the pain thrust upon a girl so tender and young. He doubted that she was aware it was he who comforted her, who held her close and drew his own mantle around her. He knew of many men whose estates had been seized, ancient holdings passed from father to son for tens of generations; but none of the men had been taken prisoner. This greed of William's, his manner of rewarding the loyalties of his vassals, was slowly eroding the fabric of Saxon existence, diminishing the race to nothing more than homeless wanderers, outcasts in their native land.

Suddenly Alysaun raised her head, glanced down into the vale, and pulled away from Kyrre. She had glimpsed her father again, caught sight of his hair glinting golden in the sunlight. His back and shoulders were so straight and proud, despite the awkward binding of his wrists, that he made his Norman captors seem his vassals. It was the last time she would see him, and deep within her, Alysaun admitted the finality of her loss.

The remaining body of troops, more than fifty well-armed knights and their commander, had stayed behind to secure the manor. Alysaun's mouth formed a bitter line. She wished her hatred could take some solid form—a plague, a pestilence, a flood of vengeance that would course down the hillside to drown the trespassing vermin and sweep the land clean of their foul bodies. But wishes were futile and little solace to a girl who had witnessed the seizing of the great, godlike hero of her childhood. Below her, all was suddenly in chaos, the guests and visitors from nearby Gloucester scurrying to their mounts, forming a great jumble of carts and jostling, nervous horses in a caravan of frightened people, clogging the stretch of road north to Gloucester. The extended family of Hanley's serving folk, many of whom had waited upon Alysaun's grandfather Alfgar in his day as lord, were herded together and forced to attend the Norman mounts while the commander sent groups of his men to seize control of the manor buildings.

Suddenly Alysaun remembered her mother. Dear God, in all her fear for her father's fate, she had forgotten her poor, defenseless dam. Alysaun bolted from Kyrre's side so suddenly that his instinctive grab for her arm missed. She ducked beneath the low branches that nearly hid the entrance to the bower and scrambled down the steep, twisting path with little heed of the scratching thistles that tore at her fine new gunna and tunic.

Less sure of the path but fearful for the girl's safety in her rash, resentful mood, Kyrre sped after her, cursing as a branch Alysaun had easily avoided whacked his forehead with a painful thud. He recovered, then followed one of the track's sharp curves, suddenly slipping on a bed of worn pebbles. He landed on his buttocks and scudded down the incline, jarring his pride as well as his rump.

At the bottom of the hill, Kyrre managed to catch up with Alysaun and close his hand around her forearm to swing her hard about. Alysaun, breathless from her run, stood panting for breath. "Let *go*. You've no right to stay me," she gasped, but Kyrre stubbornly tightened his grip, drawing her close to warn her to be cautious.

"By all we've seen, girl, the manor is lost to you," he whispered hoarsely. "I know . . . I can guess how you feel, but there's naught to be gained by insulting these curs to their faces—and much to be lost." Alysaun's mouth formed a stubborn line and she would not meet his eyes. In frustration Kyrre shook her, then reined his impatience and spoke more gently. "Alysaun . . . listen, I *beg* you. Keep a curb on your temper. If not for your own sake, then have a care for your poor mother." A Norman soldier passed by, eyeing them suspiciously before he went on toward the storehouse. "Has she not suffered enough this day? Saxon maids have been *raped* for daring to rebuke or criticize the foreigners. They think themselves your betters and take any excuse to debase our people. Would you make Lady Edana witness your violation—just to vent your bitterness in vain upon a Norman's ears?"

The sullen resistance drained from Alysaun's face, leaving in its place a frightened and vulnerable girl, thrust into sudden responsibility and trembling in its wake. "Then come with me, Kyrre," she begged, her azure eyes soft with an appeal he could not resist. "Come, take my hand in yours and be my caution, for I fear my hatred will spill over if I face them alone." Alysaun stepped closer, gesturing to the hill that rose behind them now. "There you swore you loved me. If 'tis true, then I ask that you prove it."

It was of no consequence to him that she was no longer an heiress whose wealth would increase his family's security. Kyrre knew only that he felt honored that Alysaun had turned to him in need. To answer with less than his entire being and heart would diminish his stature before this child-woman who needed his protection. He caught both her hands, raised them, and pressed a kiss upon the slender white fingers. "I've no purpose but to serve you, m'lady. If the Lord called me to his side, I'd not leave you." The grateful look she gave him swelled Kyrre's pride; he could scarce reason when all the world was blotted out by two gold-fringed eyes so full of trust.

Alysaun glanced nervously around. The soldiers were everywhere, ordering the remaining guests to depart, roughly herding them like a flock of sheep. She drew away from Kyrre, catching his hand to pull him along. "Oh, hurry, do, Kyrre—my mother, the poor lady, will need my care!"

22

They passed the pavilion, and at the sight of several knights gorging themselves on the delicacies prepared for the pleasure of her father's guests, Alysaun's anger renewed itself. They had already made themselves at home, these scavengers, these marauding war dogs, who owned no decency and who thought themselves so superior to honest Englishmen. If they had not come in such stealth, her father would have slain them all.

Edana was conscious when her daughter approached in Kyrre's company, but the dazed look she gave them held no recognition. She clung to the old bishop's hand like a confused child seeking paternal protection. When Alysaun knelt at her side and reached out to stroke her mother's pale brow, Edana cringed and huddled closer to Wulfstan. Her rejection struck Alysaun with the force of a physical blow. Expecting to offer comfort and receive it in kind for the sorrow of their shared loss, the fifteen-year-old girl found herself bereft of the solace of a mother's embrace.

Bishop Wulfstan sighed with world-weary sadness. His life had been a contentment, the satisfaction of guiding the spiritual needs of his people a source of pleasure, but God had made his earthly stay too long. These last few years had taxed his waning strength too greatly. What comfort could he offer a woman whose husband had been wrongfully imprisoned, who had in a matter of minutes lost not only her beloved spouse but the home in which she had raised her children? And young Alysaun, the last of those children to remain with her parents, how could he answer the puzzled shock in the great, wounded eyes she turned to him? Any attempt to soothe the misery she felt with a reminder of God's infinite wisdom and mercy would sound hollow.

"The shock, my child," he explained at last, still patting her mother's shoulders as if she and not Alysaun were the child. "Time will disperse the fog that mists the pain of knowledge. For now . . . if she could but rest awhile, watched over by her ladies. Sleep can be a great healer." Around and behind him, Edana's attendants sat on the chapel steps, a court of silent, weeping women too distraught to stir themselves without a directive.

Alysaun thought she understood her mother, but understanding made the utter loneliness she felt no less painful to bear. She raised her head, searching the puffed, tear-dampened faces for Lady Mora, the most sensible and trustworthy of her mother's women. As if Alysaun's silent appeal had touched her thoughts, Mora rose, the nod she gave the girl an assurance that she would see to Edana's care.

For minutes, Alysaun leaned against the solid strength of Kyrre's chest, eyes closed. The sound of her mother's voice, as petulant as a toddler's as she insisted she would go nowhere unless the bishop was allowed to accompany her, cut through her like a knife blade.

At the sound of Lord Einar's voice, strident with irritation, Kyrre tensed and Alysaun's eyes flew open. She peeked around her protector's shoulder and saw Kyrre's sister, Enid Magnusson, mounted on the white mare her father had bought her from Hanley's stock. The features that gave her brother's face a rugged strength stamped her own with a homeliness that made her awkward and shy. Her father stood nearby, feet planted stubbornly, holding the reins to his mount. His son's steed waited in the care of a groom.

There was a distant reserve in the bow he gave Alysaun, in sharp contrast to the warmth with which he had greeted her upon his arrival that morning. "You've my sympathies on the day's distress, Lady Alysaun," he said brusquely, the arch of his brow questioning his son's wisdom in appearing so openly supportive of the dispossessed girl. "Please offer my respects to your dear mother. You understand that I must take my family home to Meltonsham."

"I'll be staying, sire," Kyrre answered, and braved his father's fierce frown without regard for the consequences of his stand. "Lady Alysaun needs—"

"Pardon us, m'lady," Einar interrupted, seizing his son's arm and drawing him away from Alysaun's side. "I would have a moment's privacy to counsel with my son."

Kyrre reluctantly released Alysaun. Smiling to assure her he was determined to stay, he accompanied his father a few feet away. "My boy, you are too young yet to know the trouble you could cause us,"

Einar asserted in a low tone that nonetheless carried to the spot where Alysaun waited. "You were smitten by the girl's looks but *that* is finished now. Any association with this family is a courtesy we can ill afford. Do you wish the same fate to befall Meltonsham? Christ's eyes, lad, where have you been? Brihtric suffers not alone—the civil rights and charter of Gloucester have been stripped because of him."

Kyrre found it hard to comprehend such encompassing vengeance, but he single-mindedly pursued his desire to remain with Alysaun. "We *owe* the family our support, sire. The betrothal—"

"I signed nothing, thank God. 'Twas still under discussion. You are under no obligation, Kyrre, and I order you to mount and ride with your sister and me."

"Father, I have given my word to stand by the young lady. With all due respect for your wisdom, I'll not—"

Alysaun had heard every word of the exchange, and her face burned with humiliation at the knowledge that she was the subject of this contest of wills between father and son. "Please, Kyrre, your first loyalty lies with your father. For my sake, do as he bids you." The request was couched in so reasonable and calm a tone that both men gazed at her in surprise. In truth, Alysaun longed to raise her hand and scratch the mask of paternal concern from Lord Einar's face, to reveal the cowardice that prompted his flight from Hanley. Pride had dictated her speech and the same pride reined her tongue. If she loosed the bitterness within her, she feared her flood of screaming, blistering denunciations would make her seem as addled as her mother.

The leader of the Norman command approached, his interest aroused by the sight of a pretty girl who seemed to be in the midst of a heated argument. Einar Magnusson's attention was caught by the glint of afternoon sun bouncing off the chevalier's polished scabbard, and without another word he made for his steed and mounted. He tugged back so harshly on the reins that the large, dun stallion reared, pawing at the air with his wide, cobbled hooves, dangerously close to Alysaun.

Suddenly, from behind her, a strong man encircled the narrow span of her waist and swept her out of harm's way. Alysaun felt the hard mesh of chain mail bite against her back and wriggled indignantly to be free of a man who could only be Norman. The knight took his own good time releasing her, gently depositing her on her feet and supporting her elbow to assure her steadiness.

Although Alysaun had whirled to glare at him, William de Brieuse ignored her anger and faced Kyrre, whose sullen resentment reached out at him like a tangible force. De Brieuse removed his helmet, calmly tucked it beneath his left arm, and fixed the tall Saxon youth with a challenge of his own, his dark blue eyes never leaving the face that flushed a dull red.

"We are leaving, Kyrre," Einar's strident voice intruded. "Stay and you find yourself another home . . . continue with this whim of yours and I have no son." Einar was furious, both at his son's unusual willfulness and at the haughty disdain of a girl who no longer had a reason to be so proud.

When Kyrre hesitated, clearly torn between his promise to her and the threat his father had issued, Alysaun dismissed his wavering allegiance. "*Go*," she said simply, and though he opened his mouth to protest, she turned away.

Watching the young man's reaction, the shame that curled his large hands into tight fists, the dejected slump of his shoulders, the dragging stride that carried him to his waiting horse, de Brieuse almost felt a twinge of pity. A minute later the family rode past him, the son whipping his steed at a punishing pace, galloping away as though the Devil were at his heels.

Sir William pushed back his coif, grateful for the cool breeze that stirred his short-cropped, raven hair. The fact that he had found no pleasure in this duty of seizing Brihtric Meau's estate and arresting him did not diminish his efficiency nor impress the sullen-faced Saxons, who believed every Norman rose each day only to torment them. His gauntlets came off, slowly, as his attention was drawn back to the girl.

He couldn't remember having seen her earlier; but there had been so many in the crowd spread out across the green, and all his attention had been given over to his disagreeable task. Just who she was intrigued him. Even with a scratch across her fair cheek and the fine silk of her gunna torn in several places, she was an uncommonly lovely wench. Delicate features set in an alabaster oval, thick lashes framing . . . The girl glanced up, blushing as he studied her, and his guess that her eyes were a bright Saxon blue was confirmed. Clearly her manner, dress, and mien indicated quality. His deep bow in appreciation of her beauty seemed to offend her, and even as he straightened she was off, ignoring him as she gracefully swept toward the house.

"*Hold*, m'lady." William called out a command sharpened by the affront to his courtesy. She hesitated a second, then continued on. A curse, followed by an imperious demand that she halt, finally stopped her but she refused to acknowledge him, her features stubbornly set as she stared straight ahead.

His own obstinacy raised by hers, William purposely took his leisure, strolling over to her side and observing her profile for several minutes before he spoke. Up close she was even more breathtaking, with a complexion as finely textured as silk, the shining color of her plaited tresses hinting at the golden richness hidden by her veil. "Even if the gesture was not appreciated, m'lady, I've a mind to know the name of the girl I saved. Is there no place in the English tongue for a simple *merci*?"

Alysaun turned her head, gaze sweeping the length of this tall, overbearing Norman with icy contempt before she deigned to reply. He had spoken to her in only slightly accented English. Her answer was given in so flawless a French that his eyes widened in surprise. "I was never in danger . . . and so, owe you nothing. You trespass upon Saxon lands, rob and dispossess the rightful owner, send an innocent man to imprisonment, all without a care; but *you* are offended by *my* lack of appreciation?"

What she said was true enough. In his attraction to her, William had forgotten she was Saxon, he a Norman. He could not, of course,

27

expect her to be pleasant when he was cast in the position of oppressor. "Your point is well made, m'lady." Still, he did not know the identity of this staunch little defender of Brihtric Meau. Thinking that perhaps she was one of Edana Meau's attendants, William praised her defense. "Few men inspire such loyalty, *ma belle demoiselle*. Aside from the bishop, none of the English assembled here today, save you, have protested the man's innocence. I salute your—"

His aide, Stephen de Longueville, returned to assure Sir William that Hanley was secured. "Guards have been posted at the main entrance and the perimeters, m'lord," he stated in a respectful tone, his dark eyes staring past his commander at Alysaun. Though, to his knowledge, de Brieuse had been relatively faithful to his lovely wife, Judith, he seemed to have found a wench worthy of a brief infidelity.

Noting how the girl bristled beneath Stephen's rather lewd appraisal, de Brieuse frowned and curtly ordered him to see to the night's quartering for the troops. Alysaun, who had been unaware that he was the Norman commander, suddenly realized she had been conversing with the very man who had arrested her father. Guilt brought a stain of color to her cheeks; her fingers curled into fists as she quelled the urge to strike out at him.

"As I was saying," William began before he noticed the abrupt change in her manner. It was as if a wall had gone up between them and his frown returned, an irritation directed at de Longueville. The lad was of a good family and fought ably enough, but when it came to dealing with the vanquished race of the English, his contemptuously superior attitude was a hindrance to the King's desire to subdue and pacify the populace. "You were offended by my aide. I apologize for his demeanor. Stephen is yet a boy and he will—"

Alysaun lifted her chin, eyes narrowed in resentment. "He is no different from any other Norman, sir. Your entire race is an offense, a breed spawned by the Devil to degrade a peaceable, God-loving people. He is more honest than you, however, and does not hide his arrogance with courtesies and civil speech."

William's sun-weathered complexion darkened in anger, his patience tried too far by the brazen insults. "If I may warn you, child, 'twould be in your best interest to keep those sentiments to yourself. Reveal them to a man less temperate than I, and their utterance will bring you punishment."

Forgetting Kyrre's warning to be cautious, Alysaun laughed at the threat, a haughty, mocking sound that unleashed her companion's hold upon his temper. His fingers closed painfully around her arm, jerking her forward. She winced at the pressure of his hand, but the pain only heightened her defiance. "*Finally* you show your true colors, sir," she snapped. "Nothing you do can harm me. You have already taken all I love. My home is overrun by savages, my mother crazed by grief . . . and my father, at your command, is bound for prison. What more can you exact?"

William stared at her, stunned by the realization of who she was. He should have guessed, for the King's decree had mentioned a daughter still in residence. Her name . . . what was it? Alys . . . no, Alysaun. His dumbfounded gaze went from her indignant expression to the tight grip of his fingers and he released her, disturbed that he had handled her so violently. "I . . . didn't know," he said, stumbling over his words, at once angered by his awkwardness and sorry for the way he had treated her. "Where were you that I did not see you close to your mother's side?"

Nothing else he could have said would have cut through Alysaun more than the reminder that she had not been there to comfort her mother or kiss her father one last time. Guilt deflated her hauteur; with a lethargic gesture she indicated the hill rising to the south.

William's glance followed the sloping land to a peak crested with brush and trees, then returned to the guilt written on her face as he recalled the Saxon lad in her company. "You were with the boy."

Her head came up to refute the implication that she and Kyrre had met in a tryst, but she said nothing. What did it matter if this stranger thought she had been lying with a lover at the moment her father was seized? It would change nothing to defend her virtue. Father was still gone, the manor was forfeit to the crown, destined to be given to one of the Bastard's arrogant vassals. "Aside from the confiscation of the estate and my lord father's arrest, what else was in your orders?"

The question surprised William, then he remembered that she could not have heard Stephen read the decree of forfeiture. "Your father's lands in Cornwall, Devon, and Worcester," he answered reluctantly, "as well as the revocation of Gloucester's charter."

"And was there mention of how you should deal with his family and personal wealth?"

"Aye. Both you and your mother are to quit the honor immediately, leaving . . . leaving all behind as his majesty's property."

The news had no effect on Alysaun. After so many shocks one more made little difference. Later she would have time to reflect bitterly upon how overwhelming was the punishment dealt her father, but now exhaustion numbed her brain. Almost to herself, she softly mused, "So we are to have nothing?"

"Norman I may be, but I've family of my own, a daughter not much younger than you, in fact. My sympathies reach out but I have my orders . . ." His voice trailed off; there was nothing more he could say.

"Yes, of course . . . your orders." He owed his fealty and allegiance to the man who was her enemy. There was no reason he should disobey them for her, nor would she ask him to.

"You may stay the night and leave in the morning," William offered, "and I will see you safely escorted to Gloucester. Your father must have friends there."

Alysaun's expression was cynical for one so young. "Those who made a mad dash for the road were my father's friends," she said dryly. "And as for Gloucester, the judgment dealt the city in my father's name assures me that none will open a door in welcome to a member of his family. Nay, as soon as my mother is fit, we will leave."

"Where will you go?" He had no right to ask, but William somehow felt responsible for the girl.

"You are concerned?" The inquiry puzzled Alysaun. "'Tis odd

for an enemy to wonder over the fate of the defeated. Does it matter? I think not." She glanced past him, at the drapings of ivy and sacred mistletoe that decorated the stone balustrades of the chapel steps and framed its polished oaken doors. The sight reminded her of the joyous begining of this day, magnifying the grief of its ending. Alysaun's mouth tightened, holding in a rush of anguish. "We will go away from this home that is no longer a home. Even if it were permitted, I could not stay."

"I am heartily sorry, Alysaun Meau."

The smile she gave him was the antithesis of amusement. "*Are* you? So, too, am I . . . and my father, he is the sorriest of all." There was no answer to such a forlorn statement. For a long while Alysaun said nothing, for the first time thinking of what lay beyond her father's departure from Hanley. She had to know but it took all of her courage to ask. "Where have they taken him?"

William's gut knotted in tension. He wished that someone else had been given this duty. "To Winchester, m'lady."

"And what will they do to him?"

"Nothing. He is to be confined to a cell, allowed no visitor." This girl was taking the news calmly, too calmly. In her place, his wife, a stormy, emotional creature, would have by now wept and screamed out her frustrations, releasing her pain. Though he had no desire to handle a distraught, hysterical girl, some show of tears or fright would be more natural. "Why ask, only to increase your own grief?"

"So I may know what grace to ask of God," Alysaun replied solemnly. "My father is too noble of spirit to suffer the confinement of a caged animal. If there were a chance for him to be free, I would beg the Lord to see it done. If not, I will pray his end comes mercifully quick. For what has been taken from me with His knowledge, the Almighty owes me that much solace."

Lady Mora approached the two from the direction of the house, head bent as she grumbled to herself on the subject of Norman manners. "All over the house they were, poking into the pantry, proving the butler's stock of wines, sifting through the family's personal belongings, and grabbing at the womenfolk," she muttered.

"And that old fool even dared to pinch *my* bottom as I passed!" Some ten feet from the Lady Alysaun she stopped, and would move not an inch closer while *himself*, the Norman in charge of the louts thieving the house, stood near the girl.

Unnerved by the fatalism of Alysaun's views, William found the woman's stiff reserve a spark to the dry tinder of his mood. "Come forth, woman, if you've a message for the lady," he growled. "And if not, then cease your gawking and retire."

Mora's mouth rounded at the angry command; her small, close-set eyes narrowed over a short nose wrinkled in disgust. "Your lady mother is alert now, my sweet," she said, addressing Alysaun and ignoring the brute of a Norman cur. "She is calling for you, and *naturally*"—she shot a quick glance at Sir William and sniffed—"afraid for your safety."

"Go on ahead and inform the lady that her daughter is under the protection of Sir William de Brieuse. She will attend her mother shortly." Mora hesitated, looking to Alysaun to confirm the order. Alysaun nodded, just before a glowering William swore an oath at the woman's impertinence, sending her scurrying in a retreat that was almost comical.

"If she is well, you said, you'd be leaving immediately," he reminded Alysaun. "There's no harm in changing your mind, Lady Alysaun. A night's rest in your own bed will see you stronger for a journey."

"Nay, sir . . . for little rest would I find in a bed no longer mine. Better that we leave now than to tarry and make the departure all the more difficult to bear." Alysaun could not make a curtsy to him; all she could manage was a nod and a softly spoken, "By your leave, sire."

"Allow me to accompany you to the lady's chamber. My men may tease so pretty a maiden," William suggested, reluctant to let her go from his side.

"*Please . . . do not.* My mother is already aggrieved. To see me in your company . . . she would not understand." Alysaun turned away, walked a few steps, and glanced over her shoulder with a puzzled frown, adding, "I am not sure I do, myself." Much later when she and her mother had walked as far as they could before dusk and found a secluded spot off the road to build a fire, Alysaun had reason to regret her stubbornness in refusing de Brieuse's offer that they stay the night at Hanley. Her mother was exhausted, irritable without the comforts of her home, complaining that she knew nothing of making a fire out of doors, either for cooking or for warmth.

Neither did Alysaun, but, afraid that a fire was the only weapon to keep the forest predators at bay, she chose to try. Only a vague memory of seeing a servant light the hearth by rubbing dry wood together to produce a spark saved her from giving in to utter helplessness. The task was tedious and frustrating, but finally she had the pile of dry leaves and tinder smoldering. Hovering over that small start, protecting the spot with her hands as she blew the smoking leaves until a tiny flame caught hold—this was Alysaun's first lesson in survival. There would be many such lessons, but for now there was a certain joy in the small triumph.

Having seen the manor folk settled back into their usual work routine, and having dined with his men of rank, William de Brieuse now sat wearily slumped in a chair by the hearth. Brihtric Meau's chair fit him well; it was sturdily constructed of Norwegian fir, its high, carved backrest inlaid with gold burnished to a brilliance, the seat befitting a man of rank and importance.

William lifted the jewel-encrusted silver goblet, filled to the brim with the rich wine brought from Burgundy, saluting the man whose wealth had purchased such luxuries, honoring a man whose only crime was the keen intelligence that had garnered him these lands and others. Why King William had moved against Meau with such vindictive greed he didn't know—and didn't care to know. Such knowledge would surely sour him against the great lord he served, and William was already disenchanted with the King's policies.

Following a natural course, the Norman's thoughts turned to Brihtric's daughter. Her mother, whose gentle love had centered around her husband, he pitied less. Lady Edana had known the full measure of happiness, had spent her life in luxury, and had reared children who had gone to live their own lives. Although Alysaun's father was finished, he had had years of pleasurable memories, more than some who lived to a great age without love or company. It was Alysaun who left William troubled; and the more he drank, the more he brooded.

Alysaun was at the threshold of life, her beauty just beginning to unfold. A spirited, fine-bred woman who had been born to marry well and breed strong sons and fine daughters, she was now certainly doomed to live a hand-to-mouth existence as a wanderer vulnerable to anyone who had a mind to seize her.

Part of him mocked his idiocy at letting her go. Sober, he was a fair and an honorable man; wine made him less the cultured chevalier. He regretted having allowed her to leave. What lay beneath the silken drape of tunic and gunna could only have been more lovely than the show of slender hands and enchanting, innocent face. Aye, 'twas her innocence that gnawed at him. Without a man's protection she would lose the valuable prize of her honor, perhaps to some flea-bitten peasant who neither knew nor appreciated the gold-and-white purity he had defiled.

Down the hall someone was fussing with a viol, not really playing but toying with its strings. De Longueville, also filled with Meau's wine, was attempting to play a game of chess at a nearby table, but his sober opponent was easily winning. Childishly, the young man struck at the pieces, giving up the coin he had wagered rather than continue a losing battle.

Stephen approached his commander and, with obsequious concern, asked what had brought such a gloomy cast to William's features. A serving girl passing by gave the leering youth a wide berth, but he managed to seize her, and for a few humiliating moments she suffered the groping of Stephen's hands. Finally, with a laugh, he freed her, turning back to ask again why his leader seemed so glum. "Your family is due across the channel soon. D'you miss your lady so much, sire . . . or was it that gold-haired lovely who stirred your longing for the sweeter sex?''

More and more, William was finding de Longueville's youthful impudence an irritation. "She wasn't much older than my own Cecile," he said sternly. "As for my mood . . . you may find some humor in it, but *I* care not for turning defenseless women from their home.''

Stephen started to laugh, but a scowl from his commander silenced his amusement. "Pardon, sire, but how can you compare the two? Cecile is your daughter, a child yet. As for Alysaun Meau . . . I say you passed an easy chance to pluck what will fall to some English beggar.''

The thought echoed his own too much for comfort. He was twice the girl's age, old enough to be her father, too old to think of her in lust. "You are speaking of a lady, Stephen," he chided, and frowned into the fire. Outside, in the distant woods, an animal howled, a wolf, perhaps, and de Brieuse tensed, picturing the girl, alone but for her inadequate dam, somewhere out there with the predators that roamed the night.

"A lady, sire? Meaning no disrespect for your judgment, but the girl was, after all, only a Saxon.''

William's mouth twitched with irony. "Aye, a Saxon," he allowed, "but, nonetheless, a lady.''

PART I

East Anglia, Spring, 1068

1

Spring had come at last to green the sloping hills and gladed forests of East Anglia. In the peaceful, sweet solitude of an isolated meadow, the girl lay upon her back, basking in the sun's warm glow. She was grateful for the short respite from roads full of the hated Norman chevaliers and thronged as well by her own people, all solemn-faced and despairing.

Around her there was ample evidence that the land of England would survive this trial. The meadow pipit called its mate, and, banked by gold-green ivy and sweet grasses, the buds of meadowsweet unfurled their white velvet petals. Here, life went on unchanged, burgeoning with the same beauty it had known before the bastard duke had usurped England's rightful King, good Harold Godwineson of Wessex.

Alysaun closed her eyes against the too-bright sun, a despairing sigh escaping her parted lips. Of all the great earls, only Edwin and Morcar still lived. If they could not resist the ever-increasing domination of Norman rule, what could she do, a mere girl, orphaned and homeless? The hope that had come with spring was another of an angry God's jests, a false call to believe England might again be free of its oppressors.

Cadwyn would return soon; at least she had hope of that. In the months since Candlemas, her father's former smith had served as her protector and had never failed her yet. She had him to thank for the fact that she had not starved, that she still was clothed in the torn gunna and tunic that allowed her some measure of modesty. Alysaun sat up, her belly grumbling loudly for some sustenance. They had not eaten for a day, and before that only a crust of dried bread and some cheese begged at the house of a village thane.

The stream that rippled over mossy stones not ten feet from where she sat offered at least cool, clear water to fill the void. Wearily she rose and picked up the worn bag that contained all she owned, slipped its strap over her thin shoulder, and wandered down to the bank. Mantle discarded, she rinsed the dust from her hands, then cupped them and drank. Protesting that nothing solid followed the chilled liquid, her stomach gurgled loudly.

Alysaun sighed, a troubled, deep breath that caught high in her chest and doubled her over in a racking cough that had been with her for some six weeks now. The cycle that had begun with exposure to winter's harshest weather would grow worse if she did not eat soon. She would weaken, and the cough would strengthen, until she no longer had the stamina to continue her journey.

Dipping her hands into the stream once more, she drew them, wet and dripping, to the flushed heat of her cheeks and forehead. Where could Cadwyn be so long? It was at least an hour since he'd left her to forage what he could. Frightened that he might have fallen prey to some Norman sheriff or, worse, been killed in the act of stealing by some irate cotter, Alysaun pushed the thought away. She could not lose Cadwyn; her life now was so tied to his protection that his death would mean the same for her.

No, the burly smith could not be dead . . . or caught, only delayed because some fine catch had come his way. Perhaps he had happened on an animal snare and was bringing back a fine, fat hare or squirrel.

Of a sudden, there was a rustling in the brush, the sound of something heavy moving through the woods and hedges that hemmed the meadow. Alysaun paused, alert to danger, then whirled to dig within her bag for her only weapon, a dull-bladed dagger that provided only a semblance of defense. The noise stopped suddenly, then she exhaled the breath she had held as Cadwyn's familiar whistle sounded his return.

Relief flooded over her as the tall, broad-faced man lumbered into sight. Over his shoulder he carried a cloth bag, and the grin that nearly split his homely face in half assured her of his success.

"Good luck, I've had, m'lady," Cadwyn called, then nodded approval as he saw the knife grasped in her hand. "Anyone come by, did they?" She shook her head and carelessly tossed the weapon in her bag, expression eager at the thought of food. "'Tis a feast I have garnered for us this morn." He tossed the game bag over his shoulder and, as it landed next to her, added, "By the precious hem of Christ's robe, if we were not so starved, I'd portion it out and make the meat do for days."

Alysaun scarcely heard him. She seized the bag and pulled forth its contents, delight bringing a smile to her thin face. A fully skinned hare, and roasted no less, came into view, followed by nearly half a loaf of bread and two apples. With something akin to awe, Alysaun squeezed the bread. It was actually fresh enough to spring back and gave off such a heavenly aroma of yeast that she closed her eyes for a moment in disbelief.

Cadwyn was too hungry to exclaim over the unexpected bounty. He sank down on his knees beside her and began to tear off hunks of the rabbit meat. With a mouthful of food, he urged her to eat and quickly. "I know not whose lands these be, but I know we ain't welcome guests." As she reached almost timidly for a portion of bread, Cadwyn shifted his weight, turning so he could watch the woods from which he had emerged. The campsite from which he had stolen the meal was beyond the forest some two hundred yards, and in that glade lay the man who had so skillfully provided what they now ate. Anytime now, he would awaken, and the lump on his

41

noggin would no doubt add to his anger that his morning's repast had vanished.

Now that she knew some relief from the gnawing pains of hunger, Alysaun had a moment to reflect on how Cadwyn had come by a fully cooked hare, fresh bread, and fruit. "I was about to ask your source for this feast, Cadwyn, dear, but I think I'll restrain my curiosity." She smiled, wiping a smudge of grease from her mouth before attempting to down another portion of meat. "I hope you thanked our benefactor for his charity, though. 'Tis not often a man will share so kindly."

Cadwyn grunted, tearing another piece of bread for himself and one for his charge. Hard times these were, even for a man of humble origins, but for the lady, this hand-to-mouth existence they led— stealing, begging, and scuttling like some common dogs out of any path or pony track which saw a Norman's passing—was not the life she had been bred to expect. The just Lord Brihtric and his lady were gone now, passed beyond this misery their daughter now knew. Cadwyn was a practical man, his pity reserved for the living. And, as sweet and gently reared as Lady Alysaun had been she was more to be pitied for her present lack of rank and comfort. Perhaps some solace would be hers upon reaching the convent at Bury Saint Edmunds, where her sister was a nun.

He could only hope to God they made it there. Each passing day seemed more a trial. How could it not be when, in addition to the threatening Norman curs, so arrogant and armed to the teeth to back it up, Cadwyn had to fight his own kind for any scrap of food to keep them going? "Mayhap, we should save the apples for a later bite and leave now, before the owner of these lands chances to cross our path," he suggested, then relented at the look of keen disappointment that shadowed the girl's features.

"Well, take one and hide the other," Cadwyn allowed, rising with some difficulty after the unaccustomed repast. "Eat on it as we walk and if some'un should pass, stick it out of sight." He grinned and offered her a hand up. "We don't want t'be taken for well off, or poorer folk than us'll set upon us."

"I'll do as you say, Cadwyn," Alysaun answered his jest with a sad half smile, "but I warrant there's no one whose lot is poorer than ours." She bent, picking up her bag and slipping the spare apple between the folded blue silk gunna and gold-hemmed white tunic she had worn that last day at Hanley.

A kindly village wife had given her the clothes she now wore. Worn then but clean, now they hung about her like some garb a villein might use to adorn the stick figures that scare the crows from the planted fields. Indeed, she was now as wasted as a scarecrow; gone was the beauty that had made her father proud. Still, she kept the fine garments protected in the hope that she might make a presentable appearance at the convent.

Cadwyn started off with long strides that took Alysaun several steps to match. Pausing, she looked back longingly at the stream and called to him that she would be along after one last taste of cool water. From the shelter of a thicket some twenty yards away, a man watched her, eyes narrowed resentfully, concealing the simmering rage in irises of a changing hazel hue. The rust-brown curls at the back of his crown were matted with clots of blood the girl's thieving companion had drawn.

Brand de Reynaud took the measure of the lumbering oaf, waiting so patiently for . . . whom—his daughter . . . sister . . . wife? Whoever she was, she was about to lose the clod's company. Brand's belly growled as he noted remnants of his hard-won catch lying stripped of every scrap of meat near the stream.

Obviously the man had stolen to see the young girl fed. Had he *asked*, Brand might have been moved to share. It was the thievery, aye, and the throbbing bump upon his scalp he would not accept, even for the sake of this scrawny female in ragged dress. As she turned to join the man, Brand caught a glimpse of her face. She was not a relative of the thief; that much was apparent in the fineness of her features and the graceful, somehow haughty way she moved. Probably sired by some young lord out for a lark in one of his villein's crofts. It was common enough, even in Brand's native Provence.

43

The girl had caught up with her companion; staying well behind the cover of hedge and wood, Brand followed, hand poised comfortably on the hilt of his sheathed sword. He was outweighed some forty pounds, but this time *he* had the element of surprise and would see the giant begging pardon at the tip of his well-honed blade.

Just as he was about to declare himself and spring from cover, the muffled thud of horses' hooves sounded in the meadow, louder with each passing second. He froze, as did the couple. A minute more, and three men, unarmored but distinctively Norman with their close-shaven faces and clipped hair, galloped into sight, their chargers snorting and pawing the ground as they were reined in a circle about the two peasants. Brand waited cautiously to see what would happen.

Cadwyn pushed the girl behind him, silently cursing this new twist of fate. You could not reason with a Norman; only the Devil and another Norman could do that. He had gotten the girl and himself out of such fixes before by acting dull and servile. Alysaun knew the pretense and that it was her part to say nothing. Now Cadwyn hung his head and shuffled his feet, his gaze respectfully downcast. He could only hope this land did not belong to one of these three—the bones of the hare near the stream were evidence of poaching. The crime could bring an instant sentence of hanging.

"Well,. what have we here?" One man, older and more richly clad than his two companions, asked the sneering question. "More Saxon scum on my domain, poaching, no doubt, from my preserves. God save us, these stupid peasants know nothing but to steal." Another, a son, as the weak stamp of his sire's features on his own suggested, purposefully moved his mount closer, forcing Cadwyn to move quickly or be trod upon.

Alysaun's face burned. That these savages could move in unthwarted power in her country went against her sense of justice; that they chose two helpless souls already bereft of home and friends to taunt was a near sacrilege. In her childhood she had spent several summers at the estate of her Norman brother-in-law, Roger, near Lisieux. She understood the insults, sneeringly spoken in the *langue*

44

d'oil; and before caution stilled the impulse, Alysaun lashed out with a disclaimer.

"Nothing we ate was poached, only given us by a kind passerby. Crossing your lands, sire, is not poaching them."

The girl held her head high and so surprised them with her fluent grasp of their own tongue that the three Normans exchanged looks. Their leader turned to his son with a smile, gesturing disdainfully at her with a wave of gloved hand. "Have I not said, my boy, that if you turn over a plain brown stone on English soil, what's hid beneath it may surprise you?"

Watching from his hiding place, Brand frowned at the girl's response. If she understood what this Norman overlord was saying, she should have suffered his crude comments, the sooner to see the men lose interest and go. Brand could speak the language himself, a legacy from his Norman mother, who claimed descent from the same line that had produced England's new king. His frown deepened to a glower as the three men dismounted. The Saxon pulled the girl closer to himself, but he provided little protection against men hardened by battle and armed as well. Damn the girl for speaking, Brand cursed. He owed her nothing, and yet . . .

The Norman lord, though not so tall or broadly formed as Cadwyn, possessed a well-muscled chest and arms; his sword made up the difference in strength. He circled Cadwyn, intent on learning more about this thin Saxon maid who was as impudent as she was artful in his native tongue. There were few enough females here from Normandy to give it that soft lilt. "I say you lie, little Saxon," he said, hoping to incite her to further defense. His youngest son, Alain, and the captain of his knights, Guy de Creace, drew their swords and took a stand at her companion's back.

Alysaun, aware that her mistake in speaking had endangered Cadwyn as well as herself, now kept her gaze fixed on the ground. She hated this man—he symbolized all that was cruel and ugly in the Norman character—yet to say more, even in appeal, was useless.

Irritated by her silence, the Norman spoke again. "My name is Drogo de Villai, and by our noble king's grant I am lord of the fief of Farrisbrae. All the land you see for miles is mine, and all that cross it, whether wild hart or insolent Saxon maid, are mine to judge.'' De Villai raised his gloved hand and lifted the girl's chin. Still she would not meet his eyes, and his fingers tightened, forcing her head higher.

Her complexion was naturally fair, but recent exposure to the warming spring sun had given it a light, peachy tone. Though she was hollow-cheeked from too few meals, her features were finely formed. Long, thick lashes of a dusky gold hid eyes that were sure to be bright Saxon blue. Everything about her cried neglect; but with a little polish, this girl would shine with the glitter, and perhaps with the value, of gold.

"Your face is too rich for a peasant, girl,'' he declared, enjoying the tenseness of her body, the rapid rise and fall of small, firm breasts outlined beneath the thin, ragged gown. Still holding her firmly, he ran a hand along her arm, then casually commented to his vassal, "Guy, I would wager this one has not yet known a man. What say you?''

Guy smirked, replying he doubted any virgins were left amongst the population. Alain laughed, a trifle nervously, for he was no older than the girl. Sensing from the tone of the conversation what these Normans intended, Cadwyn stiffened and lifted his large, shaggy-haired head, his face mottled red with fury. This was the last of too many indignities; not while he still breathed would this poor, helpless child suffer violation. She had one chance—if he drew attention away from her, Alysaun might be able to escape.

Cadwyn took a deep breath and, making use of the Danish tongue many Englishmen of his age had commonly used, spoke to her in a low, calm tone. "When I shout, my lady, run. And run as if the Devil were breathing at your neck.'' Alysaun opened her eyes, found Lord de Villai staring suspiciously at Cadwyn, and drew his attention away by raising her hand to touch his. "M'lord,'' she said in a soft, pleading voice, "please do not . . .''

De Villai stared at her, wary still but lulled by this pliant change in attitude. Guy de Creace poked Alain, making some lewd remark about learning skills not taught a squire. That slight relaxation of caution was all Cadwyn needed. With a mighty roar reminiscent of a Viking battle cry, he struck backward in a powerful kick that connected with Sir Guy's loins. The knight howled, dropping his weapon as, doubled over, he fell to the ground.

Then the Saxon giant whirled, bringing his hamlike fist against young Alain's jaw in a crushing blow that knocked the youth flying. Alysaun jerked away from the stunned de Villai, gown flying as she sped for the cover of the woods as fast as her bare feet could carry her. Cadwyn bent to retrieve Guy's sword, but as he straightened with it firmly in hand, the Norman lord struck at his unprotected right side and drove the sword tip deep in a lunge that splintered Cadwyn's ribs.

Like a berserk Viking warrior, Cadwyn ignored the blood and searing pain, raising his weapon to meet and parry yet another thrust of the knight's sword. Steel met steel with a sparking clash that echoed in the quiet meadow. Wounded as he was and unskilled at combat, Cadwyn's strength and concern for the girl's safety made up the difference. His forward drive, accompanied by yet another unearthly howl of vengeance, pushed the more skilled and battle-hardened warrior backward, forcing him to raise his sword in defense.

Alysaun scrambled into the cover of the thick greenwood, brambles tearing at her gown, scratching at her face. She dared not look back, afraid one of the three was set to chase her. Suddenly she was pulled up short as a strong arm wrapped around her waist, dragging her back into the thick underbrush. A hand roughly covered her mouth, muffling the terrified cry that gurgled in her throat, and instinctively she kicked back at her aggressor, eliciting a low, angry curse.

She bit the hand that covered her mouth and found herself thrown to the ground, the man's weight rolling their bodies over several times before he came to rest atop her. For a second her struggling stopped. Through eyes blurred by tears, she saw the man was not one of the three Normans.

Clearly the girl was hysterical, but Brand could not help her if she were allowed to scream. He had watched the scene unfold and had expected what the girl's guardian would attempt even before the crazed shout sounded. The man was doomed and knew it ere he made his first move, yet his loyalty to the girl left him little choice. Now, to save something out of his sure death, the girl had to cease her weeping and listen.

"Your man back there is as good as dead," Brand hissed, regretting that he had to tighten his hand across her mouth to gain her attention. "If you care at all for him, don't make his death go for naught."

Alysaun stared up at her captor, suspicious of his actions. He spoke the Norman tongue with ease, yet he did not have the look of them. She could not think who he might be but something told her he was not their ally. Unable to speak, she nodded, and the hand across her mouth relaxed.

"Good, now stay silent for a moment and listen. If you scream, all is lost. I will not hesitate to deliver you over and go my way." Wild and wet as her blue eyes were, he could see the resistance fade from them; and when she nodded, Brand freed her mouth. He rolled away, sitting up to brush dirt and leaves from his fine tunic of dark green, then offered her his hand, tugging until she sat up next to him.

"Don't ask why I choose to interfere," he insisted irritably. "I cannot reconcile it myself. In a moment we will return boldly to face your tormentors, and I want nothing but silence from you. If one foolish word of pride escapes your lips, I will turn on my heel and walk away. Is that understood?"

Behind them, in the meadow, the Normans called to one another, and the lord's voice, louder than the others, shouted a furious command to search for her. Cadwyn must be dead. There was no time to mourn him. If she could trust this stranger, the loyal smith would not have gone down in vain. If? What was she thinking? She had no other choice but to trust him. The alternative was rape, perhaps worse, now that one of them might have been wounded. "Tell me what your plan is," she replied.

Brand sighed disgustedly. There was no time to discuss details. "You'll see soon enough. For your part, keep your eyes shuttered, your mouth shut. Oh, and if you can, try to weep a few tears. Pretend you are a lady offended."

Alysaun's eyes narrowed in chill resentment. "'Twill not be difficult, for I am," she answered with such hauteur that he almost believed the claim. He rose and drew her to her feet, reminding her again to say nothing, no matter what he claimed to the Normans. With her small hand held securely in his, he pulled her along, brushing back low-hanging branches to clear the way.

They met de Villai's knight as they emerged from the wood, his sword unsheathed and at the ready when he saw them. Puzzled for a moment at the sight of the girl holding this stranger's hand and standing slightly behind him for protection, Sir Guy kept his weapon extended and called back a shout that he had found the girl.

Drogo de Villai approached with a triumphant smile, his sword slick and crimson with the dead Saxon's blood. Catching sight of the tall, well-dressed man who stood with his prey, the Norman lord's smile faded to a frown. The man was armed, but his sword hung at his side, sheathed in a finely worked leather scabbard. The Saxon had been dispatched. Now that the wench had found another protector, he would have to be seen to as well.

De Villai opened his mouth but Brand arrogantly cut off any inquiry, his expression one of outraged indignation. "By God, travel in this heathen land grows more annoying with each passing day! *You*, sir—are you the scoundrel who dared attack my lady wife and servant? 'Twas told me that the Normans had brought civilization to these isles, yet to countenance your armed assault upon a defenseless woman—well, my cousin shall soon hear word of this savage act, I vow you that."

The lord stared, disgruntled by the haughty, aristocratic demeanor of the man. Thin lips pursed in mocking disbelief, he dryly asked who might this cousin be, that he should be timorous at his mention. Alain came up behind him, and father turned to son with a sneering,

"Next we'll hear this overbold rascal claim blood kinship to our good King William."

"How did you guess?" Brand responded coldly, arching a brow to stare disdainfully down his long, aquiline nose at de Villai. "If Cousin William believes his vassals to be justly administering his lands, he will be twice shocked to find they sport instead on a young woman bound to him by wedded kinship. Send for the sheriff, I *insist*."

"*Hold*, sir," Drogo protested, still not sure the man's claims were true. God help him if they were, for William was a stickler for proper courtesy to ladies of rank. The girl stood quietly at the man's side, sniffling occasionally. He noticed now a thin gold band upon her finger, but if she was indeed this fellow's wife, why was she dressed like a peasant? Why did everything about her announce her Saxon heritage? "I want some proof of this claim of a blood tie to William. You must think me a fool to merely take your word. I would also have your name and the reason you trespass upon my lands."

"Christ, hold my tried temper!" Brand growled, rolling his eyes heavenward in disgust, his right hand hovering over the hilt of his sword. "The name, sir, is de Reynaud, Brand de Reynaud, and I take offense at giving it to you. As for your lands, I wish to God I had never set foot upon them. I'm sure you will wish it, too, when William hears of this outrage. Don't stare at me so goggle-eyed, man. I suppose you know enough to recognize the Norman leopards?"

De Reynaud removed his hand from his sword hilt and, with a disgusted twitch of his full lips, held it out, displaying a ring. All eyes, including those of a curious Alysaun, were centered on its crest, two leopards rampant crossed by a bar sinister. "The tie is through my mother's line and, though not legitimate, acknowledged by William. Of course, no one dares make mention of the bar; my cousin has his own reasons to be sensitive on that subject."

The Norman lord swallowed hard, the proof too clear to refute. Still he sought some way to escape what would surely be a disaster for his family. "How do I know the ring is not stolen? Perhaps you took it from the King's cousin when you waylaid him."

"By all means, then, send one of your lackeys for the sheriff," Brand smirked. "I have already stated that to be my desire. You have slaughtered my manservant and assaulted my wife with intent to violate her. I demand some satisfaction for your scurrilous behavior. For such an affront I will have nothing but piteous weeping from my lady the rest of our journey." Brand squeezed Alysaun's hand tightly, and she buried her head against his shoulder with a wail, shoulders shaking with a display of crying that deepened her "husband's" frown. He slipped his arm around her shoulders, patting her gently in consolation. "Hush, my sweet, we will yet see some justice done."

"There's no need to alert the sheriff, sire," de Villai insisted, awkward at issuing an apology. "I beg your pardon and your lady's for this error in judgment. So many wandering natives do cross my fief. You understand, I must protect what is mine."

"Your apology is hardly balm for the lady's trampled sensibilities, sir," Brand snapped. "Nor will it replace the good services I lost in the servant who did defend my wife's honor. I am wronged, and you think to soothe my righteous anger with a few words of excuse."

De Villai grew more nervous by the second, expecting that if the matter should reach the sheriff's attention, it would go higher still, all the way to the King, and he would be ruined. "Let me repay you, then," he offered. "I will replace your man with one of my own or at least pay you his worth. And, if you would interrupt your journey, I offer the hospitality of my manor for your rest. I would see this settled between us here and now, so no ill will exists."

Angered by his casual offer to pay gold in exchange for her Cadwyn's death, Alysaun forgot her promise to keep still. "You have not gold enough to pardon your act, nor to buy off the name of murderer," she cried, raising her head to glare at the man with spiteful, narrowed eyes. Lost in the pretense they played, she poked a finger at Brand's ribs with an indignant, wifely jab. "For your honor's sake, sire, fight this man. You cannot think to let him harm me and go free.''

Silently Brand cursed. He almost had them out of the scrape, with perhaps some repayment for his trouble, and she boldly sought to embroil him in combat. Confident of his skill with a sword, he still knew enough to shy from a fray with three opponents. Holy Mary, Mother of God, was he going to spill his blood here for no more cause than the death of a Saxon thief and the ruffled feelings of a haughty girl in rags? If I do, he thought furiously, my mother raised a fool. "Now, hush, darling," he answered soothingly, firmly pulling her against his chest to stifle any further nonsense she might speak. "The man admits his mistake and justly offers to put to rights our lack of a servant. Have you forgotten how far we have to go? If you still have a thought to find out whether your dear mother lives, our way will go easier accompanied by a servant."

Brand raised his head to look de Villai in the eye. "My wife is gentle-hearted, sir, and will weep after the man's loss many a day. I, more practical, would rather see the last of this place, and do accept your offer of coin to hire another servant." Alysaun tensed rebelliously and Brand tightened his hold, barring any defiantly flung words that could worsen their situation.

"The offer still stands to welcome you to Farrisbrae, m'lord," de Villai said with a courteous bow, "but I can understand your wife's reluctance. 'Tis a pity this happened. Would you count ten farthings a fair recompense?" If he got away with that much, he would count himself lucky and next time be more cautious of an encounter.

"Twenty would be more his worth and soothe what rancor I will endure from my indignant lady," Brand asserted, playing the scene boldly for all it was worth. He couldn't let the man think he would be bought off so easily. "But I will settle for fifteen and the due burial of my poor, slain man. Any less and I will take my wounded pride straight to my cousin's presence for justice."

"Agreed, if the incident is forgotten." De Villai searched his purse, which hung from a belt of gold silk, and found to his embarrassment that he had to borrow several farthings from his aide, de Creace. Handing over the coins, he turned and ordered his son to ride back to the manor posthaste and to bring several stablemen to see the Saxon buried.

Brand relaxed. It was nearly over. Suddenly the girl's fingernails jabbed sharply through his tunic, and he frowned. "Bring a priest if you have one, as well," he requested. "The man was a good Christian. 'Tis only fitting that he receive a prayer for his soul's rest. Now, sir knight, I would see us left in peace. Believe me, my lady and I wish only to quit this place."

Relaxed as well, now that there was no threat upon his good name, de Villai bowed again and ordered his aide to mount. "I do wish you a safe journeying, Sieur de Reynaud, and suggest that you might suffer less trouble by keeping to the main roads." He turned and strode away, sure he had gotten off lightly in the encounter with a relative of King William's.

Brand did not release Alysaun until the two knights had mounted and were galloping away. Though he judged from the tenseness of her slender body that there was no hope of thanks, he thought she might at least be somewhat grateful for the rescue. Alysaun took a step back, her pale face stained with angry color. Hands on hips, chest rising and falling rapidly, she now vented her fury at his acceptance, indeed bargaining, of a wergeld for poor Cadwyn.

"You had no right to acquit that murderer of his guilt," she cried. "And for what? A few coins to fatten your own purse. Have you no conscience, half-Norman? To accept payment for a man you never knew?"

Brand could not believe what his ears recorded. He had risked his own life to save this girl, and she stood there chiding him. "I never saw his face, girl, but your huge friend's hand, rock stealthily grasped, did meet the back of my head. I owed him nothing. To my acquaintance he was a common thief, stealing *my* food to share with you."

Brand crossed his arms over his chest, head lowered as he took a menacing step forward. "As for you, had I not lied for you, you would be lying flat on yonder meadow grass, wearing your ragged hem for a wimple and screaming protest as each man took his turn.'' The half bow he made was mocking. "In your distress, I will forgive your lack of manners but do not try my patience by laying any guilt upon my brow.''

Alysaun opened her mouth, shut it, opened it again, and gave up. She could not deny what he said. With Cadwyn fallen, she would have been caught and raped. This man had ably come to her defense and saved her from that torture. He smiled now, but it was a chill expression, and she looked down, unable to meet the judgment in his gaze.

"I will take your silence for thanks, since you are suddenly struck dumb of gracious words, m'lady Saxon. And if you care not to be alone here when the burial party returns, I humbly suggest you run as fast as you can to the place whence you came." Brand turned his back and, with his purse now heavily weighted at his belt, moved into the woods again.

Alysaun stared after him, then looked back to the meadow, where Cadwyn's crumpled body lay in death. She could not stay and weep tears in mourning, else she would be caught again and lessen the good his dying had done. "*Wait*," she called, and saw Brand pause. He glanced over his shoulder with an impatient look. "Where are you going? You cannot just walk away and leave me.''

In all his wanderings, Brand had never met a woman or, for that matter, a man who possessed such gall. The girl's head was tilted high, her request more a command than a plea. "The Devil take you, wench," he called back in anger. "I've had my share of the trouble that travels with you. Find someone else to order about.''

Before he had finished the last sentence, she whirled and ran back, toward the meadow. He saw a flash of white legs and dusty bare feet, then she disappeared, leaving him frowning at the suddenness of her action. A curse sprang to mind, he almost turned to go after her, then stubbornly he picked his way through the hedges, heading for his camp. More than generous of spirit he had been, and at least he had something more useful for his trouble than airy words of gratitude.

Alysaun raced to the spot where she had dropped her precious bundle of belongings. She seized the bag and turned to run back and follow her rescuer, pausing only for a moment's prayer beside Cadwyn's sprawling, lifeless form. His devotion had helped her come this far. Now, because of his sacrifice, she was determined she would reach the sanctuary of the convent, else his blood had soaked this green meadow for no good reason.

Ignoring the scratch of thorns and brambles, Alysaun hastened through the thick, close stands of ash and oak, anxious to catch up with the tall, rust-haired stranger. In coming to her aid once, he had revealed a soft spot beneath his cynical, armored demeanor. If it worked to her advantage to humble herself, then she would. Travel had been difficult enough, even with a great bear of a man Cadwyn's size. Now she had lost his protection, she was too easy a prey for any man to seize, be he Norman or Saxon.

Breathless now, she caught sight of a flash of forest-green tunic ahead and doubled her pace. A sharp thorn stabbed the unprotected sole of her foot, embedded itself deeply in the tender flesh of her arch, and Alysaun stopped, leaning for a second against the gnarled trunk of a huge oak. She could not pull it free. Tears of pain and frustration flowed down her cheeks. Only the thought that he would soon be out of sight and lost to her made her go on, ignoring the jab of pain each time her weight came down on her right foot.

Finally, limping badly, Alysaun emerged from the shadowed forest and found herself at the edge of a sunlit glade. The man named Brand was kneeling on one knee next to the smoking remnants of a campfire some ten yards from her. She could see his irritation in his jerky movements as he packed his belongings in a leather saddlebag. This man was no poor traveler such as she; in fact ... Her gaze swept the glade and Alysaun smiled. A large silver-gray stallion grazed not fifteen feet from where she stood. What heaven it would be to ride instead of walk.

The stallion raised his well-formed head and shook it, snorting out a whinny that elicited a low, soothing call from his owner. Brand carelessly shoved his eating utensils in the bag, as anxious as his mount to be away from this place. The sight of spoon and knife had reminded him he had not yet eaten.

Suddenly Brand looked up, the fine hairs on the back of his neck bristling with the distinct feeling he was under observation. Turning his head, he scanned the surrounding forest but discovered nothing unusual to warrant the reaction. He was still tense from the encounter with the Normans, he told himself, and rose to carry the fastened bag to the spot where the stallion was tethered.

It was then, in a chance look up over his saddle, that he saw the girl. She stood so still, poised with the tense quietude of a forest doe, that her grayed, worn gown had blended with the background of dun-and-brown brush. Discovered now, she met his gaze steadfastly, and Brand frowned. He had thought he had seen the last of her. What did she want of him now? His frown deepened to a scowl. Likely she would issue a regal command that he give her a ride to the road, some mile and a quarter north of the glade.

Knowing she must swallow her pride to obtain his help, Alysaun emerged from the wood, limping forward slowly to favor her sore foot. Once, in days now gone forever, she had possessed the charm and appearance to persuade any man to do her bidding. What had she now, though, to appeal to a man already angry with her?

Brand noted the pitiful, limping gait. The girl was resourceful, to say the least, thinking to play upon his sympathies with the ruse. When she finally reached his side, he greeted her with a mocking bow and said, "You are quite skilled at pretense, girl. Had I not met you earlier, I might have been taken by that touching act of lameness."

It took a great effort to hold back a retort. Alysaun reminded herself that she would not go far unless he offered to take her to the road amount his stallion. "'Tis no pretense, sire. In hastening to rejoin you, I did carelessly step upon a thorn." She grasped the edge of his saddle, turning up her foot to reveal the thorn still deeply embedded in the tender flesh of her arch. A bare trickle of blood came from the wound, verifying her claim.

Made nervous by a feminine voice, the stallion nickered and

shifted suddenly, throwing Alysaun off balance as he danced several feet away. Reacting instinctively, Brand thrust out his arms, catching the girl before she tumbled. With an exasperated frown, he slipped his hands under her and lifted her slight weight, then carried her back to his campsite.

There, more harshly than was necessary, he deposited her on the grass and hunkered down beside her, withdrawing his knife from its sheath at his belt. The blade gleamed, the wicked sharpness of the tempered Spanish steel apparent as it reflected the sunlight.

"What, I pray, do you intend to do with that?" Alysaun's gaze went from the blade to his face as she resisted the thought that he meant to use the weapon to pry the thorn from her foot.

Brand grinned, his hazel eyes glinting as he hefted the knife hilt in the palm of his hand. "By rights, I should use it to bring a measure of peace to England and self by silencing your harpy's tongue that rattles only of ingratitude. In truth, I mean only to free you of the painful thorn so you may hobble on to do damage to someone more deserving than I."

Alysaun glared at him, her meek intentions forgotten. "I have my reasons for my temper, sire."

"Spare me the telling. I've problems aplenty without adding yours." His hand shot out to catch her foot and turn it up, fingers strongly gripping to secure a hold should she flinch in pain. "Don't rush to thank me," he added dryly. "The shock might set my hand to trembling ere the blade tip met your flesh."

Tensed against the expected pain, Alysaun grudgingly offered what appreciation she could muster. "Somewhere beneath your harsh exterior, some kindness must dwell, m'lord. Otherwise, you would leave me to suffer. If you must cut, do it quickly, or in the waiting I shall grow more fearful of the blade's cold kiss."

Brand's mouth curled in a mocking smile. "Girl, from what I've seen, you have yet to show the common sense that inspires fear. Now sit still and look away or you'll add fainting to the list of wrongs done me today." She frowned more deeply at his criticism but obeyed the command to look away.

He placed the point of his blade next to the stub of thorn that showed above her flesh. There was no way to lessen the pain she would feel, but it occurred to him that if he continued the conversation, the girl's mind would be diverted from it. "Don't think I act out of mercy," he went on in a calm tone. "My motives are purely selfish—to secure my freedom from your company, child."

"I am *not* a—" The word "child" was choked off as the blade reached the thorn. Alysaun closed her eyes tightly against the savage throb of pain, her teeth cutting into her tender lower lip to still an outcry.

Using the blade for leverage, Brand seized the nub of exposed thorn and tugged. A wicked spike of hard, brittle wood appeared, some three-quarters inch in length, followed by a flow of bright blood that would clean the wound of dirt. "Done, lady," he said, amazed that there had been no sound from her, not even a whimper.

Alysaun opened her eyes and raised a hand to wipe away the drop of blood from her cut lip. She glanced down at the blood flowing from her arch and paled, nauseated by the sight of so much crimson blood pouring forth. "I do thank you for your assistance," she said weakly, and glanced up to find him studying her with a puzzled expression. "No matter what the motive, I owe you that."

For the first time Brand realized how finely wrought her features were. Beneath the smudges of dirt, which a good bath would clean away, her skin was as fine as silk. From a lack of proper food, no doubt, it stretched tautly over the high, aristocratic cheekbones. Her eyes, lacking their earlier antagonism, were bluer than the sky, shadowed softly by thick golden lashes. He swallowed hard and looked away to break the luring appeal of that vulnerable gaze.

"You'll have to bind the cut, or the flesh will swell and give you fever," he explained, looking back at his mount to see if he had any cloth that would do the work. No, nothing but a clean tunic, and he was not about to rip it to pieces. Turning back, he picked up her bag, ignoring her protests as he dumped the contents on the grass.

Fine clothing, lovely enough to grace a noble lady, spilled out in a crumpled heap. On top of the pale gunna of blue silk a small cross, marked at its points by oval emeralds, winked a brilliant green in the sunlight. Beside it lay an apple, looking suspiciously like the one he had possessed earlier in the morning.

That sullen, defensive look was back upon her face when he glanced over to find her staring at her belongings. "All stolen, I presume?" Brand snapped, rust-brown brows drawn together in frowning disapproval. "The apple I believe I recognize, but from which fine lady did you thieve the cross and clothing?"

"Everything you see is mine," Alysaun asserted, "save the piece of fruit. I care not if you believe me. Take back the apple, with my blessings." She reached over and seized it, thrusting the offering at him with such haughty disdain that the act elicited a laugh from Brand.

"Ah, but the tale of man's downfall repeats itself in that offer, little thief. So Eve, on the delivering of fruit from the tree of knowledge, did bring all manner of ills upon the shoulders of man. My thanks, but knowing in advance the story, I refuse. Held this long, my hunger can yet keep awhile." The clothing was another matter. Stolen surely, despite her denial, it was better put to use to bind the girl's foot than to drape her in aspiring vanity. Before she could react, Brand seized the gunna and with his knife ripped apart the hem.

Nothing in the long, disastrous day, not even the numbing realization of the loss of Cadwyn, quite affected Alysaun as much as seeing that torn remnant of silk in his hands. Tears flowed down her cheeks. The hope that had given her the will to go on, the peaceful sanctuary that lay at the end of a bitterly traveled road, shimmered once like a dream and then vanished. How could she present herself at the convent in rags? Shoulders bowed under the weight of too much pain and bitter loss, Alysaun covered her face with both hands and wept.

Brand knew a stab of regret at the pitiful sound of the girl's sobbing. The need to keep the open cut free of dirt had seemed more important to him, but to her . . . If she had known little of such pleasures as a fine silk tunic, how dear the possession of the gunna must have seemed.

He glanced at her foot; the bleeding was slowing now. She seemed not to notice or care as he gently wrapped the ribbon of silk around her foot and tore it in half again to secure the bandage with a knot. Brand felt awkward, oddly guilty, though his intention had been to see to her welfare. Slowly did she quiet, the tears lessening to a trickle. "I *am* sorry," he apologized lamely. "I could not know such a small loss would set you crying as if your heart would break."

Alysaun drew in a deep, ragged breath, wiping at the traces of her tears before she turned her head toward him. "No, you could not know, but more was lost than a damaged gown. The past is gone—I cannot catch it back to me with wishing—but before you go your way, I would have you know that the gunna was mine. 'Tis no matter now, what I was when last I wore it, for I hold no hope of being so again."

She struggled awkwardly to stand, cautious about putting her weight, slight as it was, full upon the injured foot. Brand, moving more easily, stood and steadied her with a supportive hand. He half believed her, for certainly she was the most regal girl who ever wore such a ragged, threadbare dress. Noting the glint of sunlight that caught the jeweled cross, he retrieved it and handed it to her. "Yours, you claim. If so, it would be more secure worn around your neck and concealed by your clothing." She accepted it and closed her thin fingers around it.

"I realized just now," Brand continued, "with all the morning spent together, I do not have a name to fix to that tearstained face of yours." She raised one fine golden eyebrow that questioned his sudden friendly manner, and Brand smiled and made a short, courteous bow. "You have the advantage, having heard my name. If we are to travel farther this day, I must have something to call you."

Alysaun was startled by the unsought offer to share his company and transport. Distrustful still, she studied him for a minute before reminding him that he had earlier called her child and thief. "I do resent the term 'child,' sir. Those happy days are gone. As for 'thief' . . .'' Alysaun shrugged her shoulders, blushing at the admission that it was not untrue. Her head came up with a defiant set. "But I stole only to feed myself, and never from one with less than I."

Opening her fingers, she gazed sadly at the cross that had been her mother's, then slipped the chain over her head and settled the cross beneath her tattered, grayed gown. Glancing up, she finally returned his smile with an air of resignation. "Call me by my given name, Alysaun. The sound of 'Lady' set before it fits no longer. Now, 'tis merely Alysaun."

2

Though Brand had firmly intended only to ease the girl's way a bit by allowing her to ride to the main road, where she might seek the help of some passing Saxon merchant, twelve days' passage still found them together. Try as he might, he could not free himself of Alysaun. What galled him most of all was that she had made no pleas or demands that he continue as her protector.

Had the girl played haughty once again, he might have turned his back and ridden away. If she had resorted to weeping and thought to influence him to pity, he would have abandoned her. Alysaun did neither. Simply by her voiceless gratitude and dependent manner, she had won his continued companionship.

Still, disgruntled by what he saw as a weakness in his character, Brand was not an entirely gracious patron. He questioned what decree of fate had allotted him the responsibility for the girl. He had always valued his freedom to go where he pleased. He was independent of duty to anyone but himself, or had been until that unfortunate morning he had happened on Alysaun with the Norman lord, de Villai.

In his irritation with himself, Brand often snapped at her. She was slowing him down; he had a task she was keeping him from; she was a burden better shunted off on some gullible member of her own race. And yet, no matter what discourteous rebukes his temper tossed her way, Alysaun bore them with so stoic a demeanor that Brand found himself immediately apologetic and anxious to soften his harsh criticisms with some small kindness or a gift.

For her part, Alysaun realized the good fortune cast her way and tempered any defensive retorts with a silent reminder to herself that this handsome, well-formed Frenchman owed her nothing. Pride was a privilege of those who could afford it. No, whatever taunts Brand de Reynaud cared to fling, they were little enough distress in the face of what she might suffer without his protection.

Though she did resent his all-too-obvious attitude that she was an unwelcome burden, Alysaun had good reason to appreciate the man's basic kindness. Oh, he hid it well enough, masking his generous deeds with a hard, cynical expression, but to one who had become accustomed to a world filled with cold-hearted and ruthlessly selfish men, Brand was near a saint in the goodness of his spirit.

He was, as well, undeniably attractive. In the days of traveling with him, she had become aware of the appeal he held for her own sex. Females, regardless of their age, be they Saxon, Danish, or Norman ladies, all seemed to respond to the boyish charm of his smile, to the evidence of humor in his hazel eyes. Generally their response was to offer some kindness: a direction to the proper roadway, a freshly baked sweet roll to lessen the hunger of a stranger in their midst. He never sought, to Alysaun's amazement, any of these attentions. They merely came to him, and he accepted with a grace that left the ladies pleased.

Because she knew herself to be undone by all the mad grief and struggle of the past six months, Alysaun dismissed the physical attraction she felt for Brand. If, she thought, if only she still possessed the beauty that had just begun to blossom and unfold. Too many missed meals had left her gaunt; too much exposure to wind and weather had roughened her hands and complexion. She possessed nothing and was no longer a lady with fine clothing to enhance her looks. Because there was nothing to attract Brand, Alysaun felt awkward in his presence.

Her foot had healed nicely, aided by the herb poultice Brand had charmed from an old village crone. Sandals, purchased by Brand from a traveling tinker, protected her feet against further injuries. Washed and braided to fall across her shoulders in thick, silken plaits, her hair shone like burnished gold in the sun of early summer. Having discarded the ragged gown, Alysaun now dressed in the fine silk kirtle, tunic, and gunna. The torn hem had been repaired with a length of white silk given Brand by a merchant's wife in exchange for a few songs plucked from his lute.

With all the improvements to her appearance, Alysaun still lacked the confidence that had once been so natural to her. With no mirror to reflect the gradual return of beauty and the loss of tension that had shadowed and lined her eyes, she believed her frail, plain looks had inspired Brand to pity her.

Their travels had brought them now to Cambridge, long the seat of Anglo-Saxon England's most learned scholars. In the morning, after a night's rest at the inn where Brand had taken a room, they were to part at the city's gates. Brand was adamant about the separation, insisting he could not accompany her along the east road toward Bury Saint Edmunds. He had some task to accomplish, an avowed duty, the nature of which he would not divulge.

They had supped, and the light beyond the open, uncovered window of the loft they shared was paling to darkness now. Alysaun sat forlornly on the room's only pallet, her chin propped on her hands, despairing that the inevitable parting would come so soon. Angered by her mood, Brand paced the room, stopping several times to glower. She was not sister, mother, or wife, he thought, so why did he have the feeling he was abandoning a helpless relative to a questionable fate? "If you're worried about how you'll eat or make your way," he said finally, "I intend to leave you with enough coins to see you as far as the convent."

Alysaun glanced up, her eyes round and sad. In truth, she cared less about her welfare than the loss of his companionship. She would look the fool, admitting such a thought. "I will not take them," she answered firmly. "You have been overkind in all your dealings with me. Please do not increase the debt I owe by adding to its weight."

Brand frowned at the refusal, wondering why, in so short a period, he had become attached to this homeless waif. She stirred in him some odd sense of responsibility. By guile or not, Alysaun had managed to work her way into his feelings so deeply that he was guilt-stricken over the thought of parting. "You *will* accept the money, Alysaun," he said slowly, deliberately emphasizing each word. "I'll not have your pale, troubled face haunting me in dreams."

Alysaun's mouth quirked with impatience to match his own. "If my pale, troubled face continues to bother you, sire, I cannot drive it from your night thoughts. Have I done aught but return gratitude for your generosity? If your conscience does twinge, Lord Brand, I have not knowingly plucked at—"

Her words were cut off by an angry curse from Brand. "I have no guilt over my treatment of you, girl. If you will pardon my abrupt exit, I will walk off some of the irritation you make me feel."

He left the room before she could reply. It was just as well, for tears had sprung to her eyes, and she had no desire to be accused of using them to her advantage. If the idea of leaving her bothered him so, why did he curse and mutter at her like some savage, caged beast? Now it was Alysaun's turn to pace as she puzzled over his anger, over her own attachment to a man who had been a stranger a fortnight ago.

Finally she wiped away her tears and sighed. No amount of weeping or playing upon his sympathies would change what was to be. She wandered about the room, carefully ducking the timbered rafters, looking for something to occupy her time. She had no idea where he had gone or how long he would be absent. And no right to inquire, either, she found herself thinking.

Pausing in the corner, she spied his saddlebag and lute beneath the window. Alysaun bent down on one knee, idly plucking at the strings of the instrument. Brand had a way of strumming such lovely melodies from the simple lute. His voice was low and clear, and the poetic phrases he sang, often created almost out of thin air, had made many a night pass more sweetly.

Her attention turned to the finely wrought saddlebag. She knew little enough about his past, but from all appearances, he was too richly garbed and equipped to be the wandering troubadour he said he was. His sword, hanging from a scabbard of tooled leather, was not merely for show. He had drawn it once, when a band of men had threatened their campsite. So her mysterious Brand de Reynaud was possibly a full-fledged knight, as skilled at courtly manners as he was with his lilting songs of romance.

Suddenly it occurred to Alysaun that she might do him some service in return for his time and care. He had several tunics in his bag; perhaps one had a tear or loose seam she could mend. She drew out the tunics and took only a moment to marvel at their fine material and solid stitching before carrying them close to the single rush lamp burning near the pallet.

At first examination, there seemed to be nothing to repair. Then, on a forest-green mantle, embroidered and edged in gold silk thread, she found a torn seam. Heartened by the chance to mend it for Brand, she placed the other articles aside and rose to fetch needle and thread from her own belongings. Those, too, had been a gift from Brand, but at least her stitching was given of herself.

It was when she returned to the pallet that Alysaun noticed the short, painted wooden stick lying on the straw rushes. She bent to retrieve it, sure she had not seen it before taking the clothes from the saddlebag. On closer examination, the three-inch piece of wood was not a stick but a hand-carved shaft of arrow, broken at both ends. The design was a coiled snake, and the deep carving had been daubed with bright red paint.

67

Alysaun looked up, staring without seeing the clay and wattle wall, her thoughts confused by the discovery. This broken arrow shaft, the old Saxon emblem, could mean only one thing.

Brand had opened the door quietly, returning in good humor after a long walk that had exorcised his irritation. For seconds, as he stared at what Alysaun held, he was silent; then his fury rose at his assumption that she had dared to explore his belongings with a mind to taking something of value. When he finally moved he startled her completely, and snatched the wood from her hands so swiftly that she stepped back and cringed at his expression of rage.

"Who gave you leave to search my saddlebag?" he snapped. "Not I. It seems a fortnight of 'overkind' care and false gratitude has not cured you of a desire to thieve."

Recovering from her shock, Alysaun flinched beneath that unfair accusation, then straightened her shoulders and firmly set her mouth. "I am no thief, m'lord," she insisted, pride glittering in the wounded blue pools of her eyes. "I only—"

"Pray do not add a lie to your overburdened soul," Brand interrupted. "'Tis clear enough you explored what you had no right to see. Do you know what this is?" He held the shaft forward and saw a flicker of acknowledgment in her eyes. When she made no reply, he seized her arm, jerking her close to him. "*Answer me.* You know the significance of this discovery, don't you?"

His fingers bit painfully into the tender flesh of her upper arm. "Let *go* of me," Alysaun insisted, then, when her protest only deepened his fury and narrowed his eyes in a look of menace, she gave in. "All right . . . *yes*, I know it represents a challenge to arms. All Saxons know the symbol of a broken war arrow. What puzzles me is your possession of it."

"That was and is no business of yours, but since your petty stealing has brought it to light I will tell you." None too gently he shoved her back and Alysaun tumbled to the pallet. His gaze never left her as his hand reached to shut the door. Alysaun was poised tensely on the bed of straw, ready to flee a room from which there was little chance of escape. Brand looked angry enough to throttle her; and when he stepped forward, looming over her with a menacing scowl, she instinctively cowered, as if she expected a blow.

"I see you fear some punishment for your offense," Brand noted, sitting down beside her. He caught her wrist, a little less roughly, and pulled her forward. "Ease your fears—at least for the moment, maiden. I am not in the habit of striking women." He smiled, his lips curving in a wicked grin. "Until this point, I have not had reason to." His grin faded. "So you have discovered my secret and care to know why a foreigner carries your precious war symbol, eh? I am merely a messenger, my dear, returning a refusal of support from Keric of Cornwall."

"He paid you to return the arrow?"

"In a way. Keric once cast a pretty and willing wench my way, affording me a leisurely stay at his keep of Blackurst. Had I known then the troubled cost of those days of entertainment, I would have spurned the offer. I plan to deliver the message and arrow whence it came and quit this godforsaken country of yours."

Alysaun's eyes brightened with excitement as she leaned forward. "Then you are bound for Ely to see Hereward of Lincoln," she said, a surge of hope leaving her lips, which were parted in breathless eagerness. "Brand . . . take me with you, please. I will not be a bother. You will hardly know I am with you."

Brand stared at her in surprise, both at the fact that she had guessed the name of whom he sought and that for the first time she had appealed to him for a favor. "A rebel's camp is no place for you, Alysaun. Better you keep to the east road and take sanctuary in the convent. What would make you think they'd welcome you at a fort filled with fighting men?"

"I'll be safe there, among my own kind, and pleased to offer my help to Hereward's cause. There must be other women there. Someone must feed and mend battle-torn clothing." She laid her hand on his arm, her expression beseeching him to grant her request.

"How safe do you think you'll be? More likely, the manner of help the rebels will exact will be to answer the lust your face would stir in them. A Saxon won't deny himself a tumble just because your ancestors are of a common stock, girl. Are you ready to give up your virtue for a cause so feeble?"

"I will lose it sooner or later."

Brand smiled, intrigued by the statement. "You seem resigned to accept the loss as your fate."

"Before you found us in the meadow, Cadwyn had occasion to defend my honor. If I am to lose it, better for a belief it goes for the freedom of England." Alysaun raised her head, eyes shadowed by her long, golden lashes. "And better a Saxon than a foul, merciless Norman sweating over my bruised limbs."

Brand reached up to slide his fingers around her neck. They teased the silken wisps of gold escaping her braids, then drew her head toward him. "And what of a half-Norman, Alysaun? Do I fall somewhere between the acceptable and the spurned advances of the enemy?" He gave her no time to answer, his lips touching hers, seeking a wordless reply to the passion her soft appeal had inspired.

Alysaun struggled for a moment. The pressure of his mouth was too sweet to fight. Half-Norman or not, Brand in no way fit her image of the hated enemy. Both arms around her were strong and sure, and he twisted her body around until she lay half across his lap; it was so easily done she wondered at the unresisting pliancy of her limbs.

The girl was his to take. Her soft lips parted, yielding, offering up the sweetness of her willing mouth. More than submission, though, Brand recognized the desire that quickened in her response and found delight in the compliment to his vanity.

Even as he whispered her name and pressed light kisses across the soft white flesh of neck and throat, Brand's conscience fought a battle. She was right; her innocence would fall soon enough to some greedy man, Saxon or enemy. The thought of any man laboring to spend his lust upon this fragile, tender innocent was galling. Why not he, who would at least introduce her to the gentle pleasures of love?

But could he leave her in the morning and, knowing he had taken her to sate his own desires, not feel remorse at abandoning a girl who had one less possession to call her own? Brand swore a silent oath and groaned. Damn his thoughts, for they betrayed what his body wanted, needed. A curse on his conscience. The girl was not protesting the caresses of his roaming hands. Why was he?

Brand half rose and turned to place her on the pallet. Alysaun's eyes were half closed, her face flushed with the confusion of the strange, new feelings his artful kisses had aroused. Brand lay beside her, half his body covering hers, careful not to crush her with his weight. His fingers stroked her face, soothing, calming her even as he whispered endearments. His right leg touched her thighs, and Alysaun knew a sudden burst of panic that stiffened her entire body.

Warmed by his kisses, aware of what might follow more intimate caresses, she felt the fear inspired by reality. Her breath held until she ached, her eyes wide and reflecting the fright that coiled deep within, Alysaun whispered Brand's name.

At the sound of his name, torn from her throat in so terrified an appeal, Brand raised his head. Her eyes seemed to beg his assurances that what she offered would not be taken with pain. His sigh was more a moan as he rolled away and stood, facing away from the bed. He knew accusations would follow his false words of reassurance and that the sure ache of torn, bleeding flesh would slice through him more sharply than any sword.

He turned back to find her huddled against the wall in an effort to silence her weeping, shaking her body. Dismissing the aroused ache of his loins and the selfish desire to ignore her tears and satisfy himself, Brand sat down again and reached out. His touch was gentle, his fingers firm as he pulled her into his arms and cradled her close to his chest.

Brand's fingers, lightly stroking her head and shoulders, soothed and comforted Alysaun, and her tears slowed to a trickle as she looked up to wonder at the patient reserve of a man who had only minutes before communicated the urgency of passion. He still wanted her, she knew, and despite the fears that had halted his possession of her, she also knew regret and the remnants of her desire for him. She had wanted him to take away a memory of her when they parted in the morning, one that could not easily be forgotten. She could not bring herself to question aloud what had caused him to stop, but the puzzlement in her gaze elicited an answer from him.

"I am not one to kick dogs or snatch sweets from little children," Brand explained, sweeping a baby-fine wisp of gold back from her temples. "I will not take you this night, knowing I will ride away tomorrow and never see you again. So short a time, one night of love, however sweet it would be to recall." Still, Alysaun seemed unhappy with his reasoning. It was a time to speak plainly. "The world knows enough bastards, Alysaun. I would not leave you burdened with yet another."

Alysaun glanced down, her blush hidden by the shadows. She hadn't thought . . . Suddenly she looked up again, remembering the explanation for Brand's debt to Keric. "I think your reasoning lacks merit, sire. The woman at Blackurst—you did not take heed to seeding *that* plot."

Brand grinned, enchanted by her phrasing. "Aye, but it wasn't virgin soil, sweetling." He gave a tug on one of her long braids. "The lady in question, lovely as she was, had known a few seasons of planting . . . and I was not the first plowman to furrow that property. Alysaun, I cannot think why, when I've saved you your virtue, you argue against the act. Could it be that within that innocent breast you harbor a fine passion for me? Or is it the debt you imagine you owe?"

"Your question is arrogant on both counts, m'lord. I . . . I have not known you long enough to harbor so strong a desire. And as for the debt, which I *do* owe you, if I offered you my body"—Alysaun tilted her head and gazed up into his eyes—"would that payment not make of me a whore?"

Brand frowned. Alysaun had more than beauty. The girl's wits were as sharp as his knife blade. "Well put, Alysaun. What reason had you, then, if you deny desire and gratitude? Tell me true, girl."

She thought a moment. To admit how fine she thought him would only swell his head. Brand de Reynaud was arrogant enough about his looks and charm. "If you must have the truth, there was no reason—save that I was in an unreasoning mood, sire. I was not thinking, only feeling."

When he had fully considered her answer, Brand found a roundabout compliment in the maze of hedged words. If that were all her pride would allow, it pleased him. Though Alysaun seemed calm and recovered now, he was loath to let her loose yet. "I have never apologized for quitting the act of love," he said.

"That is understandable, Brand, if you have never quit it," Alysaun replied saucily. She much enjoyed this verbal tilting with sharp words in place of weapons.

"I haven't—" Brand moved to sit more comfortably and suddenly let out a howl, releasing Alysaun so abruptly that she tumbled backward. "*Christ*. What in the dev—" He reached beneath his leg and grimaced as he retrieved the object that had stabbed his right thigh. A needle, but where had it come from? At the sound of a muffled giggle from Alysaun, Brand turned a suspicious eye on the girl to find her red-faced at the effort to suppress her amusement, both hands covering her mouth. "Yours, m'lady?" he inquired, holding the needle aloft.

Alysaun nodded, wiping a tear from the corner of an eye. She could not help her laughter—it seemed that justice had been duly meted out for his unfair accusation that she was a thief. "I was about the repairing of your mantle, sir, when I found the piece of war arrow. If ever you assume to judge without all the facts, do recall the sharp prick of the needle point. I trust there was no permanent damage?"

"To the needle, girl, to my pride, or," he asked with a mocking brow, "to my thigh? I will recover. I was unaware, though, that any of my attire needed mending. Where is the mantle?" Alysaun dealt him a sweet, patient smile and pointed over the edge of the pallet to the floor. His dark green mantle lay there in a crumpled heap. "It does appear I've wronged you. What will you accept in the way of a peace offering?"

Alysaun half rose, leaning on one elbow. "Play me a song,

sire . . . nothing sad, mind, I've had enough of sadness. Play me a merry chanson on the lute whilst I finish what I set out to do. My needle, sir?''

Brand handed it to her, careful not to stab her with its point. "Your needle, Lady Alysaun, and my thanks. Your judgment is more merciful than mine." While Alysaun searched for the spool of thread, Brand retrieved his lute, came back to sit at the end of the pallet, and sang her a bawdy tale of a lady who had juggled her six lovers so well that not a one suspected he was not her chosen swain.

Alysaun fell asleep, lulled by Brand's soft, crooning songs, and he found a certain contentment just watching her. Lying on her side, hands pillowed beneath her head, she looked angelic, the picture of innocence. The sun had sprinkled pale freckles across the bridge of her straight, even nose. Long, thick lashes, darker gold than her bright tresses, lay feathered over cheeks as fair and smooth as a baby's. Beneath the dust of travel that had smudged her thin face the day of their meeting, had lain a jewel. Now that she was fresh and clean, attired in clothing more fitting to her rank, the jewel was polished, revealing its rare value.

Perhaps, he thought, he would take her with him to Hereward's camp on the Isle of Ely. He could enjoy her company that much longer. No, it was better to part as they had planned. The leavetaking in Ely would be that much harder, for Brand could not help but think he would be more enchanted by her with a passing of time.

Rising quietly, careful not to wake her, he crossed the small loft, ducking rafters to check his saddlebag. His tunics and mended mantle had been neatly packed by Alysaun before she lay down to rest. The arrow shaft, the possession of which he could not explain if a Norman sheriff took mind to search his belongings, she had sewn within a fold of his mantle. The hour was late and Brand was growing weary himself; but before he lay down to sleep, he drew several gold pieces from his purse and hid them within the nearly empty cloth bag Alysaun carried. She would fuss over the gift on discovering it, but he felt more at ease knowing she would have something to aid her journey.

Several hours before dawn, when Alysaun awoke, the room was dark, and she could scarcely make out the silhouette of Brand's body as he slept beneath the window. Rising quietly, she crept across the room and stared down at him. He slept so soundly, his mind apparently settled on the issue of leaving her.

The thought of watching him turn his mount and ride away from her was too painful to bear. Sure that she would betray her sorrow with tears, she did not want to leave him with that memory. Catching up her bag, she slipped its strap over her shoulder and went to the door. There she paused, trying to think of something she could leave behind for Brand. Now that her clothing was no longer stored in it, the bag lay empty and flat. Her mother's wedding band hung loosely on her thin finger, but there was too much of her father in that symbol for her to give it up.

Quickly, before she changed her mind, Alysaun slipped the jeweled cross over her head and arranged it carefully where Brand would find it. She could not guess at his reaction upon waking to find her gone. Perhaps relief that she had spared him a maudlin scene of weeping at the city gates, perhaps some regret, she hoped, that she had passed out of his life.

Downstairs, in the common room of the tavern, several drunks were snoring off the previous night's indulgence. She slipped past the room, nearly colliding with the innkeeper's wife, a squat, harried woman with a kind face. "Where be you off to at this hour, lady?" the woman inquired wiping her sweated brow with the edge of her apron. "I hain't had time to finish me bakin'. Your 'usband's still sleepin', eh? Now, hain't that typical—we're up and they's still snorin'."

In the dim light by the door, the blush that colored Alysaun's cheeks at the mention of her "husband" was not visible. If she wanted to be away before Brand woke and found her missing, she couldn't tarry. "I've no time to eat," she whispered, "but if you'd be so kind as to let me out..." Alysaun looked toward the barred door.

"O' course, m'lady. But if you don't mind me speakin' out o' turn, you shouldn't be walkin' about at this hour wi'out your 'usband's company. Why, there be all sorts of ruffians and thieves roamin' loose afore dawn lights the skies. Can your business not wait your lord's risin'? No, I see I'm pokin' me nose where it don't belong.'' The women lifted the heavy bar that secured the inn door, swinging it open for Alysaun.

"Thank you," Alysaun replied, grateful that the woman had ceased her questions. "Could I bother you for a direction? I seek the road east, leading toward Bury."

Agatha Grim's small gray eyes, almost hidden by folds of fat, widened at the query. What was this lady about, that she was leaving so handsome a husband and asking the way to Bury? She didn't look daft. "Follow the lane," Agatha directed, leaning her bulk out the door to point, "past the square and St. John's Maddermart. It'll lead you straight to the gates. The road forks there, and a turn right'll see you headed for Bury."

Again Alysaun thanked the woman, then slipped past her into the lane. It was empty now, in the gray half-light of predawn, except for a cotter urging his broken, swayed mare to hurry his fresh goods to market. She started down the cobbled lane, pausing when the innkeeper's wife called after her, "Hey, now, wha' will I say to your 'usband when 'e finds you gone?"

"Oh . . . he knows where I am bound," Alysaun tossed back, and hurried away before the woman could pin her down to a more detailed explanation. Dawn was just beginning to pink the sky when she reached the gates of Cambridge. The day would be fine and clear, making her way easier to travel. She stepped aside as a Norman soldier galloped his destrier past her, heading into the city.

The road forked some thirty yards beyond the gates, both byways beginning to clog with villagers' carts bound for the marketplace. For a while Alysaun had to fight the flow of traffic moving toward Cambridge, but as the sun climbed higher in the direction she walked the noisy rumble of carts and hayracks lessened, and only an occasional merchant passed her, leaving the town to travel on after a night's lodging.

* * *

Anxious to make home before nightfall, Esmond Rede left his lodgings in Cambridge's Borough Mews at dawn, mounting his steed to ride east, along the road that led to his estates of Havistock. The business that detained him three days in the city had been boring and, except for a brief lay with a tavern wench, dull. The Norman tax on Havistock's livestock and produce had been increased again. Only a bribe slipped to the sheriff had somewhat lessened his due.

Esmond rode for a while, carefully sidestepping his mount past the commoners headed for the city, ignoring the good-humored shouts that passed between fellow villagers. No one, least of all the serfs, had reason to be so jovial in this time of heavy-handed oppression.

At the sight of a young girl walking along the road before him, Esmond frowned. Dressed finely, yet with no veil and wimple to cover her braided, golden locks, she looked to be Saxon. What lady, though, Saxon or Norman, would be walking, without chariot or mount? Intrigued, he spurred his horse forward to come abreast of her.

The glimpse of her profile before she increased her pace was oddly familiar. Reining in his mount, Esmond paused to ponder if he might have met her in the past. Her purely Saxon coloring was common enough. Eyes closed for a second, Esmond saw the image of the golden-haired knight who had been squire to his own father and with whom he in turn had served his own apprenticeship for knighthood. Edwin Meau was dead now, gone down beneath a Norman lance at Hastings, but he had had two sisters, Alysaun and a younger girl, whose name he could not recall.

It was near two years since his father had called him and Sir Edwin north to repel the invading Norwegians. Alysaun had been thirteen, just beginning to flower with the fairness of her mother, Lady Edana. If this was she . . . the girl looked to be fifteen or so. Esmond glanced up to find her far down the road, and with an excitement that communicated itself to his mount, he spurred the horse to a gallop.

Alysaun tensed, listening to the thudding hooves of the approaching steed. One brief glance over her shoulder saw a well-dressed young man amount a horse of dark brown, determination in the set of his body as he gained on her. Her first, panicky desire to run subsided. She couldn't have run far pursued by horse, and the man didn't have a Norman look. She stopped, waiting to see what he was about, refusing to look up even at the close sound of the mare's heaving, snorting breath.

Esmond drew up the reins, bringing the mare to a halt across the girl's path. He grinned, delighted to find that it was, indeed, Lady Alysaun of Hanley Manor. "M'lady? Lady Alysaun, have no fear," he said softly, throwing leg over saddle to slide down and land before her. "Surely you remember me . . . your good brother's squire, Esmond of Havistock?"

Even before he said his name, his voice was familiar. Alysaun looked up with a blend of surprise and dismay. So changed was she, the thought of recognition from some past acquaintance was an unlikely chance that knew realization. Had he heard rumors of her family's downfall? Surely he would question why she walked the roads with no servants or protectors. She did not feel like repeating her tale of woe to a man who had known the family's better days. "Of course I remember you, Esmond," Alysaun said hesitantly, then offered him a smile. "By now it must be Sir Esmond. The sound of a familiar voice did startle me. I must seem as senseless as a village idiot."

"Nay, my lady, I am as shocked to find you here." Esmond's eyes were wide with admiration. Despite a thinness of form, Edwin's sister had matured into the full, golden beauty of her Saxon inheritance. "I cannot think what fortune directed our paths to cross but I'll not question such luck. Why, though, if I may ask, are you alone, afoot and far from home? Your parents—"

The sadness that shadowed her blue eyes was as a cloud sweeping over the sun. "Both dead, Sir Esmond, or at least I know my mother is. Hanley was seized, forfeited to the crown, and Father dragged away to prison. I hope he doesn't live. Death would be more a mercy than the harsh captivity dealt our kind by the Norman curs."

Esmond was speechless, uncertain how to offer his sympathies. "You are homeless, then, my lady? Where are you bound?" The thought of young Alysaun prey to all the dangers prevalent on the roads was like a knife blade thrust in his heart.

"To Bury Saint Edmunds, which, I was told, lies at the end of this road. My sister—you remember Aelwyna, all shy-eyed and quiet—is a nun at the convent there. I have been laboring these past months since Candlemas to reach that sanctuary and assume the veil myself."

"Aelwyna I can see in the veiled hush of chapel prayers and the company of only women. You, Alysaun, if you would pardon my opinion, are too lovely to hide away. Down the same road, before the town of Bury, lies Havistock. The estate has passed to me and is still a plot of English soil untrampled by Norman boots. You are homeless no longer, m'lady, if you would care to accept the hospitality of my manor. I know my widowed lady mother would be pleased to have you with us."

Alysaun was hesitant, for a moment too proud to accept. She turned back to look in the direction of Cambridge and Brand. He was lost to her company now, and she would be a fool to refuse the offer to dwell again in an English home, to be surrounded by the comforts that would be so close to Hanley's. She turned back and smiled at Esmond. "I most humbly accept your kind offer, sire, and pray your mother does not chide you for bringing home a stray."

Catching her hand to raise it to his lips, Esmond touched the pale white fingers in a kiss and answered confidently, "My mother can only praise the fortune dealt her son. Believe me, she will welcome you as the daughter she never had." He drew her forward, lifting her slight weight to the saddle before mounting behind her. The girl was tense at first; he sensed that as his arms encircled her narrow waist to reach for the reins. But as Edmond tugged at the mare's bit and wheeled her gently around to trot eastward, toward Havistock, he thought he heard a peaceful sigh escape Alysaun's lovely lips.

3

When the day's first light streamed through the open window above his head, Brand was too sleepy to feel much alarm at the sight of the empty pallet. He thought only that Alysaun had awakened first and gone below to see to some breakfast. He stretched tired, cramped muscles and stood, only to curse aloud as he forgot to duck the oaken rafters and his crown thudded painfully against a hardwood beam.

The sunlight strengthened now, glinting off a golden object lying on the bed. His curiosity aroused, Brand approached the pallet, brows fiercely knit as he recognized Alysaun's jeweled cross and bent to seize its fine gold chain. Still fastened, it could not have slipped from her neck in sleep. He whirled, searching the floor for her bag. Gone, and she with it, while he slept.

Brand swore another oath and slammed open the door, his booted feet thudding down the steps to the common room and his loud, angry shouts for the innkeeper startling the other patrons. The man's thickset wife waddled over, frowning over the too-early disturbance of her establishment, and requested that he lower his voice.

Brand's threatening scowl capped her own irritation, and to his brusque inquiry about his "wife's" whereabouts, the now suspicious Agatha retorted that the lady had taken herself off for other parts. She wagged a finger at him, assuming that a lovers' spat had sent the girl fleeing him. "Be you lover or 'usband," she chided, "a fine lady like that 'un won't put up wi' threats and blows. If you've a mind to make it right, though, the lass hain't been gone too long. A man on horse could catch up easy-like. Said you'd know where she's bound, she did."

Without so much as a thank-you, he turned and sprinted back up the stairs, leaving goodwife Grim to shake her head over such manners. Upstairs in the loft, Brand grabbed his saddlebag, desposited the emerald cross in his purse, and slung the lute strap over his shoulder. A quick glance assured him he had forgotten nothing, and he clumped downstairs once more to settle his debt and call for his horse.

The cobbled streets were thronged with townspeople and thick with peddlers haranguing potential customers. With a patience he didn't feel, Brand guided the stallion through the crowds and along the same path Alysaun had taken earlier. Finally he reached the gates and set out on the east road at a furious pace. Behind him the church bells of Cambridge tolled the hour of seven, calling the faithful to a mass to start the day.

Brand expected to catch her easily enough. There were other people walking, an occasional horseman or a cart, but no sight of a slim figure in blue silk. When he had ridden past the farthest point Alysaun could have made on foot, Brand went a mile farther, then stopped at last to allow his winded mount a rest. She couldn't have taken the north road by mistake, and yet . . . Apprehension tightened his muscles as he again looked up and down the road as far as he could see.

Though a pretty girl was easy prey for any passing ruffian, Alysaun probably would not have met trouble so soon. There had to be a reason she wasn't on the path; perhaps some merchant had offered a ride in his cart. Riding back toward the city, Brand questioned those traveling in the same direction if they had seen a slim, golden-haired lady dressed in a gunna of blue. As each responded negatively he moved on. It seemed, when he finally approached Cambridge again, that all hope was gone. Unbelievably, Alysaun had walked out of his life and disappeared.

At the city gates, his anger tempered by worry that she might have been dragged from the road, Brand tried one last person, a Norman chevalier who had dismounted to chat with the sentry.

In answer to Brand's description of Alysaun, the man, who boasted he was Hugo de Tracene, chief bailiff to the city's sheriff, Roger Fitz Walther, claimed he had seen the girl. "Aye, so I did, my friend. Couldn't help but notice what a pretty piece she was. Weren't afoot, though. If the girl I did see was the same, she was riding a brown mare and not alone. The girl and her companion was both Saxon. What is she to you?" His dark, swarthy face showed curiosity as Hugo puzzled over the stranger's interest.

"Wife," Brand lied, using the pretense to extract some information. He frowned and the tension in his body communicated itself to his mount. The tightening of his knees against the stallion's shoulders sent him sidestepping, rearing his head to shake his mane with a nervous whicker. Brand called his name in a low, soothing tone and stroked the silver-gray coat. "Simply because I paid too much favor to a lady at our lodgings, the girl has run, I assume, back to her mother. How long ago did you see her, sir? I would catch her ere she insults my name and honor before her gloating relatives."

"An hour or so," the bailiff replied, shading his eyes against the sun to judge its passage. "Mayhap a bit more." He grimaced sympathetically at the foreigner's plight. "These English are an odd lot, no? A tad too sensitive and overproud for my liking. Your wife seemed to have found a friend to aid her escape, though. Laughing they was, when I noticed 'em in passing, but in no great hurry."

So Alysaun had found a protector, one of her own kind, and so quickly it irked Brand's pride, even though he knew relief at the knowledge she hadn't come to any harm. He was left with a distinctly dissatisfied feeling. Her departure, so abrupt and almost stealthy, had cheated him of the chance to bid her farewell. There had been no call for her to leave the cross behind, and now, since she had disappeared with an unknown countryman, he had little chance to return it. "'Tis too great a chance, but I must ask if you know anything of this companion, his name or residence perhaps? If I find him, he'll be most sorry he chose to aid a runaway wife."

Brand's menacing scowl brought an appreciative grin to the bailiff's face. "'Tis only right to put him in his place, sir. Fortune smiles upon you. The man was in the city several days, consulting with the sheriff. The Saxon is called Rede, Esmond Rede, of a keep known as Havistock. Tried to wriggle out of what he owed the King, he did."

His luck *had* turned, Brand speculated. "And how do I find Havistock, my good man? Not that I don't appreciate your help, but I must ride hard to catch the little rebel before my honor is further compromised."

De Tracene pointed to the east road. "Retrace your path, sir. The manor is some fifteen miles short of Bury. Ride south once you pass Compley village. 'Tisn't but a few miles from the main road. Good luck to you. A sound thrashing might make the lady think ere she tries another foolish escapade."

Brand thanked the man for his assistance, then wheeled the stallion about to canter toward the crossroads. The bailiff watched for a minute, then turned back to resume his conversation with the sentry. It was the guard who a minute later pointed out the path the stranger had taken. Hugo turned back, frowning, a puzzled look in his dark, almost black eyes. The stranger was fast disappearing to the north, along the road that led to Ely.

For some time Brand kept up a hard pace, urging the stallion to gallop. He had almost taken the Bury road but changed his mind and decided to deliver the troublesome arrow to its owner before settling his unfinished business with Alysaun. Once she had her property back, he would ride past Bury to the Channel coast and take passage on a ship, bound for anywhere, as long as it was away from this accursed land.

Brand passed sloping fields just beginning to green with sprouting wheat; grassy meadows dotted by grazing sheep with a curious, naked look after the recent spring shearing; thick, verdant stands of oak and ash. In his determination to reach Ely, he saw little of the scenery. An occasional village of clustered cottages offered the chance to rest his mount and seek refreshment, but by late afternoon he was some five miles south of his goal.

He heard the shouted curses and labored sounds of the skirmish on his approach to the village of Daning Greens and frowned, nearly deciding to skirt the place as several frightened cotters ran past him. Though all of England was claimed by William, the farther north one rode, the more rebellion seethed. Indeed, after nearly two years of Norman occupation, the rich earldoms of Northumbria and Mercia still claimed their allegiance lay with the exiled atheling, Prince Edgar.

Brand slowed the lathered stallion to a walk, listening. Clearly, some rebel Saxons were harrying their enemies. The years of Danish rule had left their mark, for the wild, keening war cry of the English was akin to the battle shriek of their Viking cousins. Brand took shelter out of harm's way between two thatched cottages huddled close together.

From this vantage point he could see the fray. Several Normans, heavily armored but dead nonetheless, lay on the ground close to the stone church near the village boundary. Other defenders fought hand-to-hand, clashing with the long-haired Saxons in an effort to repel the surprise attack. The church, wealthy despite the poverty of the surrounding cottages and crofts, was the object of the assault. Even as he watched, several of the English emerged from the nave with arms full of the treasures stored within.

Brand was about to move on, to circle the melee. The fight was not his, though his sympathies lay with the Saxons. The brief defense was nearly ended—dead or dying Norman soldiers were scattered about the dusty commons, more cries of victory breaking the still air of the village. Just as he tugged the reins to bring his steed around, he caught sight of a lone Englishman, separated from his companions and backed against the whitewashed wall of a nearby cottage, with three Normans surrounding him.

The predicament brought Brand's retreat to a halt. The Saxon didn't look stupid, yet the tall, shaggy-haired rebel had allowed his greed to overshadow caution. His defense was hampered by the jeweled ivory casket clutched beneath one arm. Without the encumbrance, he might have had a fighting chance; with it, he was as good as dead.

Yet with the odds against him, the man stubbornly retained the plundered treasure and fought his losing battle, inching along the wall even as the Normans closed in. His skill with the longsword was all that kept the foe at bay; he could but parry the multiple thrusts.

Brand cursed as one of the Normans sliced the Saxon's shoulder. It was not his place to rescue the man but the underdog always aroused empathy in him. With another curse, he emerged from between the cottages, riding hard the thirty yards and shouting a wild cry that echoed the earlier Saxon whoops.

One Norman, turning at the sound, died instantly, Brand's sword half decapitating him as it sliced through the chain mail covering his neck. "Drop the box, fool," Brand shouted, wheeling to engage another of the man's attackers. Prepared this time, the Norman fought well, though with Brand's advantage of mounted height, he was as doomed as his dead friend. Backed against the wall, he managed to thrust upward and caught Brand with a slice across the thigh, just above the knee.

Ignoring the searing pain and the blood that gushed forth, Brand lifted his sword arm high and lunged. That blow dented the man's chest plate, but left him too stunned to ward off a successive strike that sent the tip of the blade through his throat. His mouth twisted, all that could be seen beneath his helmet, blood gushing from lips that could no longer form words.

All that kept the man afoot was Brand's sword point pinning him to the wall. Grimacing at the blood that spattered the stallion's neck, Brand tugged and the sword came free. The man crumpled forward and the stallion reared away from the scent of blood and death.

Brand turned in the saddle, curious to see if the Saxon had defended himself against the one attacker left him. The man stood over the Norman's sprawled body, one foot on the man's thigh as he tugged his sword from the vulnerable spot where the hauberk divided below the man's belly. The Englishman glanced up, a cocky, victorious grin widening his full mouth as he wiped the blood from his sword on the Norman's leggings.

Now the throbbing of his wound drew Brand's attention. He examined the sword cut, peeling back the ripped material of his leggings and tunic to judge the damage. The cut was superficial, only deep enough to ache and bleed, not enough to tear the muscle, thank God. He had no desire to limp the rest of his life because he had come to the aid of a thieving Saxon.

The defense was at an end. Despite the advantage of their chain mail and helmets, the Normans littered the ground, dead or dying of mortal wounds. As far as Brand could tell by a short survey of the commons, only one Englishman had fallen. Free now to carry off their plunder, the Saxons stopped only to strip their dead opponents of weapons and proceeded with the looting of the church sanctuary.

"I owe you a debt, my friend," a deep, gravelly voice said at Brand's side, and he turned back to frown down at the rescued Saxon. The man was even bigger close up, his brown-blond hair falling to the edge of shoulders so broad they reminded Brand of Alysaun's old protector, Cadwyn. Eyes of bright blue in a darkly tanned, bearded, and mustached face looked up with crinkled warmth. "I'm sorry, I am, you suffered a cut on my behest. What can I do to repay your valor?"

The Saxon tongue was harsh to his ears. Though Brand could speak and understand it, he was more comfortable with French. "For one, you may address me in Norman, if you know it. For another, retrieve your precious plunder before it goes awalking with one of the villagers," Brand snapped, irritated because of the

87

pounding ache of his leg. He pointed and the Saxon whirled to find a ragged cotter reaching for the ivory casket. A shout and the partial drawing of his sword from its scabbard was sufficient to scare the man off.

"And next time you go thieving," Brand added as the blue-eyed gaze returned to him, "see to your flanks, sir. You should never have allowed yourself to be cornered."

The blue eyes widened, then narrowed in a fierce frown that drew heavy golden eyebrows together. Without a doubt, thought Hereward, he owed his continued breath to this young man's unsought aid, but the lad's impertinence didn't sit well with a man grown used to respect. "You're handing out lessons with your help, eh, my young warrior?" Hereward retorted, feet planted firmly apart, arms akimbo as he snorted his disdain. "When you were but a sprout no higher than my knee, I had fought my first battle."

Despite the ache of his leg, Brand found this blond, shaggy giant likable. "Then you never learned what I knew before I trained as squire. 'Tis a wonder you've lasted this long with such sloppy defensive habits." Brand grinned, taking some of the edge off his criticism.

Hereward rubbed at his beard. The lad was right, he had been careless. "I would guess I'm not too old to learn from my mistakes, son, though I don't know as I care to hear them recounted. What manner of man are you, who likes the Norman tongue yet comes to the aid of an Englishman? I'd like to hear the name of the man I owe gratitude to."

Brand bowed his head. "Brand de Reynaud, a native of Provence but mothered by a Norman lady, sir. I don't seek any reward but this: Good Saxon that you are, would you know the way into the marshes that guard the stronghold of one Hereward of Lincoln?"

"Aye, that I do, but the fens are a treacherous place for those who don't know it, full of bogs and swamp holes deep enough for a man and horse to disappear in forever. What business do you have here with Hereward?"

"The delivery of a message meant only for his ears," Brand

88

snapped, foreseeing the difficulty of what had seemed a most simple task. "I'll take my chances with it, for I have no other choice. At least answer me this: What is your rebel leader like? I want to make sure my message is given to the right man."

"Oh, you cannot mistake him," Hereward replied with a smile that revealed a broken front tooth. "The man is tall and handsome, about my height and build. And so keen a warrior he'd never be cornered like I was." He looked over his shoulder; the plundering done, his men were mounted and ready to ride. "We're bound for Ely ourselves, son. I'll not lead a stranger in to see Hereward, but there's a village chapel near enough to the fens where you can wait to see if he'll come to you."

"Wait here," he ordered, starting off on foot toward the church, where his men were waiting. "I'd best acquaint my fellow . . . thieves, as you deem us, of the decision so you'll not be obliged to fight any more frays."

It wasn't likely, Brand thought as he watched the man stride off. The next time he heard any sound of an altercation, he would turn and ride the opposite way. While he waited he tore a strip from the hem of his ripped tunic and gently bound his thigh. The bleeding had ebbed, but the dust of the road would do no good to an open cut.

An hour's ride north, past another huddle of thatched cottages and more cultivated fields bordered in hedgerows, brought Brand and the company of Saxon raiders to the chapel Hereward had mentioned. Beyond it lay the low, damp marshes that the rebel Englishman had chosen for his island fortress of Ely, a place so inaccessible that no one could guess how many Normans had disappeared in the attempt to locate it.

Hereward dismounted and ordered his men to watch the road. As he had warned them earlier not to mention his name in Brand's hearing, they knew what he intended now. Coming around the man's gray steed, he offered him a hand down, seeing how the young man winced at the stiffness of the wound he had received in Hereward's aid.

"How long will this larger-than-life hero of yours keep me waiting?" Brand asked, grimacing as he climbed the chapel steps with a hobbling gait and gingerly placed his weight on the sore leg. "I've no patience to sit in an empty church for hours, hungry and tired, while he decides to grant me an audience."

Hereward held open one of the double doors and gestured to the dimly lit nave. "Hereward is more courteous than you deem him, Sir Brand, though I know your wound sets your tone." Inside, he led Brand into the sanctuary and across it to a stone well covered by a planked oaken lid. "Have a seat, son," he offered, and Brand gratefully sank down, easing the weight from his right leg.

Hereward took a stand opposite Brand's seat, a few feet away. His arms crossed over his massive chest, he looked down and drew Brand's attention by clearing his throat. The action did nothing to lessen the deep, rough rumble of his voice when he inquired again what message Brand carried to Hereward.

Brand looked up, his mouth tightening with irritation. "You would make a weary man waste his last strength, sir. I have said my message is for Hereward of Lincoln and no other."

"Then give over the message, son, for it is Hereward who stands ready to receive it." He smiled sheepishly and shrugged off Brand's narrow-eyed, disbelieving frown. "Aye, none other, and I am regretful of the ruse carried this far. There's a fine price set on this shaggy-headed outlaw. I grow more cautious with each day I live past another raid. To die defending England would give me pleasure. To risk a spy or traitor turning me over to the Normans . . . well, I would rather fall upon my trusty blade and end all with dignity."

"I only have your word, sir," Brand asserted. "Not that I think you lie, but what I carry is too important to hand over to a man who *says* he is Hereward. If you are truly he, you might understand my own caution."

Hereward pondered for a moment, raising a hand to scratch at his beard. "I can't say I've ever had to prove who I am," he commented, then his eyes widened with the glimmer of an idea. He took a step closer and removed one of the three brooches that secured his mantle. Offering it to Brand, he pointed out the raised insignia of a coiled snake worked into the round copper brooch. "If you know anything about me, this is the emblem I use."

Brand stared at the brooch. The snake design mirrored the one carved into the arrow. He sighed and glanced up. "I believe you, sir, but this exchange could have been done at an earlier time. I have traveled from the south coast of Cornwall—"

"Lord Keric sent you?" Hereward interrupted, hoping against hope that the message meant support from the young lord.

Brand was probing the lining of his dark green mantle, searching for the spot near the collar where Alysaun had hidden the arrow shaft. "Yes, 'twas at Keric's"—he smiled, fingers touching the stiff broken shaft— "at his bidding that I came to return your war arrow. The blasted thing is here, if I can pull it free." He tugged a little harder and, with a ripping of stitches, produced the arrow for Hereward. "Keric humbly submits that he is unable to offer men, arms, or even coin to further your cause, m'lord. His holdings now are half what they were a year and a half ago, and the rest may go to a Norman overlord within the year."

Keen disappointment made Hereward pace the sanctuary in long strides, shaking his head and grumbling in a low voice Brand couldn't quite make out. "I'm sorry to bear such ill tidings, sire, but it would seem to my view that England will never shake off the Normans because . . . because anyone with anything left is too busy defending it against forfeiture. Your men fight with valor, Hereward, but they do so with nothing but their lives to lose."

"I agree with you, my boy. If I could see every Saxon keep and bailey seized, I'd have my fighting strength and whatever we could steal back or pillage would add to our chances. Now we only pick at the enemies' flanks. Like summer bugs that sting and fly away, we are vulnerable to a strong slap." He sighed heavily and cleared his throat once more. "At least I still have Edwin and Morcar, and a chance the Danish king will invade and add to William's problems."

"Edwin and Morcar?"

Hereward looked up, having forgotten his companion was not a native son. "The border earls, lad, Northumbria and Mercia. Their holdings are still strong enough to lend money and supplies, if not men. Despite their youth, the two brothers are wise enough to know their only chance to save their earldoms lies in rebellion.

"Well, enough of this," he added, his mood optimistic despite the disappointing news. There were yet other pieces of the war arrow scattered over England. Until they all came back, there was a possibility of support turning up. "We're very close to home, Brand de Reynaud. My dear wife, Torfrida, no doubt has a hot meal waiting. Aside from saving my hide, you've done me a good service in returning the arrow and Keric's message. Come with us. Frida will clean and bind your wound and see you're given every comfort we can offer."

"I accept, sire, with eagerness that does not become me. Whatever the accommodations, 'twill seem a palace to me." Brand eased cautiously off the well lid, his leg stiffer for the inactivity. Limping over to Hereward, he held out the broken arrow and brooch. "These are yours, sire."

Hereward accepted only the arrow and moved past Brand to open the well and drop the wood within. A second later there was a sound of a splash and the creaking of the lid. He returned to Brand and insisted, "Keep the brooch, son. You'll offend me if you don't. It's small enough compensation for so selfless an act of bravery. If mayhap you find yourself in danger or dire straits one day, return it to me with a message, and I'll come storming to repay my debt."

"I will, Hereward, for if your wrath should come down on me, I'm not sure I have the strength to defend myself. Here, I'll pin it on." Brand secured it next to the plainer cross-shaped brooch that held the gathers of his mantle to the right. "There, now your men will know not to push my mount and me into one of those deep sinkholes you mentioned."

"Oh, I doubt they would, Brand. No, if they considered you a threat to me, you'd be dispatched long before we started into the fens. Now come along, lad. The sooner we make Ely Isle, the better you and I both will feel."

Hereward led his stalwarts toward the marsh, Brand riding at his side until the rebel leader suggested he drop back behind him. There was no path, only small mounds of dry land rising above the puddled waters, thick ferns, and mosses. The way was difficult enough in the strong sunlight of day. Now, with darkness falling, a thick mist was rising off the marshes. Brand's respect for Hereward's wisdom increased dramatically. Only a fool or an Englishman familiar with their many pitfalls would attempt to cross the fens, day or night. Supplied by his sympathetic countrymen, Hereward and his warriors could hide within the bogs forever and escape capture.

Never in his life had Brand guided a steed so cautiously. Even with the torches carried by every other man, he had to strain his eyes to follow Hereward and keep the stallion to the same tracks the rebel's mount had laid down. At last an eerie glow seemed to light the shifting layers of fog ahead. A tired, halfhearted cheer went up from the men behind Brand, and Hereward called back to him that a warm, welcome fire and hot food were but a stone's throw away now.

The horses' hooves suddenly echoed against wooden planking. They were crossing a short, narrow bridge over a river that ran through the fens and surrounded the Isle of Ely. On solid ground after the bridge, the company spurred their mounts to a faster pace, moving up a slight incline. Not much more could be seen of the fort than the torches flickering above the pointed timbers of the palisade.

At their approach, the heavy gates creaked open. Inside, a number of people crowded the bailey to welcome them; and as a grinning Hereward stood in his stirrups to give a wolf's howl of triumph, a strong cheer rose at another successful raid against the hated Normans. Wives hurried up to assure themselves their husbands had returned safely; grooms and squires came rushing to quarter the horses.

Brand stayed mounted for several minutes, studying the joy of those reunited one more time, taking in the sturdiness of the two-story stone and timber keep. Hereward had built the structure on an existing stone foundation, the ruins of an abandoned ancient monastery. It was well he had made it so large, for there seemed to be at least a hundred Saxons living in the fort; knights, wives, squires, servants, and the homeless mothers and sisters of several of the dispossessed knights. Just to feed and quarter so many was an arduous task; it was no small wonder that Hereward sought to repossess the wealth that had belonged to his people before the coming of the Norman conquerors.

Hereward had told his wife how Brand's valiant charge had saved his life. Now he approached with his arm around Torfrida's slight shoulders, to introduce her to Brand. Upon dismounting, Brand winced at the stiffness of his wounded leg. Still, his bow was as courteous as if he were greeting a queen. "'Twas my pleasure, m'lady," he replied when the petite, raven-haired woman thanked him for the rescue. Questioning her accent, he found she was a native of Paris, far to the north of Provence. "I've seen the wonders of that city, madame. It far exceeds any splendors to be found in my province."

"Then we will speak of what we know in common, sir," Frida replied with a concerned smile, "while I tend to the wound you received in my husband's behalf. Come . . . Hereward, assist your friend within."

Brand was about to deny the need for such coddling, but one awkward step on his sore leg assured him he should humbly accept the offer. Though the rebel leader towered over his wife by at least a foot, it was clear that Torfrida was one of those women who ruled those around her with quiet, gentle persuasion, who found her requests obeyed instantly because of the soft, reasonable way she made them.

Inside the hall, the tables had been set for the arrival of the hungry, exhausted troop. Even while servants rushed by with deep bowls of a hearty beef and bean soup and platters of roasted chickens, Brand was escorted to a chamber specifically set aside for the care of the wounded. Others, most of them injured no more seriously than Brand himself, were lovingly tended by wives or mothers. Cleaning the cut above his knee was almost more painful than receiving the wound had been but while Frida cautiously soaked away the blood-encrusted, makeshift wrappings, Brand's flagging strength was fortified by a goblet of heated wine Hereward brought him. When all was said and done, Frida was able to assure him that the herbs she had applied beneath the linen wrappings would draw out any infection caused by dirt. "You'll have a scar, but more to show your courage to your wife or lady," she said as she tied the bandage.

"Then she'll have to view an old scar," Brand answered with a weary attempt at a grin. "I've no one to care for me as you do for Hereward."

"No one? How can it be that so handsome a man has no lady to bless his life?" Torfrida's dark eyes twinkled mischievously. "There are several here who would be delighted to attend your cares, sir. Perhaps, ere you leave us, you may find one of the ladies to your liking."

"Leave the man be, Frida, he's suffered enough already," Hereward chided gruffly, then affectionately squeezed his wife's shoulders as he apologized to Brand. "Frida would love to spend her days in quiet matchmaking, away from all the bother and worry of the cause I fight."

"'Tis only natural," Brand replied, "but I value my freedom too much yet to bind myself for life. Besides," he added, "I've yet to meet a lady as sweet and gentle as yours."

Three days later, when Brand was lying abed with a fever born of his infected wound, Frida had reason to recall that disclaimer and doubt its veracity. Though he had at first been quartered with several of the single knights, Frida had insisted, upon the onset of the delirium that accompanied the fever, that Brand be brought to the small chamber adjacent to their own room. When she emerged from the room with a worried frown, Hereward looked up and questioned Brand's progress. "How goes he, my sweet? I would be loath to lose so courageous a newfound friend."

"The next half day will tell," Frida replied with a heavy sigh. "I would never have expected so much festering in a mere flesh wound. But in fevered dreaming, Brand has spoken a truth his lips earlier had denied.'' At Hereward's puzzled look, she added, ''He calls repeatedly for a lady lost to him, a girl named Alysaun.''

4

To shorten the length of Brand's journey, Hereward had suggested he ride southeast to Bury Saint Edmunds and take the road leading west, toward Cambridge. To further accommodate the young man, who had in the passage of four weeks become a friend, he had sent one of his most trusted companions to accompany Brand as far as Bury.

Thinking that Alysaun might have gone on to the convent in Bury, Brand stopped there and inquired. The abbess, Mother Christina, knew nothing of the girl but recognizing Alysaun's family name, offered the information that one of her charges had been Aelwyna Meau. *"Had* been?" Brand had asked. "Then she's gone off to another holy order?"

Beneath her white woolen veil, the abbess's face had taken on a shadowed expression of sadness. "No, my son, soon after Christmastide, the girl fell ill. 'Twas a wasting fever, leaving her weaker until, just after Easter, she passed on. A sweet and gentle child, she was, my Aelwyna. She is buried near our gardens, a spot she loved well and tended.''

So there was one more blow to add to Alysaun's distress. Brand's irritation with her, nurtured in the time spent at Ely, lessened with that sad news. He had thanked the abbess and, after leaving a donation for a mass to be said in Aelwyna's name, rejoined his companion, Leofric of Lincoln.

Leofric was but a few years younger than Brand's twenty-five, but the quiet, solemn young man seemed older. Of all Hereward's company, he was the least likely warrior. Brand had been told by Hereward that Leofric had been raised for the priesthood. William's invasion and the fact that Leofric had lost his father and brothers at Hastings and seen his younger sister raped by the marauding Normans had changed his vocation.

After sharing a meal at a tavern on one of Bury's quiet, narrow streets, Brand and Leofric made for the city's west gate. Leofric had stubbornly insisted he would accompany Brand farther, at least to the point where the track to Havistock branched off the main road; but, just as stubbornly, Brand had denied the suggestion, claiming, ''You've done enough, my friend. I've traveled enough on my own to make my way. The journey thus far was made more easy by your companionship. Return to Hereward and Ely with my thanks and good wishes. We may yet meet again, Leofric, and clasp hands in friendship.''

Leofric had reluctantly given in and headed north while Brand turned the stallion due east, his quest for Alysaun once more nearly at an end. Just before the scattered crofts and cottages of Compley, he had turned south. The path he traveled now was little more than a pony track that led through a rise of gentle hills. The area was heavily forested, and on this heated midsummers day the cool shade was most welcome.

Though the village had sprung up to serve the manor of Havistock, there were other cottages a mile farther along the track. The unrest that shadowed England seemed more distant here. Barefoot children, shrieking in a racing game of chase, paused to watch him pass, their eyes widening at the sight of a stranger.

Just beyond the cottages, the track widened, and on a steep, broad plateau, surrounded by tall poplars and an orchard heavy with fruit, sat Havistock.

In his travels from Cornwall to Bath, from Oxford to Cambridge, Brand had kept to the main roads and seen little of the Saxon estates hidden away in the countryside. More used to the tile-roofed, pastel-shaded manors of his native Provence and the storied grandeur of Norman fortresses of stone, he was still taken back by the simple rusticity of the English homes. Built in the style of Viking long-houses, Havistock was a squat, thatched building of oaken timbers interlacing daub and wattle plaster covered with a fresh whitewash.

In the yard that stretched before the manor's story-and-a-half entry doors, two men were engaged in mock combat, exercising their skills with swords whose sharp edges were blunted by cotton wrappings. They paused, wiping sweat from their eyes, as two hounds raced down the hill, announcing Brand's arrival with loud, yelping barks.

"*Hold,* Bracken, Dalian," the taller of the two men called and, when the dogs kept racing, added a curse that drew a laugh from his companion. "*Hold,* you hellhounds. The stranger is no Saxon, but neither looks he a dark, scurvy Norman."

The hounds bounded around the stallion's forelegs until a whistle from the Saxon brought them coursing back with protesting whines. Brand waved a hand, though clearly one mounted man was no threat to the practicing knights. Finally, when he had led his steed up the incline and across the yard, he took a moment to catch his wind and announced his name.

"Where d'you hail from, foreigner, and what business brings you to this manor?" asked the taller of the knights, who had given his name as Edelbart.

Brand dismounted. "I'm a Provençal, friend Edelbart, but travel-ing through your land these past seven months. This is the keep of

Havistock, is it not? A villager did direct me here, upon my inquiry as to a patron who might offer lodging in exchange for services."

Edelbart's gray-green eyes swept over Brand's face and form before he rather contemptuously inquired what those might be. "I am a poet, sir," Brand replied, ignoring the smirk the Saxon gave his companion, "and, like many of my provincemen, a troubadour. Perhaps I was wrong to pause here . . . the English care less than the French for civilized advancements of lay and carol."

His jibe had its desired effect. "You're wrong on that, Sir Troubadour. Lady Elfleda has always welcomed traveling minstrels and jongleurs to Havistock." He turned to hand his sword to his companion. "Here, Olan, be a good lad and see to my sword. I've a mind to escort this foreigner to the lady myself, just to prove we are more than heathens."

Brand suppressed a smile and left his mount in Olan's care, following Edelbart into the manor. Beyond the entry, a long, beamed hall extended the length of the house. Sweet herbs hung in wrapped bunches from the rafters, and the air was further freshened by rushes sweetened with dried rose petals. On either side of the hall, lit dimly by the open windows at both ends, a colonnaded aisle of oaken timbers provided passage to chambers for the family, attached knights, and guests.

Edelbart led Brand down the right aisle to the last room, which cornered the rectangular building. "Wait here, minstrel," he ordered, and knocked at the door to Lady Elfleda's solar. A moment later the door opened and a dark, petite young lady slipped out into the aisle. Her manner was all modesty, though she did risk a quick, curious glance at the sight of a stranger. "This man seeks lodging in barter for an evening's entertainment of song," Edelbart said, embarrassed that he was sweaty and dusty from his exercises. Yet unmarried, he was fond of the maiden Morwena, hoping to pay court to her before the year ended.

The girl gave him a sweet smile and nodded, taking another look at Brand before she said she would ask if her lady was interested. A few minutes passed before she came out again to announce, "Lady

Elfleda will see you, sir. Please follow me within." For the enamored Edelbart, she had a quick, flirtatious glance before thanking
him for his efforts.

Inside the spacious room, well lit by windows whose shutters lay
open to admit the sunlight, the widow Elfleda sat before her
embroidery stand, working her silk-threaded needle through a linen
hanging that would, when finished, grace the wall of her chapel.
Several other ladies of varying ages surrounded her, passing the day
in sewing a new gunna of scarlet samite.

Brand stood before the lady several moments before she deigned
to look up and greet him. Appearing younger than her thirty-four
years, the widow had the milky, translucent complexion that so often
accompanied red tresses. Indeed, Brand could see wispy curls of
bright auburn poking from the edge of her veil. Yet with her hair
braided in coils and hidden by wimple and veil, only the pale,
arched brows of auburn and her milky skin betrayed her Irish
coloring.

Before she spoke, Elfleda took a second to study the man. Not
often these days did a singer of lays pass by, and never had one
combined good voice with so noble an appearance. Despite his
broad shoulders and height, he had a natural grace of carriage and an
air of gentility. His request for employ intrigued her.

"You look more a courtier than a man forced to sing for his keep,
sir," she said, and drew in a sharp breath as his smile revealed
strong, even, white teeth. "How came you to believe that we might
desire your services?"

Brand bowed, still smiling, mustering all of his considerable
charm to flatter the woman. He recognized appreciation when he saw
it. Often women older than this one had granted him favors because
of his ability to play upon their vanity. "Not every manor can boast
of so lovely a chatelaine, my lady. Your repute has spread farther
than the surrounding countryside and, like the gentle rippling of the
brook, washed your praises as far as Bury."

"Ah . . . and is it also rumored that I fall easy prey to a handsome
gallant with a little flattery?"

"Nay, m'lady, only that you possess a keen appreciation of the finer pleasures in this hard life."

"If your voice is as charming, sir, I think we may have a pleasant night's entertainment from you," Elfleda replied. "You seek only lodging, no compensation in coin?"

"Your hospitality for a night and the delight of playing my lute is payment enough, Lady Elfleda. In such hard times, I would not tax your purse further than a meal and a night's rest untroubled by the company of the forest creatures."

Pleased by his respect for economy, Elfleda turned to address her companions. "Ladies, I think we have a treat in store. Make it a point to have your husbands at hand, to take advantage of the troubadour's songs of love." To her youngest lady-in-waiting, Morwena, she added a request that the girl escort the minstrel to the servants' quarters. "No, no, that isn't fitting," she amended, thinking aloud. "We've extra guest rooms. Morwena, dear, show our songster to the chamber fronting the north corner of the hall."

Morwena's eyes widened in surprise at the special courtesy awarded the man. Clearly her widowed mistress had been taken with the troubadour's easy wit and good looks. She curtsied; and as he bowed to the lady and turned to follow Morwena, she herself was seized with a trembling excitement born of attraction.

At the door, Brand paused when the lady called out to him. "Wait, sir. With all our conversation, I still do not know who is to entertain us this eve. How are you called?"

"Brand, m'lady, Brand de Reynaud," he replied with another flashing smile, then turned and followed Morwena through the portal.

Well used to masking her emotions before others, Elfleda covered her shock at the revelation of that name and, claiming she wished time to herself, sent her ladies out of the solar. Only when she was alone did the mask of calm drop to reveal the play of conflicting emotions she felt. Lady Alysaun, the homeless waif her Esmond had rescued from the road to Bury, the younger sister of the now dead knight, Sir Edwin Meau, the fragile child who had poured out her sorrowful tale to Elfleda's sympathetic ear, had claimed the loss of a recently wed husband by the name of Brand de Reynaud.

The man could not be the same. If they had been separated by an attack of Norman soldiers as Alysaun claimed, surely he would be searching for her, asking information at every manor and village. And yet, the coincidence of a foreigner of the right age, bearing the same name, and appearing so close to where the girl had lost her husband was too great to dismiss.

In her early compassion for the girl, whose family had ranked with Elfleda's own and exchanged social visits over many years, Elfleda had welcomed Alysaun as warmly as her son had predicted. Making sure the girl's wardrobe was increased to offer her some change of color and style, clucking over her slenderness, insisting she take adequate rest, the widowed mother of one had offered Alysaun a mother's tender care.

Now, though, after some four weeks of watching her son moon over the girl like some love-struck, glazed-eyed peasant, Elfleda's tenderness toward Alysaun had been hardened by anxiety. Oh, Alysaun had done nothing to encourage his attentions, but with her bright, golden beauty growing more enchanting with each passing day of rest and nourishment, she hadn't had to encourage Esmond's ardent attentions.

Esmond had ignored her on the subject of his possible betrothal to Aelgifu of Dalstoun and, when pressed about the match, protested that the Northumbrian heiress, of twelve, was yet too young to wed, adding that from all accounts, she was also too ugly for him to think of bedding her. Her reply that all women were comely in the dark brought only a grimace to Esmond's sullen face.

Having seen the seeds of a possible rebellion in her son's attachment to Alysaun, Elfleda had the previous week sent a message to an old friend in London, asking that inquiries be made about the possibility that the girl's eldest sister, Edana, might be in England. It was a chance; her husband, Roger Fitz Henry, was a small landholder in Normandy. If they were over the Channel from the dukedom, her letter had requested, send the pair posthaste to Havistock to take into their care the lady's orphaned sister, Alysaun.

Elfleda returned to her needlework with a smile. So skilled was she at plying her needle through the cloth, her attention could be directed to her thoughts without lessening the perfection of her stitches. The work always calmed her, allowed her to clarify her problems. Now, with the arrival of this man, who must be Alysaun's husband, there was little reason to worry over whether the Fitz Henry couple would come to fetch the girl. Fate seemed to have delivered an answer to her prayers.

The problem was . . . were the two really wed? That part of the lady's tale hadn't rung quite true. Still, why would Alysaun add such an embellishment to her story? 'Twas sad enough in reality. If they weren't married . . . that put Elfleda back into the same quandry of deciding how best to rid herself of the girl. One way or another, she would see the matter settled to her satisfaction.

Brand spent the two hours before the evening meal in the yard behind the house; an awed group of servants scattered about his seat beneath an ancient spreading oak, listening to him practice the lute. The music was a rare treat for them, and he was rewarded in turn when a few casual inquiries elicited a rattle of household gossip. Yes, there was an English lady visiting Havistock, a most sad but beautiful girl, the recently wed and widowed Alysaun of Gloucester.

She had lost all, family and fortune, to the despicable William, the so-called King of England the butler said. Due to the kindness of their mistress, Elfleda, Lady Alysaun had finally found some respite from her dire straits.

" 'Twouldn't surprise me none should the young master, Esmond, decide to take her to wife," added the loquacious Selwen, explaining that while the girl was bereft of land and dower, Lord Esmond was so smitten by her beauty, he could not care less if she added to his wealth.

"Aye, but it won't come to pass," interjected one of the maids with a sniff for Selwen's opinion. "Lady Elfleda would ne'er let him waste the chance to add to Havistock's holdings. Besides, the lady herself is too grief-stricken to accept an offer. 'Tis a shame how she's suffered.''

Occupied with tuning the lute, Brand looked up to pose a question to the maid. He was intrigued by Alysaun's claim of widowhood. ''Did she love the fellow so much, then, to mourn his passing after so short a marriage?''

''Aye, you'd think they were wed a lifetime, not mere weeks. Whenever 'tis mentioned to her, the lady's fair face is overshadowed by her sorrow. Still, life must go on . . . she is too young and fresh to weep forever.''

Brand was amused by Alysaun's imaginative ruse of a husband. Apparently she hadn't claimed to see him die, only made her marital status ambiguous by his suspected demise. These servants, just from listening closely to conversations, had learned more about the girl than she had revealed to him. That her parents were dead he had known; yet if half this gossip was true, she had also been deprived of the luxuries afforded her by her father's many estates. 'Twas no wonder she had seemed so haughty that day in the meadow.

Seated out of the way of the cook and her apprentices, Brand took his meal in the kitchen. The servers bustled past carrying trays of bread and cheeses, deep platters full of herbed peas and steamed leeks, all bound for the trencher tables that had been set up in the hall. Despite Sir Esmond's complaints to the sheriff about overburdening taxes, Brand noticed there seemed to be no lack of nature's bounty for the family and retainers of Havistock.

Because he had played several bawdy songs expressly for the cook's delight, the tall, skinny Ula had arranged a special meal for Brand. Even while she efficiently ordered her help to serve a light, meatless supper to the diners in the hall, she fussed over him, insisting that a generous helping of roast duck from the midday meal would better serve a man his size.

He had yet to see Alysaun and wondered aloud to Ula that the young lady hadn't passed by sometime in the day. ''She keeps to her chamber, then . . . perhaps in brooding sorrow?''

''Oh, no, sire,'' Ula denied, turning to swat a girl who had attempted to snatch a fat, juicy strawberry from the garden basket. "More likely, the lady spent the day with Lord Esmond. They do so like sharing the master's company, but now . . . 'tis better than lingering housebound."

Selwen came in, returning several empty wine decanters to the kitchen and snatching a berry. He ducked the swing of Ula's broad palm and skirted her chopping table to tell Brand the servants were clearing away the tables. "The Lady Elfleda is anxious to hear you play, sir. Didn't say so, just nodded all regal and 'requested' your presence, but I ain't seen her eyes sparkle so since the old master were alive."

Brand retrieved his lute from beside his long-legged stool and stood, his wink bringing an unaccustomed blush to Ula's lean cheeks. "Shall I play her the one about the lovers under the bridge, good Ula? Nay, I'd best behave myself or risk embarrassing Lady Alysaun." He was no longer nervous about a reunion with the girl, just curious about how she would react when she saw him.

Selwen, returning to the hall with a tray of sweet apple in silver goblets, led Brand through a passage that ended in a latticed screen. The butler left him there, going on to serve the eighteen or so knights and ladies in the hall. Brand studied the company from the cover of the screen, searching for a glimpse of Alysaun. Lady Elfleda stood across the room, her cloth-of-gold gunna highly visible among the plainer gowns of her ladies. Young Morwena, she of the dark eyes and dimples, stood close to her mistress with Sir Edelbart at her side.

Most of the party were ranged about the long room, quietly conversing in small groups of two or three. Brand couldn't locate Alysaun, though, and stepped to the screen's edge. The circular stone fireplace, centered in the hall, had blocked his view. When the sandy-haired young man sharing one of the benches drawn up beside the hearth moved, Brand had his first sight of Alysaun.

Gone were the deep hollows beneath her high cheekbones. A plain gold circlet secured her veil and wimple, covering her hair completely but for the thick, silken plaits that hung forward across her shoulders to her breasts. A gunna of deep purple covered a graceful tunic of white, embroidered at the hem with a Greek key design worked in purple silk to match her gunna.

Once Brand had seen a glimmer of beauty in a thin, plainly attired Alysaun and desired her. Now, with a comely fullness to cheeks kissed golden by the sun, she sparkled like a polished jewel, enhanced by a setting more natural to her breeding; and Brand knew more than desire. A stir of possessive passion dried his mouth. The butler, passing him with several untouched goblets on his tray, gave up one at Brand's hoarse request, watching in puzzlement as the troubadour downed the full cup in several successive swallows.

Aside from easing the dryness of his throat, the sweet, full-bodied wine helped quiet the racing of his pulse. Ignoring Selwen's questioning stare, Brand moved beyond the screen and began to strum at his instrument. He paused, frowning as Alysaun blushed over some whispered remark from her companion, then started again the melody of an old love song.

It was his clear, deep voice more than the simple strumming of the lute that brought a hush of quiet to the hall. He strolled across the room, ignoring Alysaun as he directed his song to Lady Elfleda. The widow listened raptly for a few minutes, enchanted by the favor Brand directed only to her, then remembered Alysaun and glanced to see the girl's reaction.

At the first sound of that all-too-familiar voice, Alysaun stiffened, her face paling noticeably. Other than the tenseness of her body as she stared forward into the fire, there was little more to indicate the turmoil set in motion by the troubadour's haunting voice.

Esmond pondered the bright, beaming smile his mother gave the troubadour, sensing something in it that bode trouble for him. He thought the song a silly fluff of nonsense and turned to whisper the same into Alysaun's ear. She was very still and tense, teeth worrying at her bottom lip as she gazed trancelike into the fire. He might have been across the room for all the attention she paid his comment.

His song finished, Brand bowed to Elfleda and asked whether it had pleased her. Her eyes glittered with especial brightness and crinkled at their corners with the pleased smile she gave him. "It did indeed, sir, so much so that I will reward you with a surprise ere you continue your artful playing.'' The lady slipped her hand within the crook of his arm and led him toward the fireplace.

"If you are truly the man you claim to be, sire, then I have the pleasure to present you your wife. She thought you perished, sir, and now I have the joy of reuniting two lost lovers.'' Having drawn him to the bench Alysaun occupied, she added, "I trust you did not suffer a loss of memory when the Norman troop attacked your person?''

Alysaun closed her eyes, wishing by some magic incantation that she could disappear. She was discovered, and the harmless lie she had told would make her appear an ingrate to these kind people who had sheltered her. Any second, Brand would deny the marriage, causing her no end of misery, and it was all her own fault. She really couldn't blame him if he exposed her. *Where on earth had he come from . . . and why turn up here, of all places?*

"No blow from a Norman sword could so destroy my mind or derange me enough to forget my bride's lovely face, m'lady,'' Brand said calmly. "In truth I spent the last weeks recovering from a fever brought on by a slight flesh wound. My lady and I had so little time to share ere we were rudely parted, 'tis almost as if we were never married.'' Alysaun's pale, shocked face finally turned to look up at Brand. "You see how unsettled my appearance has left her,'' he went on. "I feared for this, that after our separation my Alysaun would become resigned to her beloved's demise.''

"But you are well—and against all odds have found each other,'' Elfleda replied, her features flushed with satisfaction at the outcome of her little surprise. "My prayers for dear Alysaun's happiness have been answered. How strange that fate should bring you to the very manor where she did take shelter.'' Ignoring the look of intense frustration on her son's face, mottled now by ruddy splotches of color, the widow smiled down at Alysaun. "Child, none of our company would deny you deserve it if you would seek to leave us for the privacy of a reunion in your chamber.''

"I've yet to hear some joyous claim of recognition from Lady

Alysaun's lips,'' Esmond asserted, scowling at both the troubadour and his mother. "Mother, why do I sense this is all a game, some charade you have arranged?"

" 'Tis no game, Esmond,'' Alysaun said, breaking her silence at last. She had lied and now Brand had joined her in collusion—but why? Withdrawing her hand from Esmond's tight, perspiring grip, she offered a weak, apologetic smile. "When first I heard my husband's voice raised in song, I could only account the sound as the ghost of my longing.'' Alysaun looked up at Brand again. "Forgive me my lack of warmth, sire. I had accepted your death. Now I need a moment's pause to realize that you stand before me."

Esmond still disbelieved the resurrected husband his lady mother had produced for Alysaun. There was an unreal quality of make-believe in the air, as if the three were acting for his benefit. The thought that what he had come to desire so strongly was slipping from his reach was infuriating. Willing to forgo the match his mother desired for him and wed the penniless Alysaun, Esmond now found himself without that choice.

"I suggest that my . . . wife be allowed to retire to recover from her shock,'' Brand said, and offered Alysaun his hand. Hesitant, but not daring to ignore him, she accepted and rose. For the second that their eyes met, she saw a subtle amusement in his steady gaze, and a hint that soon enough he would have her explaining the reason they were acting out the pretense. Raising her hand, Brand pressed a lingering kiss upon her upturned palm. "I'll stay behind to play for your enjoyment, Lady Elfleda, and then, by your gracious leave, retire as well to renew my too-brief acquaintance with my bride."

"Oh, yes, I quite agree,'' Elfleda replied, most delighted by the settlement of her problem with Esmond's misplaced affections. "You're most considerate, sir. 'Tis a quality seldom found in husbands. Mark it, Esmond, my love, for in this couple you may see how married life should be, but more often is not."

"Ah . . . but we are not your average pair, m'lady,'' Brand explained, still holding Alysaun's hand in his. " 'Twas love at first glance, a match made in heaven. Still, how I ever won the lady's favor leaves me humble . . . and puzzled.''

Alysaun blushed at the ironic phrasing, snatching her hand away. Caring only to retreat from this farce and Esmond's morose study, she curtsied to his mother and asked, ''By your leave, my lady, I'll follow my husband's suggestion. 'Twould indeed be a kindness to be alone with my . . . my newfound joy.''

''Granted, child. You have my sympathies. In your place I would be even more unsettled. Be not embarrassed in the sight of others—a brief kiss of welcome is expected after so hard a separation.'' Elfleda tugged at Esmond's sleeve and, when the lad reluctantly rose, tucked her arm in his to stroll away.

''Well, sweet?'' Brand stepped closer and caught Alysaun's wrist, pulling her into his arms. Bending his head, he whispered close to her ear, ''You began this for the sake of appearances. Continue the pretense a few moments longer. Think how happy you are to see living, breathing flesh in place of a supposed corpse.'' She had only a moment before his mouth brushed hers, then all thoughts of a reply were swept away by a long, lingering kiss that left her breathless and dizzy.

Brand released her and, in a voice loud enough to carry to Elfleda, said, ''Run along, my love. I'll keep you waiting but a short while.''

Alysaun whirled, gathering her skirts to flee from his side. Once within the safety of her bedchamber, she leaned against the solid oaken door and closed her eyes. Her chest was tight, constricted by the nervous tension of the past quarter hour. For some reason of his own, Brand had covered her lie, but now she had him to deal with. It occurred to her now that in exchange for his compliance, he might expect some reward; with a slow-dawning horror, she realized what form of payment Brand would exact.

Quickly Alysaun moved about the room, gathering her possessions, preparing to flee rather than face exposure to Elfleda or Brand's injustice. Soon everything she owned was folded on the bed, a pitifully small pile of clothing but more than she had had on arrival.

She was leaning over the edge of the bed, folding her last garment, when the door opened and shut. Alysaun straightened, heart beating rapidly as she nervously clutched the mantle to her breast. Without turning, she said, "I did not hear your knock, m'lord."

His footsteps echoed as Brand crossed to the bed and paused behind Alysaun. "You forget, dear, a husband has no need to announce himself." His glance took in the pile of clothing. "Were you planning a journey?"

The fine, downy hair at Alysaun's nape prickled, fear blending with anger at Brand's unnecessary sarcasm. Turning abruptly, she faced him, chin raised in defiance. "You have my apologies for borrowing your name, sire, and my thanks for not revealing me to Lady Elfleda. Now I think it best for all concerned if—"

"You run off? How would it look, dear, so soon after we are happily reunited?" Brand seized the mantle she held at her breasts like a shield and tossed it carelessly onto the bed. "Before you do anything, I would have an explanation from you." With mocking courtesy, he gestured to her to be seated on the bed. "Pray take a moment to collect your thoughts. I can scarce wait to hear what prompted you to claim you were my widow."

Though spoken politely, the request was more a command. Alysaun sighed; she owed him the truth. Already resigned to leaving its comfort behind, she sank onto the down mattress and sighed once again. Refusing to meet his gaze, she hesitantly voiced her explanation. "Esmond and I met on the road from Cambridge, the same day I left your company."

"I know that," Brand snapped impatiently. "Why leave so stealthily, though? You could have waited to bid me a proper farewell."

"I . . . I couldn't," she replied, remembering the sadness she had felt at departing. "I was afraid I would embarrass myself by crying if we said good-bye at the city gates. I did leave you my cross, though."

"Yes, that was one of the reasons I came after you." Brand drew up the leather pouch hanging from his belt and extracted the cross. "I never asked for any payment, girl. Here, take it back." He dropped the chain and cross into her lap as if its possession irritated him.

"I never thought to see you again. 'Twas a gift, to give you pleasant memories of our sojourn." Alysaun's mouth formed a stubborn pout as she looked up at him. "How could I know you would turn up here? If memory serves me right, you advised me to find a protector."

"Aye, but I thought it would take more than an hour's walk. What other falsehoods did you offer that poor, beguiled youth?" Brand's mouth was set in a hard line, a pulse ticking at the edge of his clenched jaw. He had worried over her welfare for a month, and all the while she had been cozily ensconced in the comfort of Havistock.

Unaware of his worry on her behalf, Alysaun found herself indignant at his accusing tone, resentful of his insinuations. "Only the truth, aside from that one small lie, and I do regret its inclusion. Why are you so begrudging? 'Tis unseemly that you condemn me for so slight an error of judgment."

"Slight, is it?" Brand was angry now. The girl should be seeking his forgiveness in a less haughty manner. Instead, she had the gall to accuse him of being ungallant—a mistake, to be sure. The bed sank beneath his weight as he sat next to Alysaun. Her chin was stubbornly set as she stared across the room, her fingers nervously twisting in her lap. " 'Tis not for *you* to measure the weight of your misdeeds.

"*I* am the injured party, m'lady. In assuming my name, you took what was mine to give." Further angered when she ignored his rebuke, Brand seized her shoulders and shoved her backward, easily pinning her to the bed with the strength of his arms. Alysaun stared at him, blue eyes wide with alarm. " 'Tis a favor I'll grant to a lady of my own choosing and not to be appropriated by a lying little thief."

The description stung sharply. Alysaun glared back at Brand, hating him for the cruel title that even to her own mind had a ring of truth. She had lied and, in the past, stolen to survive. She was what he had called her, and yet, with reason. "Yes, I am what you named me," she responded finally, and in such a meek tone of resignation that Brand raised a brow, questioning the sincerity of the admission.

He had expected more of a defense and perhaps a list of righteous excuses. The surrender defeated his fury, leaving him at odds with himself, suddenly guilty instead of injured. "I should have added, full of guile, as well," he went on, hard put to let go of his irritation. "This mild manner you've adopted doesn't suit you, Alysaun. 'Tis a ruse to dull my anger. What other tricks do you hide behind that mask of wounded innocence?"

"I told but one lie and you condemn me so harshly, sire. I grow faint at the thought of what justice you would seek for a greater offense. I have no tricks. To hear you speak, I am as cunning as Delilah; but since you have come away without shorn locks, still strong enough to overpower a mere girl, I decry your accusations."

The angry stain of rose upon her cheeks enhanced the pale ivory of her complexion. Eyelids shuttering the look of blue resentment, the brush of golden lashes dusted those rose cheeks with all the innocence she claimed. Brand's eyes slid to the softness of her mouth. Why did he feel it was he who owed an apology?

"If we continue to play out this farce to your benefit, will you also grant me the privileges of a husband?" Brand's voice was serious and teasing at once; he ran his fingers down the softness of her braid, then reached up to tug at the wimple that covered her throat. Alysaun's eyes flew open, as she became wary of the game he played. His fingers lightly stroked the slender column of her throat and she raised a hand to protest the caresses. "A throat so lovely should not be hidden from view. Your skin is as soft and smooth as silk."

"Leave off . . . I *beg* you," Alysaun exclaimed, and her breath caught in a sighed protest. "Brand, why do you torment me so? I've made my apologies and my remorse is real." His fingers slid upward, teasing the tender spot beneath her earlobe. "You have no right—"

"As you did not when you unthinkingly made use of my name," Brand interrupted. "If you would have me stop, then rise and accompany me to Lady Elfleda. Tell her the truth and all will be set right. Continue to lie to save face and I will exact the pleasure that accompanies my position as your spouse."

Brand's arms no longer bound her, though as she raised up on one elbow to stare at him, his fingers still curled beneath her veil, toying with the wispy curls that had escaped her braids. "What munificence you reveal in offering that proposal, m'lord," she replied with cutting sarcasm. "If I choose confession, I am again homeless. If I stay silent, I lose all to you. Who would think one simple twist of truth could bring about so ignoble a fate?"

" 'Twas not I who chose to lie," Brand reminded her, eyes locked on her mouth as his hand cupped to press her head closer. Alysaun tensed, her hand pushing against Brand's chest. At the moment when their lips first touched, a knock sounded at the door, drawing a loud curse from Brand.

Alysaun heard Morwena's voice call out his name and Brand's sharp, snapped inquiry as to what she wanted. He rose and crossed to jerk open the door; the conversation was muffled as he stepped out and closed the door. In a reprieve she was sure would be short, Alysaun tried to sort out her flustered thoughts. She touched fingers to her cheeks to find them heated as if from fever.

It seemed inconceivable that both "choices" Brand had offered her would end in her disgrace. How could he be so determined to take advantage of her plight? Where was the gentle poet now, the protector of innocents? Tears would avail her naught; they would not even rust the armored arrogance that had hardened his heart.

No, there was no appeal in that quarter. With an exasperated sigh, Alysaun rose to straighten the pile of tunics scattered in their tussle. She would confess to Lady Elfleda and ask her forgiveness for the deception. She, at least, might be more merciful than Brand.

The door opened again and Brand looked in, his narrowed glance taking in her activity. "Be not so quick to pack, m'lady. Your field of choice may be narrowed ere I return. I'll be gone but a short while. Do not try my patience by thinking you can run. I would find you no matter where you chose to hide." With that, he slammed the door shut, leaving an astonished Alysaun staring at its shuddering oaken planks.

Alysaun couldn't begin to guess what had elicited his angry threat. Indeed, with her temples beginning to pound with a headache, she could scarce think at all. Giving up the attempt to interpret Brand's behavior, she lay down upon the cover and curled her knees up against her belly. Her fate was not hers to decide; it seemed always to rest in another's hands and, of late, had been as capricious as the changeable weather.

By the time Morwena had admitted him to her mistress's solar and quietly withdrawn, Brand was in control of his irritation at the lady's untimely summons. His bow was polite, his curiosity masked by an unconcerned expression. "Though I never balk at spending a pleasant hour's conversation with a lady fair," he said, "I was . . . ah . . . occupied in an even more pleasant manner, m'lady."

"Be seated, sir, and soon enough you may, perhaps, return to your lady's bower," Elfleda requested, and, with a nod, indicated the chair opposite hers. There was an air of contest in the room, and as Brand took the seat each seemed to measure the other's mood.

Elfleda leaned forward, elbows resting on the arms of her chair, palms pressed together as if in supplication. "I will not play coy nor mince words, Sir Brand. Don't think me heartless to pull you from Alysaun's arms at such a tender moment. I am fond of romance myself, though practical enough to know it seldom lasts. If you profess true love of Alysaun, it will stand the test of an hour's wait. What I would discuss cannot."

Brand raised a brow and settled more comfortably in his chair. "And that is?"

" 'Tis a matter that I must see settled or I shall not rest easy in my bed. I ask that you swear an oath upon whatever you hold most dear to attest to the truth of the marriage claimed by yourself and the lady. It grieves me to doubt that vows were exchanged, but my concern for the girl's welfare insists I do so."

115

"Concern? You said you would not speak coyly, Lady Elfleda. If we are both to shed light on the truth this eve, I respectfully submit that your concern lies closer to your own hearth." Though he had adjudged her son to be a spoiled, indulged whelp, it was clear that the widow was no one's fool. "Alysaun has lost family and home to the King. If she were free, young Esmond might prove quite determined in his desire to wed her," Brand continued. "And that, to a mother desiring to increase her family's fortunes, would be a disaster." He smiled, hands clasped loosely in his lap. "You are too modest, m'lady. I understand and do salute your practicality."

Elfleda returned his smile. She genuinely liked this handsome, astute Frenchman. Were she ten years younger... well, such thoughts were useless. "Pray don't make me out to be entirely cold and heartless, sire. I *did* accept the girl into my keep, even after learning of the rancor King William holds for her family and name. Her parents were fine people. Alysaun's father I remember with especial fondness. Brihtric Meau was as honorable as he was handsome."

For a moment Elfleda's face softened in a sad reflection on the vanished past. "He was what England bred before the oppression of our Norman overlord. Ofttimes I do wonder if our vanquished race will not disappear, buried beneath William's heavy tread. Well, 'tis no matter now. I cannot change what is by wishing." She glanced up, her eyes hard and speculative once more. "You haven't answered my inquiry. I know you and the girl were together once, but was what you shared blessed by the words of a priest?"

Brand hesitated. The lady's motives were singularly selfish—she didn't care to see Alysaun available to tempt her son to rebel against her will. He could lie and please her or tell the truth and... what? Have her attempt to bribe him in some way? He chose the truth, more to see how she would deal with it. "The girl is still a virgin, or was when we did part. I cannot vouch for the interim, especially since she was allowed to spend so many hours alone in the company of your lovesick Esmond."

"That doesn't worry me," Elfleda said. "Esmond pants after her too much to have been granted what he seeks." Her pale auburn brows drew together as she digested the admission Brand had made. "Your greetings in the hall were too constrained for lovers wrenched apart and then delivered to each other's arms." Elfleda didn't bother to add that she had had a servant eavesdrop on their argument. " 'Tis amazing how genuine was Alysaun's grief over your 'loss,' sire. Her mourning had a touchingly melancholy effect upon me. Does this not indicate to you that the girl had learned some affection for your person during your time together?"

Brand straightened in his chair, disliking the direction the conversation had taken. "Nay, lady," he denied. "It indicates only that Alysaun possesses a facile imagination and an ability to pretend. She was forced to live by her wits until a short time past. No doubt they have been honed as sharply as a war sword, but I do not intend to feel their edge or lessen your worries over Esmond's vulnerability by sacrificing my freedom."

"Ah, but you should reconsider, troubadour. There are few ladies of her quality and beauty available. True, she does not come with dower, but to see the issue settled to my satisfaction, I would sweeten the offer of her hand from my own funds." Brand's handsome face was set in a stubborn line, his firm jaw clenched. "Be not hasty," Elfleda cautioned him. "Such an offer is generous and well you know it."

"I will choose my own bride, thank you. When that time comes, I'll not care if she's an heiress or penniless." Brand nodded, acknowledging the widow's determination. "I wish you good fortune in finding Alysaun a mate, though. With what you have to barter, it should be an easy task."

Elfleda sighed and shook her head. "I had hoped you would accede to my wishes. Your obstinacy is matched by my own. My priest is even now in the chapel. Another half hour's passage will see you wed to the Lady Alysaun."

Brand stood. He had had enough of this annoying battle of wills; the woman was beginning to irk him no end. "Then tell your priest he'll not be needed, Elfleda," he said, arms crossed over his chest.

"If you think me as easily handled as your stripling son, think again."

Elfleda glanced up. He really was a magnificent catch, this young knight-troubadour from the south of France. 'Twas almost a pity to waste so charming a creature on a slip of a girl who couldn't possibly appreciate his worth. "Sit down, sir. I am not intimidated so easily. We have minutes yet for your considerations of the match's advantages. Let's discuss a different subject, cool our tempers a bit. I think that brooch of yours a most handsome piece. Its emblem is a match for the insignia of a wild Anglian rebel named Hereward, a Lincolnshire thane who has troubled the King for some time now. Think you that the sheriff, Sir Fitz Walther, would believe you innocent of the Saxon's marauding raids against the crown's holdings?"

Brand stared at her, then glanced down at the brooch securing his mantle. In truth, he had forgotten the gift from a grateful Hereward. Now it seemed it would be his undoing. There would be little he could do if the lady chose to carry out her threat. Brand had no desire to join the multitudes who had been imprisoned in the stone keeps William had raised throughout the countryside. His claim of kinship to William was too weak and distant to save him as it had in the past.

Brand bowed and sat down. "My choice is clear, m'lady. I like this body I've worn these twenty-five years too much to see it consigned to rot in a dungeon. You have a bridegroom, however reluctant, and an answer to your problem. I wonder, though, how Alysaun will react to your plans. And Esmond—is he to give the bride away?"

He had finally struck a nerve. "In exchange for dower and bride, I want your silence on that point. Esmond is too young to know his mind," Elfleda answered. "He retired to his room thinking the lady your wife and he will awake in the morning with that belief a fact."

"Keep the dower, Elfleda," Brand insisted, not caring to have his honor further insulted by a bribe. " 'Twill soon enough, I think, belong to one of William's loyal vassals. He moves methodically to

118

reward his men. What befell Alysaun's father and so many others will no doubt roll around to you. Now, enough of talk—I'm weary of it. Let's see the deed done.''

Elfleda didn't like his insolence or the suggestion that her lands and Esmond's might soon fall forfeit. Her earlier delight in arranging the wedding vanished, replaced by fear of such a Norman encroachment. That ugly possibility had lain with her many sleepless nights, but until de Reynaud had voiced it in retaliation, it was only a shadowy thought. She rose, smoothing her gunna with a trembling hand before she swept to the door. ''As you wish, m'lord. I, too, am weary.''

Calling to Morwena, who waited in the aisle, Elfleda ordered the maid to escort Lady Alysaun to the chapel. ''Quietly, Morwena, and with as little fuss as possible. I would not have my son's rest disturbed. Tell the girl nothing save I request her presence immediately.'' Morwena curtsied, hesitant about her duty; she opened her mouth but thought better of it. She started down the aisle, her reluctance evident in the slow, dawdling pace. ''*Quickly,* girl,'' Elfleda ordered impatiently.

Brand came up behind Elfleda, startling her when she turned around. He looked down at her with a hooded gaze and she could feel his reined temper radiating over her like the waves of heat rising off a banked fire. The refined, aristocratic face masked a raw power she found fascinating. For a brief second she knew a wrench of desire no man before him had ever aroused.

''So you fear your son's interference in this scheme? As bewitched as the boy is, it wouldn't do to have him wake and hear Alysaun protestingly dragged to her wedding, eh, m'lady? You must be less confident of your ability to handle him than I'd guessed.''

Infuriated by her desire for this tall, contemptuous foreigner, Elfleda drew herself up and defended herself. ''As long as I am able, sir, I will defend my late husband's legacy to Esmond and his future heirs. The girl is a threat to his . . . to our security. He sees only her face. *I* see the ruin that shadowed her own family's fall from grace. Mayhap Havistock will go in the same manner as her father's estates, but in these uncertain times, my fate, as well as yours, is in others' keep."

"If that pretty speech was uttered in the manner of an excuse for this night's injustice, I care not for your reasons," Brand replied, raising an arrogant brow as he gestured to the aisle. "Shall we go, m'lady? I should not be tardy for so important an event . . . my bride would surely consider it rude."

5

Alysaun hesitated before the arched, carved door of the chapel, a drawing fear rooting her to the spot. Asleep until awakened only minutes before by Morwena, she struggled to understand her summons. Elfleda's attendant had offered no explanation for the strange request that she come to the chapel at this late hour. Indeed, her apprehension had increased because of the girl's silence. In the month Alysaun had been at Havistock, the two had come to be friends. Morwena, ever gay, always found some amusement in the dullest task. Now her unusual solemnity added to Alysaun's feeling that she was a lamb bound for the sacrificial altar.

Morwena pulled open one of the divided doors, holding her sputtering candle high to light the shadows, lips pursed in righteous anger at a brief glimpse of her friend's pale, distraught face. Though the French troubadour, Sir Brand, was a bridegroom any girl would desire, this stealthy, forced ceremony was an ugly business. Still, Morwena's avowed duty lay in following her mistress's commands; there was little she could do to protest the injustice soon to be done.

"Come, Alysaun," she insisted with a troubled sigh, offering her hand in support. "Lady Elfleda awaits within." Morwena's eyes, the color of autumn chestnuts, offered sympathy as well as a plea for Alysaun's forgiveness.

With feet that felt weighted by lead, Alysaun moved to enter the chapel. The nave was dark. Beyond the stretch of sanctuary the apse was lighted with the glow of flickering lamps. A shadowed figure, tall and lean-legged, stood at the stone altar. Alysaun caught her bottom lip between her teeth, trying to still the rapid poundings of her pulse.

Lady Elfleda stepped from the shadows to order her attendant forward to join the reluctant bridegroom and the priest, but Morwena hung back, hovering protectively at Alysaun's side. A sharp, waspish order and a shove finally sent the hesitant maiden on her way.

Alysaun looked as if she were in a trance, her wide blue eyes fixed on the shadowed apse. "You summoned me, m'lady," she said at last, turning her head to glance at Havistock's mistress. "'Tis a late hour for services. I could not think why you bid me come to the chapel and not your chambers."

"Because, my dear child," Elfleda answered in a hushed, irritated tone, "a wedding ceremony cannot be performed in my chambers. I have . . . spoken with the troubadour, the man you falsely claimed as husband. Out of respect for your dear parents, I do intend to see their daughter's virtue protected. It is beyond me to puzzle why you made the claim, taking advantage of the shelter I have offered, of the warmth of hospitality given you at Havistock."

Alysaun flushed with embarrassment. So Elfleda knew the truth . . . she would have learned it soon enough from her own lips. "If I lied, m'lady, and I cannot deny I did so, then I cannot compound my mistake with solemn vows spoken in the house of God. Your concern is touching, but I would take my leave of your keep rather than further distress you."

"Oh, 'tis no distress to see the proper act done, dear. My conscience would allow me no rest if I did not proceed in your best interests. Your husband-to-be awaits you in the apse." Elfleda gestured. "He is impatient now—see how he does pace before the altar."

"*No.*" Alysaun's outcry was more in disbelief than rejection. Surely the kind, generous Lady Elfleda could not mean to force a marriage ceremony against her will. Brand didn't want her . . . why had he agreed to this mockery? "I have no dower, m'lady, nothing to bring a husband. Brand knows this."

"Hush, child, fret not over your impoverished state. In my fondness for you, I have settled that question. All is arranged to the groom's satisfaction."

Brand had no need of money or other grants, yet it seemed he had accepted Elfleda's unduly generous offer. "No bans have been issued," Alysaun said, desperately seeking excuses why the marriage should not go forward.

"Because of the unusual circumstances, I cannot allow for that delay. My priest, Thomas, knows the situation and is agreed that it warrants haste. This will be done *now*, Lady Alysaun. Accept your fate and play out your part with the grace with which you were reared."

"Grace, m'lady?" Alysaun's glance at the older woman was indignant at the use of the word. "How can you speak of grace when I am under duress to marry? Though I did abuse the warmth and kindness of your hospitality, you have no right to force me into an undesired match."

"Come now, your innocent protests are exasperating me, Alysaun," Elfleda snapped, retrieving an oil lamp from its place on a nearby chest. She lifted it high, then firmly grasped the girl's arm with her free hand. "Come along. I'm tired, as we all are."

"*No.*" Alysaun twisted away with surprising strength, backing away toward the chapel doors. "I will *not* be a party to your plans, however you cloak them in righteous words of duty and responsibility." Elfleda had nearly dropped the lamp in surprise at Alysaun's rebellious nature. Her growing impatience intensified by the chit's ingratitude, she stubbornly seized her arm again and tugged.

Suddenly a figure loomed out of the darkened sanctuary. Brand took a step closer to the struggling women, his features sharpened by a menacing scowl. "Let her go," he ordered in so commanding a tone that Elfleda instantly obeyed. "I warned you, did I not, that Alysaun would not accept this easily? Have the courtesy to leave us, Lady Elfleda. Your priest could use a word of encouragement. Though he is your man more than God's, even he questions the reasoning behind this too-sudden event."

"*Fine*." Elfleda's expression was cold, haughty as she laid the lamp back upon the chest. "But do not tarry overlong, sir. My patience will not last beyond a few minutes' delay."

Brand's gaze followed the woman as she disappeared into the darkness with a rustle of silk, his eyes contemptuous of the patience she claimed. He turned back to find Alysaun staring at him, resentful and stubborn, clearly frightened enough to attempt flight. This she did, backing away several steps until the heavy solidity of the chapel doors halted her.

"Do not fight this, Alysaun. It has been decided." He rubbed a tired hand across his forehead and down one cheek. "You have nowhere to turn, other than to me. The ceremony will be over with soon."

" 'Tis not the nuptials I fear, m'lord, but the close captivity that will follow on its heels. I may be beggared but I'll not give up my freedom so easily. How is it that you are so resigned? The lady spoke of a settlement. I did think you too much your own man to be persuaded by a bribe. Not an hour ago you arrogantly reminded me that 'twas your right to choose a wife. At what cost have you bartered away that privilege?"

"Too dearly, it seems on second thought. I'll not acquaint you with the details yet, but I've no more enthusiasm for this farce than you. That makes allies of us, does it not? Neither having a choice, I would count it a victory against our cunning hostess if we proceeded with some dignity." Brand held out his hand, and after some hesitation, Alysaun reached out to take it, joining him with a heavy, frustrated sigh.

"Good," Brand said approvingly, and smiled down at her. "Now if you will also offer me your trust, we'll see this through, and, once away from the lady's domain, find a priest to annul our forced vows."

Alysaun raised her head, her slender, golden brows arching in a puzzled frown. "For that to be granted, Brand, there must either be some close tie of blood or proof the marriage was not consummated. Am I to accept your word you will hold the latter as our measure of release?" Alysaun held her breath as he scowled again, then tucked her arm within his.

"I don't take pleasure that is not offered in return. Exhale your breath, my bride, or you will be too faint to repeat your answers to the priest."

Alysaun accepted the vaguely worded reply as what she had sought. "I wonder, sire," she asked with so sudden a calmness in her voice that Brand bent closer to puzzle out her expression, "of the two of us—which will choke upon the words 'I do'? I think it will not be I."

Later all the ritual and words were a blur to Alysaun. In truth, she was numb. It was some other girl who repeated vows in so clear and self-possessed a voice. Brand, too, answered the priest in a firm tone. Morwena witnessed the ceremony with less distress than she had known earlier. No one would guess the pair were under constraint. Brand was so tall and virile, and his dark, rusty-brown curls and deeply tanned skin were a perfect foil for his bride's slender, golden-ivory beauty. Perhaps, she thought, the marriage was a blessing in disguise. Fortune often united two reluctant people who later found themselves delighted with the arrangement. For Alysaun's sake, she prayed it would be so.

Playing out the farce to the fullest degree, Elfleda brought the newlyweds to her solar and ordered a sweet May wine to celebrate. Brand accepted the drink because the woman's guile had left a bitterness in his mouth, but he ignored the toast she offered to their happiness. Alysaun accepted the cup from him, nervously swallowing several gulps of wine to still her anxiety about the moment that would come all too soon, when she was alone with the stranger she had wed.

"I'll not keep you long, but one word of caution, Alysaun," Elfleda said, ignoring the bemused smirk on Brand's handsome face. "Esmond need not know of this hasty ceremony to realize your claims of wedlock. The servants have been warned as well to curb the wagging of their tongues. My son is truculent enough of late. I have no desire to listen to his complaints."

"If I had thought of him, m'lady," Alysaun replied haughtily, no longer innocently believing the woman had acted out of anything but her own selfish interests, "I would have screamed to waken Esmond and brought upon you the havoc of his protests. But 'tis too late now. I shall say nothing to destroy his filial devotion."

Brand yawned and made a show of stretching his long arms high above his head. "'I do not intimate that your company is less than charming, madame, but I have known better endings to a day."

"Understandable, sire, in the light of this evening's affairs, but I think perhaps it is more your wish to retreat and share your bride's company in private. Stay a few minutes longer and allow Alysaun to retire with some modesty. We'll share another cup to salute your good fortune." Brand shrugged, the gesture a negligent acceptance of the offer.

Alysaun blushed at the arrangement and looked to Brand for some indication that he meant to keep his promise not to consummate the marriage. He busied himself with pouring the wine, taking longer than the task required. She looked daggers at his broad, well-muscled back, sure that he was purposely avoiding her gaze.

"Drink well into the night, if you care to," she spitefully suggested, and though he raised his head and allowed her a glimpse of the irritating smile that curved his mouth, Brand did not acknowledge her. "I am worn by the late hour and the constraints upon my patience," she went on. "Pray do not stumble when you enter my chamber, for I have need of my rest."

Brand slowly turned and raised his cup to her. "*Our* chamber, sweet," he replied. "How easily you forget that we now share *everything.*'' Alysaun blanched and her mouth tightened as she cut off another angry retort that would have only added to his amusement. She bobbed a curtsy to Elfleda and whirled with a furious swish of skirts to stamp across to the door. "Do leave a lamp burning, though. I won't be long," Brand called after her, and was rewarded as his bride paused, back stiffening in righteous indignation before she swept open the door and slammed it in answer.

"The girl has a temper," Elfleda commented wryly, accepting a full cup of wine from Brand's hand. "I had not seen it ere now."

"Until now, you've given her no cause to show it," Brand replied, clinking the edge of his silver chalice against hers. "I'll wager even now she is wondering how your benevolence did so suddenly change to malice."

"That attitude will change soon enough, m'lord, once she is settled to the thought of the bliss that marriage can afford. You look mellowed, Sir Brand. Why do I feel that despite your protests to the contrary, the union does not displease you?"

"I am practical, Elfleda, and accept what I must. And I cannot deny I find my bride lovely, no less for that she was pressed upon me against my will."

"Then I salute your practicality, sire," the lady replied with an appreciative smile. "Perhaps we are more alike than you think."

"I doubt it, madame. Forgive my reluctance to drink to practicality . . . it has cost me enough this night."

Escorting Alysaun to her chamber, Morwena was hesitant to speak, guilty over her part in the evening's proceedings. At first she had difficulty keeping up with the girl's angry stride. Then Alysaun slowed her pace, seeming to realize for the first time that she had company.

At the bedroom door, she turned to Morwena and offered her a wan smile. "Go and rest, Morwena. You must be as tired as I." The maiden hesitated, embarrassed to meet her gaze. "Don't think I blame you, dear. Truly I know you had no choice. 'Tis yet another bond that unites us in friendship. Don't worry, the worst is done." Impulsively, Alysaun reached out and hugged Morwena close.

When they parted, Morwena smiled. "Worse matches have been made, Alysaun. At least your lord is handsome and well formed. And I think he cares more for you than you guess."

"Aye, there are less pleasing men to be had for a husband," Alysaun agreed. "The morning will discover, though, if I judge him too honorable. Now go—I must have some time to think."

Once inside, Alysaun leaned against the door, less brave than she had been before her friend. Brand had promised to come soon to her; she didn't want him bursting in to discover her half dressed. That thought spurred her to action and she moved quickly to disrobe. It did occur to her to retain her kirtle, but if, when he joined her, he was moved to break his vow, the thin shift would be no protection.

The night air, sifting into the room through the oiled-lambskin window coverings, was chilly. Alysaun hurried into bed, pulling the coverlet up over her bare flesh to the chin. Then, thinking the gesture silly, she adjusted the sheet beneath her arms and sat up to unwind the long plaits of her braids. Laying aside Esmond's gift, the golden fillets that had secured the braids, she ran her fingers through the tangles, combing them free of snarls as best she could without a comb.

Warmer now, Alysaun snuggled down beneath the covers, securely tucked beneath their thin weight, one arm free. Apprehension made her restless and she tossed several moments, trying to find a comfortable spot, finally turning on her side to face the drawn bed curtains. Eyes closed, she said a silent prayer that Brand might change his mind and stay to imbibe so much wine that he could do little but tumble into bed and fall fast asleep.

But even as that maidenly prayer winged heavenward, the chamber door opened and she heard Brand's footfall across the floor. In a panic at the realization of her fears, she tightly closed her eyes and pretended to be sleeping. Moments later a soft breeze ruffled the wispy tendrils of gold at her temple as Brand swept aside the curtains.

Brand smiled at the ruse; Alysaun's eyes were shut too tightly for sleep. For a while he was content to study her, the delicate lines of her face in profile against the feather pillow, the gentle curve of shoulder, white and smooth beneath a tumble of burnished curls.

Alysaun heard him move away and found it a blessing to release her held breath. Lying still as she could, she listened curiously at the sounds Brand made as he moved about the room, wondering what he was doing, what he meant to do. The clump of boots hitting the floor was followed by a rustle of clothing.

Brand parted the curtains on his side of the narrow, canopied bed and, as the mattress sank beneath his weight, saw Alysaun stiffen tensely. Plumping the pillow to a comfortable position, he slid beneath the covers and leaned back. As he adjusted the sheet over his legs, his hand brushed her bare back, and his bride flinched, retreating to the edge of the bed. "You may cease your pretense of sleep, my love," Brand announced. "That brief contact, though sweet, was unintentional."

"Not that I doubt your word, m'lord," Alysaun answered, "but if I feel more secure upon the mattress's edge, you will not think me discourteous?"

"Do as you please, Alysaun, but if flesh should accidentally meet flesh again, I think you have not far to go ere you land upon the rushes. I do not intend to spend a long night worrying that my presence offends your modesty."

Alysaun raised her head and risked a glance over her shoulder. Brand was leaning against his pillow, arms crossed over a muscular chest covered with wiry brown curls. Instinctively she blushed, warmth flooding her face, grateful that the lamp cast a dim enough glow to hide her reaction. "Can I take that to mean you will leave me to seek rest, sire? I still have not been given a satisfactory answer to that question."

"I answered you in the nave, girl. I want pleasure *given* me in exchange for my efforts, and do not care to extract it from the cringing limbs of a cowering innocent. I am curious, though, as to what you would do if I chose to press my rights. Have you thought it out?"

"Of course, I've thought of very little else, sire." Alysaun laid her head down again, sighing. "I could not resist you and would submit without struggle, but before dawn came to light the room and my dishonor, I would flee you."

"What, again? And how would you live? I'd wager you wouldn't have another chance meeting with a love-struck fool like the stripling Esmond. Will you go back to dressing in rags, begging or stealing to live?"

"I . . . I have my mother's cross and ring." Alysaun touched the thin gold chain around her neck and drew some comfort from the thought she possessed something of value. "The emeralds are valuable, they would bring—"

"No, Alysaun." Brand's voice cut her off, chillingly possessive. "Give it to me now. Anything—"

"But it's mine. You came back, you said, to return it to me," she protested.

"Ah, but circumstance has made it mine again. As I was saying, anything you have is mine. I will not see what is mine employed to effect your escape. Go . . . and you take nothing but your clothing."

Half rising before modesty and Brand's interested gaze made her remember her nakedness, Alysaun clutched at the sheets, glaring resentfully at his cool, arrogant expression. "Will you leave me nothing?" she asked. " 'Tis little enough I have to call my own." Her mouth was set in a stubborn pout, the dim glow of lamplight reflecting off the shimmering waves of gold covering her bare shoulders.

"You have me, dear wife, and with nothing else, are rich. If you can find any solace in a title, for the moment you are the lady of the Count de Chevercé, a title older than any in England." Brand knew a moment's pleasure in the surprised widening of Alysaun's eyes, then he reached out to seize a curl, testing its texture to see if his memories had enriched how silken and fine was her hair.

If anything, the weeks of care and attention to diet had increased its softness. The back of his fingertips brushed the hollow beneath her slim throat, then slid down to tease the enchanting curve of flesh above the spot where she held the sheet to cover her breasts. "I remember another time you most willingly offered yourself to me, Alysaun. Then I knew only your name, no more. Now, from a stranger's lips, I have heard your worth recounted." Brand's fingers curled over the edge of the sheet and tugged. "I have a mind to see what treasures were purchased by granting you my name."

Alysaun scrambled back, tightening her grip on the thin protection the sheet offered, pushing at his hand, digging her fingernails into his wrist. "Brand . . . you have no right." She stopped, realizing that he had every right; her own voice had promised it him before the altar of God. "Please . . . Brand, don't or you will have me hating you. We will part, we both agreed—please, do nothing that will make the annulment impossible."

Brand pulled, and as the sheet came free and flew back, his gaze swept from the enchantment of gently rounded breasts to the shock of Alysaun's expression. He had meant to tease her, to make her aware of how she had played into his hands because of that one, simple lie she had told; but with the exposure of her slender, trembling body, desire flared deep within, banishing all other thoughts.

For the seconds that Brand's eyes moved over her naked form like an intimate caress, Alysaun was frozen, immobile with indecision. Even as she turned to roll away, his hand shot out, strong fingers encircling her wrist to pull her toward him. Flesh met flesh, the softness of Alysaun's lying half atop Brand's, molded to his lean chest by the pressure of his other hand against the small of her back.

"Let loose of me, you devil," she swore through tightly gritted teeth, more furious than frightened at such a boldly presumptuous act. As she realized her struggles only increased his pleasure, Alysaun lay still. "I'll scream . . . I *will*."

"Scream, then," Brand dared her, with a grin that flashed whitely before his lips came down to touch the hollowed V at the base of her throat. "Everyone will think you cry with delight. 'Twill only add to my repute, love."

Alysaun kicked out and Brand's hand slid over her derriere to secure her struggling thighs. If she dared try to kick again, his hand would slip between them and only add to his crowing delight at her helplessness. Alysaun was still again, breathing hard as she tried to think of an escape. Only the thin coverlet and sheet covering his hips separated his manhood from the flatness of her belly.

Clearly she couldn't influence Brand with struggles or pleas. "Since you have already raised up memories of our sojourn, m'lord, I do recall how your conscience twinged, how you hesitated to take my innocence once because you feared to leave a child on me," Alysaun reminded him.

"Ah . . . but, my lady, we've said our vows before one of God's priests," Brand replied. "Now a child would have no taint of bastardy, having been conceived within the bounds of holy wedlock."

"But you would make a terrible father, Brand de Reynaud. If a wife burdens you with responsibility, think how much more a child will add weight to your carefree life. If you mean to leave me, pray do not also leave a babe."

Brand smiled, his fingers lightly tracing the swell of a curved hip. "I've decided to keep you—for a while, at least—until you love me enough to know some regret at my departure. That may take weeks or, seeing how obstinate you are, months. Months full of long nights spent tutoring you in what I find pleasing, in learning what delights you, my sweet."

"Do not waste months seeking what I can tell you in seconds," Alysaun said, her voice deceptively warm and eager. "What I would find most pleasing of all—"

"At last some willingness. Go on, love, be not timid."

Her head cradled against his shoulder, Alysaun smiled. "I would welcome your leave to travel on to the convent, there to spend my days in the unsullied peace of prayers. Before you came back to find me, I was resigned to that decision."

"As your legal guardian, m'lady, I cannot grant that request," Brand said, disappointment tingeing his voice with a shade of gray irritation. "It doesn't suit my plans or my desires for you. If you are

132

not willing, then I will make you so. Once I succeeded in that purpose. Think you that I cannot stir the embers of that fire to flame again?"

"Either way, you win, sire," Alysaun sighed, all hope of release dead. She had one defense and knew not its power. Her defiance had made Brand determined to subjugate Alysaun; her tears would have made him free her.

"You are coming to know me, Alys. I like to win and I mean to come out of this forced union to some advantage."

"I thought . . . you *said* you would seek an annulment. If you spend your lust upon me, you will lose the grounds to see it done." It was a desperate, last-ditch effort to dissuade him.

Brand kicked his leg and the sheet slipped down; another kick freed him of the encumbering material. He rolled and pinned Alysaun to the bed, the warm flesh of his body covering hers from breasts to toes. "Not so, though I do admire that bit of logic, love. I can have you at my leisure and still secure an end to this mock marriage. There are other grounds. The church has reason to dissolve our vows if you are abandoned."

"But that could take *years* to prove," Alysaun protested incredulously. "Abandon me now, if you mean to, before I am ruined." Brand's face was only inches above her own, his handsome, bold features arrogant in the power he wielded. "I . . . I thought you cared for me, Brand. Once you were kind."

"As once you were the sweet innocent," he answered, his eyes narrowed by the memory she had called up. "One time I played the fool, and that was your doing, girl. A second time 'twould be my own fault. I would not have it so."

Brand's mouth lowered slowly, intent on silencing the lips that parted in another protest. Alysaun turned her head, straining away, her body stiff with resistance. Close to her ear, in a voice whose measured reasoning underscored a threat, Brand ordered, "Yield up your mouth, dear wife, or I will, in moments, lay siege to your maidenhead. Pain need not accompany surrender."

A shiver passed over her. To possess her was his punishment for some imagined wrong. There were no entreaties left her that would soften his stony determination to have his way. She chose to obey him and turned her face back. For a second her eyes met his, accusingly, before she shut them tight. "You, sire," she whispered softly, "are in the brotherhood that contains the Norman, de Villai. Be gentle or savage like he, I am resigned."

Brand frowned. Alysaun had the innocent look of a martyr on her pale, tight-lipped face. The trembling of her body, so soft beneath him, angered Brand as much as it excited him. His mouth came down hard against her tender lips, crushing them in a bruising kiss, his fingers tangled in the long, silken waves that framed her bare shoulders.

Frustrated at the lack of response, he drew back, teasing the rounded slope of a breast, cupping her head to raise it with his free hand. "Open your eyes, Alysaun," he commanded. " 'Tis my right to take you, yet I would do it so that you know what pleasure can be found in the union of two bodies. Look, see how your nipple rises, eager to meet my fingertips. Protest now that you care not for my touch and your own flesh will make you a liar."

Crimson with embarrassment, Alysaun stared at Brand. Her breast tingled, firming with the gentle, circling strokes of his fingers. A twist of remembered desire coiled in her belly. "You are more cruel than de Villai," she said condemningly, "for he sought merely to use my body to sate his lust. You want more—you would take all, leaving nothing, not even the belief that I am your unwilling victim. Proceed, Brand. Your point is won, press home your advantage."

The warm length of male muscle moved against her belly, trapped between their bodies in restless desire. Alysaun tensed, so stiff and, for all her bravado, so afraid. "You are too beautiful, Alysaun," Brand whispered hoarsely. "Though I have a poet's way with words, nothing I say could do justice to your face. My lips will tell you of the passion you inspire."

He touched the dark rose peak of her breast in a kiss. "Would you make me beg to see your answer? I wanted you once and reined my desires. Now that it is my right, must I wring the passion from you?

'Tis you who art cruel, to deny the pleasures I would have us share.''

Alysaun was close to tears, frustrated by her body's betrayal. She wanted Brand, knew a rise of yearning so strong it choked her breath. More than desire, though, she needed some assurance that he cared, that the passionate encounter they would share was more than just a salve to his vanity and masculine pride. Why could he not want *her, what she was*, not just the shell of a body that reacted to the unnerving pleasure of his caressing hands?

And how could a man so warm with life contain a heart so cold and ruthless? "Victory is yours, my lord. My heart beats fast, my flesh is weak and shivers under your assault. Take me and end this torment of my senses. Do not prolong my agony with questions. 'Twill make you no less a conqueror to see the deed done with dispatch.''

Brand raised his head. "Of all the women I have known, girl, you puzzle me most." He retreated to study her, his upper body supported by well-muscled arms. "In the room we shared at the inn, you were mine for the taking. Why now, in a marriage blessed by God, must you withdraw what you so freely offered then?" His long, sculpted lips turned down in a scowl and he rolled from her and dropped back to the mattress with a disgusted sigh. "Just before the ax did fall, m'lady, you have been reprieved. Rest easy—I will not demand my conjugal rights. Your virtue is yours to retain. I find it too chilling to embrace.''

Alysaun stared at Brand in stunned disbelief. *How* could he make her admit to damning desire and then reject her? "A thousand pardons, sire," she answered acidly. "I thought you too full of ardor to notice my lack of warmth. If my virtue is too chilling, may I suggest you draw the covers over your frostbitten limbs?''

Brand started to laugh, a chuckle at first, then came a deep, helpless rumble of laughter that echoed in the chamber. He doubled over, then flipped onto his belly and muffled his amusement at her haughty retort with the feather pillow.

Only when her open palm slammed into his back did he cease his chuckling. Alysaun struck again, fingers closed in a small fist, doing little damage despite the fury that prompted the blows. Brand raised his head and turned to find her on her knees, rage sparking in the deep blue of her eyes.

"If you've a mind to, tell me why I deserved that attack," he asked, further infuriating Alysaun with the puzzled innocence of his raised brows. "I'm waiting, girl. 'Tis not often I give someone the chance to explain an attack upon my person."

"You . . . you are without a doubt the devil's spawn," she raged, hands still clenched into fists. "I want not your name nor your attentions, sir, and especially not your mockery. You may not credit me with it, but my breeding is as pure as yours. I will not be near-raped and then ignored like some frigid shrew. I'll not, d'you hear? You *cannot* treat me thus."

Brand almost laughed again, amused by the righteous claims of injustice and wounded dignity, by the fiery defense of honor. He suppressed a smile as she pouted, one hand raised to strike again. "Hold your blows, madame. The accused has a right to answer without the threat of more violence. By God, I'd be the laughing-stock of all England *and* France if anyone had witnessed this scene. A slip of a girl, beating upon her poor bridegroom—and all because she's not been properly bedded. What is the world coming to?" He smiled as Alysaun's mouth rounded into an "oh" of indignation, tensing his muscles to seize her if she pounced again.

"I'm a reasonable man, sweetheart. If I've left you aching with desire, I'll put the problem to rights. All you needed do was ask." Brand's eyes twinkled merrily at her offended gasp, then narrowed in appreciation as she flounced back, her high, proud breasts bouncing delightfully before she presented her back and lay facing away from him.

Brand reached out, drawing his fingertips down the velvet skin of her back, no longer amused but enchanted by the gentle curves of Alysaun's derriere and hips. He slid one hand between her shoulder and the mattress, the other trailing down her back to insinuate itself between the warmth of her thighs. As he had expected, she whirled at the encroaching, intimate touch and was trapped, pinned close to his chest by the hand that had encircled her shoulders.

"Why don't we start anew?" Brand suggested. Brushing his cheek against the soft spill of golden curls, he swept them aside and planted a kiss at the tender fold of skin where her breast and shoulder met.

"*No.*" Alysaun wriggled but found herself firmly captive. "You'll not do that to me again—stop it, please." Against her will, she giggled as Brand's tongue teased along her shoulder, swirling tiny circles near her throat. "Oh, stop . . . please, Brand, that tickles so."

"What is it, Alysaun? Must you hear me say how much I want you? That much should be evident. Or should I whisper sweet words of praise in your lovely ears?"

"I want *nothing.*" Brand's sigh brought Alysaun's head up and she gazed into his eyes, trying to measure his mood. "Don't trouble yourself with lies, Brand. I need not hear you say you love me. I . . . I would think a less possessive touch and . . . ooh, how you confuse me when you gaze at me like that."

"Like what? I cannot help wanting you. Alysaun, you tease me overmuch. Your scented skin, so soft and firm, draws from me a need to know all its secrets. You may not know men, but know this—I cannot stay the night beside you and keep from reaching out. Speak plainly what you want. I cannot guess at your thoughts."

"Some sign that . . . that I am more than just a body, something to use and then discard. I have feelings—too many, I sometimes think." Now she sighed. "I don't know what I want of you, Brand. How can I tell you when I do not know myself?"

"I've never told a woman I love her," he answered. "I'll say it if you wish, but God's truth, Alysaun, I may not mean it."

"Then lie to me, Brand. Let me have that much and your kisses will lull me into believing. Oh, Brand . . . I need someone to care for. There has been little enough reason to go on the past year."

Alysaun turned, cuddling against his chest, and Brand, resisting the ties that accompanied the claim, whispered that he loved her. Her head came up, mouth parted in surrender, and the kiss that passed between them was the sweetest of moments. "Sweet Jesus, I think I do," he affirmed in wonder at the depth of his feelings.

Very gently he pressed her onto her back, then bent his head to engulf a nipple with his lips, eliciting a breathless whimper from Alysaun's throat as the rose peak of breast blossomed under his tender sucking. Her hair tangled with the restless movements of her head, a froth of goldspun lace to frame features sharpened with desire.

Brand's fingers replaced his mouth, lightly massaging her breasts. Moving lower, he teased the fullness beneath each aureole with feathery touches of his tongue, nipping at the firm, silky globes with little love bites. "You taste of a wine so sweet and heady, no man ever knew such a thirst as I," he whispered, then laid his cheek against the comfort of her breasts, fingers tracing a pattern of circles on the spareness of her waist and belly.

More urgent now, he traveled the gentle, sloping road from navel to a golden mound of curls nested between her thighs. Alysaun gasped in shock at the gentle exploration and tensed, but the soothing, light contact of his fingertips soon relaxed her modest reaction. Brand's fingers combed the soft curls, stroking, caressing, slipping ever lower until they found the petal-soft folds of flesh that hid her maidenhood.

The restlessness called up by the sensations Brand's caresses elicited was strange and new. Alysaun wanted more, desired something beyond the stir of passion, and yet was afraid of what lay beyond. She called out his name, once, then again as his fingers toyed with the warm, yearning flesh hidden by her curls.

Her thoughts, shocked by the teasing trespass, went unheeded as her body responded to the intense pleasure of the contact. She moaned as his fingers circled and divided the sensitive folds, thighs parting slightly as a rush of heated, liquid feeling curled in her belly and spread like honey throughout her limbs.

A cry escaped her and, unknowing, she closed her teeth against the knuckles of a hand. Waves of peace washed over her as her hips twisted and arched, seeking all it could draw from searing intimacy of sensation.

As dazed as if she had drunk wine, Alysaun went limp, enveloped in a cloud of dreamy contentment. A rustle of bed linens and Brand was beside her, his leg cast possessively over hers, the tumescent length of his penis pressed against her hip. With that contact, the sense of languor fled and she again knew fear. "Brand—I am frightened," she whispered. "Pray, do not hate me. I know it will hurt, it *must*." She fought the panic, afraid he would be repelled by her apprehension.

The tender kisses Brand played out upon her throat and lips helped to ease her fears. "I will not hurt you, love," he pledged, knowing, even as he spoke, that such a confident claim was false. Of her chastity he had no doubt, Alysaun's trembling was born more of shadowed imaginings of the physical act than of anticipation. For some time longer he merely held her, slowly arousing her desires with whispered praises of her beauty. Warm and wet, his mouth sought her breasts again, tongue flicking at their taut points until Alysaun was beset with wild abandon. She wasn't even aware of his movements, only of the pleasure mounting as his hands caressed the length of her body.

Kneeling now, he kissed and nibbled at her belly, his fingers kneading the firm flesh of white thighs. The head of his shaft rose, seeking the heated sheath hidden by the nest of golden curls. Brand leaned forward, his arms slipping beneath her shoulders to lift her and allow him to kiss the lips that pouted in a pretty curve of longing flesh. Her arms went around his neck, fingers splayed through the short, wavy length of auburn hair.

His tongue battled hers, swirling, plunging, drinking in the sweet nectar of her breath. Alysaun's breasts touched his chest, and like tiny fingers, her nipples stabbed the lean-muscled surface. His kisses found her throat and all the soft, hidden hollows, and a low groan, a rumble of need, broke from his lips.

Urgency replaced the languor of drawn-out caresses. Brand's hands slipped beneath her to cup the rounded globes of her buttocks, lifting as he eased into position. Passion riding high, he poised above that vulnerable display of soft flesh and knew a certain humility in the realization that from this moment, Alysaun would always belong to him.

Brand thrust his hips and with one hard lunge tore past the delicate skin protecting her virginity, the tight, silken sheath yielding before the deep penetration of his swollen shaft. Alysaun's body arched with the pain, her scream of protest silenced as Brand sank forward to cover her mouth with his.

Tears spilled over Alysaun's cheeks as a dull, throbbing ache replaced the first searing shock of Brand's entry. She fought his mouth, her hands pushing at his chest, nails digging into his skin in an effort to free herself of him. Finally he raised his head and she took a deep, gulping breath that came out as a sob. "You said..."

"I know, sweet," Brand whispered, tenderly wiping away the damp traces of weeping, "that it wouldn't hurt. The hurting's done, there is only pleasure from this time on. Alysaun, that proud flesh had to be torn asunder, else you would forever be a maid. And you are too much a woman to be denied the sweet rapture that can be given you."

There was no longer any sharp pain, but Alysaun could feel the warm trickle of blood dampening her thighs. "You are..." She couldn't bring herself to say it but the size of him overwhelmed her, filling the softness within her.

"Full within you," Brand finished with a smile. "And buried where no man has gone before me." He kissed the last tears from the outer corners of her eyes, stroking her hair away from her temple. "'Tis the way of all women who came before you and all who will come after, my love. Your tears are as common as the outcry against the pain. Only once that pain, though, then a lifetime of pleasures follows." He frowned. "Your mother left you unprepared, dealing you a disservice in keeping such knowledge from you."

"With knowledge it would not have hurt less, Brand—mayhap more," Alysaun replied. "I hesitate to sound untaught, but... is

140

there more to it?'' She blushed, coloring at the naiveté of her question.

"Aye, more, much more," Brand answered, easing his hips back, watching her face for a flicker of pain. Alysaun was wary, too, but more curious than frightened. He lowered his head to her breast, sucking in its nipple and more, until his mouth was full of soft, ivory flesh. She stirred, enchanted by the nibbling of his teeth, the caress of his sweeping tongue, and laid her hand upon his head.

Legs stretched straight, weight supported by his arms, Brand began a slow pattern of withdrawal and entry. So tightly did her softness hold him, he glanced up, worried that he was hurting her. Alysaun was not in pain. Her head twisted from side to side, her breathing so rapid it left her panting.

Brand increased the pace of strokes and groaned as her hips, loath to lose what gave such pleasure, rose to follow his retreat. No longer the controlled, detached lover, Brand was wild with a need to capture the fleeting dream of power. His hips ground against his wife's twisting, whimpering form.

Tears coursed down her cheeks again as Alysaun came to know the ache of too much pleasure. The only relief from the savage yearning came when Brand was deep within her. Her skin burned, all senses keyed to the one goal she and Brand sought together. She called out his name, then caught her breath and held it, savoring the flow of warmth that spread outward from the core of her being, leaving her straining muscles as weak as a newborn kitten's.

Striving to exact the full degree of pleasure, Brand arched backward. Alysaun watched her lover, her body still but for the buffeting assault that continued until Brand paused, his features sharpened by the surge of brief, immortal power. A low, husky groan accompanied one last, triumphant lunge forward.

Slick with sweat, the lovers seemed to merge as one. His head resting on the soft pillow of her breasts, Brand listened to the wild drumming of Alysaun's heartbeat and smiled. "The siege is done, m'lady," he whispered. "Can you make accusation of any cruelties committed?"

"None, sire," Alysaun answered softly, her fingers stroking his damp brown locks with a tenderness born of their passion. "Save one—if I had known such bliss existed, I would have surrendered sooner."

The confession added to the sweet contentment of the moment, deepening Brand's realization of his affection for Alysaun. Though still he chafed at Elfleda's high-handed manipulations, his anger had been lessened by the surprising sensuality of the innocent girl he had taken for his wife.

Withdrawing reluctantly from the sweet prison between her thighs, Brand slid up to lie next to Alysaun and drew her into his arms. "You seem contented, sweet. Does the idea of an annulment still hold so strong an appeal?"

Alysaun hesitated. To her shame, it was her fault they were trapped in this marriage, her simple falsehood that had drawn Brand into Lady Elfleda's schemes. "If this forced alliance still pricks at your pride, m'lord, I can understand your resentment," she answered. "A man has more say regarding whom he chooses to wed, a woman much less. The issue is yours to decide."

Brand tightened his arm around her shoulders and smiled. "Then I say, though Elfleda acted selfishly, the lady did more a service to me than herself. I am content as well . . . for the moment . . . to let lie the issue of parting."

6

In the dense weald of gnarled oak and ash surrounding Havistock, the weary night hunters sensed the coming of the new day and welcomed it. The hour before dawn's light illuminated the shadowed sanctuary of greenwood was alive with the scurrying of those animals that shied from the passage of man's heavy foot.

A lynx passed the fog-wreathed pond, carrying her lifeless catch of plump hare toward the den where her kittens still slept. Chasing new-hatched minnows, a large pike suddenly jumped, sliced through the pearl-shrouded mist in a wriggling arc of silver-green, and landed with a loud splash that startled the feline predator.

The large cat crouched possessively over her catch, tufted ears tensed forward, yellow eyes glaring in the waning moonlight. A low, guttural growl whined from her throat before the mother lynx realized that the sound she heard held no threat to her or her bounty.

Above her, perched securely on the highest fork of a spreading, thick-leaved oak, a tawny owl hooted, warning the bobtail cat that his talons were as sharp as her claws, communicating in a treble call that he stood guard over his mate's nearby nest of three downy owlets. Regally ignoring the warning, the lynx sank her needle-sharp teeth deeper into the bloody, matted fur of the hare's torn throat and hefted it, continuing her homeward journey.

A small fox, long, pinched nose twitching along the ground as he followed the trail of fresh blood along the pond's bank, paused at the echo of the lynx's snarl. His jaw hung open, the soft red fur lining his muzzle wet with saliva at the scent of freshly killed meat. He was too young to tangle with a full-grown lynx; for a second the hunger of an overlong, unsuccessful night's hunting nearly tempted him to try to wrest her prey away. Instead he raised his pointed nose to the lightening golden sky that heralded the end of his night's hunting and yelped in self-pitying protest.

In the yard before the manor, a cock's crowing awakened the snoring night watch. The man yawned and stretched, then rose to stumble around the house and relieve himself against a tall, spiky bush of woodruff growing wild around the manor's foundation. He was back at his post, tired but looking alert, when his relief man emerged from the house.

Inside, the servants were astir, eyes dull with the shadows of receding sleep, as they went about their morning tasks. There was always much to do before the family rose to attend the new day's mass and break their long night's fast.

In her chambers, the Lady Elfleda slept soundly, the peaceful, dreamless sleep of one content with the previous night's proceedings. Her son slumbered as deeply but, besotted by his late-hour indulgence in wine, dreamed that the lovely Alysaun shared his bed; his dream was so vivid that the warm spill of passion's fluid wet his thighs, bringing him awake with a groan at the fact that he slept alone.

Exhausted by well-spent passion, Brand was slow to wake. When the bright stream of sunlight finally penetrated the linen bed curtains, he sat up, sinews rippling as he stretched firm-muscled arms high over his head with the tautness of an arising leopard. Memories of the long, sweet night brought a contented smile to his full, sensual mouth, and he turned to kiss the sleep from Alysaun's eyes, only to find her gone from his side.

All traces of sleep vanished as he bolted upright with a frown, thrusting aside the bed curtains to call out her name. No answer. His irritation deepening, Brand swung his long legs from the bed and stood, gripping the bedpost with a tension that whitened his knuckles, as his gaze swept the chamber in a search for his missing wife. The door swung open suddenly, and a young serving maid started into the room, then halted as she saw him standing naked at the end of the bed. She gawked at him for a minute, mouth hanging open, and finally lowered her gaze, a dull red blush suffusing her thin, lean features.

"What is it?" Brand grumbled, not bothering to cover himself. "Have you any knowledge of Lady Alysaun's whereabouts?"

The girl stammered, shuffling her feet nervously, certainly afraid to glance up and too timid to explain her presence. "I . . . I was . . . m'lord, the lady did rise early and is finishing her bath. I were asked to see . . . to see if you was yet awake, sire."

"Obviously, I am," he snapped. The maid raised her head and, following an awkward curtsy, stared at him with the wide, fixed gaze of a frightened rabbit. "Cease your gaping, girl, and fetch me back my wife."

"Yes, m'lord . . . yes, I beg pardon for . . ." The girl whirled and nearly collided with the returning Alysaun. Backing off, the flustered maidservant squeaked an apology and bolted as if the Devil were hot on her heels.

"In heaven's name, what has seized the . . ." Alysaun turned and at the sight of Brand standing there so bold in all his naked glory, she blushed and raised a hand to cover her smile, no longer puzzled by young Gerta's embarrassed confusion. "Oh, m'lord . . . 'tis no wonder you frightened the child. Without the cloak of dark night to provide modesty, you near scared me."

Brand sheepishly returned her smile. "If it's modesty you want, love, then close the door and fetch me my undergarments. After what passed between us last ev'n"—his smile deepened rakishly—

145

"you cannot blush at the sight of what delivered up your cries of rapture." He saw her blush more deeply at the recollection and moved to sit on the edge of the mattress. "Come, Alysaun . . . I would hear from your own lips why I did wake to find myself deprived of your company."

Alysaun hesitated. Her hair, freshly washed and scented with lavender, curled in damp, burnished waves across her shoulders, making a pretty contrast against the azure color of her gunna. A plain, cross-shaped brooch, unadorned by jewels or design, fastened her white mantle at the shoulder. She sighed and crossed the room to find his garment, unable to put off the moment when she would again view the evidence of Brand's sex.

Undergarment in hand, she turned and found her husband studying her and the amusement he showed in the green glint of his eyes added to her reluctance to approach him. Brand crooked a finger, beckoning, one brow raised as he questioned her hesitation. "What am I this morning—a fierce and terrible ogre who frightens all females? Come, my sweet, attend to your wifely duties."

Alysaun came to him, keeping her gaze fixed upon his face, not daring to risk glancing lower than his chin, offering the undergarment and turning away slightly to allow him to don it. A second later Brand seized her wrists and tugged. "The object of your desire is covered now," he teased. "Come, you may look and not blush, sweet. I still have not your answer to my query of why you left me sleeping." He would not admit that for the most fleeting of moments, he had believed her gone from him, and thought her pleasure in lying with him had been feigned. With her skin all aglow from the bath, Alysaun was a sorely tempting sight.

Able to face him now that he was partially clothed, she found herself disturbed still by the stir of desire that rose at the sight of his firm, broad chest and lean, tapering waist. "I . . . after all that happened last night, sire, I felt a necessity for greeting you and the new day with a fresh start." Alysaun tossed her head, sending her curls cascading over one shoulder as she offered Brand a tentative smile. "If you would care to follow suit, m'lord, I will . . . if it

146

pleases you . . . be most happy to assist your bathing, to wash your back and . . ."

"And all else modesty forbids you mention?" Brand finished with a grin. "I am unused to such pampering, Alysaun. You will spoil me. Next time, wake me." He decided to admit his apprehension and added, "It did occur to my sleep-drugged mind that you had taken advantage of the early rising to flee from me."

Alysaun was shocked at the assumption. "Oh, *no*, m'lord. You've given me no cause—" She suddenly realized he had tricked her into reaffirming her fidelity, and pouted in dismay at the ease with which she had been handled. "I can see that I must make a study of you, Brand, else you will have me in a constant turmoil. How can you suggest—"

Brand tugged once more on her hands and, taken by surprise, Alysaun tumbled forward into his arms. With easy grace, he rolled and she was pinned to the bed. Though she made no struggle, Alysaun's raised brows questioned the purpose of his actions. "Don't look so skittish, wife," he protested. "I mean only to apologize for doubting your pledge of faith and begin our first day of wedded life with a kiss from your sweet mouth." His face hovered close over hers, a wide grin crinkling the corners of his eyes. "No more than a kiss, even if you beg me, love. 'Twould be a sacrilege to tarry in bed and miss attendance at the morning mass."

Alysaun wasn't sure which shocked her most—the idea of making love in the full light of morning or Brand's suggestion that she might swoon so over one kiss that she would insist upon more. "Pray do not mock me, m'lord. I am new to this state of marriage."

The fragrant scent of lavender rose from her hair, and, burrowing his face against the silken tresses, Brand was tempted to follow through with what had only been a jest. His lips gently touched the softness of one shell-like ear. "I, too, am new at it," he whispered, "but find it an increasingly pleasant manner of captivity. That I can, by right, stay long past sunrise in a married lady's bower is a pleasing novelty. By experience, I have had to leave the warmth of bed linen and clinging arms before an irate husband appeared."

147

"Oh? And mayhap the novelty wears thin... will you then be seeking other beds to explore, sire?" Alysaun's voice trembled with indignation at his callous revelation.

Brand trailed his fingers down her back and over a rounded hip, then looked into her eyes with a hooded smile. "Nay, my sweet spouse, not as long as you look as you do now. Why would I seek out any other when these proud curves shelter what I desire? Grow fat and neglectful and I will reconsider. Till then, Alysaun, I will find solace only in your bright, golden beauty."

The answer pleased her; a woman could ask for no more of a vow of constancy than Brand had offered. She relaxed, enjoying the quiet security of his arms. "And you, Brand... if with age you grow broader at the belt, have I the same resort? It would only be fair."

"Life is not always fair," Brand replied. "I have played amorous in many a lady's chamber, but should I ever find you disporting with another man, I would run him through with my blade and see you locked within a tower to await my pleasure or punishment. No man can take what is mine." Even to himself the claim sounded fierce, and Brand softened the threat with a rueful grin. "I'm a jealous hound... see how you've done me in? Ne'er before have I worried over straying ladies. Now that you share my name and bed, I am savagely determined you will dishonor neither."

"You think to warn me, sire, with harsh threats of retribution? That is both unnecessary and an insult. Even if... if we shared no warmth, I would still honor the vows I uttered. Of the two of us, I have no past to boast of or to shame me. I ask the same question you plied earlier. Why, when your kisses stir in me a shameless abandon, would I seek a stranger's bed?"

"I trust you, Alysaun, and therein lies my weakness. If you would turn away your mouth from mine and deny me the release of passion your sweet body does inspire, I cannot guess at the rage I might know. Mayhap time will reveal the devotion you have pledged with words." Brand smiled down at her, lips curved upward as he studied the solemnity of her expression. "A kiss now would melt my doubts, weak as they are."

"If that will ease your mind, m'lord," Alysaun answered, "I would that there was some other, more powerful token to show you my loyalty." Slipping her hand behind his neck, she stroked the soft russet curls that lay at his nape, feeling the strong, corded muscles beneath her fingers as she urged his head lower and raised her lips to meet his.

Alysaun's mouth parted to allow his tongue to enter and possess, even as he had taken his possession of it in the darkness of the night. Her willingness to please him was evident in that one lingering kiss. As his fingers played through her hair, combing it away from her temples in tender, caressing motions, Alysaun's breath came short and fast.

Her eyelids fluttered open; she brought her hands up to frame Brand's face and reluctantly pushed him back. Brand's hazel eyes were warm with desire, shadowed by the resistance that had risen suddenly in her. Lips red and bruised, complexion suffused with a flush of rose, Alysaun was so tantalizing Brand could think of nothing but the urge to take her, to possess again what was his. Her long tresses, drying now, lay spread around her in a tumble of glistening curls. Within the bright blue of her irises, a reflection of his desire danced; she wanted him as much, though the protest she gave him denied it.

"Oh, Brand . . . we cannot, not now," Alysaun whispered. "The mass begins soon . . . perhaps after the morning meal?"

"No, love . . . now," Brand insisted. "I will not be so blasphemous as to sit through the service and think only of how I want you. The others may wonder . . . let them."

"But, Brand . . . I'm bathed and dressed. How will it look to appear all disheveled and . . ."

"Lovers are forgiven much," Brand replied, and cut off any further protests by the pressure of his mouth against hers. She shivered as the wings of desire brushed her skin, giving up any attempt to argue against the impious impropriety of spending the morning's prayer hour at so wanton and sensual an activity. "If it makes you rest easier, my lady wife," Brand teased, drawing back

149

from her with a flush of triumph at Alysaun's surrender to his will, "after our passion is spent, we will share a bath. No one will reproach a morning spent in private worship."

The look she gave him doubted they would escape totally unnoticed. A resigned sigh broke from her as Brand tugged at the hem of her tunic. The material slid upward, slowly exposing her thighs and the flatness of her belly. His fingers caressed her bare flesh, tracing light circles across her thighs. Another sigh heralded her whispered, teasing reproach, "Lord Brand, you *are* a rogue."

"Aye, but you would not have me otherwise, my darling," came Brand's arrogant reply before he covered her trembling body with his.

Three idyllic weeks followed that first morning of missed prayers, a time when, for all her past sorrows, Alysaun was once again carefree and lighthearted. In attending to her husband's needs and desires, she had found a new joy in the deep greening of an England ripe with summer. Though her heart still grieved for her family and her hatred of the Norman bastard had not lessened, those emotions were less consuming.

Brand was a demanding lover but Alysaun had convinced him it was improper to miss matins, so after rising early of a morning, they spent an hour in the chapel with Lady Elfleda, Esmond, and the manor's retainers. Following a brief meal, the rest of the day was theirs. Elfleda, now that she was duly satisfied that Alysaun no longer represented a threat, was benevolently gracious in her insistence that they stay as long as it pleased them. Brand, still cool and reserved with the manipulative woman, accepted the invitation only because Alysaun seemed so happy in the midst of her own people and customs.

With the coming of the midsummer feast of St. John on June 24, the hay harvesting commenced. The preceding eve had passed in a night-long celebration in honor of the summer solstice, but dawn found every able-bodied cotter and villein in the hedged fields working the longest days of the year at a task that would keep them busy for the five weeks until Lammas.

With everyone who lived on the estate so occupied, Brand and Alysaun were free to explore the lush glades and rolling meadows of Havistock. Mornings passed quickly in long, invigorating walks past cottages backed by furrowed strips of land thickening with vegetables the cotters grew for their families and to barter at market, past groves of oak entwined by ivy and the sacred mistletoe. The trees provided a cool respite from the heat of the midday sun; a quiet, sheltered bower to share a light meal of fruit and cheese.

Lazy afternoons lying on the mossy banks of the millstream came and went as the newlyweds shared each other's memories of childhood and youth. Brand, surprised to learn Alysaun was one of seven children, held back the information about her youngest sister's death. Alysaun, puzzling over his absence from the duties burdening a man who had inherited a title of count, discovered her husband was the black sheep of a conservative and religious matriarchal family presided over by his dowager grandmother, Lenora. They were Cathari, a Christian sect of growing popularity in the south of France, whose beliefs harked back to the simplicity of the church's early days.

Legally his grandmother had no power to strip him of his rank or its privileges, but such was her sway over the family that Brand had been ostracized for his too-worldly disposition toward the sensual. The girl he had seduced had quietly taken the veil, but Brand's punishment had lasted the past four years, a sentence of exile from his native county until, in Lenora's lofty estimation, he had learned to restrain himself.

Despite retiring quite early each night, Brand's strong desires were not fully sated by the long hours spent in his bride's arms. The first time he suggested making love in the open air of a sun-dappled meadow, Alysaun balked, horrified at the thought that someone might pass by and discover them in feverish coupling.

He won her over to the idea, though, as he always did, and never by a show of strength. With charm, he never failed to persuade her she was safe and secure in his company. What soft, wooing words could not effect, he accomplished with such tender kisses and caresses that Alysaun became lightheaded and pliant.

No one discovered them that first day, and in her newly awakened thirst for the pleasures she knew at his embrace, Alysaun grew more bold. She could deny him nothing, and, basking in the warmth of his loving attention, she no longer worried over the risk of shame that would accompany the revelation of their open trysts. It was as if Brand could not possess her enough, as if each time he took her only increased his desire to establish his dominion and leave her body and soul indelibly etched with his name.

Esmond had made a show of accepting the fact of Alysaun's marriage and her husband's presence at Havistock. The long, arduous years of apprenticeship as a squire served him well; to wait upon the full-fledged knights who trained him in arms and horsemanship, to groom their steeds and suffer the indignity of cleaning the horse stalls of malodorous droppings, all these duties had required a discipline of will and demeanor, a mien of humility to mask the unpleasantnesses of a life that became rewarding only after one achieved knighthood.

No one, not even the mother who thought she knew him so well, realized the frustration seething beneath Esmond's placid exterior. Like the wasp galls growing on the leaves of the host oak tree, jealousy and envy had fixed upon his heart, nurturing the twin emotions of love and hate. Esmond was quiet in his hatred of Brand, watching, waiting, hoping for some cruel or stupid act that would lose the man his wife's affections.

Because the object of his desire had been so abruptly snatched from his hold, Esmond found Alysaun even more desirable. Her every movement enchanted him; a chance look from her set his heart pounding and slicked his palms with sweat. If, before Brand's arrival, Esmond had been willing to defy his mother's wishes and make Alysaun his wife, he was beyond that single-minded determination now, living each day only to brood upon how he might steal her affections from the Frenchman or, failing that, destroy the man.

The month of June had passed in a preoccupied expending of energy. He hunted with his falcons, attempted to concentrate on his steward's boring recital of accounts, and kept to his mother's company as little as possible. Her joy had been too great at the reunion of the parted lovers; still, in the darkest moments of his sullen spells of resentment, the suspicion of her stealth lurked. He could not find evidence to support the sense of conspiracy that had colored that night, but the near-miraculous appearance of Alysaun's presumably dead spouse suited Elfleda's own desires too well to be coincidental.

A drawing, obsessive curiosity to know how the lovers spent the long days away from the manor seized hold of Esmond. One day he followed the pair, keeping well back and covered by the lush growth of bushes and trees thick with the verdancy of midsummer. Reynaud led his wife along a forest track, apparently familiar with the path that ended at the mossy banks of the stream that crossed the property.

For a while they paused by the stream, just below the millrace. The Frenchman lounged against a large, worn boulder near the water's edge, his face lifted to the warmth of a sun that turned his auburn hair to a fiery red. Alysaun lay on the cool, grassy bank, her head cradled in her husband's lap. Above the deep grasses of a meadow that sloped gently from stream to hillock, long-stemmed daisies bent their white-gold heads, stirred by a breeze to a swaying dance of wildflowers. The air was heavy with the rich fragrance of sweetbrier roses and honeysuckle, with the insistent hum of bees from Havistock's hives, busily collecting the nectar from the snowy scattering of clover blossoms.

It was a day made for lovers, Esmond reflected bitterly, hidden by the thick green boughs of the cherry tree against which he leaned. A snatch of warm, intimate laughter drifted back from the bank to torment him; and as Esmond absently plucked the hard, ripening fruit of the tree, he brooded that it was not he who had elicited Alysaun's melodic, tinkling laughter. It should have been he who brought a smile to curve those soft, bow lips, who held the delicate hand Alysaun offered so trustingly to de Reynaud.

Esmond chewed the hard flesh of several cherries, barely noticing their tart sourness, so bitter was the taste of gall that had risen with his reflections. He squatted down on his haunches and, discovering a gooseberry bush bowed with the weight of ripe, green berries, thrust a handful into his mouth. The sweet, succulent fruit only made him thirsty and he rose, thinking to quench his thirst farther upstream, where his presence would go undetected by the lovers.

There was no longer a need for such caution. The bank was abandoned; while Esmond had been so mired by his melancholy reverie, Brand and Alysaun had slipped away. Heedless of the noise he made, he hurried down the slight incline, brushing at the heavy branches that scratched his face and impeded his progress. Esmond cursed, searching the meadow with eyes shaded against the bright glare of the sun. Remembering his parched throat, he went down on one knee and cupped his hands to bring the cool, clear water to his lips. He drank heavily and, after rising to his feet, felt the volume of liquid that pressed like leaden weights upon his upper belly.

Once more he searched the sea of undulating grasses for some hint of the direction the two had taken. He was about to turn away, his shoulders slumped in disappointment, when a flutter of something white caught his attention. Esmond backed away from the open ground of the stream's bank, stepping behind the slim trunk of an ash tree that shaded the water. From his vantage point he could now make out the two figures standing in the isolated shelter of a sun-dappled copse across the meadow. Brand's mantle of forest green had blended with his surroundings to make him almost invisible. Alysaun stood before him, her burnished tresses bare of the silken veil that had drawn Esmond's attention as it drifted to the ground.

Brand's arms encircled his wife's narrow waist and as he bent his head to kiss her, Alysaun's slim white hands curled around his neck, fingers clutching at the russet curls covering his nape. Alysaun was arched on her toes, her body molded to Brand's, and even as far from them as he was, Esmond could feel the abandonment in her attitude, the surrender of will to the passion that made her cling to de Reynaud's strong shoulders, weak and pliant from his kisses.

Brand broke the kiss with evident reluctance and smiled down at his wife before removing his mantle to spread it on the grass. He sat down and, gazing up at Alysaun, beckoned to her with his offered hand. Her eagerness was apparent as she slipped her hand in his and sank down on her knees beside him. Brand wove his fingers through the rippling masses of golden hair and, as she melted against him, rolled their bodies so that he was lying half upon her supine form.

Esmond wrenched his gaze from the lovers' tryst, a wave of overpowering desire washing over his body. His loins ached with need; his member was swollen above the heavy sac of his testicles. A flood of saliva filled his mouth, preceding the nausea that rose in a sour belch of gorge. Esmond doubled over, heaving, spewing forth the contents of his belly in convulsive, racking coughs until there was nothing left to expel. Sweating from weakness, he stumbled to the bank and splashed water over his face, sucking in a mouthful to rinse the bile from his tongue, then spat it out.

For minutes he was too weak to stand. He dropped back to rest, covering his wet eyes with an arm to shield them against the harsh sunlight. The threat of nausea receded, leaving behind the cloying need to release the passion stirred by Alysaun's brazenly sensual surrender on the hillside. Finally, when his heartbeat had slowed somewhat; Esmond sat up, wiping his mouth with the edge of his sleeve.

His stride as he made his way back along the wooded path was a stagger, the unsteady lurching of a besotted drunk. By the time he reached the clearing before the thicket, his gait was more even. Esmond, passing the fields where his tenants toiled at the harvest, ignored the looks of curiosity his purposeful, scowling expression drew from the sweating workers as he pursued his intention to seek some relief from the throbbing of his groin.

Except at the holidays, when he was expected to make a show of lordly beneficence to his estate people, Esmond knew little of how their lives passed. Occasionally a young peasant wench had caught his eye; but under his mother's watchful presence, he had had little chance to take a moment's pleasure. The shouts of younger children filled the air as he walked beyond the huddle of cottages, seeking a more isolated spot to spend his backwash of desire. The last cottage was set some distance from the others, little more than a rundown hovel that could have used a good coat of whitewash. In the dusty, weeded yard before it, a young girl crouched over a strip of leafy vegetables, her dirt-smudged face frowning in concentration as she freed the soil of choking weeds.

The girl, startled at his hail, had pale gray eyes fringed with light flaxen lashes that matched the white-blond of her long, plaited braids. Somewhere between a child and young woman, she appeared to be eleven or twelve years of age, the outline of her dirty, torn tunic just beginning to swell with the buds of breasts.

As Esmond approached her she stood, not daring to glance directly at the man she knew to be her father's lord and master. Her feet, bare and dusty, were suddenly a great embarrassment. Esmond glowered at her awkward shuffling and almost turned away to head back to the manor. Beneath the unwashed face there was a hint of pretty features and the thought that her mother or older sister might, though just as filthy, share her looks prompted him to stay. "Where is your mother, girl?" he asked. After a brief, shy glance, when she seemed too tongue-tied to answer coherently, he snapped, "Fetch her. Tell her Lord Esmond would have a word with her."

The girl, flushing a dull red from her embarrassment before the lord, sprinted off, her long legs flashing whitely in the heat of midday. Depending upon his ability to stomach the woman's appearance, Esmond meant to be blunt about his needs. These people owed him too much to deny any demand he made.

The woman who emerged from the low portal of the cottage was no more than five years older than Esmond, but early breeding and a hard-scratch existence had lined her face with premature weathering. Her braids, a darker shade of flaxen than her daughter's, were wound around her crown in a coronet, evidencing some degree of

156

care for her appearance. Despite the weary set of her features, her body still had a youthful firmness Esmond found pleasing. She was short; another five years would find her fat as time dragged at her flesh, but the spread of her rounded hips seemed to Esmond's greedy gaze a pillow of flesh that would draw off the passion weighting his stones.

A fat, red-haired baby rode the woman's left hip, his chubby arms bared to allow him some relief from the heat rash spotting his skin. The child stared at Esmond and trilled a gurgling cry, the only one present who was not awed by his importance. The boy waved a fist, then brought his hand back to settle on his mother's breast, drawing Esmond's attention to the large, engorged teats that strained at the covering of gunna and tunic, spreading a stain of leaking milk around her nipples.

Merganthe recognized desire in the heavy, hooded gaze of the young lord; and in the warmth of her sun-splashed yard, she shivered. Her husband and son were laboring in the fields. Neither would be home until dusk. A drawing fear clutched at her belly, and, sensing her sudden tension, the baby began to wail. "Give the boy to your daughter," Esmond ordered, and glanced past her to where the girl shyly peered at him from the shelter of the doorway.

"Alys . . . come, take Ned to play in the garden," Merganthe called back without taking her eyes from Esmond's face. When the girl had obeyed and hefted the screaming tot into her arms, her mother added a warning to seek out shade if the boy fussed with the heat. "Stay there till I call you, hear?"

For her daughter's sake, the woman made a show of inviting Esmond into her home and apologized loudly for its humble furnishings. Esmond followed her, studying the roll of her hips, the swell of her buttocks. Her understanding of what he sought made his goal that much easier to attain, and she showed a certain intelligence by not making weeping protests, which would have only angered him. Though not a slave, the woman knew her family's continued residence and well-being at Havistock depended heavily on the patronage of its liege.

Within the hovel, the odors of unwashed bodies and acrid smoke combined with the stale, stagnant air to deliver a blow to Esmond's senses that was as staggering as a physical punch. He choked on the stench and, swiping at his offended nostrils with his sleeve, turned back to the door to suck in a deep breath of fresh air.

Somewhat recovered, he turned and moved into the single room, searching the darkness for the woman's figure, eyes unaccustomed to the gloom lit only by the dying embers of a cooking fire. Suddenly she was in front of him, her expression sullen, betraying her resentment of the lust he chose to spend upon her, of his indifference to her vows of fidelity and marriage, of the haughty arrogance and power that allowed him to make use of her as only another animal among the manor's livestock.

Esmond reached out to lay his fingers across the damp peak of one of her breasts and smiled at the realization that his hand could not span the breadth of the heavy globe. Encouraged by her silence, he fondled both breasts, cupping and testing their fullness. "Bare them for me, woman," he insisted, his voice hoarsened by the urgency tugging at his loins. "I'll not offer a reward, but if you please me . . ."

Merganthe had none of the lord's learning and polished manners, but neither was she a fool. "If you leave me an' mine in peace, sire, 'twould be enough reward," she said in answer to his implied offer of a bounty. "I cannot give you what is my husband's right to know. If you must, take what you want and leave me the small comfort of my unwillingness."

Esmond cared not whether she knew pleasure at his touch or feigned a response. As long as he needn't overcome her resistance by force or spend effort muffling her screams, he would come away satisfied. Her tunic was split to the hem, the gunna laced over it to the waist, allowing her the convenience of baring a breast for the babe to nurse. With fingers that fumbled in their impatience, Esmond tugged roughly at the laces and finally loosened them enough to thrust the two layers of clothing down over her shoulders.

Merganthe stood still with as much dignity as she could summon up with her arms pinioned by the confining material and her full, pendulant breasts exposed to Esmond's lewd appraisal. She heard him suck in a deep breath and closed her eyes, tensing against the rough, pawing exploration that followed.

Esmond grasped a handful of plump flesh and kneaded, marveling at the length of the woman's nipples, flattened and drawn by the baby's suckling. Each press of his fingers against the huge, tawny-hued aueroles brought a flow of sticky, bluish-white milk trickling from her teats. Vague memories of the wet nurse who had suckled him from birth aroused his curiosity. He cupped one breast and raised it, lowering his head to draw in the elongated, oozing nipple, tightly banding her waist with his left arm to cut off her indignant struggling to escape.

Tears slipped down her cheeks as Merganthe gave up the attempt to protest his lips against her tender breasts. Her milk, her babe's nourishment, was drawn from her despite the tension of her muscles. Lord Esmond's teeth pressed painfully against her, and despite her revulsion for his callous treatment, the rough texture of his tongue lapping at her sensitive nipples brought a flood of warmth rushing outward from the pit of her belly. Without realizing, she raised her hand and rubbed at her other breast, massaging it to release the pressure of engorgement, sighing when the steady drip of milk eased its ache.

Sensing the musky perfume of arousal, Esmond bent the woman back, his hand sliding down to fondle the flaring hips and mold her to the growing bulge between his thighs. She moaned in shame at her easy manipulation, at the passion that flamed as his hands seized hold of the cheeks of her buttocks and lifted her until her toes barely touched the packed earthen floor. He slid her weight down hard against the steady grinding of his hips, the hard promise of his sex stroking her mound.

More than he could have guessed, the pleasure of nursing at the fullness of a warm, pliant breast heightened Esmond's desire. He let the woman slip back to the floor and took his mouth away only to bury his head against the softness of her right breast and capture the neglected peak. Modesty forgotten, she clutched his head with both hands, encouraging him to continue. More than the sweetness of the liquid, the forbidden delight of a comfort reserved for those innocents too young to appreciate it made him linger.

Finally, roughly pulling her hands away from his nape, he raised his head, contented that her whimper of protest now centered around the loss of his warm lips. He was smiling as his fingers closed around her arm; she was past caring that there was no gentleness in the grip that jerked her around and pinned her back against his chest. He drew up her skirts, tucking the bunched material into his belt of rough hemp, his breath hot against her neck as one hand slid beneath her arm to squeeze her breasts, the other curling around the breadth of hips to probe the pouting lips hidden by the mound of tight, blond curls.

Merganthe was panting, whispering breathless, unthinking words of encouragement, her bared thighs parted and straining against the stroking of her lover's fingers. Just as the pleasure mounted to an unbearable peak, the hand withdrew and she groaned in frustration.

No longer caring to waste precious time in leisurely exploration, Esmond tucked his own tunic within his belt of golden links and freed his engorged shaft from the chafing linen undergarment. Grasping her breasts for leverage, he pulled her back and teased the cleft of her cheeks with the hard length, drawing an impatient gasp from her before she tried to turn and position herself.

Esmond had no desire to grapple in the dirt and choking dust of the floor. Close by a small table served as the family's dining place, the rough wood bench positioned before it their only seating. He drew Merganthe over to the bench and ordered her to straddle it, then pushed her head down and with the full, white cheeks an easy target, thrust forward and sank deep within the slick, welcoming cushion of flesh.

His penetration brought a muffled scream from the cotter's wife and a clamping of muscles that sucked on his member as he withdrew. Esmond bucked his hips, hunching forward like a stallion amount a heated mare, one hand gripping her shoulder, the other caressing belly and breasts. With his eyes shut tightly, an image of Alysaun's face floated before him and he uttered a hoarse, guttural cry as the rush of passion she had inspired spilled deep in his partner's womb.

Merganthe wept tears of pain and frustration as her lord collapsed, crushing her against the planked bench, heedless of anything save his own sweated satisfaction. "Please . . . the babe, he'll be hungry," she gasped, using the only excuse she could think of to free herself.

Esmond rolled away, unsteady on his feet for a moment. The woman started to rise, but he pushed her down again, pulling her tunic and gunna free and using the material to wipe away the vestiges of his spent seed. "He'll have to wait anyway, won't he?" Esmond smirked and reached down to run his fingers over her bare ass. "Give him my apologies for robbing him of a meal. Still, with those great udders, he'll be fed soon enough."

He arranged his clothing and strolled toward the doorway, glancing out to see the daughter sitting cross-legged beneath the shade of an oak, bouncing her little brother on her knee to keep him contented. His head turned back, eyes sweeping over Merganthe, smiling at the wanton picture she made, half risen on the bench, the bounty of her breasts and hips still uncovered. "I was pleased by you, woman. I've a mind to settle an honor on your husband and take you into service at the manor."

"*No.*" Merganthe sat up, drawing up her clothing to still the crawling of her skin. She didn't care if her defiance aroused Lord Esmond's anger; she would not agree to such an "honor"—her husband had been cuckolded enough by this day's work. "I said all I wanted was to be left be, m'lord. If I pleased you, then for God's sake, take your pleasure and leave."

"How old is the girl? Perhaps *she* would benefit more from exposure to the manners of her betters. Ripening quickly, your daughter is." He smiled again, more a leer as he looked out the door.

Gripped by terror for her daughter's innocence, Merganthe knew the defeat Esmond had meant her to feel. "I . . . if 'tis your will,

161

sire, I will come to serve at the keep," she said in a soft, despairing tone. No doubt my Edward will think it a great honor."

"You will in time, also, woman," Esmond boasted, and yawned as he stretched his arms in contented exhaustion. "Of course you will have to learn to wash more often. My lady mother frowns upon any member of her household who is not spotlessly clean."

Merganthe rose and straightened her clothing, cheeks burning at his humiliating tone of hauteur. " 'Tis no reward you offer, sire, but a punishment. If you were truly a great lord, you would give me something of worth."

"Ah, but I have," Esmond claimed, raising an arrogant brow. "If nine months hence you bear a child stamped with my features, you will have the pleasure of seeing it raised within the manor. I could use a loyal bastard or two."

Esmond dismissed her from his thoughts, bending his head to pass through the low portal and emerge into the sunlight. The girl glanced up at him, curious over the visit paid her mother, awed by the honor the liege lord had paid their family in passing by. She dared not risk staring at him and shifted uncomfortably for a few minutes as she felt the studied interest in his gaze. When he finally walked on, moving up the path, she stared after him, taking in the fine cut of his clothing, the natural grace with which he moved. Only when her mother appeared at the door, eyes strangely puffed as if she had been weeping, to snap a curt order to come in, did she tear her gaze away from the grand, important figure disappearing down the road.

Esmond's temperament was much improved as he strolled toward his manor. The jealous poisons aroused by Brand's possession of Alysaun had been dispelled, left behind in the depths of the cottage wife's womb. He realized he had taken his pleasure upon her and left without learning her name, but that was of no importance. He knew where she lived; his steward would fetch her to work at the manor, perhaps as a scullery maid if Ula found her material for proper training. Whatever the tasks assigned her, the cow's main duties would be to make herself available for his needs. Esmond smiled, the taste of milk still sweetening his mouth. Once again Havistock's lord would have a wet nurse.

There was nothing much to occupy the rest of the afternoon. In the yard, several of his retainers were exercising their mounts, wheeling the chargers around a padded stick figure, to practice feints against an imaginary enemy. He dawdled there for a while, drawing pleasure in laughter at Sir Edelbart's expense when the knight brought his bay gelding too close to the figure and the animal reared, nearly unseating the man.

Later, finding his belly settled and growling with hunger, he wandered around the thick figure, to practice feints against an imaginary enemy. He dawdled there for a while, drawing pleasure in laughter at Sir Edelbart's expense when the knight brought his bay gelding too close to the figure and the animal reared, nearly unseating the man.

Later, finding his belly settled and growling with hunger, he wandered around the long building, heading for the kitchens to insist Ula find him something worthy of his empty belly. Hearing someone say his name, he paused straining to hear more. Often, the servants were a source of gossiped secrets that never reached his or his mother's ears. The man who had said his name was Selwen, the butler. The other person was a woman, but Esmond couldn't hear her voice clearly enough to match it with a face.

"Aye, and if the master finds out, I faint at the thought of his mother's fury," Selwyn went on in warning his companion. "You well know she don't like to be crossed. Thomas only let on t'me once he was in his cups. Mistress swore him to an oath of silence, she did, and Morwena as well. 'Twas her, y'see, what fetched Lady Alysaun to the chapel that night."

"But I thought they was wed—evr'body thought so," the female replied. Esmond still couldn't recognize the voice, but it hardly mattered. The revelation that Alysaun had been free and likely still a virgin the day of de Reynaud's arrival stunned him. His suspicion of his mother's stealthy manipulations had a firm basis now. Knowing how much he had wanted the girl, Elfleda had moved against him and denied him with her selfish, ambitious plotting the chance to wed Alysaun. "So the girl was forced into it, eh?" the woman continued. "What about the Frenchman? He seems right pleased with the arrangement."

"Well, he weren't at first. Our Thomas, lax as his morals be, said he were sorrowed by so hasty an arrangement. Had somethin' on him, Elfleda did. Don't know what, but it were enough threat to make him agree. She may be my mistress, but mind you, the woman's a wily fox when it comes to gettin' her own way." There was a pause and then Selwen added, " 'Tis the young lady I pity. I say 'tisn't right to use her like a pawn, make her suffer more'n she had already."

"Oh, *pshh*," his companion chided. "She don't look like she's sufferin' any more'n I do. Ev'n if the lady had no say in it, she's resigned to the marriage now. Don't go wastin' pity on your betters, Selwen, they makes their own rules. 'Sides, she ain't been done by so badly. T'my mind, he's a fair and handsome catch." The woman laughed and added, "If she wants to give him up, I'll take her leavin's anyday."

Esmond did not wait to hear more. He turned and retraced his steps, his face transformed by fury, his mind so set on vengeance that he ignored Edelbart's call in passing and stalked within the house to seek his room. His first inclination was to confront his mother with her deception, to see her strong, willful features pale beneath his righteous accusations. For an hour or more he paced his room, going over the conversation between the servants, trying to sort out what he could do to spoil his mother's triumph. Of one thing he was sure—she'd not get away with her underhanded scheming. Somehow, some way, Alysaun would be his.

7

It had taken Esmond a while to sort out the intricacies of his plan. Nothing in his manner revealed his discovery of the forced marriage. If anything, moving in imitation of his mother's masked slyness, he kept his temperament amiable, pleasing Alysaun with the sudden acceptance he showed Brand. Now he engaged his guest in conversation at the table, now he kindly asked Brand to join him in hunting the forests with his falcons, all the while drawing him to speak of his life in Provence, evidencing interest in his experiences since arriving in England.

Morwena had proved to be a fount of information about the details of Alysaun's wedding. His first rash thought had been to summon her to his room and threaten her into revealing what she knew. As a party to his mother's conspiracy, she would be punished as well. Then, realizing that he needed time to develop his own plan, that he must come to know his enemy before he could dispatch him, Esmond reconsidered and decided to make the young girl into an ally.

Without drawing his mother's attention, Esmond began to pay court to Morwena. She was, at first, flattered and confused by his compliments. The girl was one of five daughters of a poor, landless knight. Her position as his mother's lady-in-waiting had been a boon to a family with so many daughters to marry off. She had little of her own and, at the most, could expect to marry a knight or thane, trading on her pretty face and gentle upbringing to secure her a husband.

Esmond had her when he first began to talk of marriage. They had taken walks together, danced at the merrymaking on the eve of his birthday fête, which fell on Saint Swithin's Day in mid-July, and had ridden out together to explore the terrain of his properties. He confided his irritation with his mother's plans to marry him to the ugly little Northumbrian heiress, his dissatisfaction with her reluctance to let loose the reins of authority at Havistock.

When she had assured herself that Esmond no longer brooded over losing Alysaun, Morwena found reason to believe the young lord could be interested in her. Elfleda would approve of her no more than she had of Lady Alysaun, but Esmond showed signs of a new maturity, an assertiveness he had lacked when he had made known his desire to wed the lady. The thought of becoming Havistock's mistress would be a dream come true. Once she was his wife, Elfleda could no longer order her about in so haughty a tone. Aside from the position and wealth he offered, Morwena found him handsome, his admiring glances a balm to the indignities of her present position.

She was surprised to find he knew the details of Alysaun's marriage to Brand, and the lack of concern he affected served to reassure her again that he no longer cared. Basking in the warmth of his attentions, she freely answered his questions about that night, revealing what she knew of the reason Brand had acceded to Elfleda's demands.

Once he knew what form the blackmail had taken, Esmond had the key to separating Brand from his wife. He knew from his own inquiries that the Frenchman had suffered a wound in coming to

Hereward's aid, that Brand had spent some time recuperating at the rebel's camp on Ely Isle. This, in itself, was little reason to see him named a rebel, but his possession of the Saxon leader's symbolic brooch was all the evidence the Norman sheriff would need to arrest and hang him for treason against the crown.

Though she balked at Esmond's request that she search Brand's possessions and bring him the brooch, Morwena was too chary of losing his affections to deny him. Feeling like a thief, she crept into the bedchamber one morning while Brand and Alysaun were attending mass and found the piece of jewelry hidden beneath layers of clothing folded away in a wardrobe.

She brought it to Esmond after the mass was over and puzzled over his desire for it. "I intend to see my mother blush when she denies she had a hand in arranging their marriage and I produce the threat she used against the poor fellow," he lied, smiling at the round copper brooch she had placed in his hand. Then he drew her into his arms and let his kiss banish any doubts she still had. As he drew back, he tossed the damning piece of evidence high and caught it again.

"The good Lady Elfleda will trouble neither of us any longer, my sweet," he pledged. "My mother will have no choice but to accept my firm decision to see her retire to her dower estate of Aswold, near Cambridge. I intend to escort her there myself within the week." Esmond kissed Morwena again, and she mistook the triumphant excitement that welled in him for the trembling of an eager lover. "Then you and I," he added in a whisper, pressing a kiss upon her throat, breath warm with ardent promise, "will be free to pursue our own plans."

Esmond made good his promise. While Morwena attended a midsummer's fair at the market town of Herriston, some ten miles southeast of Havistock, enjoying an unexpected outing in Brand and Alysaun's company, Esmond sought out his mother in her solar and in a quiet, firm voice revealed what he knew of her ruse. As he had predicted, she denied any knowledge of such goings-on and righteously insisted that he reveal who had told him such an outrageous tale.

Esmond produced the brooch, grinning at her effort to cover her recognition with an innocent protest. When she saw that he did indeed know the truth, her mask of pretense dropped. Elfleda thought to sway him from anger by claiming her concern over his welfare. She pleaded and wept dramatically, ranting at the cur who had betrayed her, pacing and wringing her hands in an effort to make him see that she had acted only in his best interests.

"I'm sure you thought so, Mother dearest, but I now take responsibility for my life. Your days as chatelaine at Havistock should have ended with my father's death. Now, because of your own ambitious pride, you will cease your hysterics and dutifully accompany me to your retirement at Aswold." Esmond smiled, enjoying the shock that drained his mother's face of color. "I act only in concern for your continued good health, madam," he added slyly. "I could not be responsible for my temper if you stayed to try it further with your tricks."

Elfleda, wanting revenge of her own against the person who had caused this rift between mother and son, stalled for time. "I cannot possibly be packed for such a trip in less than a day or two," she claimed, then blanched even more when her son informed her that while they spoke, the servants were loading the traveling carts with her belongings. No longer had she the power to resist this suddenly cold and ruthless man who wanted her gone from the home that had been hers for over twenty years. Elfleda seemed to wither before his eyes, and for the first time Esmond saw how illusionary her strength had been. Using guilt and the strong bonds of filial devotion, she had ruled and guided his life too long. Now it was his turn to rule.

A half hour later the procession of carts led by Esmond and his mother on their mounts began the day's journey to Aswold. Esmond left word with his steward to tell Brand and Alysaun his mother was sorry to depart without a farewell but for reasons of health had decided to seek the peace and solitude of her own small estate. "I should be back late tomorrow," he added, "or Tuesday morn at the worst," then he joined his mother, who did appear in need of a respite from her burdens, her puffed eyelids shadowing a dull, glazed resignation.

Esmond returned home on Tuesday, having made a brief stop at Cambridge. Alysaun expressed her surprise, on greeting him, that his mother had so suddenly decided on the journey. "She has put on a brave face to cover her melancholy since my father's demise, Alysaun," Esmond explained with a worried sigh. "When I realized that living here with so many happy memories haunted her nights with sleeplessness, I took the only action a loving son could. Believe me, my mother will rest easier without me to worry over. My only regret is that I did not act sooner."

At least that much was truly spoken, thought Esmond, smiling as he took Alysaun's arm in his to escort her within the keep. Had he realized before that his mother could act with such cunning, Alysaun would even now be his wife. In the hall Brand came up to them and asked after Elfleda's health, his query understandably lacking true concern. Reminding himself that a little while longer of patience would see the matter of possession turned to his favor, Esmond gave Alysaun's hand to Brand's keeping and answered with the same information he had given her.

That night he was in an exceptionally good mood. Although Morwena's usefulness was finished, Esmond continued the farce of plying her with compliments, ensuring her loyalty if he needed to call upon it. Alysaun seemed puzzled by the attentions he devoted to the girl, who by rights should have accompanied her mistress to the seclusion of Aswold. She worried that Morwena would be led to believe there was a chance for her to marry Esmond.

Alysaun could not announce her worries or risk offending the girl she still considered a friend; and in her frequent, troubled glances at the girl's flirtatious clinging to his arm, Esmond read jealousy. It encouraged the exultation of his mood and he made a request that Brand bring out his lute and entertain them with something romantic; Esmond planned to increase his attentiveness to test Alysaun's reactions.

Any doubts Morwena had entertained about the promises Esmond made her were banished by the warm desire in his gaze. He had cautioned her to keep his offer of marriage to herself; but with this open show of affection, it was as if he were shouting his yearning to make her his bride. She took no notice of Alysaun's disquieted looks; Morwena felt the evening slip by too quickly in a haze of contentment, planning how graciously she would command the domestic duties of the lord's wife, thinking how she would secure a charm to assure her their first child would be a son, an heir.

The evening ended early when Esmond claimed weariness from his trip. He escorted Morwena to the room she shared with another maid attendant, sloughing off her suggestion that she should take a room of her own, as befitted her rise in status, insisting that there would be many changes in the weeks to come and that he was too tired to discuss them.

Emboldened by her near-betrothal, Morwena wanted to make him aware of her loyalty. She kissed him, not the prim, virtuous pecks she had allowed earlier, but a lover's kiss with lips parted to show her willingness to please him. The answer of his tongue thrusting deep into her mouth, of his hands sweeping over her figure, both frightened and stirred her. She was breathless when he released her, willing to seal their love even before he spoke the vows that would bind them in wedlock. Surprising herself, she admitted the thought aloud, sure that he would accept the suggestion that she share his bed.

"Nay, I will not spoil you before our wedding night," Esmond answered, declining the startling offer and wondering over his sudden surfeit of bed partners. In the past week, the cotter's plump wife—he now knew her name to be Merganthe—had come to serve in the manor, leaving her babe to be wet-nursed by a married cousin. For the past two hours she had awaited his leisure, summoned to his room from her duties in the kitchens. He could hardly take advantage of Morwena's willingness, though the thought of entertaining two women, so different in temper and appearance, tantalized him. He raised Morwena's hands to his lips and pressed a respectful kiss upon her upturned palms. "That night my pleasure will be heightened by the knowledge I checked my passion to have you," he lied, and, despite the bounty awaiting him, showed his regret at leaving her side in the lingering look he cast back as he walked away.

In his room, Esmond found Merganthe prepared, her new tunic neatly folded on a table. By his orders she bathed as often as his other serving people and the difference a good washing had made in her appearance was startling. She lay on one side of the large, canopied bed, the sheets drawn over her bare flesh only serving to enhance the hillocks of her large breasts. Her hair, freshly washed and unplaited, lay across her plump shoulders like silk the color of thick cream.

Esmond stripped off his clothing, excited just by the sight of her. He still felt nothing for her, but Merganthe had become an obsession with him; she satisfied a craving he recognized and found vulgar. Even after Alysaun became his wife, he would not put the woman away, only seek her out more discreetly. Slipping into the bed, he pulled the sheet away and stared at her breasts. They were all he wanted of her; the plowing of her fat, cushioned womb was almost an afterthought.

Because of his strange desires, Merganthe was now dependent on Esmond. Without her babe to draw off the milk, her breasts were bulging with an excess, painful and tender from the swelling. She could not press enough out with her fingertips, the only relief lay in having him suckle. She sat up now, wincing at the tenderness as the heavy mounds swayed with the opening of her arms. Esmond came to her, sliding into the welcoming embrace, his lips opening to draw in a long, swollen finger of a nipple, his upper body cradled against Merganthe's chest. Heedless of anything but the relief she knew at the steady flow of milk, she closed her eyes and gently rocked, crooning a low, soft melody as if she held her own child.

A week later, staying up late to drink in shared companionship before their morning hunt, Esmond offered Brand the woman's strange services. Alysaun had retired several hours earlier, somewhat put out by the endless talk of hunts and methods of butchering prey, by the lack of attention she received from Brand.

171

Brand stretched out in his chair, lounging back with his feet propped up against the stone wall surrounding the fire pit, his curiosity, if not desire, aroused by Esmond's description of Merganthe's breasts. They were both past the point when they should have ceased drinking. Brand showed only a slight inebriation in the relaxed posture he assumed; Esmond's voice was slurred by a tongue thick and awkward, a tongue that felt as if it did not belong in his mouth.

"Truly, I swear it, the woman could nurse an army of brats and still have enough for me and ten others," Esmond boasted, leaning forward in his chair to try to show the size of Merganthe's breasts with his hands. His hands wavered, and he gave up the effort. " 'Tis something you have to see to believe," he said, and belched, ignoring Brand's laughter and searching the floor beside his chair for the wine decanter. "Alysaun needn't find out." The wine slopped over his cup, staining his tunic. " 'Twill give you some measure to compare her with."

Brand frowned, disliking the path Esmond's conversation was taking. "Alysaun is bountiful enough, thank you, and I do not care to have her discussed as if she were an ill-bred sow."

Esmond held up a hand to pacify Brand and spilled more of his wine, drinking from the cup before he wasted what was left. "My apologies, sir. I . . . have the greatest respect for Alysaun's worth. I just thought you might . . . care to avail yourself of a different kind of . . . of pleasure." He started to hiccup, then gulped what was left of his wine to silence the annoying tremors in his throat.

"I appreciate your hospitality, Esmond, but I was weaned years ago. 'Tis not a mother's image that arouses my passion. I fancy a slim ankle and a comely face before a thick-waisted cow. If she lasts that long, your mistress'll have her nipples banging at her waist after a year of having a full-grown man pull at 'em." Brand smiled and shook his head, drawing his own cup of wine to his lips to take a sip. He hadn't figured young Esmond to be so odd in his taste for women. He'd had his share of big-breasted females himself, but he found them a touch too common. A nice balance of curves like his wife's was far more enchanting and lasted past the age that dragged

172

at a too-bountiful bosom, flattening them into the image of unleavened loaves of bread.

"The offer stands if you grow curious. Now she's cleaned up, the bitch isn't half bad-looking. All soft she is, full-fleshed." Esmond grinned and chuckled, confessing, "Of course she's had three big brats. A man has to have a care he don't get swallowed up."

Brand finished his cup and dragged his legs to the floor. The hour was late; Alysaun would be in a snit if he stayed longer. "Your company was pleasant, sir," he said, nodding to Esmond, "and the conversation was"—Brand had trouble finding a word that accurately fit the tone of their talk—"most certainly interesting. If I do not hie myself to my bedchamber now, I'll not be able to stay amount for the morrow's hunt."

Esmond smiled and reached down for the decanter, cursing as he knocked it over. "Then, by all means, Brand, take yourself to bed. If Alysaun awaited me, you can be sure I'd not have tarried *this* long." He retrieved the decanter and shouted for his butler. "Since she doesn't, I will console my loneliness with more drink and then settle my mouth on sweet Merganthe's teat." He flashed a grin at Brand's unsteady stride and yelled again for Selwen.

Though he was not drunk, Brand was close enough to that state to move in the drunk's slow, methodical manner, every gesture and act seemingly executed with precision when, in reality, they were exaggerated. He found his own room only by counting off the doors as he came down the aisle, then opened it with the quiet stealth of a thief and cautiously crept across to the bed, drawing aside the curtains to make sure he hadn't miscounted.

In the dim, flickering glow of the rush lamp, he could just make out the familiar outline of Alysaun's features. Pleased with his progress thus far, he sat down on his side of the bed and started to pull off his boots. One went sailing across the room to land with a loud thud against the wall as he started at the sound of his wife's voice, fully awake and tense with irritation.

"If you must come in at such an ungodly hour, have the courtesy to close the door after yourself, m'lord."

Brand looked back. Sure enough it was still wide open. He frowned, sensing condemnation in the silence of the room, then swore a casual oath on the heels of a weary sigh and crossed back over what seemed like a longer distance then his trip to the bed, shoved it closed, and set the latch. The third crossing seemed to take forever and was further complicated when the bed moved away from him, forcing him to stop its flight by grabbing the end post.

"You're *besotted!* Holy Mother of God, Brand—how much did you drink?"

Still clinging to the post with his left hand, he scowled at the accusation and bravely loosened his grip to execute a swinging right turn that brought him sprawling across the bed to land with his face in Alysaun's lap. Brand would have been content to lie there—indeed, he smiled and nuzzled his cheek against the firmness of her thigh—but Alysaun had other thoughts.

She shoved at his shoulder with all her might, just barely managing to roll his weight away from her. Still, he was lying at an awkward angle and seemed inclined not to move. A silly grin crossed his face as the fingers of his left hand walked across the bed linen to climb the curve of her thigh. "Don't touch me—*get away*," Alysaun ordered, and swatted at him as he tried to insinuate a hand between her legs.

Offended by the rejection, Brand rose up on one elbow and glowered. "Since when, m'lady," he inquired, "do you take exception to your husband's touch? Expecting warmth and welcome, I return to my bed only to find a coldhearted harpy who screeches protests at what is mine by right to explore."

The injured indignation of his tone was the last blow. Alysaun slipped as far from him as she could without falling off the bed and glared at Brand. "If you cared so greatly to exercise your rights, sire, you would have swilled less and come seeking me at a more decent hour. Apparently Esmond's companionship was more interesting than mine. Go sleep in *his* bed—if he's had as much as you, the wine fumes will not bother him."

"Can't," Brand insisted, and grinned. "Esmond has company

already, a kitchen wench with great, soft breasts to pillow his head. Offered her to me, he did." Alysaun's eyes widened in shock at the admission, then narrowed with fury as her mouth pursed. "Well . . . I *did* decline the offer," Brand said defensively. "Told him yours were comfortable enough. No man needs more'n a mouthful."

Brand truly thought he was giving his wife a compliment, but the idea of his discussing her attributes with Esmond infuriated and humiliated Alysaun. "So . . . above the fact that you lurch into my bed at so late an hour, you openly boast about the dimensions of my figure, bandying my name about as if I were a whore." Alysaun's eyes shimmered with a glaze of tears. "Oh, Brand—how *could* you?"

" 'Twas couched in the most respectful of terms, dear, and I refuse to feel remorse. You *are* my wife. I can say what I please." Brand frowned, feeling her resentment wash over him. "Damn, I *should* have taken Esmond's offer. Whoever she is, the woman must be warmer than you. I've never seen you so oversensitive, Alys. You are showing signs of becoming a shrew."

Despite her attempt to hold them back, the tears gathering in Alysaun's eyes spilled over. She wiped at them with the back of her hand, not sure if they evidenced her anger or the hurt she felt at his callous treatment. Her head tilted up, chin stubbornly set. "The honeymoon had to end sometime, sire. More than just lovers, we are husband and wife. I . . . I thought you had more care for my feelings. If you find me so disagreeable, then go and take Esmond up on his kind offer. I'm sure 'tis not too late to change your mind."

"Aye, nor too late to see an *annulment* set in motion." Brand regretted the words directly they came spitting forth, but he was in no mood to apologize and recall them. "You'll have the solitude to consider your temper, m'lady." He rolled and sat up, sobered a bit by the harsh accusations they had both flung, trying to remember where his boot had landed.

Across the room, he retrieved his boot and stalked to the door. "Where are you going?" Alysaun asked, her voice at once petulant and apprehensive.

He wasn't sure himself. "To lay my tired body someplace warmer than your bed, madame," Brand snapped, and pulled open the door with a jerk, slamming it as he left.

Alysaun stared at the door, her mouth open in dawning dismay. Her tears flowed heavily as she imagined Brand wrapped in the arms of the plump, buxom woman Esmond had offered him. Then, turning onto her belly, she sobbed against her pillow, beating it with her fists. Damn Brand, damn Esmond, and all men—they were nothing but animals, each and every one. *He had no right to make her out a cold and shrewish wife ... hadn't she proved how much she loved him?* And after trusting him with her affections, he dared to bring up the near-forgotten threat of an annulment.

Brand had stood in the aisle a few minutes, brooding over the trouble his loose tongue had wrought. He almost turned back to make up with Alysaun, but the sound of her muffled weeping beyond the door halted the action. Tired as he was, he didn't care to spend an hour apologizing only to have her use his own guilt against him. The thought of passing the night smothered by the ample form of Esmond's woman was equally unappealing. Taking a moment to draw on his boot, he moved off through the darkened aisle and made for the hall. The chair he had vacated earlier was uncomfortable to sleep in, but at least it was close to the fire pit and warm.

In the morning, Brand was stiff and more irritable than he had been the previous night. His head ached, his vision was blurred, his tongue felt coated with a cottony fuzz, and the smell of food cooking in the kitchen pots drew a strong protest from his unsettled gut. He made for his room, hoping that a good scrubbing with soap and water would wash the ache from his skin. Alysaun was fixing her wimple beneath her chin when he entered; and though she gave him a quick glance, she returned to her task with a cold, disdainful reserve that assured him she had neither forgotten nor forgiven the night's argument.

With his body so beset by the effects of his overindulgence, Brand was even less willing to plead for understanding. He crossed the room, ignoring her, and searched the wardrobe for fresh clothing, leaving the neatly folded pile of tunics and breeches in a careless jumble in his quest for what he wanted.

Brand's back was to her; Alysaun frowned at the way he burrowed through the clothing and was about to rebuke his lack of concern for the care with which they'd been arranged. Her lips tightened and she bit back the criticism, unwilling to engage in another argument when she was already late for mass.

Finished with her toilet, she swept toward the door and paused, reconsidering her sullen attitude. One of them had to make an attempt at breeching the distance; and though she was as stubborn as he, Alysaun knew a twinge of sympathy for the pallor and queasy look on her husband's face. He was no doubt suffering the effects of his drinking bout. "I was about to leave for the chapel," she said hesitantly. "If you wish—"

"Go on, then," Brand replied without turning. "I've no patience to suffer an hour's chanting. If you have any care left for me, though, say a prayer for my throbbing temples."

Alysaun stiffened at his curt tone of voice, incensed that Brand lacked the courtesy to turn and address her to her face. "I'll do that, m'lord," she promised, "and pray as well that the Lord might give you a lesson in humility, for you are sadly lacking that quality. If I do not see you before the hunt, you have my wishes for an enjoyable day's outing."

Brand slowly turned, his brows drawn together over the scowling set of his features. His wife turned to go and then glanced over her shoulder with a shuttered look of reproach. "Oh, m'lord . . . I do beg your pardon. I was remiss in not inquiring how pleased you were with the kitchen maid's services. If you are missing again tonight, I shall know the answer, shan't I?"

Before he could open his mouth, Alysaun swept out, and Brand's string of oaths resounded behind the closed door. He stalked across to the bed, kicking at a stool in his way, and threw his change of attire on the mattress. He should not have let her get away with such an impudent speech. Brand found himself wishing he had taken advantage of the woman offered him; he was condemned now for

177

breaking his vows of fidelity but with no memories of such an indulgence to console his solitude.

There were men who kept their wives in line by beating them into submission. He had always considered violence an unnecessary weapon; but, then, he had never taken into account how exasperating a wife might be. Now, as Brand pulled his tunic over his head and discarded it, to move across the room and wash in the cold water of the basin, he found himself reconsidering his views. Perhaps what Alysaun needed was a few well-placed smacks across her derriere, a reminder to control her sharp reprimands and show a little respect for her lord.

In the sanctuary, Alysaun drew a puzzled look from Esmond when she appeared so late and without Brand. She slipped quietly beside him and when he bent his head to remark upon her dark, frowning demeanor, she glanced up at him with so furious a look of resentment that he took a step back, unable to think what had happened to alter her usual sweet mien.

Alysaun said nothing, afraid that her anger would erupt and she would not be able to stem it once an accusation passed her lips. How dare Esmond play the innocent, when he knew full well how his vulgar, crude sharing of that woman's services had come between her and Brand. His feigned surprise at her righteous anger was an added insult. The service continued, Father Thomas's voice droning on in the Latin liturgy, and when it was finally over, Alysaun tried to slip away; but with unusual determination and assertiveness, Esmond caught her arm and insisted in a hushed whisper that she explain what had prompted the look she had given him.

Alysaun flushed with embarrassment as the others attending the morning service passed them and gave curious glances at Esmond's hold on her, at her own posture stiff with tension. Finally the sanctuary was emptied of worshipers. Her cheeks colored by a blush, Alysaun glanced down at his hand, then up at him, and Esmond released her.

"Alysaun, what have I done to deserve your anger?" Esmond

asked, putting the question to her with such a bewildered gaze that she flared anew, indignant at his pretense of ignorance.

"Exactly how am I to accept the lure you cast before my husband, Esmond? I've not been married long but I did think I would hold Brand's fidelity longer than I seem to have. Until you threw this serving woman upon him, he was content not to stray. I . . . I thought you were fond of me, that you cared enough not to thrust such a humiliation upon me, Esmond."

Esmond restrained a smile. Apparently Brand had picked an argument with her and slept elsewhere, though he could vouch for the fact that Brand was innocent of his wife's belief he had taken advantage of Merganthe's lush warmth. Esmond himself had fallen asleep sprawled atop her plump body. He could not say for a fact that Brand hadn't found some other wench to fondle but, more likely, the man had curled up in some corner of the hall and spent a most uncomfortable night.

This development worked so well into his plans, Esmond hung his head and made a show of remorse. "I was beyond clear thinking when I offered the woman," he admitted. "Truly, I would never have suggested it sober-minded. 'Twas a jest, in truth, the kind of boasting generosity men indulge in when a cup is shared in companionship."

" 'Twas more than a cup, sir, and Brand accepted your jest seriously, in fact with an eagerness that makes me doubt how lightly you made mention of it." As she spoke of the betrayal Alysaun's eyes filled with tears. "How can he be so careless of my feelings? I thought he . . . Esmond, did you not believe his love for me was sincere? I did, but now . . . if he can flaunt this in my face so easily, what will follow? I could not bear . . ."

Tears slipped down Alysaun's cheeks and Esmond drew her against the comfort of his shoulder, patting her back, a bit awkward at finding himself suddenly cast in the role of friend and protector. "Hush, sweet . . . don't cry. Men think less of such matters as faith. Their lusts are too great to confine to marriage. 'Tis more common

179

than you know, and should have no effect upon your continued bliss unless . . ."

She was beginning to feel a little easier, her tears ceasing, when Esmond's unfinished statement brought her head up sharply. "Unless what?"

"Well, my father loved my mother and yet I know he often found pleasure in a change of partners. I don't mean to suggest doubt that Brand loves you; but from all I've heard of his travels, his appetite for women has always been tempted by a variety of choice. For such a free soul, it may be difficult to settle for one morsel, no matter how delightful."

What Esmond was hinting at was the chance that this was only the first infidelity, that she must allow Brand the freedom to roam or lose him. Alysaun stared up at Esmond and saw pity in his eyes. A lump of misery blocked her throat; she wanted to be alone with this painful new idea that she must endure Brand's escapades and, somehow, ignore them.

"Go to the solar, Alysaun. The room is yours to make use of, now my mother is gone." Esmond found it difficult to act so somber when he felt like leaping for joy. "Since I am partly to blame for tossing temptation in Brand's path, I'll do what I can to make him see how it's hurt you. Trust me, Alysaun . . . you know I have your best interests at heart."

Alysaun wiped at her tears and gave him a tremulous smile. "I know, Esmond. Tell him . . . do tell Brand that I said the argument was partly my fault. I don't know what's come over me of late. It seems that I spark at any small slight."

"Nonsense, you're an angel," Esmond insisted, lifting her chin with his fingertips. "I only wish . . . well, if you were mine to care for, I'd never give you a moment's worry over how deeply I was devoted."

Neither of them noticed Brand standing in the shadows by the open chapel doors. He had come looking for Alysaun, thinking he should apologize before the rift that lay between them widened. Now he saw only that his wife was standing close to Esmond, too close for his liking, that their conversation was low and intimate, and that her expression was trusting as Alysaun gazed up into Esmond's eyes.

His first inclination was to approach the two and indignantly inquire what they were about, his pride insisting he come between what had the appearance of a lovers' tryst. No, he thought, no matter how guilty Alysaun thought him of straying with a common serving girl, she would not seek to revenge her hurt by seeking out Esmond. Brand turned and walked back toward the hall. He'd find out soon enough from Esmond exactly what that scene had meant.

8

In the wide, cleared yard that stretched before the manor, all was in readiness for the morning's hunt as the participants waited only on the arrival of Esmond. The day's quarry was deer, specifically the harts who had grown fat over the long summer's grazing. The assembly of grooms and attendants was far greater than the number in the hunting party.

The huntsman and his aides had all they could do to hold the leashes of the dogs. In the absence of the usual huntsman, a role lost to Esmond while he recovered from a wound received in an earlier hunt, Edelbart was serving in his place. He held three limers at leash, the bloodhounds eager to be at their work of finishing the bayed stag, snarling at the smaller brachet hounds and staying well back from the large, sleek greyhounds who could fell a deer with one lunge of sharp-toothed, snapping jaws.

None of the hunters was in the jubilant, eager good humor that usually accompanied the excitement of a chase. Edelbart, forced by his duties to walk the dogs into the wood instead of riding with the other members of his rank, snapped churlishly at his aides. Brand was off by himself, his expression warning everyone away from his dark, brooding mood. Only a distant cousin of Lady Elfleda's, Sir Keir McClenna, visiting Havistock from his home across the Irish Sea, seemed amiable, and even he was put off by having to wait upon his cousin Esmond.

Finally Esmond emerged from the house, calling an apology to his companions for his delay. His groom held the big bay gelding steady for his master to mount, and Esmond gathered in the reins, wheeling the steed around to blow one short blast on the carved-ivory oliphant, which signaled the start of the hunt. Taking the lead, Esmond called Brand to ride by his side and set a hard pace for the clearing a quarter mile to the north, where they would rest until Edelbart used the limers to search out the spoor of a stag.

Esmond made little attempt to speak with Brand until they had reached the clearing and dismounted. His cousin, who had come along reluctantly, tethered his mount to a nearby oak and sat beneath the tree to doze until the dogs had found a good track. Brand's expression was tense; a pulse ticked in his firm, tightly clenched jaw. Aside from the effects of the previous night's indulgence in drink, his gut churned with the fiery acid of anger and resentment. If not for his desire to hear Esmond's explanation of his meeting with Alysaun, Brand would have begged off attendance on the hunt.

"I've a matter to discuss with you, friend," Esmond said in a cheerful tone that showed little distress from his own heavy imbibing. Brand glanced up, giving up the attempt to tighten his saddle girth with a grimace of disgust for the fumbling of his fingers.

"As do I," he replied, and turned his frown on Esmond, "and what I have to ask cannot wait. You know my wife and I had a falling out late last evening?"

"Aye, but—"

"How did I know she told you?" Brand was too impatient to have Esmond's explanation to be polite. "I happened to pass by the chapel door, searching for Alysaun. Would you care to tell me why I saw her in your arms, sir? 'Tis one matter to offer sympathy, yet another to console a man's wife in an embrace.''

For a moment Esmond was speechless, then it dawned on him that Brand's jealous, mistaken impression of the scene could work to his advantage. " 'Twas not what you thought, Brand,'' he protested, a purposeful, nervous shifting of his gaze making his protest seem false. "Alysaun was upset. I could not ignore the tears that sprang to her eyes. She truly believes you lay with my Merganthe after leaving your chamber.''

Brand's frown deepened to a menacing scowl. "And I suppose you 'neglected' to tell her that such was not the truth, that you, yourself, occupied the woman's attentions?''

With a pretense of wounded dismay, Esmond denied the insinuation. "I swear by all that's holy, Brand—I did my best to convince your wife of your innocence. Alysaun chose to believe I was covering for you. Even after I apologized for throwing the temptation your way, she seemed to think we were in league to abet your infidelity.''

"And yet she turned to the comfort of your shoulder to weep out her frustration, eh?'' Brand still believed there was more to the meeting than the simple portrayal of solace Esmond made it out to be. "If Alysaun wishes to confide any problems we have in the future, you may direct her to confess them to the priest or seek out Morwena,'' he asserted. "Whatever your motives, Esmond, save your sympathies for someone else's wife. Alysaun and I will work out our disagree—''

Brand's statement was cut off by the sound of several short, successive horn blasts to the north and the distant baying of the hounds. The brachets and greyhounds, held back in the clearing, began yelping and bounding, eager at their brother hounds' call of scented prey.

Edelbart emerged from the thicket surrounding the clearing, approaching Esmond to display the "fumes,'' the droppings he had collected in a horn, their size evidence of a large, heavy-bodied hart. Brand had moved off, his tender stomach protesting at the sight and smell of the fumes. "There are two good sets of tracks, one leading north toward the Bury road," Edelbart said, "the other southeast, back toward the manor. The fumes are from the southeast track, a big buck, from the height of his antler rubbings. The limers gave little mind to the other tracks. I think it may be a spring buck, a forkhorn too young to leave much musk."

"Direct your huntsmen to take the rest of the hounds along the north track," Esmond replied, and both the command and the feverish excitement of his eyes puzzled Edelbart, who was bold enough to question the decision to take after the less challenging of the two deer. "I don't care to have my orders questioned by you or any member of my keep," Esmond snapped. "If you don't wish to risk my anger, Edelbart. then see to them at once."

The knight bowed respectfully enough, but as he turned away from his lord his irritation showed in his scowl and the long, stalking gait that carried him across the clearing to the spot where his attendants held the chase hounds. Edelbart had more than this minor incident to fuel his disgruntled feelings for Esmond, though. Morwena had shown him interest until Havistock's lord had begun to pay her court. Now she scarcely knew Edelbart was alive, so little did she acknowledge him.

Esmond called Brand back to him and, at his approach, clapped him heartily on the shoulder in a show of warm friendship. "Forget your quarreling for the moment, Brand. On our return, you and I will seek out your Alysaun and explain exactly how innocent your night's activities were. Now we have a hart to stalk, a great stag by the looks of the spoor he left leading north. Once we have him at bay, you may have the honor of the killing lance thrust." Brand raised a brow, questioning Esmond's sudden, benevolent generosity, but the younger man tugged on his arm with an eagerness that was catching. "Don't think I'm so selfless," he added with a grin. "My pleasure will come from watching the hart panic as the hounds close in, from that moment he realizes he is trapped."

Brand had always hunted to provide food. Though the stag would provide meat for the tables of Havistock, Esmond's bloodthirsty eagerness to see the proud animal brought down was not to Brand's liking. Brand thought, as he followed Esmond's hard-set pace, that when that moment came, he would decline the offer of such an honor.

Awakened by the hounds' barking, Sir Keir scrambled up from his bed of leaves beneath the oak and hurried after the others. Shorter than the other two men, his legs had to pump twice as hard to catch and match their long-legged strides. Ahead of them the dogs followed the tracks but seemed to lose interest, yelping mournfully as if in disappointment. At the crashing rustle of last winter's fallen-leaf cover, a variety of small forest creatures scattered, hares darting for the safety of the thick, bramble underbrush, squirrels chattering angrily at the trespass as they scurried up to the highest branches of the trees. A swallow dived across the rough path several times, screeching a diminutive cry of warning as the hunters passed her nest.

Edelbart had reached the slope leading to the crest of the road and now waited, angry about the wasted time spent tracking a young buck barely weaned. The limers pulled at their leashes, bounding in their eagerness to be free of restraint and heading south, where their keen sense of smell told them the real quarry lay.

Esmond was the first to reach the spot. He ignored his knight's request to loose the hounds and let them lead the party through the forest, in a circular path back toward the manor. Instead, the young lord of Havistock searched the road, climbing halfway up the incline, looking left and right until he finally turned, a pleased look in his light eyes. "Take the hounds across the road, Bart," he ordered. "*Now.* My senses tell me we've a wily foe, and he taunts us from the weald beyond."

Edelbart frowned at the nonsense but obeyed, using all of his strength to drag the reluctant dogs up the hill and onto the level ground of the roadbed. It was only there, when the hounds' reluctance turned to eager barking, that the knight saw what his lord had searched so keenly for and found delight in. A troop of well-armed Normans waited some twenty yards down the road in the direction of

Cambridge. The sheriff, recognizable even at that distance by the banner that floated from his couched lance, led the soldiers. By the restlessness of their chargers, the men had been waiting some time. Unable to reason at first why his master would have dealings with the sheriff, Edelbart turned back to question Esmond.

Too late it occurred to him to recall Lord Esmond's passion for Lady Alysaun, his strong desire to wed her before de Reynaud's appearance made that impossible. Too late did he remember thinking that Esmond was not one to give up what he wanted without a fight. Everyone at the manor knew of the Frenchman's involvement with the rebel, Hereward of Lincoln; it had even brought him a grudging acceptance from Edelbart.

In those few minutes when the pieces fell together and the Saxon knight realized his liege lord's plans, his mind recoiled from the ruthless betrayal. A cry of warning echoed in his head but as Edelbart opened his mouth to shout it, concern for his own welfare silenced his voice. The hunters were climbing toward the road, Esmond leading with a vigorous stride that betrayed his anticipation of the trap about to spring.

When they reached the crest of the road, Edelbart loosed the hounds. They sped away toward the mounted troop, drawing the hunters' attentions to the Norman presence with loud, growling yelps. Like a man entranced by the visions in his dreams, the knight hung back and watched the evidence of Esmond's treachery unfold with infinite slowness. At a signal from the sheriff, the men of his command urged their chargers down the road, spurring them to a gallop until coming abreast of the hunting party. Then they moved to encircle it, closing off any attempt to escape.

Brand said nothing and though he shared the tension that rose in his companions, he had no reason to believe that he was under threat. The sheriff drew off his helmet and brought his steed a few steps forward to study their faces.

"Which of you is called de Reynaud, Brand de Reynaud?" Sheriff Fitz Walther inquired in a demanding tone. He recognized the man he sought by the description given him by Sir Esmond, but his question was designed to cover the Saxon's duplicity.

Now Brand was more than tense. Though his apprehension at hearing his name was masked by a calm expression, he was wary and poised to flee, his eyes searching the ranks of guarding soldiers for an escape route. "I am de Reynaud," he answered, "but your purpose in seeking me out leaves me puzzled. Hunting on the property of a friend can be no crime, sir, not even in King William's mind."

"Aye, but aiding the Saxon dog Hereward *is*, and for that crime against his majesty will I take you into custody. Do not waste my time denying your treason, de Reynaud. Come quietly or you'll make the journey back to Cambridge bound across one of my soldiers' saddles."

"What proof have you of de Reynaud's guilt?" Esmond demanded to know, the flush of triumph on his face taken as the coloring of a man indignant over the arrest of a friend. "De Reynaud is a guest at my keep of Havistock. You've no right to seize him without some evidence, especially on my land."

"We are on common ground belonging to England's crown, sir, and administered by myself as William's sworn vassal. I need not show you proof. My seal set upon a warrant is all justice requires to see this rebel questioned." Fitz Walther smiled, amused by how well the Saxon played out his righteous defense of the man he had betrayed like a Judas. "However, I am a tolerant man, aware that you might doubt the judgment that a guest allotted your hospitality had engaged in acts of rebellion. Here, m'lord, I'm sure you'll recognize this."

The sheriff tossed down a round metallic object that caught the sunlight and flashed with a coppery glint. Esmond caught it easily, turning it over in his hand to study the incised design. Brand stared at the brooch, feeling the cold fingers of the treachery its presence revealed close tightly around his heart. No show of bravado, no claims of kinship to William, would see him free of this cautiously set snare. Again he had reason to regret the late hours spent in drinking. As the sun beat down on his aching head and the knot of unreasoning fear increased the queasiness of his belly, the senses that should have been sharp and ready to serve him in an escape seemed now to become dull and unresponsive.

"What manner of proof is this?" Esmond scoffed. "With all due respect for the office you hold, m'lord sheriff, this brooch is scarcely an indictment of my friend."

"And I submit, sir, with the same respect for your defense, that the possession of that piece proves a bond between its original owner and the man to whom it was given. Enough of this talk, now. De Reynaud's face clearly shows his recognition of the brooch given him by Hereward." Fitz Walther signaled to his chief bailiff, the same man who had months earlier directed Brand to seek his "wife" at Havistock.

Coming out of the shock that had dulled his instincts, Brand moved to draw his sword. Even though his mount was tethered in the clearing an eighth of a mile behind him, even though there was no chance to outdistance the mounted soldiers, his pride drove him to make a bid for freedom. Esmond shouted a warning not to resist and the sudden flare of tension among the soldiers sent their chargers nervously sidestepping, breaking the tight wall of horseflesh surrounding Brand.

The air reverberated with the sharp commands issued by the sheriff, with the answering calls of his sergeants and aides. Brand saw his chance to slip past a skittish, dancing charger and further widened the route by using the flat surface of his drawn sword to strike the gelding's haunches. The gap widened and freedom beckoned in the chance to sprint into the woods and make his way through the thick weald, where none of the huge, heavy Norman chargers could follow.

It was a desperate bid and Brand might have succeeded if an equally desperate aide of the sheriff's, anxious over the wrath that would fall upon him if he let the prisoner escape, had not wheeled in the saddle, striking an awkward blow against Brand's skull with the heavy shaft of his lance.

The bright greenery of the wooded sanctuary faded to a dull gray-brown as Brand was thrown forward by the force of the object that slammed against his head, just below the crown. There was only a second to perceive the gritty taste of dirt and know he had failed before a wash of black drowned awareness, mercifully cutting off the shock of pain that pulsed from his torn, bleeding scalp.

Esmond pushed past the mounted soldiers, then stood watching in silence as several of them dismounted and dragged Brand's limp body across the road to hoist him over the saddle of the horse they had brought for him to ride. At Fitz Walther's order, the prisoner's feet and wrists were tied with a strong hempen rope, securing him for what would be a long, jostling journey to Cambridge.

The others in his party had retreated from the road, stunned by the abrupt, apparently lawful seizure of a man whose only crime had been to aid one of their countrymen, but Esmond kept to the stand he had taken, seemingly awed by the realization of what to this point had been only an airy scheme. The sight of his rival trussed like a piece of baggage, delivered over to what counted for Norman justice, brought him no great joy, only satisfaction with the accomplished deed.

Before he issued an order for his troop to form ranks, Sheriff Fitz Walther urged his charger toward Lord Esmond at a walk, coming up slightly behind and to the man's right. A firm tug on the reins brought the steed's long nose down and, in reaction, up to bump the Saxon's shoulder blade. Esmond stumbled forward a step and wheeled, his glare losing its strength when he found the sheriff looking down at him, his long, thin lips pursed as if the sight of Esmond left a sour taste in his mouth.

"What will you do with him?" Esmond asked.

"Does it matter, sir?" Fitz Walther replied, then gave a disgusted sigh. "I see, you are not yet satisfied. We will ask the prisoner to tell us about the strength of Hereward's forces, who gives him support, by what path we can enter the fens and locate his fortress. And when de Reynaud does not answer, he will be lashed, beaten, starved, perhaps blinded."

Despite the fact that both Rede and de Reynaud were his enemies, the sheriff felt nothing but contempt for Lord Esmond's falseness and a grudging respect for Brand, who had honorably followed his heart in aiding the rebel leader. Still, justice would come to Esmond, perhaps in some degree more painful than torture. There was, in Fitz Walther's Cambridge quarters, a copy of an order from King William, acquainting the sheriff with the fact that the Saxon estates of Havistock and Aswold had been granted to a loyal vassal, one Sanson de Bourney. When the man arrived from Reims in a month or two, Fitz Walther was expected to assist him in any problems he might have securing his fief.

The sheriff called out a command to form ranks for the homeward journey, and as the man turned his mount away Esmond called to him. "*Wait*, m'lord sheriff." He held up the brooch and offered it to Fitz Walther. "You'll be needing this, sir. 'Tis evidence."

"I have no need of it. The word of an honorable Saxon lord is enough condemnation." Fitz Walther smirked, his gaze contemptuous before his helmet came down to hide the expression. "Keep the piece for your services. 'Tis not worth thirty pieces of silver but, then . . . you have delivered over a man, not Christ."

Esmond said nothing in reply; indeed, the sheriff turned and rode to the lead of his assembled troops before the young Saxon lord could think of a properly scathing retort. He stared after them for a moment, then wheeled around and stalked back to the spot where Edelbart and Keir stood. Only Keir seemed visibly unsettled by the episode, his milk-white complexion more pale than usual under his thatch of carrot-red curls. "By God, we must do *something* for the poor fellow," he insisted, wondering how his cousin could remain so calm. "Esmond, surely you can appeal the seizing of de Reynaud?"

"Much as I regret my impotence, I have no power to sway the Norman Fitz Walther," Esmond answered with a dolorous sigh. " 'Tis informing his widow that leaves me faint."

"Widow?" Edelbart questioned the use of the term. "You condemn the man faster than the enemy, m'lord."

"We all know Norman justice too well, my friend. Do you

believe Brand will live after their torture? If they deal him too much pain, we should all hope to God that it's followed by the mercy of death."

It was amazing how Esmond played his role of grieving friend so artfully, thought Edelbart. Though they had never been friends, he had respected de Reynaud, would have fought for him if there had been half a chance to resist the Normans. He could do nothing now but use his knowledge of his lord's guile to his own advantage. "Odd, is it not, how that damning brooch came into the sheriff's possession?"

Esmond's head came up sharply, his eyes narrowed at the implication. Without taking his gaze from Edelbart, he issued an order to his cousin. "Fetch the hounds, Keir. I must get back and perform the sad duty of informing Lady Alysaun of her husband's fate."

"By my faith, I'm no dog handler, Esmond," Keir protested.

"No, but you *are* a guest and cousin whom I have entertained and asked little of in return. Don't argue, Keir—my temper has been tried enough."

Reluctance dragged at his feet but Keir obeyed. When he was out of range of their voices, Esmond asked his retainer to explain his comment about the brooch.

"I have not your learning, m'lord, but can cipher well enough to add together the desire you once showed for Lady Alysaun and the convenience of her husband's capture. Your purpose became clear to me when, after insisting we follow a northerly track, I came upon the road and saw the waiting troops."

"Assuming that your ciphering is correct, what are your intentions?" Edelbart shifted nervously and, impatient to hear what demands the knight would make, Esmond snapped, "Speak up, man. I would hear you out before my cousin returns."

"Well, sire, you saw this deed done to steal the lady from her husband. Lady Alysaun will doubt your innocence unless I add my assurances that you did protest his capture."

"And in exchange for such assurances . . . what is your reward?"

"Morwena, sire. You never meant to honor her with marriage.

She may have even assisted your intrigues, however innocently. Renounce any claim to her—I want the girl for my wife.''

Esmond started to laugh as relief flooded over him. He had expected some demand for money or privilege. ''With my blessings may you have her, a virgin still, for I was too occupied to take advantage of Morwena's offer to share my bed.'' Pleased by the unexpected presentation of an ally, Esmond's mood lightened. ''Come along, then, but mind you don't weave too colorful a tale of my wrenching despair at Brand's loss. 'Twould ring false to a girl whose beauty hides a discerning and facile mind.''

The two waited a few minutes until a grumbling, cursing Keir came back with two of the bloodhounds in tow, claiming the other had gone deep into the weald across the road and could perish for all he cared. ''Send one of your servants after the cur,'' he complained to his cousin. ''That's what you've got 'em for.''

Edelbart took charge of the limers and the three men retraced their path through the thick woods to the clearing. The servants were no doubt curious about Brand's absence and the lack of any game, but Esmond chose not to enlighten them. There would be gossip aplenty when word reached the manor.

An hour later Esmond was alone with Alysaun in the solar, Edelbart having departed soon after he had recounted how valiant were his master's efforts to save Brand. Expecting tears and all manner of weeping and fainting, Esmond found reason to admire Alysaun's composure.

What he had taken for Alysaun's well-disciplined resignation was in truth an instinctive measure of protection to cover her shock. At first she could not believe what Esmond related. She heard him say that Brand was arrested, that he had been dealt a head wound in an attempt to escape the sheriff's men; but the words didn't penetrate, and when they finally did, a dull, numb feeling stilled any protest. The tenseness of her body showed in the whitened knuckles of her tightly clasped hands, in the strain that shadowed her eyes. If one tear escaped her eyes, Alysaun knew, there would be no end to the flood, and weeping over his fate would not help Brand.

She glanced up now, to find Esmond studying her with a concerned look. "There must be something we can do, Esmond—*think*. I cannot just let them take him, not *Brand*."

"Was there anything to be done for your father, dear?" Esmond asked, and saw her wince in pain at that memory.

"Perhaps, but I was too weak to save him. I will not let Brand suffer his fate. I'll *not*." Her voice had a sharp, hysterical edge. "I will go to the sheriff. Since Brand isn't English or Norman, he doesn't fall under their jurisdiction."

"Anyone who consorts with an acknowledged outlaw is considered an outlaw himself. And I refuse to let you go, Alysaun. You are his wife, for God's sake. You'll put yourself in danger. Do you think for a moment that they'd believe you didn't know he was with Hereward? No, you cannot go."

Alysaun was close to tears, so close she brought her teeth down sharply against her bottom lip to draw her attention away from the overwhelming desire to give in to weeping. "Then what can we do? To know he suffers at their hands—"

"Only this morning you were furious with Brand. Perhaps the Lord saw the pain of your tears in the chapel and means Brand to suffer for his broken vows."

She stared at Esmond, her brows drawing together in a disgusted frown. "How can you mention *that* now? I love Brand. He could go to that woman every night if only I knew he was safe from those devils."

Esmond turned away, irritated by her declaration of love. He clasped his hands behind his back and paced a few steps. "There is a way," he said, and turned to face Alysaun again. The hope he offered was reflected in her eyes. "Hereward is his friend—indeed, the cause of his troubles. If I were to ask his help in freeing Brand . . . Of course such a meeting would make me vulnerable to the same charges your husband faces." Esmond shook his head, showing signs of reluctance. "'Twould be asking me to take a great risk."

Alysaun couldn't believe he would hesitate. "Esmond, Brand is no Saxon, yet he gave aid to one of our own. You drank in companionship with him, sought his company in the hunt. Have you no thought for his pain . . . for mine?"

"And what of *mine?*" For the first time Esmond dropped the mask of friendship and admitted the bitterness within him. "No one cared to consider my feelings when you wed him, least of all my loving mother. Yes, I know about it, though both you and Brand were in league to keep that night a secret. Now you ask only that I risk my own life to free the man you were forced to marry."

"Esmond, 'tis true that we married under duress, but I *am* his wife, I love him. I cannot alter either fact, nor can you."

"Then let him *rot.*"

The tears Alysaun had restrained spilled over, coursing down her cheeks at the shock of that callous statement. "Esmond, please . . . I beg of you. If there is anything I can do to change your mind, *anything* . . ."

"I'll take the risk of seeking out Hereward only if you agree to annul your marriage to Brand and wed me." Esmond let out the deep breath he had held. All his long weeks of planning had come to this. If Alysaun refused, the responsibility for Brand's torture and death rested with her. "Do not think your tears have any effect on me, girl. I love you and only want my chance to prove how well."

"If you truly loved me, you would go to Hereward without demanding what I cannot give you."

"But you can and will, or Brand faces the whip and death. Can you live with the knowledge that you could have spared him that? *Can* you, Alysaun?"

"No, I cannot." Her crying slowed as the numbness returned. "I have no choice, sire. I will annul my marriage but take no vows with you. If you force me to accept you, your domination will not be blessed by the church." Alysaun looked up, the dull, glazed look leaving her eyes for a moment as they flared with anger. "How long do you think to keep me once Brand is free? He will seek you out and make you pay for the insult to his pride and mine."

"*If* he still lives when Herward comes for him, Brand will be naught but a broken shell, my love, an outlaw who must keep to Hereward's den like a cowering hound or risk recapture. No, fear of his retribution will not leave me tossing in sleepless nights.''

"I'll go with you to meet Hereward," Alysaun said, unable to trust Esmond to keep his promise. If she had to share his bed and suffer his attentions, it would not be for anything less than the assurance Brand would be free.

"Then accompany me, but before I arrange a meeting, Father Thomas will see the annulment fixed with your name or we do not leave Havistock."

Alysaun seemed to hesitate and Esmond reminded her that each moment she procrastinated was drawing Brand closer to torture. "Should I describe the methods used to extract information, Alysaun? First, the guards will strip away his tunic and bind his wrists to—''

"*Stop it.*" Alysaun covered her ears to muffle the cold, ugly words, and shut her eyes as well. Moments later, Esmond was beside her, seizing her wrists to jerk her to her feet.

"If the thought distresses you so, I suggest we find the priest, the sooner to meet with the rebel and put your mind at ease."

"There are no grounds for an annulment. Father Thomas—''

"Will do as I ask," Esmond said confidently. "I own his loyalty, m'lady. He well knows your marriage was a farce—'twill soothe his conscience to know it is dissolved.''

"You have all the answers, don't you, m'lord? I think no one but I understands the depth of your cunning.''

"Not cunning, my sweet, desire. I have desired you from that first moment we met upon the road, and I have suffered seeing you in de Reynaud's arms. Now I will have my turn at knowledge of your sweetness, my chance to tempt sighs from those soft lips.''

The corners of Alysaun's mouth turned down in contempt. "Your arrogance is overbearing, Esmond. Only one man can move me to answer his desires with such contentment. Whether Brand is a captive or free, my heart is his.''

"Then I shall have to console myself with what is left. If I had the choice, Alysaun, of owning your heart or body, I'd not hesitate to choose the latter. Neither, I think, would Brand." Esmond bent his head to kiss her and Alysaun turned her head aside.

"There will be time for sweet kisses later," he asserted, releasing her wrists so abruptly that Alysaun stumbled back and sank into her chair. "You've a half hour or so to collect yourself before I bring Thomas to witness the annulment. Content yourself with the knowledge you will be helping to free Brand."

Once Alysaun had signed the hastily drawn-up document of annulment in an angry, barely identifiable scrawl, Esmond proceeded quickly to fulfill his part of their bargain. While servants packed a change of clothing and the bare necessities needed for a day's journey, he wrote a short message that would precede them to Peterborough, the abbey some eighteen miles northwest of Ely, where Hereward's uncle, Brand, was abbot.

It was Alysaun who, worried that Hereward might be wary of a trap and refuse to emerge from his stronghold, suggested that the brooch he had given Brand accompany the message. Esmond knew a moment's unease, wondering if Morwena had replaced the jewelry as he had ordered her to. All mention that it had been in the sheriff's possession that morning was cautiously censored; Alysaun did not know the brooch had been out of the wardrobe, much less carried to Cambridge and back.

When they arrived at the abbey, Hereward's men ringed it, staying mounted and well back amongst the trees, but their presence was nevertheless a warning of their leader's cautious attitude.

Abbot Brand had courteously allowed his nephew the use of his chambers for the meeting. Hereward was seated in his uncle's heavily carved, high-backed chair when they arrived. One of the monastery's cowled monks opened the door, which was flanked in the aisle by two Saxon knights armed with sword and battle-ax. Expecting only the English lord of Havistock, Hereward rose to his feet out of respect for the young lady who accompanied Esmond Rede. He did a quick perusal of her comely face and slender figure and smiled.

Brand had never confided the reason he had left Ely to seek the manor of Havistock. Now Hereward had an inkling of what had lured his friend there. "Lord Esmond, I assumed we were to meet alone," he said, his expression more serious as his glance turned to the slim, pale stripling who had inherited his fief too young to appear so commanding. "Lovely as she is, you have put me at a disadvantage. Before we go further, I would know the lady's name and why she accompanies you."

"Because it was I who sent the brooch you gave to Brand," Alysaun answered before Esmond could open his mouth. Hereward's mouth quirked in amusement as Esmond's face flushed ruddy. "My name is Alysaun, daughter of Lord Brihtric Meau of Gloucester."

To cover his surprise at recognizing her father's name, Hereward offered her the abbot's chair and stood beside it, forgetting Lord Esmond's presence for the moment. "I knew your father by reputation only. 'Twas sad news to hear of his imprisonment. You have my condolences, m'lady. You lost a father and England lost a good man." Brihtric Meau's fate was common enough, but the tale of his harsh treatment at the bastard duke's hands had spread across England. William's vengeance had gone beyond stealing Meau's estates. The town of Gloucester had lost its charter merely because he was one of its citizens.

Now his daughter, with the golden-haired, fair-skinned beauty of the Saxon race, had appeared, claiming posession of the brooch Hereward had given Brand. The connection intrigued the rebel. "How came you by the brooch piece, m'lady?"

Esmond, tired of being ignored, asserted himself now and chose to answer for Alysaun. "Alysaun . . . *was* de Reynaud's wife, sir. Two days past he was seized by the Cambridge sheriff, Fitz Walther. 'Tis why we came seeking you, to ask you to redeem the pledge that was issued with the brooch and rescue the man."

Hereward stared at Esmond, disliking his manners. The lad could be no more than twenty and, like a pup, thought himself more important than his size or age warranted. "What was the charge?"

"His association with you, sire. De Reynaud is considered one of your rebels."

"Then why in the name of hell's master didn't you send me more than a message with his name?" Hereward crossed his arms and glowered at Esmond before he paced across the room and back, his thick brows forming one solid line as he considered Brand's chances. He paced back and stopped before the chair, including Alysaun in his anger at the time already wasted. "Rede said you *were* Brand's wife. What occurred to change your state?"

Resentment flared in the depths of Alysaun's blue eyes. The first warmth Hereward had shown her had turned to cold, suspicious accusation. " 'Tis a tale overlong in the telling, and the more time we waste, the more Brand suffers in the enemy's keep. Wed or not, I want him free."

Hereward turned on Esmond so suddenly he flinched as if preparing for an attack. "And you, m'lord, what is your interest in this affair? You are no relative of Brand's. A friend, perhaps?"

"Lady Alysaun *and* her husband were guests in my home." Esmond looked past Hereward, warning her to say no more. Hereward glanced over his shoulder and for the first time saw the strain that formed tiny lines around her eyes and mouth. There was something feral and possessive in the lad's attitude toward Alysaun Meau, as if he were a mongrel cur who had stolen a choice delicacy from the table and now jealously guarded his prize. "Though their marriage is ended, the lady's tender heart was aggrieved to hear of Brand's arrest."

Again Hereward ignored Esmond, turning his back on him to address Alysaun. "If anyone can see Brand de Reynaud free, 'tis I, m'lady. Once we have him, though, he'll be a wanted man, an outlaw, and most likely will join our band. Have you a message for him?"

"She has no message," Esmond insisted.

Without deigning to turn, Hereward silenced the young man with the coldness of his voice. "I asked the *lady*, Rede, and if I care for a message from you, I'll address you directly." He turned with an intimidating scowl. "Why do I feel your interest in the lady's answer goes beyond that of gracious host?"

To his mind, Esmond thought Hereward a great, lumbering ox, and an insolent oaf at that. He straightened his shoulders and spoke as he would to one of his serving men. "You assume much, sir. Lady Alysaun has annulled her marriage, and since she has no male relatives, I have the honor of acting as her protector. If my hopes prove out, she'll become my wife." Esmond paused, wondering if Alysaun would issue a denial. When she said nothing, he added, "Alysaun is quite free to speak for herself."

A fleeting frown passed over Alysaun's features, gone before Hereward faced her again. "I . . . " She sighed, unable to voice what she truly wanted to say. "If anything, sir, tell Brand . . . tell him I will pray that he finds happiness. It lies not with me. What we had, thought we had, is lost." There was not much more she could say with Esmond hanging on her every word, selfishly measuring them as if they were coins from his own purse. "Wait—you may give him this"—Alysaun slipped the thin gold band from her ring finger and passed it to Hereward—"and say I am returning it." The ring was her mother's; Brand had never given her one. "'Twas his mother's," she lied. "And what it represents belongs to him still."

"I'll give it over to him, m'lady, but is there nothing more?"

"Nay, the return of that symbol says more than I can put into words." For a moment she closed her eyes, and when she looked at Hereward again, he glimpsed briefly the underlying pain in their misted azure gaze. "Though Brand has a poet's heart and voice, he was trained for knighthood, m'lord. Even forced by circumstance to fight your noble cause, he will prove a valiant and steadfast member of your band."

Again, Hereward had reason to puzzle over the contradiction between the girl's actions and her speech. She had put aside her marriage vows, a drastic step unless she felt Brand's arrest had placed her in danger, and yet she did not seem the type to abandon a man just because he had fallen on hard times. Her praise for Brand's worth implied no loss of affection for him. Hereward closed his fingers around the ring, still warm from her flesh, and gave her a smile that was strangely gentle for so gruff and brusque a fighting man. "He'll have your message, Lady Alysaun, and, by my oath, his freedom ere long. I cannot warrant, though, that he will not seek you out to question himself why your marriage is over. Will you be at Havistock?"

"I will, sir, but beg him not to come there. If he should be so foolish as to fall into Norman hands again, then he cares little for his life, or for what I have done on his behalf."

Hereward dropped the ring into the leather pouch hanging from his belt and drew her hand to his lips. "You have assured his rescue, for as I live and breathe, Brand will be freed. Still, I think the man will find his freedom an empty joy without you to share it. In truth, I am loath to be the bearer of such ill tidings, but I sense you had good reasons for your actions."

Turning, he offered the clasp of friendship to Esmond. "I imagine that someday in the near future you will be joining our fight, Rede. You still hold your estates intact but the Bastard's greed is endless. We are in need of support, if not more fighting men. You may yet save your lands from seizure if your coin can extend the cause we espouse, England's freedom from the oppressor."

"Though my debt to the crown's coffers weighs heavily against my reserves, I will send one of my men here with a pledge." This Esmond replied, hoping that his generosity would bring him Alysaun's favor. "I can promise fifteen pounds ten, if that will aid you."

"'Tis a goodly amount, more than I had reason to expect, Lord Esmond." Hereward grinned, pleased that the youth had redeemed himself by showing some concern for protecting his Saxon heritage. "There are times when I feel more beggar than warrior. Of late, I've had to spend as many hours badgering my countrymen for gold as I do in stealing it from the Normans."

Hereward made his exit first, caution too ingrained to allow any man, even a Saxon lord, to see the direction he and his men took. His parting words were a promise that Brand would know freedom within a day, two at the most. He took with him a troubled mind that wondered over Lady Alysaun's true feelings and the nagging sense that the girl was under duress. She was too tense and the slight puffs beneath her eyes bespoke sleeplessness and weeping.

Outside, as he called to his men and mounted, it occurred to him that the harder task would not be rescuing Brand from the Norman keep but relating the news that Lady Alysaun had chosen to dissolve her marriage to him.

On the journey back to Havistock, Alysaun was silent and subdued, feeling that a door had closed, separating her forever from the man she loved. Esmond, pleased with her restraint at the meeting, allowed her the mood and busied himself in conversation with Sir Aiborn, one of the young knights who had trained as his squire.

Finally, when they were riding up the path toward the manor, Esmond interrupted her solemn reverie to ask if she did not admire and approve of his pledge to the rebel. "I did not have to offer such an amount, Alysaun. The manner in which you carried yourself did please me, and prompted my generosity."

Alysaun's gaze barely hid the contempt she felt for him. "You have pledged only, sir, not delivered. Make no claims that 'twas done in my behalf. England is our homeland. If you loved it as much as you do yourself, you would have offered more than gold."

"Mean you my knights and my own service?" Esmond asked in an incredulous voice. "Nay, m'lady . . . I have a different cause to forward. The time may yet come when I am forced to the field to defend my honor, but for now, no one could fault me for a desire to stay close to my hearth and you."

9

Following the matins service performed by the new priest Esmond had taken on at Alysaun's insistence, Alysaun stayed behind to seek Father Michael's counsel. The priest was young but far wiser than the malleable Thomas. His moral strength could not be corrupted by fealty to the lord of a manor; Michael owed allegiance only to God, and for that reason Alysaun trusted him with all her heart.

Just five days past the feast of Lammas, Havistock was a busy hive of workers toiling in the fields till evening to harvest the late-summer crops of oats, barley, and rye. Despite Esmond's absence, the harvesting proceeded well under the watchful eye of his steward, Harivig. For eight days now Esmond had been gone, summoned to his ailing mother's bedside at her estate of Aswold, south of Cambridge. Though prayers were said daily for Elfleda's recovery, Alysaun could not sincerely repeat them; it was one of the problems she had stayed behind to discuss with her confessor.

Everyone had doubted the messenger's claim that the lady was near dying, that though she had recovered from the cold that had sent her to bed, she grew weaker each day from an affliction of the spirit and languished for her son. Believing it another attempt by Elfleda to prey upon Esmond's sympathies and effect a return to Havistock from her exile, Alysaun had urged the reluctant Esmond to go to his mother's side. The first easy breath she had known since Brand's capture by the sheriff had come when she had watched him ride away from Havistock in the company of one of his knights.

No, Elfleda was most likely hale and hearty, but Alysaun could imagine the lengths to which the woman would go to convince her only son of the cruel toll his banishment had exacted from her. No doubt she had powdered her face pale for his arrival and lain abed bemoaning the maternal loyalty and devotion that had made her act in his behalf.

What mattered to Alysaun was that Elfleda's summons had given her some respite from Esmond's company. For the first fortnight after Hereward had made good his promise to pull Brand from the sheriff's clutches, she had been able to keep Esmond at bay. Using every possible excuse, even a blushing admission that she was in the grip of her monthly bleeding, she had managed to keep him at arm's distance.

Then, two weeks later, he had burst into her room late one night and, made bold by the wine he had been nursing, ignored her tearful pleas, taking her by force. Esmond had laughed at the scratches that left his arms bleeding and when she realized that her struggling only added to his enjoyment of the possession so long denied him, Alysaun had ceased any attempt to defend herself and submitted, tightly shutting her eyes to block out the image of his triumphant, sweating face.

After that there were no excuses and despite the intercession of Father Michael on her behalf, Esmond continued his nightly assaults. The only satisfaction she derived lay in the petulant frustration he showed at his inability to extract any response to his lovemaking. Whether he treated her roughly or praised her softness in tender words, Alysaun lay still and unaroused beneath him, giving up nothing of herself. Once only had he moved her to a response— hysterical weeping when he had dragged her along a familiar path to the meadow above the millrace. The sweet memories of the bliss she had known there in Brand's arms were too much to bear.

Perhaps Esmond had thought the backdrop of open sky and lush, fragrant grasses would move her to repeat the abandoned, sensual offering up of herself as she had to her husband, but that special place had the opposite effect on Alysaun. From Esmond's thin lips the expression of his longing for her had an ugly, hollow ring, like an atheist praising the wonders of God's creations. And, too, the sight of his pale, wiry frame exposed in the bright splash of sunny copse, in comparison with Brand's lean, superbly muscled body, made him appear all the weaker. His hands, possessive and yet hesitant, searched the surface of her flesh, seeking some hidden lock that would release her and arouse the woman she had been for Brand.

He might have been one of the hated enemy for the disgust his touch aroused. Alysaun fought him with all her strength, battling though it was a useless effort, and a portion of her mind blamed Brand for what came to a sordid, shameful violation of her body and a rape of her senses. Much had she given to secure his freedom and in return he had abandoned her to Esmond's selfish, rutting lusts.

Though Father Michael had assured her Brand was still her legal spouse and had chastised Esmond for taking her forcibly in adultery, Alysaun was sure that if Brand were to appear now, she would turn her back on him. Impossible as it was, she loved him still and hated him all the more for the longing she could not deny.

Strongly entrenched in ascetic celibacy, the priest could not offer solace to a girl who had known delight in the physical act of wedded love. If Alysaun had not been introduced to such knowledge, Esmond's lack of expertise and skill as a lover might have been disappointing, but surely not so keenly distressing or, in comparison, so repugnant. What she had shared with Brand was a perfect union of flesh and soul; Esmond's laboring over her unwilling body called to mind the frantic, mindless questing of a rutting beast of the forest.

Beyond his attempts to make Esmond aware of the danger to his mortal soul in breaking one of the holy commandments, Father Michael could effect little remorse in the young lord. As easily as the corrupted Father Thomas had been replaced, he, too, could be sent upon his way. Deplorable as his morals were, Esmond ruled this small parcel of English soil. With youth's callous disregard, he worried more over his earthly liege, King William, than for the sorrow he dealt his heavenly Lord.

"Perhaps now that the first heat of this devilish passion has worn thin," the priest said now, breaking the heavy, melancholy silence as he strolled across the chapel sanctuary with Alysaun, "Lord Esmond will heed the call of his soul and temper his desires." A sideways glance at the girl's face revealed a twinge of impatience with his naive hopes. Michael touched her shoulder; and as they paused beneath one of the high, vaulted windows, a sudden flood of sunlight enveloped them in its warmth. "As the clouds roll back to reveal the sun's brightness, so the darkness shadowing Esmond's soul may yet recede. No one, my child, is beyond redemption until a last breath signals his destiny."

"Fine words, Father, and meant to comfort, I am sure," Alysaun replied with an effort at an appreciative smile, "but you trust too much to miracles. I fear only a divine stroke of lightning would change his selfish heart. Esmond is too much his mother's son. Strong wills and strong desires run cold in Rede veins, in place of the crimson warmth that serves the rest of us as life's blood."

"I know your suffering, m'lady, yet would I remind you that our Lord Jesus called upon us to leave judgment to His—"

The offering up of yet another scriptural homily was interrupted by a sudden, noisy commotion in the hall beyond the chapel doors. They were just as suddenly flung open to admit a storming Elfleda, who swept forward with a vengeful stride, a white-faced, shaken Morwena trailing in her wake.

For a minute Lady Elfleda was so beset with fury she could not give voice to the accusation glaring from her narrowed eyes. She sputtered and, taking in the sight of a strange young priest hovering protectively close to Alysaun, in place of her familiar Thomas, pointed a finger at the girl. "You . . . you ungrateful *slut*—what have you done with him? Answer me at once or I'll rip that hussy's face of yours to shreds." Elfleda took a menacing step forward and Michael stepped bravely between the two ladies, shocked by the older woman's behavior in the dwelling place of God but determined to save Alysaun from harm. "You've even seen to your own priest, eh? How quick you've gone from protesting innocence to sly and wicked guile. I repeat, slut, where is my boy?"

Father Michael frowned at the woman's language and opened his mouth to warn against its further employ in the sanctuary; but Alysaun's voice, far more chilling than anything already said, cut off his rebuke. "How strange, m'lady . . . the good father and I were just speaking of miracles. You appear exceedingly vigorous for a lady who, less than a fortnight past, heard the fluttering of Death's wings beyond your chamber door. Truly, the prayers offered for your recovery were answered with dispatch." Alysaun's expression revealed little of her surprise at Elfleda's abrupt arrival. She faced the older woman with a resolute determination not to be intimidated. Whatever this nonsense was about Esmond, she knew nothing of it. "Father Michael, this woman who cannot keep a civil tongue within the holy chapel is none other than Esmond's mother, Lady Elfleda. Assure her, please, that he left Havistock quite as healthy as she appears to be."

Michael's sympathies for Alysaun increased as he stared at the haughty, spiteful creature who had given her so much heartache. "If you'll accept my word, m'lady, as a man of God," he said, inclining his head in a stiff nod of acknowledgment, "I do attest to the truth of Lady Alysaun's statement. Your son left here eight days past in the company—"

"The only thing I'll accept, priest, is that this cunning chit has cast her spell upon you," Elfleda interrupted rudely, "as she did on my poor, bewitched Esmond. Wear he a tunic or the drapings of a devout, a man can be a gullible fool. Try my patience no further by claiming my son rode forth to answer my call, for if he had, would I have come seeking him?"

"Wherever your son is, madam, he is not in my care," Alysaun insisted, offended by the continuing vilification. "If he has come back, 'tis without my knowledge. Think you still that Esmond is here, I would suggest you begin a search in the buttery. Your son has an inordinate fondness for strong drink." Alysaun touched the priest's arm and, when he turned, curtsied. "Father, I thank you for your words of comfort and beg your understanding of my wish to retire to the solitude of the solar."

Father Michael bowed, the courtesy drawing an indignant sniff from Elfleda. "Go with our Lord's blessing, my daughter, and forget not that I am always here to listen."

Without a glance at Elfleda, Alysaun swept past the woman and toward the doors. *"Halt,"* Elfleda commanded, once more assuming the powers denied her by Esmond's harsh decree of banishment from Havistock. "I will tell you when to take your leave, woman, and I deny you the use of my solar. Go to your room while you occupy it still."

Alysaun had paused, listening to the haughty orders with a stiff posture. Now she turned and smiled at Elfleda, speaking firmly as though to a child. "My lady, I answer you only out of respect for your age. Esmond left Havistock under *my* care. If you doubt it, the steward, Harivig, will confirm my authority. What had been your bedchamber was granted for my use, as the solar was allotted for my privacy. If you intend to visit until Esmond's return, I'll see a room prepared but I'll not permit your petty grievances to disturb the household. Good day, m'lady."

Her momentary glimpse of Elfleda's stunned visage was a brief triumph to savor before she made her exit. Outside the nave, Alysaun leaned against the support of the heavy oaken doors and took a deep breath. Though she had spoken truly in stating that Esmond had left her in charge of Havistock, the boldness she had shown in asserting herself before the manor's former lady had surprised even herself.

Yet if I had not, Alysaun thought as she started off toward the solar, the woman would have trodden upon me as if I were dirt. Too much had she already suffered to allow Elfleda that pleasure and right again. In the solar, she found Morwena seated near the window, sewing upon the hem of a new tunic. The girl started to rise but Alysaun stopped her with a gesture. "Continue with your work, Morwena. Despite your old mistress's return, nothing has changed. I'll join you in the task, if only to keep my thoughts occupied."

The maiden nodded, teeth worrying her lip, then bent her head to resume her sewing. Serving Lady Alysaun was almost as difficult as waiting upon Elfleda. Once Esmond had revealed his true intent, Morwena had been mortified by her role in his scheming. It was bad enough that she had offered her virtue in exchange for airy promises of marriage, but her stealth on Esmond's behalf had torn Alysaun and Brand apart. The guilt she carried in her heart strained the friendship.

Alysaun took a seat next to her attendant and resumed the intricate beadwork appliqué on a lavender band of brocade that would edge the tunic's sleeves. For weeks she had sensed the reserve in Morwena's manner and puzzled over it. The only excuse for the distance that had sprung up between them could be the girl's disapproval of the relationship between Alysaun and Esmond. If so, it was understandable but unjust. She was his mistress. The servants whispered about the shame of it, but Alysaun refused to feel guilty. The fact that it was not by her choice made Esmond's domination no less embarrassing.

"M'lady?" Morwena's hesitant voice interrupted her brooding thoughts, and Alysaun glanced up to find the girl's dark eyes gazing into her own. The maid flushed and looked away, and again Alysaun was embarrassed. "What . . . what can have happened to his lordship? Lady Elfleda thinks . . . she acted as if there was some plot afoot to harm Lord Esmond."

"I know, dear. I'm sure her accusations were loud enough to carry to the hall." Alysaun sighed. "I am untroubled by his seeming disappearance. Selfish as it may be, I care only that his absence has afforded me some peace. Wherever he may be, Esmond may stay there and trouble someone else."

"I'll add my prayers to yours on that account, m'lady," Morwena said without thinking. Suddenly realizing the hostility in her voice, she looked up and blushed at Alysaun's curious perusal. "I . . . 'tis not my place to comment, m'lady, but his treatment of you has been a . . . a disgrace. To my sorrow—" About to confess her part in Esmond's selfish plotting, she hesitated, unable to bear the thought of the anger such a revelation would stir. "Forgive me, Lady Alysaun. I had no right to speak so bluntly." Ashamed of her cowardice, she took up her stitching once more with fingers that trembled so nervously that Alysaun reached out and laid a hand across hers.

"Leave off your work for now, Morwena, and calm yourself. I do appreciate your concern but you needn't worry so." Alysaun patted the girl's hand and smiled. "Do me a favor now, if you would. I, somewhat rudely, informed the Lady Elfleda that I possessed her chambers. Unfortunately, until Esmond makes an appearance, we must put up with her company. Please see that she's given a room — one as far from mine as possible." Suddenly, with an impish grin that brightened her features like the sun coming out of cloud cover, Alysaun leaned forward and confided, "I'd see her quartered in the stables if I could get away with it."

The image of the haughty dame suffering such an indignity brought a giggle from Morwena. For a moment she was her old self enjoying the companionship of a girl her own age, then a shadow of guilt brought her back to reality. She had no right to the innocent trust Alysaun had in her. Morwena stood, expression solemn once more. As she dipped in a respectful curtsy, a loud, insistent knocking came at the door. "I'll see who it is, m'lady, and attend to your wishes," she said.

The door opened to reveal Harivig, his jowled face all white and pasty as he demanded to see Lady Alysaun. Morwena turned back with a questioning look and, as her mistress nodded, granting the request, stepped aside to allow the steward to enter.

Harivig paused in front of Alysaun, starting nervously at the sound of the door closing after her attendant. Usually he was an overconfident braggart, puffed with the importance of his responsibilities, but now he appeared ill at ease. What could it be now, thought Alysaun, finishing a stitch in her beadwork. Most likely Elfleda had made some attempt to resume her former control. "What problem makes you seek me out, Harivig?" she asked impatiently.

"Sorry to disturb you, m'lady, but a message did come and I thought . . . well, I wasn't sure, with Lady Elfleda home again, whether to give the news to you or her." Harivig shuffled his feet, staring down as though he had never seen them before. A quick glance upward at the irritated expression on the lady's face brought another apology. "Seems the master's gone and got hisself captured by Hereward and his band. They plan to hold Lord Esmond till we come up with the money they say he pledged 'em, some fifteen pounds. You'd think, would you not, that they'd leave their own kind be."

Alysaun was more startled by Hereward's method of extracting the pledge than by the information that Esmond had reneged on it. "Is there enough at Havistock to pay the ransom?" she asked. It served Esmond right to suffer so ignoble a position, she thought, and wondered if Brand had not instigated the idea.

"Aye, I can gather it, but there's a catch, m'lady. The man who delivered the message insisted you was to come with me to the meetin' at Grouneswold Forest tomorrow at dawn." The steward flushed a dull red and looked sullen. "Perhaps Lord Esmond didn't trust me to bring so great a sum by m'self."

"No, 'tis not the reason I'm to accompany you, Harivig," Alysaun replied. Brand had a hand in this; she knew it now by her being included in delivering the ransom. She smiled, toying with the idea of refusing to pay the ransom. For all she cared, Esmond could rot; they had him, let them keep him. "I don't think his lordship would care to see the sum handed over. As Esmond is a Saxon, they'll not harm him.''

"Well, no, m'lady, but they did say that if we didn't come up with the money, they'd raid Havistock. The lord would lose far more'n any fifteen pound should the manor be torched.''

Alysaun's mouth was pursed. "What time did you say the meeting was arranged for?''

"Tomorrow morning at dawn, m'lady.''

"Then gather the coin and bring it here to me. I'll see it secured in pouches and allow you to carry it to Grouneswold in the company of Sir Edelbart. There's no need for me to go along. The ransom alone will see to Esmond's release.'' If in the past month Brand had not seen fit to come to her, she would be damned if she'd answer his hidden summons.

"Yes, m'lady, whate'er you say, 'twill be done," Harivig replied with a short, awkward bow before backing toward the door. He paused and scratched at his scalp. "Y'don't think they'll harm him, Lady Alysaun?''

"The only harm will be to Esmond's purse and pride, steward, and the latter could use a blow or two. Now see to it and keep a closed mouth. There's no reason to alarm the household, *especially* Lady Elfleda. There's time enough for her to weep and wail when Esmond's safe at home.''

When he was gone, Alysaun's smile deepened. So Brand thought she cared enough for Esmond's well-being to run to his aid, hmm? She would have given anything to see his expression when she failed to appear. If not for the threat to Havistock, she'd have refused the ransom demand. Still, it was not even ransom, only the support she herself had heard Esmond vow to give Hereward's cause. It pleased Alysaun that they would receive it despite his broken promise.

That night the pledge money was readied. Still unable to discover anything reassuring about her son's disappearance, Elfleda had taken to her bed, apparently hovering close to death once more. Alysaun enlisted Morwena's aid in sewing the linen coin pouches closed and, for safekeeping, carried them to her bedchamber. There they were securely tucked between the mattress and the leather underframe supporting it.

Alysaun was asleep for several hours when the sounds of loud shouting echoed in the great hall. Her first, sleep-dulled thought was that Brand hadn't trusted her to turn over the ransom and so had convinced Hereward to raid the estate. A woman screamed and, recognizing Morwena's terrified voice, Alysaun bolted up to scramble for her clothing.

Before she was out of bed, her door slammed open, shuddering under the strong kick that had broken the latch. Alysaun cowered, frantically grabbing at the bed linens to cover her bare flesh as Morwena stumbled in, nearly falling from the push she had been given. A tall, armored Norman followed her, pausing to survey the room for any defenders before his gaze settled on the bed.

Alysaun felt her heart sink. It was happening again, as it had to so many Saxon families, as it had to her own beloved Hanley. The King had finally granted Havistock to one of his vassals. The Norman knight shoved Morwena aside and approached the bed, leisurely drawing off his gauntlets and thrusting back his hood of chain mail before he drew aside the curtain that partially hid Alysaun from view.

The knight was close to her father's age, his pale red-gold hair beginning to streak with silver-gray. It clung damply to his head, sweated by his mail and helmet. In the dim light his eyes seemed pale but cold and merciless as they took in the sight of Alysaun clutching at the thin sheets, her face pale and framed by glistening waves of gold.

"This wailing maid claims the Saxon, Esmond Rede, is not in residence," Sanson de Bourney said in halting English. Morwena, cowering against the foot of the bed, had quieted to sniffling and sobbed anew at the reference to herself, drawing a scowl from the tired knight. The girl who occupied the large, ornately carved bed showed none of the maid's fear. Only wary resentment burned from eyes the color of the sky. "Are you his wife?" he asked.

Alysaun made no answer and de Bourney swore an oath, turning to address a young man who stood in the shadows behind him, remarking in his own language, " 'Tis a shame these heathen English can't speak a civilized tongue. It will be all the harder to make good use of them." The younger man, a pale, thin version of his crude companion, stepped forward. Alysaun's gaze flickered over him for a second, and she recognized a hint of sympathy in his wide gray eyes.

"I understand your speech," Alysaun admitted finally, her command of the Norman French far better than his awkward use of English. "But from my viewpoint, when spoken correctly, the English tongue is far more civilized. I suppose you think you've the authority to enter my private chambers and terrify the manor's occupants?"

"I do, by the rights granted me by his royal majesty, King William. The manor is mine now, wench, and all that surrounds you." Sanson's surprise that this lovely, golden-haired girl spoke his tongue did not alter his dislike for her insolent tone. "Answer me—are you Rede's lady?"

"No, a guest only. Lord Esmond is away on business."

"Then the man is a fool who deserves to lose his demesne," he boasted. "Well, whoever you are, m'lady, I am the new lord of this fief and this is my son, Brian. De Bourney is our family name, and if you expect to stay the night, have some respect for it. I've a decree to prove my title and William's royal seal to mark it legal."

"The seal of a bastard usurper is not legal to English eyes, sire. What you are about is outright thievery. A *curse* upon your claims of legality."

"Saxon *bitch*. You should have your tongue cut out for uttering such slurs." De Bourney's hand moved toward the knife sheathed at his belt, but his son's hand stayed any attempt to draw the blade. Sanson glowered at Alysaun, angrier because she showed so little fear. "I should deliver you to his majesty's care. William would not allow such insults to pass your lips. He—"

"I know well enough what 'justice' he metes out," she interrupted. "I have experience with Normans, sir, and the breed knows nothing of mercy or justice. Send me to him and word for word will I repeat what I said to you."

"Father, the lady is not our enemy," Brian asserted. "Can you blame her for the resentment she feels at awakening to see strangers who deny her even the courtesy to dress before demanding she answer their queries?" Brian's gentle, soothing voice was often the only balm that would lessen his father's rash temper. It worked now, as the tension flowed out of Sanson's taut, hard-muscled forearm.

Not so with the girl, though. Brian sensed a hint of trembling anxiety beneath her exterior show of calm. He stared, unable to pull his gaze from the delicate oval of her face, from the proud and sullen set of her lips, the vulnerability hidden in the depths of her blue irises. That quality stirred a protective instinct within him. "Let us retire to the hall, sire," he prompted, "and allow the girl a few minutes to collect herself."

Though she was grateful for the suggestion, Alysaun's hatred of the Normans was too encompassing to allow even an acknowledgment of the kindness. On the heels of his son's temperate voice, Sanson's harsh, deep tones grated upon her ears. "Well enough, then . . . get some clothing upon your back, young woman, and be quick about it. I've men to be quartered and fed who will not wait upon your toilette."

Alysaun's "Yes, m'lord" was as sarcastic as it was curt. The older man stared at her, suddenly seeming to notice how her bare shoulders gleamed ivory in the candlelight. At the flare of lust that sparked in his eyes, Alysaun drew the covers higher, for all the meager protection they gave against the Norman's hot, greedy stare.

"If you give nothing else civil, m'lady, at least surrender your name," he insisted. "Else I will choose one of my own liking that you may not find so pleasant."

" 'Tis Alysaun, sir, though I am loath to offer it and hear the good Saxon name butchered by a Norman cutthroat."

"I'm not here to please you, Alysaun. For a Saxon wench, you

217

are more finely formed than most, and as you implied, we Normans show no hesitation at taking what we want.'' Sanson turned to his son with a wicked leer and clapped Brian soundly on the back. '' 'Twould be an added bounty to think she comes with the holdings, eh, m'boy? To practice your bed skills on so comely a frame would soon see you in fine mettle for a Norman bride.''

Sanson chuckled, amused by the thought and pleased that his words had brought a blush to the girl's cheeks. He was still laughing when he turned and crossed to Morwena's side, pulling her to her feet to drag the cringing girl along with him to the hall. His son stayed a moment longer, ill at ease with his father's lusty suggestion and embarrassed for the girl.

"You'd best dress quickly, demoiselle. It would not do to try my sire's temper any further. As much as I can, I vow your honor will be safe.'' The assurance was awkwardly given but seemed sincere.

"Do not feign courtesy, sir,'' Alysaun protested, irritated by his lingering. "If you wish me to attend to your father's commands, leave my chambers. I'll not move a hairbreadth while you continue to gawk at me.''

Brian bowed and his thin, blandly attractive features betrayed how deeply her disdain had cut. "I beg your pardon, Lady Alysaun. 'Twas your unexpected beauty that did slow my leavetaking.'' He turned and strode away, leaving Alysaun somewhat puzzled by his gentle mien and feeling almost guilty about her sharp rebuke.

Once the door was shut, she scrambled to dress, keeping a wary eye on the portal. Her fingers shook so she had to fix the drape of her wimple twice before it lay right, frowning at the vanity that made her take such care for her appearance before a host of despicable, crude Normans. At the door, she suddenly remembered Harivig's dawn meeting at Grouneswold Forest and hurried back to the bed to assure herself the coin hoard was securely hidden.

What would be Hereward's reaction when no one from Havistock met him? Brand would probably urge him to attack the manor, as they had warned. Alysaun chewed nervously on a fingernail and worried over the possibility. Only de Bourney and his son had come into her room, but the older man had mentioned men who needed to be fed. Perhaps there would be some way to send word and warn Hereward about the seizing of the manor.

It wasn't Esmond she pitied. He had held his property longer than many of his fellow countrymen and had done nothing to help those who resisted the hated Norman overlords. No, her concern lay with the estate people, the servants and landsmen whose lives revolved around Havistock. They had a new master now and, by the look of him, a harsh one. And she, herself, had once again fallen prey to the whims of one of the enemy. Esmond had lost the least of all.

A Norman soldier lounged outside her door. He straightened his posture when Alysaun appeared, his hooded gaze sliding over her with a leering appraisal that made her stomach muscles tighten in apprehension. Sanson de Bourney was not the only threat she faced. These Normans, be they lords, soldiers, or serving men, were all animals, rutting after any female who crossed their path.

Anxious to escape the brazen stare that seemed to strip her naked, she slipped past the man and hurried toward the hall. The trestles had been set up and Lord de Bourney and his men were busy swilling wine from Havistock's buttery, gorging themselves like gluttons on enough food to serve a troop ten times their size. The two retainers Esmond had left to guard the manor were securely trussed, and bloodied, but alive, and their ladies trembled at their fate as they hurried to attend to the Normans' demands.

Sanson was seated at the high table, lounging in the lord's high, carved chair. His son sat to his right, in a less ornate chair, which had once been Elfleda's. That proud and haughty lady was poised stiffly on the bench to Sanson's left, her expression full of disgust at the man who had taken over her son's rightful inheritance.

The Norman caught sight of Alysaun and gestured imperiously for her to join him. With as much dignity as she could manage, Alysaun made her way to the dais, her cheeks burning from the stares and loud, ribald comments of de Bourney's men-at-arms. Elfleda gave her a look that seemed to say this humiliation was all her fault, then tipped her nose upward in a display of disdain. Sanson kept his seat but Brian courteously rose and offered her his chair, waiting until she had taken it before seating himself on the bench next to it.

"We've just been discussing you, Lady Alysaun," Sanson said, his speech garbled by the mouthful of mutton he chewed. "Rede's mother here"—he gestured at Elfleda with the half-consumed mutton leg—"claims you are her son's mistress. Does the widow speak the truth, or does she merely bear you some malice?"

Alysaun glanced past the Norman, and Elfleda sniffed righteously, as if daring Alysaun to deny the truth. "The woman has a penchant for twisting words but in this she did speak truly." Alysaun looked full into de Bourney's gray-blue eyes and lifted her chin, unashamed of the admission. "Under duress, I did share Esmond's bed. He is quite his mother's son, selfish and immoral."

Elfleda looked huffy at the insult and started to speak, but Sanson warned her with a menacing look. Alysaun, startled by a gentle touch upon her sleeve, turned to find Brian offering her his wine cup. Feeling imprisoned between father and son, she refused and stared straight ahead. The knights seated at the tables below the dais were, in a reflection of their lord's mood, making themselves at home. Hunger sated, discipline loosened by the free flow of wine, they turned their attention to the women.

Sanson stared out across the hall with the attitude of an indulgent father watching his children at play. His men had made a game out of challenging each other to see which one could take the most liberties with the females serving the tables. Excepting the two ladies who sat beside him, the manor's other ladies of rank had received no deference. The two knights who had put forth so weak a defense could only struggle against the strong ropes that bound them to one of the aisle timbers and watch in red-faced humiliation as their wives fell prey to the lusty grappling of the Norman soldiers.

The scene took on the noise and color of a battle as the jostling camaraderie between the men evolved into sharp rivalry. Tempers flared in loud arguments as the more powerful of de Bourney's knights vied for possession of the younger, prettier women. Toward the front of the hall, a grizzled, battle-scarred warrior had grabbed

Morwena, only to be challenged by a tall, young knight whose *coif de maille* had been shoved back to reveal a short crop of raven hair.

Other women had been seized, but the sight of Morwena struggling against the older man's grip cut deeply into Alysaun's heart. She knew the girl's panic as if she were a part of her at that moment, and fought down the nausea that threatened her stomach. It mattered not who won the fight for supremacy—Morwena lost whether it was the old warrior or the young lion who would drag her off into the shadows.

Alysaun turned to Sanson, steeling herself to forget pride and ask his favor. "M'lord?" He had been watching the noisy, lusty scene with a grin, and at the sound of her voice, his eyes met hers. "I have a boon to ask . . . the dark-haired maiden . . ." Alysaun glanced down the length of the hall and de Bourney followed her gaze to the girl cowering in terror as his trusted aide-de-camp, Fitz William, sent young Walter de Shailles sprawling with a heavy blow to the chin. "Spare her violation, sire. Morwena is so young—"

"No younger than you, m'lady, and I see no reason to deprive my men of the prize for which they struggle. 'Twould be a blasphemy to snatch away the victor's reward. Why do you beg mercy for her?"

"No woman deserves such treatment, sir, but Morwena . . . she is kind and gentle. She has never known hate, and that I would ask you to save her from."

Sanson shrugged, unable to understand such reasoning. "All women must come to know a man's desires, Lady Alysaun."

"Rape is not desire, Lord Sanson."

"Aside from serving man, woman was put upon this earth to pleasure him. My men have fought ably and well. I would be half the man they thought me if I denied them these simple comforts."

"No." Alysaun shook her head. "You would be more a man for exercising mercy, sir, and sparing innocence so abrupt and harsh an end. Please . . . I beg you reconsider."

"Why? Oh, I know your reasons, but tell me, girl, what do you give in return for the granting of your plea?" Stirred by the cries and protests of the maids resisting his men, Sanson's own passions were aroused. The girl was even lovelier in the full light of the hall, her complexion flawless, her bright tresses rippling over her shoulders.

The question tightened the grip of apprehension clutching at her belly. "My gratitude and respect, sir."

"You seek to barter something of which I have no need," he sighed in disappointment. "If you had offered yourself, all sweet and willing, I might have saved the chit." Sanson looked down the hall and found the matter had been settled. De Shailles was bloodied but triumphant, and one arm firmly encircled the girl's waist as he stood over the prostrate body of his opponent.

Alysaun's shoulders slumped as she, too, saw the outcome. To the cheers of those men who had wagered on his winning, the young knight bent Morwena back and claimed a kiss, then swept her up into his arms to carry the struggling girl from the hall. For a moment Alysaun turned her face to the Norman's and a mix of anger and contempt blazed from her eyes. "Only one man has had my willingness, sire, and in loyalty to him and myself, 'twas not mine to bargain away."

Sanson frowned at her and tossed the rest of his wine down his throat, calling for more before he leaned forward and seized Alysaun's wrist, the marks of his fingers reddening her white skin. "You flaunt your contempt unwisely, girl," he warned, smiling at her wincing in pain as he jerked her arm and pulled her closer. "If I chose to turn you over to my men, I'd warrant their pawing would make you less haughty."

"Nay, sir," Alysaun denied, her head held high despite the pain of her tightly gripped wrist. " 'Twould only underscore my knowledge that Normans are a savage, unprincipled race of blackguards. In fact, the deed is so predictable, I find the threat amusing."

Brian de Bourney stared down at his nearly untouched food with a puzzled frown. The girl was tempting fate with so bold an answer. It would not take much to move his father to hand her over for such punishment. The thought of this gentle beauty falling prey to the lewd, groping hands of his father's men made Brian's stomach lurch in protest.

"Amusing, eh?" Sanson said. "You've a biting, shrewish tongue, young woman." He might have admired the proud defiance in a lady of his own kind, but in her vulnerable position this one's speech was foolhardy.

"I've been told that, m'lord. If my words wound you too grievously, mayhap I might retire and save you further pain?"

"You'll go only when I give you leave to, girl," the Norman lord snapped irritably. "How came you by so fearless a mien, little Saxon? In your place I would be shaking with terror, yet you show a more valiant defense than your fallen defenders."

Alysaun glared at him and Sanson released her arm. "I've nothing left to fear, m'lord. Your bastard duke, in his ambitious greed, has conquered my land, stripped my people of their rights and freedom, and killed my parents. You and your kind have raped my country. The violation you threaten would be merciless but, then, savages know nothing but torture and force."

"Ah, but we do, though . . . you are mistaken," Sanson claimed. "Our own ladies are so gentle and soft we have only to woo them with sweet words and presents."

"There's a name for that type of woman in any language, sir," Alysaun retorted. "If it were your daughter who sat in my place, threatened with rape, would she not also wonder at the brutality of her captor? Would a show of tears make such a savage pause to consider this arrogance?"

Sanson grinned, delighted by this battle of wits. "I have no daughter, Lady Alysaun, and, I think, you've no tears. For all your valor under such constraint, you would have made an admirable enemy. Still, I would not wish you a man. I find your face too comely for such a waste." Still in his prime, the red-bearded Sanson entertained the thought that this bold, spirited girl might enliven his own bed. At the moment, with the image of her scratching and fighting him, it mattered little that his own son was gazing at young Alysaun with the look of a moon-eyed calf.

"Would that I had a man's strength and skills," Alysaun sighed in despair. "As for my tears—long before your lord arrogantly disposed of Esmond's estates, I spilled the last of them." Rashly, Alysaun tore at her wimple and exposed the white column of her throat, daring de Bourney to draw his knife and end her misery. "The sharpness of your blade will bring no tears, nor will you hear a plea for swift mercy. 'Tis a better fate than what you have suggested."

Leaning close, Sanson studied the resolute set of her features. "I vow 'tis *you* who have no mercy, m'lady," he said in a low, husky tone. "I have erred in judging all Saxons to be simple-minded and dull, just as you have in lumping all Normans in the same bushel. A woman is a woman, no matter what her race or blood." He raised his goblet and added, "I salute your beauty and your brave spirit, and say you are as fine as any Norman lady of my acquaintance."

"Save your 'praise,' Lord Sanson. To my ears your compliment is akin to naming me a whore. I have little but my honorable name, and you sully it with so foul a comparison." Brian stared at her, swallowing hard before he risked a glance at his father's face. This time the lady had gone too far. God only knew what his sire would do to see that proud look vanish from her face.

"Once you may have thought your name honorable, Alysaun," Sanson snarled with a menacing scowl, "but when I've had my fill of laboring between your thighs and allow my men the same pleasure, you'll not hold your head so high. If you still manage a haughty demeanor after thirty men have known you, then, by God, I'll offer up an apology and give your pride its due." The first hint of her fear brought a pleased chuckle from him. "Shall we see it done here or retire to the privacy of the lord's chambers? I, for one, would find the cheers of a gallery an enhancement to the contest."

Her composure unsettled, Alysaun trembled, though she tried to keep her expression calm. Her earlier sympathy for Morwena's terror now washed back upon herself. The humiliation called up by de Bourney's boastful intentions sucked the defiance from her. She bowed her head, praying for some measure of rescue, knowing it was beyond her. Suddenly, from the least expected source, help came.

"Father, you did say earlier that I must sharpen my skills ere I wed," Brian said in a firm, bold voice. "I choose this time and this girl as my partner, and am eager to attend my lessons."

Sanson stared open-mouthed at Brian, the meekest of his sons, and, out of the corner of his eye, saw Alysaun raise her head. She was staring at Brian, her lovely mouth set in disbelief at his assertive calm. Apparently she had thought him a weakling and the least of her worries. His Brian was finally showing some signs of manhood; there was hope for the lad yet. Sanson faced Alysaun, a pleased grin baring his teeth.

"No, I will *not*," Alysaun said.

"Yes, with my heartiest approval, you *will*," Sanson insisted. "Or my Brian will break you like an untried filly and spill his seed before the lusty appreciation of our company. You've my leave to make the girl yours, son. Ride well but mind the chit's knees and nails."

"I'm well able to see the lady bedded without harm to myself, Father," Brian bragged as, rising, he seized Alysaun's hand and drew her to her feet. Some of the knights who had overheard the exchange were openly snickering over her predicament and laying bets on how well the match would proceed. Alysaun struggled against Brian's hold and found his long, thin fingers surprisingly strong. She tried to pull away from this newest indignity, but Brian bent with easy grace to catch her beneath arms and knees and raise her into his arms. This act elicited applause from the gathered throng of soldiers and brought a crimson blush of shame to heighten the angry color of Alysaun's cheeks. Fury prompted her to strike out at him but Brian avoided the blows and tossed her over his shoulder, carrying her off like captured plunder to the cheering encouragement of his fellow Normans.

Outside her chamber door, Brian bent to lift the latch, and Alysaun's fists thudded against his back. In French and English both, she called him every manner of vile dog and devil. Ignoring the stream of epithets, the young man crossed the room to deposit her upon the bed and left her to retrace his steps and secure the door. When he came back to stand beside the bed, Brian took a deep

225

breath and held up his hands in a show of peace. She looked all wildcat, muscles tensed to fight, azure eyes spitting fury. Her expression dared him to come closer and suffer the sharpness of her ready fingernails. "Pause and think before you vilify me further, m'lady," he requested. "Better I than my father and his company. You had little choice, but I was the best of that lot."

"You—you're no different," Alysaun insisted, indignant at the "choice" offered her. "Your manner wears a mild cloak, but what you seek is still rape. If you touch me I will . . . I will . . ."

Clearly she couldn't think of a properly intimidating threat, and her sputtering brought a laugh from Brian. "I'll not touch you, Alysaun, or take you against your will. 'Twas only a ruse to see you safe out of my father's company. You must admit your attitude drew his wrath upon you."

"I admit nothing but that I see through your continued pretense. You think to calm me with reasoned speech and then . . ." Alysaun shook her head in denial that he had spoken the truth. "No . . . why should I expect mercy from a Norman? You are as uncivilized as the wolf who sired you."

"Truly I am sorry for the troubles that have made you hate us so. We're not all barbarians—we Normans sing and dance, bleed and die in the same manner as your race. 'Tis a pity you've had no chance to see how lovely Normandy is. Savages could not have raised the spired cathedrals that soar heavenward with such grace nor create the sweet sounds of monks chanting of God's glory."

"I've seen your Normandy," Alysaun protested. "Why could you all not have stayed there and left us in peace? Your talk of God is strange for one spawned by such a heathen lot. How can you speak His name when your people stand on stolen soil and proclaim it theirs? William carried the pope's banner, but a man responsible for the rape and slaughter of innocents, who seeks to displace those who only defend their freedom and land, such a man cannot possess the Lord's sanction. And if he gave it them, then He is not *my* God."

" 'Twas a man, in the name of Christ, who settled that banner on King William," Brian claimed, disconcerted by her rejection of

God. "Men may err, but God cannot. If you repeat what I say, I'll name you a liar, but I have some sympathy with the suffering of the English. Too much blood has been spilled in God's name, too much spreading ambition justified by calling upon Him." Brian sighed, tired and weary from defending himself. "But these things always have been, and will be. Think not that you can change the nature of man."

"You speak the Lord's name with the reverence of a cleric. Am I to believe you feel none of the lust common to man, or do you wear your piety only to mask your base urges?"

"I was reared for the church, though fate has altered my plans to seek its peace. My two older brothers have died in the quest to secure England for Normandy, and my sire now looks to me to fulfill his desire for another generation of de Bourneys. Thus far, I have been found sadly lacking." He gestured toward the hall with a tilt of his head. "That business there—at this moment my lord father is crowing with the pride of a gamecock. He thinks you properly chastened for defying him and is doubly pleased that I finally have shown signs I am his true son and not a chaste monk."

Alysaun believed him and it showed in the relaxation of her taut muscles and the curiosity in her expression. "You . . . care nothing for women, then?"

Brian flushed at the unintentional insult to his virility. "Oh, I care," he said. "This is flesh, equipped with all the desires born to man. I see you think that because I do not assault you I am less of a man? You *are* a harsh judge, Alysaun. No, I find you very desirable, with features so alluring they could tempt a holy hermit from his vows."

Sensing now that she trusted him, Brian moved to sit next to her on the bed. " 'Tis only that my desire is well reined by years of temperance and study of the Scriptures. The great monastery of Cluny was my only passion, and now change comes slowly. I think . . . at some other place and time I would have pursued and tried to win your favor. We cannot, fair Saxon, change what we are,

227

but I'll not add a brutal, senseless violation to your misery, nor by some act of mine increase your hatred for my kind.''

Despite her relief at such unexpected courtesy, Alysaun was despondent. ''So we are allies for the night,'' she said with a wan smile. ''Come morning, what will you have to say to your father? Will you, who seem so honorable, lie to save face? Or shall I lie for you and blushingly admit how well you pleased me?''

Alysaun was teasing him but Brian had very little experience of a woman's humor of coquetry. He flushed, unable to look at her. ''Nay. I'll say naught but that the company was sweet and that we were both well pleased by what passed between us. If he is allowed some measure of pride in my accomplishments, 'twill keep him from harming you, m'lady.''

''You've a keen command of a well-turned phrase, Lord Brian,'' Alysaun said in praise. ''It calls to mind someone I once knew, or thought I knew.''

Brian looked up at the bitter sadness in her voice. ''Who was he, that the memory of him brings such an ache to your tone?''

''My husband, sir, though the marriage was dissolved and put aside. Brand had a way, when first we met, of plucking at my heart as easily as he did his lute strings. 'Tis all past now, come to naught.''

''I think he matters more than you admit, Lady Alysaun. ''Is he a Saxon?'' Alysaun shook her head. ''*Surely* not a *Norman*.''

His exclamation over that possibility evoked a broad smile from her and a careless shrug of her shoulders. 'Half-Norman,'' she explained. ''Just enough to be heartless. The other half was pure poet, all charm and wicked rogue.''

''There is no chance to mend your differences and—''

''Nay, none at all,'' Alysaun said curtly, cutting off his question. ''Brand has gone his way. If he did, indeed, love me, his love was shallow and fleeting. Too much has passed between us for me to hold hope of recapturing what was a pleasant interlude.''

Brian thought he glimpsed a hint of tears in her eyes, but a moment later she was smiling again as she changed the subject to his training for the monastery. Even as he related the dry, dull details of his long preparation to enter Cluny, he sensed he had only half her attention. Alysaun's eyes sparked with interest, but her thoughts were far off as she brooded about the man she believed she had lost.

10

Though Hereward and Brand had waited well past the appointed hour, no one from Havistock had appeared to exchange the ransom for Esmond's hide. Two weeks had passed, and with no word forthcoming, Hereward's patience was now at an end. In his disappointment, sharpened by the expectation of seeing Alysaun for the first time since the morning of his arrest, Brand had demanded that they ride down on Havistock immediately, but, removed from such emotional involvement, Hereward had vetoed the idea.

Now, though, he had finally agreed that, Saxon hold be damned, he'd extract the promised pledge from the manor's coffers, even if the looting meant its destruction. His men were gathered about a table of counsel in Ely's hall and though their leader's word was final, the planning of the raid was open to discussion.

"I suppose it's possible the steward was waylaid," one of the men suggested. "Or stopped by an enemy patrol and questioned."

Frida slipped quietly to her husband's side and refreshed his ale tankard, retiring to a spot near the hearth to listen to the talk. For the first time her son had been allowed the privilege of joining the counsel, and she was more worried by the thought that he'd soon want to accompany Hereward on one of his raids than by the subject under discussion. Devon had his father's broad shoulders but at twelve still had a way to go before he attained Hereward's height and brawn. His face, touched by an eager longing to be a man, still had the soft, rounded set of boyhood.

"Something's amiss," Hereward answered, raising the tankard to quench his thirst. "I know it as sure as all my scars ache." He didn't care to move his men in any raid without accurate, advance information of their objective. "You know the lay of Havistock," he said with a resigned sigh, addressing Brand, who sat to his right. "Acquaint us with its features, and we will ride against it on the morrow."

Brand grinned. This was the moment he'd been waiting for. When Alysaun had failed to appear at Grouneswold, Esmond, bound to his saddle by ropes, had taunted him. "I told you she wanted nothing to do with you," he had claimed. "What more proof do you need to accept the fact you've lost her?" Brand had come to believe it, but he had to see her one more time, to demand an explanation of her faithlessness, to make her believe the scorn of his own repudiation of her.

Brand described the approach to the manor and the small number of its defenders, and was finishing his account of the manor's layout when a loud commotion in the bailey beyond the keep disturbed Hereward's concentration. "A curse on such noise," he growled, and looked around for his wife. "Frida, see who is disturbing us and command them to be quiet."

Frida hurried out of the hall, her son scrambling up from his seat at the table to satisfy his own curiosity and follow. Five minutes later she was back, leading two men to the head of the table where her husband sat. Recognizing the shorter of the two, Brand leaned closer to Hereward and apprised him of the fact that the man was Esmond's steward, Harivig.

Harivig paused before Hereward and tugged respectfully at his forelock. "Beggin' your pardon, sir, I was supposed to meet wi' you at Grouneswold a fortnight past. Harivig I am, steward of Havistock."

"How did you come to find Ely . . . and what reason have you for failing to make the exchange?" Even with his tall, broad figure seated, Hereward could be fiercely intimidating. His deep, gravelly voice and dark scowl set the steward quaking in his boots.

"When I said who I was, sire, one o' your men brought me through the marshes. I'd've ne'er made the way myself." He swallowed hard as the rebel leader frowned more deeply. "Sir, I had to get through t'you. You needn't think I know the way in—your man was careful to cover my eyes wi' a blindfold."

"Enough, man. Why was the ransom not delivered?"

"Havistock is in Norman hands now, sire. Lord Sanson de Bourney arrived with his heir and men-at-arms the night before we was t'meet you at dawn."

Brand abandoned his reserved study, tensing as he leaned forward to question the steward. "Why didn't Lady Alysaun send you sooner?"

"I managed to get away late that same night, sir," Harivig replied, coloring with shame as he explained his delay, "but I stopped in Daning Green to 'borrow' an apple from a market cart and the bailiff tossed me in a hold. Just escaped last night and made m'way here right off."

Almost reluctant to ask, Brand inquired how Alysaun had fared with the new owners of Havistock. "If they've harmed her . . ." He let the threat dangle, realizing how much time had passed since this fellow de Bourney had taken over.

Harivig hesitated to admit what he knew. Brand de Reynaud was no longer the lady's husband, but clearly he still cared. With others listening, the recounting of her fate would only deepen the man's anguish. "She . . . seemed to be bearing up, m'lord, but . . ."

"Finish your tale, man, or my knife will—"

Hereward turned to Brand and cautioned him not to be so rash.

"Harivig will be a help in taking the manor," he said in a hushed, calming tone. "Go on, steward. Lady Alysaun is well but...what?"

"De Bourney is no better than most of his countrymen, m'lord. After his men had glutted themselves on Sir Esmond's stores, they were allowed to take whichever of Havistock's women they found pleasing." Harivig lowered his gaze, his pudgy face mottled with shame at the memory. "Lady Alysaun was given over to the new lord's son, a gift brazenly offered before all those assembled in the hall."

Hereward's men had accepted Brand as one of their own. Though they knew little of what had severed the relationship, it was common knowledge that the lady in question had been Brand's wife. Now, in their sympathy for him, an embarrassed quiet settled over the table, a quiet broken only by the scrape of the bench as Brand abruptly stalked away, his hands clenched furiously into tight fists that corded the muscles of his arms.

Behind him, Hereward's voice mirrored his friend's frustration. Brand heard nothing beyond a terse command to Harivig to sit at the table and answer their questions. The torture of the whip applied to his bare back at the sheriff's command was as nothing compared to the pain Brand knew now. He had endured each whistling crack of the lash in silence, the thought of Alysaun's face a buffer to the strokes that sliced into his flesh.

When Hereward's daring midnight raid had secured his release from the filth and darkness of the stone outbuilding behind Fitz Walther's headquarters, Brand had been barely recognizable. The lash stripes crisscrossing his back had not been attended to and were black with dried blood; his face had been a mass of reddened bruises from the morning's beating, his eyes swollen shut above the straight, aquiline nose that had been broken in two places.

The first days of sanctuary at Ely had been a blur. Hot and feverish from the infection that festered in his torn back, he had tossed in a wild delirium, fighting so strongly Torfrida's efforts to draw the poison from his flesh that Hereward had him tied belly down on the bed. The rebel leader had alternated shifts with his wife, watching over him until the poultices of yarrow, saxifrage, and comfrey had eased the festering wounds and the daily doses of a buckbean and honey infusion had lessened the heat of his fever.

Only when Frida pronounced him well enough had Hereward spoken of his meeting with Alysaun. During his brief, hard captivity, Brand had bitterly reproached himself for his own gullibility. The sheriff's possession of the brooch meant someone at Havistock had plotted against him, and the only person with the means and guile to set the trap was Esmond. At first, when Hereward had told Brand of the annulment, he was so crazed by the news he unthinkingly called his friend a liar. Hereward had been tolerant, recognizing how deeply Brand loved his wife, trying to explain his impression that she hadn't seemed to be acting of her own free will.

With Alysaun's ring in his hand, Brand had heard nothing, only the echo of his own heart naming him a fool, an idiot who had seen love where none existed, a man who had trusted only to have trust betrayed.

At first he had hated her enough to want her dead. Any woman who possessed the power to make a man senseless with longing and then to cast him aside as easily as she had done did not deserve to go on breathing. And yet, when he'd had time to think, to remember, Brand found it hard to believe she had been so artful. Memories rose to haunt him and mock the core of bitterness that set him brooding, memories of a girl whose pride and beauty had shone brightly even when she was draped in rags. Memories of a laughing Alysaun, her cornsilk waves crowned by a wreath of wildflowers, teasing him in a game of chase across a grassy meadow touched with daffodils. And of Alysaun reclining on a sun-dappled bed of sweet grass, her eyes so blue they shamed the vault of heaven overhead, suddenly becoming serious as she lifted a slender arm to offer him a spray of violets and, more, herself.

Oh, yes, he had thought himself the bold, the accomplished lover who with controlled emotions would take his ease with the bounty cast his way and come away sated but free of commitment. No woman, regardless of her beauty, could bind the carefree, arrogant spirit who wandered where he pleased and took to the road when a female showed the slightest hint of possessiveness. Yet in those leisurely, contented weeks Brand had spent in making love to Alysaun's sweet, yielding body, a subtle, unheeded change had crept over him.

A sudden glance from beneath her thick golden lashes set his heart racing; each shift of silk that had artlessly displayed the curves of her body and aroused desire as well as the jealousy that had made him glower suspiciously at any man who, with a look or word, seemed to find her beauty an enchantment.

He wanted her back; his pride demanded satisfaction for the many long nights he had lain awake and tormented himself with visions of Esmond making love to her. The thought of that lean-haunched youth grunting and sweating over Alysaun's fair, delicate form became an obsession that haunted even his waking hours.

Esmond had played the role of friend and lured him into a trap; Alysaun's betrayal was far more cruel. She had used her feminine wiles to snare him, making of her soft vulnerability and sweet voice the fetters that bound him to her, chains that could not be struck off unless he faced her with his anger and his own rejection.

Now, to add insult to injury, another man had lain with her. Though it seemed a just punishment, Brand could take little pleasure in the idea that someone else had known Alysaun, possessed her, even if he had been dealt scratches from her long, oval nails as she fought him.

Brand came out of his brooding melancholy at the sound of the wooden benches scraping the stone floor. Still, he faced the hearth, unwilling to meet the sympathetic glances of his companions. Only when the shuffle of booted feet had ceased and the hall was quiet did he turn, to find Hereward staring at him with an odd look of tried patience.

He approached Brand and started to speak, then gave up the effort with a heavy, disgruntled sigh, his thick, wiry mustache twitching as the corners of his mouth turned down in a grimace. "If you've some complaint to make," Brand snapped, his temper barely reined by the bond of fellowship they shared, "then spit it out, man. If we ride at dawn's first light, I've my weapons to sharpen."

Hereward frowned, at odds with his own temper. Brand had reasons aplenty to be bitter but this dark, indulgent brooding of his was unseemly for so fine a man. The marks of the lash had healed over with scar tissue; the swelling was gone from the breaks in his nose. Rather than destroy the straight, handsome angles of his face, the slight crook of his nose had given Brand the fierce look of an eagle; ladies would no doubt find it a virile face, and men would think twice before stirring his wrath.

Seldom at a loss for words, Hereward was unsure of how to phrase his feelings of disappointment with Brand's recent indulgence in self-pity, with his sullen musings of revenge against Alysaun. "You may not need them, son," he said finally. "My conscience would trouble me less if you stayed behind on this raid. I don't know that I care to ride with a man whose value as a fighting man is diminished by preoccupation with his own selfish goals."

The color drained from Brand's face. How could Hereward claim to be a friend and deny him the right to fight the Normans who had, in taking possession of Havistock, seized what belonged to him? The color returned, spreading a dull, red flush of anger across his features. "Annulment be damned—Alysaun is still my wife," he insisted indignantly, "and I will have her back. I've given you no reason to doubt my loyalty or to believe that I would not repay the debt of gratitude I owe you with loyal service."

" 'Tis not your loyalty I doubt, Brand. Nor do I find you ungrateful. Your aims are too much at odds with my purpose in plundering Rede's manor. I seek the money still hidden from de Bourney's greed, and I want to free Lady Alysaun from the harsh captivity she's known at those bastards' hands." Hereward tucked his thumbs into his belt, his broad shoulders stiff with challenge. "You, on the other hand, care only to effect her rescue and make her suffer for the imagined humiliation she has brought you."

"Imagined?" The reply was more than indignant, it was voiced in such a wounded tone of hauteur that Hereward stared in open-mouthed dismay at Brand's narrow, self-serving view. "I gave that . . . woman my love and respect, both of which she tossed aside when they no longer served her, and you mock my right to feel slighted, to call the lying bitch to task for her part in seeing me fall victim to the sheriff's 'justice'?"

"I know well how much you suffered, but you've nursed your wounds past the time needed for recovery. If anyone should know your anger, spend it upon Esmond's head, for I believe with all my heart that your wife was as much his victim as you." Gathering what remained of his patience, Hereward made a last attempt to reason with Brand.

"Hear me out, my friend," he said in a slow, measured tone, as if he were dealing with a stubborn, recalcitrant child. "If you had acted stealthily to rid yourself of someone's company, would you make any effort to secure that person's freedom? No, yet this is what your wife did. If there was the barest chance that the person would be free to exact revenge for your guile, would you not let him rot and assure your own safety? Your wife, the woman you intemperately call a bitch, traveled miles to see that I learned of your capture. Such effort, despite the little she could say in Rede's presence, spoke of her love more eloquently than any words could."

The reasoning was sound, finally penetrating the stony fortifications Brand had raised to protect his feelings against further pain, the shell that had isolated him in misery. Still he was reluctant to let go of the righteous indignation that had been his sleeping companion all the many weeks since his rescue. "If she loves me so well, why has Alysaun not sent some message of concern for my well-being?" Brand inquired. "She knew how to reach you at Peterborough, she sent Harivig here to give word that the ransom was still safe . . . if the love she professed for me is real, she shows an odd reticence to reassure me of its existence."

Hereward sighed, pleased that at least he had Brand doubting how fair and true his judgment of the lady had been. "If I were to hold the same measuring stick to both of you, Brand, 'twould be a close call as to who was more proud. 'Tis my guess that since she went to some trouble to see you saved, Alysaun expected some word from you. None forthcoming, she likely found reason to believe you blamed her for your ordeal. In that belief, the girl was correct in assuming your silence condemned her.''

Brand hadn't taken a moment since the shocking news of the annulment to think of Alysaun's feelings. Aside from their argument that last morning, she had given him no reason to consider her discontented with their match. Indeed, between the time of the wedding and their parting, Alysaun had shown every sign of a woman well pleased with her lot, her beauty seeming to unfold in answer to his attentions like a blossom warming to the sun. ''If Alysaun is innocent of involvement,'' he said in glum admission, ''then I have lost her by my own mad recrimination. How strange it is that love stirs us to be both generous and selfish.''

''Verily, 'tis a two-headed coin,'' Hereward agreed with a wide, ear-to-ear grin, ''but the decision as to which side you present makes the difference, lad.''

''Ah . . . easy advice from a man who feels secure in his wife's devotion,'' Brand said. ''I can only hope the distance to Havistock muffled the piteous grumblings of my wounded vanity.'' He shook his head, his deep frown directed inward at his own folly. Finally his eyes met Hereward's in a sheepish, regretful glance. ''I see it now—I've been a bastard, a selfish, thin-skinned bastard.''

''Aye, but just how much o' one, Alysaun need never know,'' Hereward replied in a harsh but warranted criticism. ''For all she knows, you've been abed all this time, recovering from your wounds.'' Like the paw of a great, oversized bear, Hereward's closed hand dealt Brand a good-humored punch at his shoulder as he teased, ''I wouldn't worry too much, lad. One look at your newly reshaped beak and Alysaun'll forget all thought of reproach.''

Brand had forgotten the change in his appearance. Hereward's jest called up an altogether different worry. What if she found his face ugly? He swallowed hard as he imagined her shrinking back at her

239

first sight of him, raising a hand to touch the still-tender breaks in his nose.

Realizing his error, Hereward moved quickly to mend it and reinforce Brand's vanity. "The nose gives you a warrior's look, son. Just last week, Frida mentioned how the crook did add character to a face she thought too finely handsome." Brand looked doubtful. "Come and ask her if she didn't say so. And you know full well how the Breton lass, Maud, has been mooning over you. 'Twas only in your brooding that you ignored her passionate sighs."

Hereward looked so eager to convince him that Brand put aside his worry. He was the same man who had aroused Alysaun to abandoned cries of passion. If she loved him still, a nose with a different angle would not make him any less capable a lover. In fact, as he asked his friend to be seated again and apprise him of the exact details of their raid against Havistock, it occurred to Brand that Alysaun might find the difference in his looks more to her liking. Certainly, as Hereward had claimed, it would be a visible reminder of what he had suffered because Rede had so coveted her beauty for himself.

Alysaun had lain awake for hours, tossing restlessly in the comfort of her soft, wide bed. Though she was weary when she retired, the moment her head had touched the pillow, her mind had turned to worrying, the closeness of the shadowed room adding to the ever-present fears that were diminished in the bright sunlight of day.

Sighing in frustration, she sat up and brushed aside the bed curtain to glance at the glazed window. Such a luxury was rare and costly but, then, when Elfleda had taken her rest in this spacious chamber, she had spared no expense to increase her own comfort. The dark of night still blackened the world beyond the window, but it could not be too much longer before the sky would lighten with the new day.

Alysaun lay back, frowning. Another day approached and lessened her hope that the message she had sent to Ely by Harivig had been delivered. By now there should have been some response, a reply in one of the lightning assaults on the manor for which Hereward had gained a bold reputation. He would have come immediately; the fact that Havistock still remained in Norman hands over a fortnight past the arrival of its new lord meant some mishap had befallen the steward.

Pulling at the thin material of her kirtle, bunched around her thighs in testimony to her uneasy tossing, Alysaun straightened the shift and drew it down around her ankles. She was unused to sleeping with such an encumbrance, but with Brian sharing the chamber, modesty was far more important than the comfort of a sheet covering her bare skin.

Wondering if she had awakened him, she peered through the curtains to her right. No, he was resting peacefully, his chest rising and falling in shallow, even breaths. The look of an innocent child, Brian had. Despite what must have been a very uncomfortable arrangement, he had slept on a makeshift bed of fur throws covering the rush-and-earthen floor since that first night, the night he had saved her from his father's sure intent to see her ravished. The arrangement could have been reversed, but Brian was too considerate to insist upon the bed for himself.

Each morning Alysaun rose early, before the servants could enter and discover their ruse. By the time the household was awake for the new day, the fur throws had been stored away in the chest that lay at the end of the canopied bed. She owed him much, this gentle, good-natured young man. In his own way, Brian was as much a victim of ambition, his father's and the King's, as she.

Brian had his own cross to bear in being denied the peace of a life in the monastery. He bore his father's crude jesting with uncommon forbearance and tried to act as a buffer between Sanson's violent temper and the people upon whom it was released. Never had she met so learned a man. Even the learning of her own father, who had traveled extensively across Europe and could read and write four languages, could not compare with Brian de Bourney's wealth of knowledge.

Brian was a natural storyteller, a young man with the gift of weaving tales of magic kingdoms with hero-kings and dragons threatening fair maidens. Usually quiet and unassuming, he would become a different person when he recounted these tales; his pale gray eyes would light with warmth and his voice would rise and fall in an enchanting timbre that made the far-off lands and people seem real. He knew the lives of the saints as well, and would also quote Vergil's *Aeneid* and the words of Aristotle and Herodutus, Homer and Plato, offering an endless stream of ancient wisdom that left Alysaun awed.

Alysaun had come to realize in that fortnight that a man and woman could actually be friends, as much companions as two men. She had told him about Brand, everything except the fact that he was with Hereward at Ely. In answer to his inquiry about her parents, Alysaun had confided the entire, dismal story and, touched by the empathy he showed her, had wept unashamedly until the bitterness she had retained was exorcised by the spent tears. Brian found her as interested in his life and confided his worry about how she would fare when his father finally demanded he marry and bring his bride over from Normandy. He pledged that when that day came, he would see her safely escorted to a convent.

The other women at Havistock had not fared so well as she. The ladies of rank were taken by several of de Bourney's knights. When their husbands refused to swear fealty to Sanson, he had them dragged into the manor yard and executed by sword. Elfleda, ever one to find the best advantage in any situation, by suppressing her arrogant demeanor had achieved some rank in the hall by plying Sanson with such dulcet coquetry that he took her into his own bed.

And Morwena, poor girl, she had resigned herself to the jealous hold of the young, raven-haired knight who had fought over her and won her that night in the hall. Though she had been allowed to attend Alysaun in the daylight hours, her evenings were spent under

Walter de Shailles's watchful, possessive guardianship. On occasion, when he thought her gaze had lingered too long on another man, Walter was not above reprimanding the girl with the back of his hand.

Alysaun drifted back to sleep now, but it was an uneasy, light sleep, troubled by shadowed dreams of bloodied men hacking away at each other with swords and axes, filled with the wailing terror of women who cowered from the fighting, their fear mutiplied by the knowledge that they were the spoils that would fall to the victors. Late hours turned toward morning and when Alysaun startled awake out of her nightmares, the light beyond the window showed a dark violet. Her hair was damp with sweat, clustering in ringlets around her perspiring forehead and temples, her shift clinging to her skin.

She lay back, willing her racing pulse to slow. In the quiet of the room, her breathing sounded like the panting of a frightened animal. Across her slightly rounded belly, a tiny ripple of movement, as gentle as a breeze-swept wave washing the surface of a pond, drew her hand there. An odd blend of wonder and fear widened her eyes and glazed the blue of their irises with a sheen of tears. Only two people knew her secret—one had guessed; the other she had told.

At first Alysaun had ignored the signs that she was carrying a child. She had been sick only once, the night following the morning of Brand's capture. That, she had thought at the time, was a physical reaction to her distress. The cessation of her monthly flow of bleeding had been a relief, and again she had rationalized that it must be from her anxiety over Brand. Morwena was the one who had guessed, and when she had brought up the possibility, Alysaun had snapped at her with uncustomary sharpness, then dissolved into a fit of weeping that had confirmed the girl's suspicions.

The slight curve of her belly, the quickening that alerted her to the baby's first efforts to stretch its tiny muscles, this growing evidence of the seed planted in her fertile womb made her at once proud and terror-stricken. There was no doubt the child was Brand's, for she was too many months along to worry that Esmond might be its sire.

When Brian had hesitantly mentioned her unsettled temper, Alysaun confided her plight. At first he was shocked, then angry because, for whatever his reason, her husband had abandoned her. The surprise of hearing him swear an oath for the first time since she had met him brought her out of her melancholy, self-pitying despair; and with a laugh, she had teased him over the unusual, impious cursing. That had been yesterday afternoon. She had discussed her pregnancy with him several times and had rejected all his suggestions, especially the idea that she should send word to Brand to see if he chose to acknowledge his responsibility.

Though the thin, nearly transparent curtains and shadowed darkness made it impossible to see Brian except as a vague, curled form asleep on the floor, Alysaun turned her face toward him with a fond smile. In his kindness, he had offered to brave his father's temper and scorn to request that he be allowed to wed her. It was a sweet gesture, typical of his good-hearted warmth, but one she had adamantly rejected.

Somehow, deep in her most intimate thoughts, Alysaun still hoped Brand would come for her. It was a vain hope after so long an absence without any word, without any show of concern for her fate, but a hope she clung to. Soon enough there would be no way of hiding her swelling belly, and the shame of bearing a child alone and bereft of its father would add to her misery. Still, her pride ruled her emotions; she would *not* send to Ely and let Brand know he had left her with child. After all the bitterness of their separation, she wanted him back but not merely to acknowledge his paternity. If he came at all, he must come because he loved her. Alysaun sighed. Beyond the window the light had altered from deep violet to mauve, heralding the beginning of another day. Closing her eyes, Alysaun turned on her right side and brought her knees up, snuggling beneath the sheet in a determined effort to rest, if only for the baby's sake.

Outside, in the woods surrounding the manor, the usual sounds of the forest denizens were muted. In this hour before dawn the misted weald was always alive with birds calling and the keening cries of predators stealing home before the sunlight exposed their vulnerability to the two-legged animal who inhabited the timbered den on the hill. Now, though, they sensed the presence of Hereward's raiders, ranged throughout the heavy brush that edged the manor, and moved in caution.

A guard on night watch wearily paced the yard, an eye trained on the eastern horizon, eager for the sunrise, which would end his duty. He yawned and stretched, exasperated by the need to stay awake the night long and guard against . . . what—the stupid, dull-witted peasants? The slack-jawed English commoner posed no threat to a keep fortified by stalwart Norman warriors.

He glanced at the sky again and smiled. Only a few minutes more and the sun would crest the trees, ending his watch. He wandered around the side of the building, yawning widely one more time as he fumbled at his tunic and chausses, for he was overdue to answer nature's call. He had only a moment to feel the relief of pressure against his full bladder before a hand shot from behind him to cover his mouth, a half second to recognize his error in leaving his post before a wickedly sharp blade sliced across his jugular vein and silenced all perception.

The night watchman slumped to the ground, his life's blood pooling from his gaping throat, his sightless eyes fixed in a wide, surprised stare, his cheek against the dirt he had wet like a dog.

Brand slipped around the corner and, keeping close to the shadows of the eaves, paused before the heavy oaken door. Behind him, Hereward and the others, hidden by the brush, were ready to spring forward and attack once the guard within the hall had been dealt with. Boldly striking the door with his fist, Brand called out a gruff demand in Norman French, acting out the role of the yard watch, belligerent and impatient to end his long duty.

Inside, the guard, roused out of his fitful dozing on an uncomfortable bench near the entry, grumbled that he was coming and cursed his watchmate Ragnar's insistent pounding to be let in. Still dulled by sleep, he lifted the heavy bar securing the door and swung it open. One deep thrust of Brand's ready sword silenced the man's startled cry of warning. It gurgled in his throat and came rushing out of the corner of his mouth with the stream of bright crimson flowing down his rumpled tunic. With the sword point buried in the guard's neck muscles, Brand had to use his free hand to shove the body free.

Dismissing all thought of the guard's crumpled form, Brand poised tensely, alert for any other signs of defense. He had expected the house dogs to come running, howling at the scent of blood, but the hall was dark and silent. The Saxons' timing had been perfect— even the early-rising servants were still abed.

Retracing his steps, avoiding the slick of blood that matted the rushes near the dead guard's body, Brand stepped to the door and signaled Hereward with a whistling call. He waited just a second to see the rebel lead his men up the hill toward the yard. They emerged like wraiths from the heavy, shifting layers of ground fog that sparkled now with the reflection of the sun's bright rays.

The raiders kept to Hereward's command for silence, streaming into the hall behind Brand. Brand headed for the chamber he had shared with Alysaun while the others moved to plunder the great hall and the storerooms of any valuable pieces that could be carried off. Now that it was a Norman keep, there would be no hesitation about torching Havistock, but before the firebrands could be tossed to light the summer-dry thatching covering the roof, the Saxon occupants would be herded to safety and a battle fought with the defending Norman retainers.

Brand's heart was in his throat as he approached the door to his old room. At this hour Alysaun and the man who shared her bed would be asleep, but just the thought of coming upon a man lying next to her, close to Alysaun's bare flesh, so enraged him that for a brief, dizzy moment the door faded in the black haze of his fury. To his left past the timbers dividing the aisle from the great hall, a bloodcurdling howl issued from the throat of one of his companions, the old war cry of the English warrior, so reminiscent of the Viking's savage call to battle, as the man met in a clash of swords with one of the alerted enemy.

Now that their presence was discovered, more wild, unnerving cries echoed. The house awoke and defenders streamed into the hall.

246

Brand roused himself from his momentary trance and kicked at the door. It shuddered with the force of his kick, the latch splintering, the leather hinges ripping near the top of the door to leave it hanging at a crazy angle. Sword in hand, knife at the ready, Brand plunged into the shadows, crossing the room and avoiding objects more from memory than by vision.

At the splintering of the door and the noise beyond it in the hall, a furiously sputtered string of oaths issued from behind the bed hangings. Brand changed direction, sweeping around the bed to the left, pausing warily to see if the man sprang forth armed with a weapon. The swearing ceased, and the curtains were tugged back by a broad, freckled hand covered by wiry red and silver hair.

Though he had recognized the sounds of an attack, the sight of a fiercely scowling raider poised next to his bed with a two-bladed sword directed at his heart sent a shiver of alarm rippling down Sanson de Bourney's spine. His own weapon lay an arm's length away. Without thinking or asking quarter, the Norman lord lunged for the sword hilt, his forward surge impaling him on the point of the raider's sword, slipping through muscle and lung to pierce his heart.

Brand knew not whom he had killed, only that the man was a fool to have tried for his sword. The weight of the Norman's body burdened Brand's wrist and he put his knee against the massive, barrel chest and pushed, freeing his sword. Thrusting back the curtains again, he reached within and found a slender wrist, calling out Alysaun's name to ease her fear as he pulled.

It was difficult to say who was the most dumbfounded, Brand or Elfleda. Neither had expected to see the other. Brand reacted first, dropping her hand as if he had touched a snake, his brow knit in puzzlement that rapidly changed to anger. For once the woman didn't appear haughty—she couldn't in the face of her nudity and the bluish bruises on her neck where her Norman lover had drawn the flesh against his teeth in passionate kisses. "How the mighty hath fallen," Brand sneered. "Where is my wife?"

Bridling under his contemptuous gaze, Elfleda toyed with the idea of refusing to answer. Though he had awakened desires long suppressed, she had no thought for her dead lover. Brand sensed her thought and laid his sword point, still smeared with Sanson's blood, against the still-firm white flesh of her breast. "The bitch is in the chamber that was mine," she admitted grudgingly, pale at the cold prick of the sword, at the even colder look in Brand de Reynaud's eyes. The sword moved and she held her breath, but Brand only wiped the blood across the sheet bunched at her breasts and turned away. "You'll not find her alone, de Reynaud," she called after him in a taunt. "These days Alysaun's thighs part for another, for the son of this bastard you did me the service of silencing."

Already, during the time he had spent in the chamber, the hall was beginning to fill with smoke from small, scattered fires started by the spill of oil from lamps carelessly knocked aside in the one-to-one skirmishes between the raiders and Havistock's Norman defenders. Brand hurried along the aisle seeking the large bedchamber near the solar that had been Elfleda's when she was the manor's mistress. Suddenly, out of the billow of acrid, choking smoke, a Norman knight stepped into his path. Brand's set mouth was grim as he took on his opponent and met him in a charge that sent his weapon clashing against the defender's steel with a metallic ring and a spark of metal against metal.

When the first wolflike howls penetrated her room, Alysaun startled out of her exhausted sleep, unsure whether she had dreamed them. The brightness of the morning sun streamed through the glazed window, leaving the portions of the room where its rays did not reach shadowed and dark. Then the shouts of men fighting, the dying cries of the wounded followed—all were too real to be a nightmare.

Throwing the bed covers aside, she slipped out of bed to find Brian awake and dressing, buckling on his scabbard as she paused near the end post, still bewildered by the sudden disruption of her sleep. She rubbed her eyes, trying to clear her head of the fog of weariness that dulled her thoughts. Who would . . . the answer to her silent question hit her with the force of a gale wind, blowing away the dazed, muddled feeling in a cold rush of reality.

Hereward had come at last, and Brand. He must be out there somewhere. Just as suddenly as her mind had cleared, she realized the danger to Brian. Hurrying to his side, Alysaun clutched at his arm, desperate to stay him from leaving the safety of her room. "Brian... please, stop, you can't go."

"Must," he replied, breathless from rushing. Still half asleep himself, it did not occur to him that anyone mounting an assault against the manor would be her people, only that she was a lady in need of protection, only that his father needed his sword arm to repel the raid. "Get back in bed, Alysaun," he ordered firmly, drawing his sword and checking to make sure his knife was handy at his belt. "With any luck—"

Alysaun clung stubbornly to Brian's arm, tears spilling down her cheeks. "You do not understand," she insisted as she stamped her foot in frustration. "Brian, those men fighting without are—" The rush of explanation was abruptly cut off by the sound of a mighty thud against the door. It slammed open, rocking with the force of another kick, and Hereward's huge shape filled the portal, his shoulder-length blond hair and thick mustache damp with sweat and grayed by soot, his sword, the mighty, two-handed battle sword, smeared with blood. Puffs of smoke drifted into the room from the aisle as he paused to wipe his eyes and clear his throat of the smoke.

The first sight Hereward's smoke-filled eyes took in was Alysaun, clad only in a thin shift, her face so white and terrified his only thought was to save her from the young Norman lad who stood beside her, his own face as pale as Alysaun's despite a grip so strong upon the hilt of his drawn sword that it reddened his knuckles. Alysaun screamed, stretching out a hand as Hereward stalked toward them, cautious of Brian's every movement. "No... *don't*... he's my—"

Brian thrust her away and began to raise his weapon. For a second's pause, an eon of a second, during which he considered

Alysaun's recognition of the wild-eyed giant and her cry of warning, it occurred to him that he might be facing Brand and he hesitated.

At the same moment that Hereward took advantage of the youth's pause to thrust his sword arm forward, Alysaun threw herself in front of Brian. Hereward saw her move, the flash of white silk slipping between his weapon and its target and even as his mind recoiled at the foolish act, he stayed his thrust, cursing her with an angry exclamation as the sharp blade tip sliced through the silk and nicked her shoulder.

Time seemed to spin out with shocking slowness as Brian saw the blood well out of the cut on Alysaun's shoulder, the spreading stain contrasting with the white of her kirtle. With that sight he knew a rage so great it overwhelmed him, an ugly coil of hatred that was utterly foreign to his gentle soul. Again he pushed her away, determined to kill the man who had marred her perfect beauty with a wound.

Brian lunged forward, revenge strengthening his grip, and sparks flew as his blade struck against Hereward's. The man outweighed him by thirty pounds or more and towered some six inches over him, but in defending Alysaun, Brian knew no weakness. Again and again the metallic clang of steel meeting steel rang out. Alysaun had slipped to her knees, her back against the bed, unaware of her own sobbing as she watched the struggle, unable to shout for them to cease for fear Brian would turn at the cry and fall with Hereward's sword through him.

Thick, white smoke tinged with charred black debris poured into the room, lending an unreal, nightmarish effect to the battle. Suddenly a figure emerged from the aisle, a tall warrior who bent over in a fit of choking before he could clear the smoke from his nose and throat, a man whose reddish locks were tinted gray with ash. His appearance drew Alysaun's attention for a moment, and she had only vaguely recognized Brand when a grunt of pain brought her sharply back to the fight. Brian was doubled over; the length of Hereward's sword had gone through his ribs, its bloody point protruding from his back.

The lad was done for, but he had put forth a valiant effort. Hereward pulled at his blade and caught the man's shoulder, easing him down to the floor. There was a noise behind him and he whirled, expecting to find another Norman at his back, but as he recognized Brand's soot-streaked face his defensive move to raise his sword slacked.

Oblivious of them both, Alysaun stumbled to her feet and came to where Brian lay, his features twisted into a mask of pain, his eyes clouding as he stared up at her. She sank down, her arm throbbing but forgotten in horror at the blood that soaked his tunic. His fingers were cold when she grasped the hand he raised; his voice spoke a rattle of words so soft she had to bend close to hear.

"Fai . . . led you w-when . . ." Brian's voice was so weak it took every ounce of concentration to make out his stuttered, broken phrases. "G-God keep you, Alys . . . I . . . pray . . ." There were no more words, only a cough that sent a tiny river of blood flowing from his mouth as his head canted, features slack.

Alysaun was aware of nothing. Brian's head lay against her lap, his lifeless fingers clutched tightly in her grasp, clutched to her breasts. Somehow she felt the tears that fell from her cheeks would bring color flooding back into his drawn face, life back into the loose sprawl of limbs. Rocking slightly, she whispered his name over and over, calling him in a voice dazed by shock.

The misery in her posture, her anguished repetition of the name Brian, cut through Brand more painfully than a sword thrust. He gaped at her, ignoring the thickening smoke that drifted like the fog of the marshes. He was totally bewildered by Alysaun's grieving and glanced away to find Hereward as puzzled as he was.

"Take her out or we'll all choke to death in this damned heat and smoke," Hereward ordered brusquely, adding, "Mind you, her right shoulder's bleeding . . . and watch the bodies in the aisle." Calmer than anyone else in the room, he crossed to the bed and tore at the curtains, tossing them to Brand to use as cover against inhaling too much smoke. Then, as if there were no fire licking at the timbered hall, he took the time to lift the mattress and recover the linen pouches heavy with the clink of coins.

Brand moved to obey, still benumbed by the sight of his wife, his Alysaun, weeping as if the light had gone out of her world. Even while he felt the ugly emotion of jealousy settle over him like a pall, Brand knew a certain respect for the dead Norman. Something in him, some quality he had possessed, had deeply moved Alysaun. Brand stepped forward and gently slipped his hands beneath her arms. She made no protest as he drew her to her feet and lifted her unresisting body into his arms. Like a woman blinded, she accepted help without seeing his face or acknowledging him.

Covering her mouth and nose with the ripped linen, Brand moved cautiously into the aisle, making his way from memory past the timbered columns, brushing against one occasionally to give him a reference point in the clouded air. The heat was scorching, burning at his lungs with every breath, panicking Brand with his inability to draw clean air into his throat.

Hereward followed on his heels, the money bags clinking with each loping stride of his long legs. Just as he reached the front of the hall and the door, a roar of splintering wood sent a wall of flame rushing at him as the vaulted roof of the great hall collapsed. Moving in unbelievable speed for a man of his size, the rebel gave a leap beyond the doorway and landed ignobly on his rump, rolling to smother the cinders that had begun to burn his mantle. Beyond him, gathered in small groups facing the inferno consuming the manor, the people who had served as its staff watched the gray columns of smoke rise, awed by the occasional belch of red-orange flames. Hereward scrambled to his feet, holding the rescued pledge money aloft, and at his exultant grin, a common cry of triumph went up from his men.

The cheering was cut off by a shouted command from their leader. " 'Twas a good morning's work, my stalwarts, but unless we make haste to seek our stronghold, the smoke of yonder fire will have the sheriff alert to our work. Mount up . . . we're for Ely and a celebration the likes of which you've never seen.''

Hereward moved amongst the throng of Havistock's people, offering sanctuary to the homeless ladies, and bed, board, and a share of future spoils to any able-bodied man willing to join his cause. The servants were told to disperse and seek the help of the nearby villagers of Daning Green, many of whom were their relatives. They could not be blamed for his work; and to make sure the authorities believed he had led the raid, he slipped off one of his brooches and cast it in the dirt of the yard. Turning back, he found the throng solemn-faced, and cheered them with the call, "One less Saxon keep for the Norman bastards." To a man they cheered the statement, and the crowd broke, still proud of their heritage despite the loss of home and work.

Hereward turned slowly as he searched the yard for Brand, finally spotting him stretched out beneath a huge gnarled oak, his clothing singed and blackened, his face strained with the effort to draw in the cool, fresh air. Alysaun lay at his side, looking as though she had fainted, but as Hereward approached he saw her raise a trembling hand to her forehead and wince at the pain the movement dealt her injured arm.

Moving out of the dispersing crowd, Morwena came over, gazing down at her mistress before she turned to Hereward and asked about Brian de Bourney's fate. Hereward didn't know who she was but pitied her immediately for the purple-red bruise that stretched across one fair cheek, marring the pretty face with puffiness. "The lad died, but Lady Alysaun here nearly died for him." He shook his head, still unable to understand Alysaun's wild effort to protect the man who was her enemy. "Took a cut from my blade, she did, stepped right between him and me."

Brand sat up, curious to hear Morwena's response. Her gaze went from Hereward to him and back to the rebel, and her weary sigh seemed to indicate her belief that they would not understand. How could men understand the degradation of rape or the undying gratitude one could feel for being spared that brutal violation of spirit and body? "Lord Brian was kind . . . of all of them, he was the best. No—*more* than the best. He was a man who was Saxon in all but name and blood.'' That explained how fine he had been in a language these two men could understand.

Morwena ignored the look that passed between Brand and his friend, bending to rip at the hem of her gunna, tearing a long strip of material free before she rose and walked around Alysaun to kneel by her side and wrap the wound. Alysaun was aware of the gentleness of the hands that lifted her shoulder and carefully bound the sword wound, but she remained silent. Only when Morwena had finished her task did she acknowledge the kindness with a tremulous smile. The look that passed between the women, a communication that was thoroughly feminine and unintelligible to the two men watching, spoke of shared sorrow and strength.

Brand stood, his legs still wobbly from the flight through heat and smoke, his thoughts still occupied by the scene he had witnessed in Alysaun's room. The expectation of a loving reunion had made his spirits soar; now one glance at his wife's pale, withdrawn expression sent them tumbling in deep despair. Morwena rose and came near, walking with him to a spot some distance from where Alysaun lay.

''The Norman was her sworn enemy . . . why is she so over-wrought at his passing?'' he puzzled aloud. ''She looks almost . . . . guilty.''

''M'lord, she feels it her fault that Brian died. 'Twas she who sent word to Hereward.'' Morwena shrugged. How could she explain what had passed between Alysaun and Brian? ''I think she meant to ask mercy in sparing the man's life and, failing that, has accepted responsibility for his death.''

Brand couldn't deny he felt bitter over his wife's devotion to a man she could barely have known. ''And was he so consummate a lover that a fortnight's passing made Alysaun prize him?''

''You may choose not to believe me, sire, but truly she allowed him no physical comfort, and neither did he ask it.'' Morwena took a brief glance back at Alysaun's pale, drawn face and then returned her gaze to Brand's eyes, which were shadowed by his inability to understand. ''If your lady prized anything in Brian, it was his gentleness and the solace his companionship offered.''

Brand found the explanation hard to accept. Had he not been gentle with Alysaun? Had she not enjoyed his company? Later there would be many questions to ask, but now, with the threat of retaliation hanging over their heads, they had to make for Ely. "My wife will ride with me," he said brusquely, taking the girl's arm to lead her over to Hereward. "We've no time to pause and laud a dead man's virtues." With that, he stalked away to search for his mount, missing the disappointed frown his comment brought to Morwena's face.

11

Avoiding the possibility of encountering a Norman patrol on the main thoroughfares, the raiding party set across the open country between Havistock and Ely, following back roads and pony tracks that had been in use since the days of the Roman occupation. The pace Hereward set was hard, but with women and a few children traveling along, they would not be safe until they reached the fens. An hour before the sun was at its zenith, he ordered a short rest stop, more to accommodate the women than his own saddle-hard men.

Brand drew his mount to a halt a short distance from the main body of troops, the better to share a few minutes' private conversation with Alysaun. She had been quiet during the five-hour ride, huddled against him, wrapped in his mantle. Now, as he dismounted and reached up to help her down, their eyes met and it was Brand who looked away, awkward and strangely shy at the first close contact in so many weeks.

Alysaun failed to notice his reserved, distant attitude. She knew it was Brand at her side and yet it might have been a stranger. Her thoughts were still upon Brian and his dying words. He believed he had failed her, but how far from the truth that was. She had failed *him*, brought about his death as surely as if she had held the sword in place of Hereward. Moving, speaking, stretching tired, cramped muscles, all these actions were carried out instinctively, without thought. Like a sleepwalker, she went on with life, later remembering little of what she had done or said.

The gulf that time and distance had stretched between them had widened, and Brand found it difficult to find some method of bridging the gap. She was a stranger, a fragile child-woman whose expressionless features masked pain and grief. He suggested she sit beneath the shade of a tree and Alysaun obeyed; he offered her water and she drank. Finally, in frustration, Brand walked away.

Alysaun drew her knees up and lay her head against them. So tired she was, and exhaustion was only a small part of the dull, gray apathy surrounding her. Eyes closed tightly, she saw Brian's face contorted with pain and heard again the rattle of death in his last gasp. Her mouth trembled, then tightened into a line. His last effort to speak had been a wish, a prayer to God for her. How could there be a God when everyone she loved was snatched away from her?

Tears squeezed from between her eyelids and Alysaun lifted her head, opening her eyes. She saw too much remembered pain played out when they were closed. Nearby, the stallion grazed, his graceful, muscled neck stretched low to nibble at the grass. The memory of the first time she had seen the animal, grazing in a clearing like this one, made her blink and clear the tears that blurred her vision. Glancing around for his owner, she discovered Brand leaning against a tree trunk, shoulders slumped in a weary posture.

It was an effort to rise. Her arm ached and drew her attention and for a moment her stomach queasily protested the sight of the dried, caked blood that crusted the wrapping. She couldn't recall who had tended the wound . . . perhaps Brand. Again, as she drew his mantle over her bloodstained shift, she looked at him. As she started toward him her knees nearly gave out, but she paused only a second to gather her strength and went on.

To his left, behind him, a soft, familiar voice spoke his name and Brand turned. Alysaun's face was white and streaked by blood and cinders; her eyes were puffed and shadowed purple from her crying but for the first time, she looked at him with eyes cleared of dazed shock. "Are you all right?" he heard her ask, and puzzled over the question, for it was she who had suffered a wound.

"Well enough," he replied stiffly, an answer so bland it seemed unfeeling even to his own ears. "Your arm—does it give you much pain?" So inadequate, so indifferent a query.

"No—yes, it does," she admitted with a puzzled frown. "I don't know why I first denied it. The cut hurts awfully." Alysaun glanced down at her shoulder and then up at him with an arched brow. "I don't suppose it will heal without a scar, but then . . . I should have a reminder of this day."

Hereward had told Brand how Alysaun came to receive the wound. He couldn't hold back his curiosity. "How is it you defended the Norman so boldly? I would understand why you took so great a risk for the enemy you have hated for so long."

Alysaun's face tilted up defensively. "I'd have done the same for you, Brand."

"But I am your husband. Yes, Alys, the annulment you signed was never valid. To defend your husband so rashly would be a show of love . . . but to risk death for a man you knew—"

"I knew him well enough," Alysaun insisted. "We talked so . . . oh, how much time we passed in conversing. Brian did not deserve to die. It all happened so quickly. I did but move as my heart bid me. Am I to be tried and judged guilty by you, Brand?" The air of defiance went out of her expression, and was replaced by sharp sadness. "Well, m'lord, you are too late to pass sentence. I am guilty of causing his death, and you cannot punish me more than I myself." More to herself than to Brand, she puzzled softly, "Why must I lose . . . and lose again? Everyone I care for is denied me."

"Not everyone, my sweet. Esmond is at Ely." The caustic remark sprang to his lips before he could stay it. Alysaun winced as though he had slapped her.

"You truly think I love him?" Her voice was incredulous. "I will say this but once, Brand. *I do not love* and never did feel anything but disgust for Esmond. If you believe it still, then you are more the fool. You once professed to love me, as I did you. You cannot love me any longer. Jealousy is only an echo of love." Her eyes sparkled with tears again, but Alysaun willed them not to fall. "I am heartened to learn how little you care. 'Tis dangerous to love me. Those who did are dust or ashes now."

She turned to leave him but Brand caught her arm and circled to face her again. "Not so hasty a leavetaking, m'lady. I've a question to put to you. You believe yourself cursed by ill fortune. It's true—you've lost much. I cannot be in danger, you say, because I don't love you. But by your reckoning, 'tis those *you* love who are struck down. Do you love me still?"

Alysaun refused to look up. In the distance, Hereward's voice called out a command to mount. "We must go—"

"Alysaun, do not evade me. Answer . . . or we will stand here forever."

Finally she glanced up. She should answer no, for in loving him she surely doomed Brand to certain death. Yet, despite their parting and the weeks of trying to convince herself that what they had shared had been some kind of enchanted dream, Alysaun knew she would always love him. It frightened her to admit it. "I do," she answered simply, gazing past him with an exasperated expression. "Now that you've had it from me, sire, do not be surprised if the clear sky should cloud over and lightning bolts find you." Brand was silent and the lack of any response to her admission drew her gaze back to him. "And you, Brand, what motive makes you insist I am still yours? I had thought by your long silence that you had found the annulment a desirable form of release."

"No motive have I . . . save perhaps that I love danger. If 'tis true that your love is accompanied by some risk, then I will meet it and fight to live. Loving you, m'lady, has become too much a part of what I am, as natural as breathing. The end of either would still my heart's beating."

Alysaun stared at him, wanting to believe his confession yet too shy of such bold claims of lasting love. Brand had changed. Physically he seemed to have hardened, and though the effect of the pain he had endured at the sheriff's hands had altered his visage, it hadn't lessened the strength and attractiveness of his face. She sensed other changes, the tempering of arrogance, the ability to understand the suffering of others because of his own suffering, the willingness to give, not of his possessions, but of himself.

If Hereward had not ridden up to them, Morwena perched wearily before him in the saddle, Alysaun would have told Brand about the baby. He wanted *her*, and that was the assurance she had needed before she could reveal what had flowered from their physical love. But Hereward interrupted their privacy with a peevish, overtired complaint. "Have some feeling for the rest of us, Brand," he begged. "We're all done in and with miles to go yet ere we make the comfort of Ely's hall."

Brand saluted the request with a nod of his head, his good humor evident in the smile that quirked his mouth. "I can find no fault in your logic, m'lord. Now I have Alysaun to share it, the hall will seem twice as inviting." Morwena smiled to see how happy the pair looked, wondering if it was Alysaun's news of the child that had effected a reconciliation. Certainly the rancor that had earlier marked Brand's mood was gone.

Riding on through countryside that evolved from heavily wooded hills into the more level, open land that led to the fens and, finally, the seacoast, Alysaun nestled securely in the strong circle of Brand's arms, as quiet as she had been earlier but more contented. Before they approached the salt marshes, she was asleep. Though Brand knew the maze of paths to follow, he urged the stallion forward, pressing effort from the worn animal in a desire to catch Hereward and the others.

The day had grown progressively more cloudy and as the group of raiders wound their way past bogs thick with reeds and along a shallow, swampy trail attempted only by the brave, the clouds towered into swirling columns, darkening to a gray that rumbled a warning of a tempest. Brand cocked an eye at the changing weather, remembered Alysaun's statement that her love would have lightning seek him out, and grinned to himself as he rejected the idea that he was under some curse. Still, when the rise of Ely suddenly appeared out of the dark gloom of the mists, the sight was more welcome than usual.

The strident trebling of a horn sounded from the fort, startling Alysaun awake. For a moment, as the stallion's shod hooves clattered across wood, she could not think where they were. Snorting with the effort, the animal galloped through the swirling layers of fog, nostrils flared and steaming as Brand raced him up the hill toward the torchlight flickering through the open gates of Ely.

A cheer of welcome had gone up as Hereward led the troops through the gates. It still resounded when Brand and a few stragglers trailed in. Hereward stood in the middle of the bailey with a proudly beaming Frida at his side, trying to appear humble as he acknowledged the acclaim lavished upon him by those who had waited and worried for their loved ones. The throng of enthusiastic supporters parted as Brand walked the stallion to Hereward's side.

Brand slid down from the saddle, his flagging spirits revived by the thought of the food Torfrida no doubt had ready. Though she was equally comforted by the journey's end, Alysaun knew a moment's shock as Brand reached up to lift her from the saddle. The woman with Hereward, presumably his wife, held the familiar linen money bags that had lain undiscovered beneath Alysaun's mattress the past two weeks. She hadn't realized Hereward had saved them, and the thought that the money would lend support to his cause deepened the smile she gave the rebel as he came forward.

"Frida, you've wounded to attend to, including this tired young lady," Hereward reminded his wife, giving her shoulder an affectionate squeeze. "Would that I only had more men with her spirit and we'd be sending William scurrying back across the Channel without e'en wetting his boots."

Frida offered a welcoming smile to the girl, studying her bedraggled appearance while Hereward went on. This was Alysaun, the girl who had set Brand to brooding for so long, his wife. Even with Brand's arm tightly circling the girl's shoulders, she looked unsteady on her feet.

Recalling Alysaun's distress over her young protector's death, Hereward cursed silently for his blunder in reminding her of it. He gestured to the keep. "Welcome to Ely, such as it is, Lady Alysaun. My wife, Torfrida"—he smiled down at the petite woman with him and continued—"will see you comfortably settled." He took the bags of gold and hefted them, bowing to Alysaun. "And I thank you for securing these for us. Every coin we gather continues the hope of expelling the Bastard from our homeland."

"They were not mine but Esmond's," Alysaun replied, raising a trembling hand to touch her aching temples. The day had been too long and full of fear and tension. Of a sudden, she felt dizzy and embarrassingly like fainting. "I . . . am . . . glad . . ." The words trailed off in a whisper, and as Hereward saw the color drain from her face he stepped forward and caught her.

His experience with fainting ladies was limited to the first months Frida had carried Devon. Alysaun went limp just as his broad hands caught hold and he lifted her into his arms before she sank to the ground. Brand hovered close, his own face going white with alarm, and, as Hereward carried Alysaun toward the doors of the keep, trailed in his wake, looking utterly helpless and panic-stricken. Frida, calm and efficient in any emergency, hurried to open the doors for her husband, directing Hereward to deposit Alysaun on one of the linen-covered tables already set in the hall for the meal that waited upon their arrival.

"Shoo—away with you," she chided now, pushing at her husband's brawny shoulders and telling him to keep Brand busy. "I'll see to his wife . . . she'll be fine, I swear." Dismissing him from her thoughts, Frida turned her full attention to Alysaun, calling to the servants to bring fresh linen wrappings and water, as well as her box of herb medicines.

With the requested materials at hand, Frida bent to the task of cleaning Alysaun's arm wound. Since the girl's pulse was strong, there seemed no harm in waiting to revive her until the wound was clean and treated. An ugly, puffed cut appeared when Frida pulled the last of the bloodstained wrappings free. The wound was just below the shoulder bone, a two-inch gash in the flesh; the slice had been deep enough to leave a scar but not to tear muscle.

As gently as possible, she swabbed the cut with water and applied a paste of powdered yarrow and Saint-John's-wort, bound together by the silky threads of a spiderweb. Carefully blotting excess moisture, she bound the wound firmly with fresh wrappings. Alysaun moaned, moving her head to the side, then quieted again. At Frida's side, a young voice, full of awe, whispered, "Christ's blood! Is she dead?"

Without turning, Frida rebuked Devon. "Do not take the Lord's name in vain, m'boy, and use your eyes. Would I be wasting such care on a lifeless arm? The lady's only fainted from loss of blood and exhaustion. Her wound will heal."

"Father said 'twas his blade what cut 'er, but he wouldn't tell me why. Is she a Norman?"

Frida bathed Alysaun's face, washing away the blood and soot with gentle strokes, all the while reminding herself to be patient with her son. " 'Tis only natural you're curious, dear. Come around and look. There's nothing Norman dark in this girl's face. A pretty Saxon is hidden beneath those smudges."

Devon had edged around his mother and stared. "Surely is," he agreed. "I'm glad she ain't dead—she's too beautiful, she is. Who is she?" Bravely he peered closer, marveling at the heavy sweep of golden lashes, then he jumped back like a startled fawn when her eyelids fluttered.

"Lord Brand's wife," Frida answered in a hushed tone. "Now, enough of questions. She'll be frightened enough at waking in a strange place. Be off and tell your father she's come to." She stroked the mist-damp curls away from Alysaun's temple, a hint of their burnished color showing through the dusting of ash that dulled the gold. "Poor girl is likely to faint again."

"What's her name?" Devon persisted, reluctant to leave. He thought Brand a most fortunate man to have so lovely a wife.

"Alysaun . . . *Lady* Alysaun to you, whelp. Now, *go*."

"Fits her," Devon said approvingly, then, at his mother's stern look, added, "I am going. I am." He wandered off, glad the lady had not been awake yet to see how his mother treated him. Heading for the entry, where he had last seen his father, he wondered aloud when his mother would finally realize how much a man he was.

Alysaun's first conscious thought was embarrassment at the weakness her fainting spell had revealed. Never in her life had she succumbed to such dizziness, and though the loss of blood and the long, tiring journey could be used as an excuse, she was sure it had more to do with the strain of carrying the baby. Torfrida hovered over her, fussing with a maternal air despite the difference of only some ten years in their ages.

"I am truly sorry to be so troublesome, madame," Alysaun apologized, sitting up with the help of Frida's firm support under her arm. Noting the blood that stained the sparkling white of the linen tablecloth, Alysaun was moved to apologize again.

"Oh, please, m'lady . . . 'tis nothing. A good soak in water will see it out," her hostess protested. With the hall suddenly beginning to fill with Ely's residents, Frida remembered that she had a ravenous lot of tired and deserving men to see fed. "Let me show you to your husband's room. I'll see you settled and bring a portion of our meal for you to eat in privacy. The food's plain fare, I'm afraid, but nourishing all the same."

Though she hadn't eaten yet in the course of the day, the idea of food was unappealing, Alysaun's stomach was so tender. With Frida's arm around her shoulders to guard against the possibility of another faint, she was taken from the hall and up a short flight of steps to the timbered second story. Frida chattered on, the soothing tone of her voice more important than what she said. Already Alysaun felt at home. It was delightful to be coddled and cared for, a luxury after the responsibilities and worries of her position at Havistock.

The room Frida led her into was spare, clearly an austere bachelor's abode, and the good woman apologized for its lack of comforts. The walls were whitewashed plaster, the oaken floors covered with fresh, herb-scented rushes. A table and chair and narrow pallet against the outer wall were the only furnishings. "To one so wearied in spirit as I, m'lady," Alysaun commented with a smiling sigh, "'tis as well appointed as a king's chamber." She reached out and caught Frida's hand, pressing her plump fingers in gratitude. "You have been most gracious but, then, having met your husband once before today, I expected his wife would be as kind and good as he appeared."

Frida blushed at the compliment, covering a rush of warmth for the tired, pale young girl by urging her to lie down and rest. "I won't be but a short while with a tray, dear. Meantime, just close your eyes and forget your troubles. You are safe here at Ely now, with nothing and no one to harm you."

Alysaun sank onto the pallet but declined the offer of food. Frida wrinkled her brow in concern, thinking it better she eat something to build her strength but reluctant to push the issue. Only Alysaun knew how well her stomach could take a meal, no matter how light or bland the food. "Well, I'll be back to see how you're faring. Mayhap after a bit of sleep you'll feel more inclined to have a bite."

Outside the room, Frida paused in the hall. She had so much work awaiting her, but with an efficiently trained staff, all would proceed without her direct supervision. The room would have to be made more comfortable. One couldn't expect a delicate girl like Alysaun to live the spartan life of a fighting man. And clothing—that, too, would be a problem. Her own clothing was too small for the tall, willowy girl. Who amongst the women at Ely was of a similar height and weight, Frida mused as she walked toward the hall.

As she expected, her help had seen that everyone had a seat, and the hall was noisy with the loud chatter of reunited wives and husbands, busy with the servants scurrying from table to table in an effort to keep up with the demand. The men were eating like starving wolves—understandably, in the light of their strenuous day's

266

work and journey home. Even the ladies Hereward had brought along seemed to go at their portions with unusual zest. Frida was about to take her seat next to Hereward when she remembered that Esmond was still bound in his room, under guard since Hereward and the men had left; to keep him from causing her any trouble.

Hereward caught his wife around the waist, pulling her back to his side with a loud complaint. "Now where are you off to? Wife, of late you never stop long enough to share a meal with your own lord." Pleased as he was with the day's successful raid, the rebel was in a decidedly amorous mood, and his hand caressed his wife's rounded hips.

Frida batted at the exploring hand and reprimanded his bold overtures in a hushed voice. "For shame, sire—you are setting a fine example for your men to follow. There's time aplenty for such play in the privacy of our chamber. And I would not be too busy to share a meal if you didn't choose to increase our population with every raid." Frida's small, bow mouth was pursed in mock dismay. The people Hereward brought to Ely were unfortunate and homeless, but if his generosity continued, they would be hard put to feed and quarter everyone. "Soon you'll be having all of England's populace crowded on our isle. 'Tis *one* way to defeat William—stealing his subjects away until he's left with no one to rule."

Hereward's deep, gruff laughter boomed out, but he would not release his wife until she informed him where she was bound. "To see to the feeding of your Saxon prisoner, m'lord. Or is he no longer to be kept bound and under watch?"

"Ah, Christ, but I'd forgotten the wretch." Hereward scowled, wondering what he should do with the arrogant fellow now he had no place to call home. "Sit and eat a meal in peace, love," he insisted, then called to his son. "Devon, be a good lad and send one of the serving girls to our 'guest's' room with a tray. I don't care to have his sullen face spoil my supper." He handed his wife his goblet of mead and turned to ask Brand's opinion of the problem Esmond presented. "Since the sheriff doesn't know he wasn't part of the raid, I'd say he's as much a wanted man as any of us here."

"If you're considering letting him stay, Hereward, think on it again," Brand replied curtly, washing down his bite of roasted chicken with a swallow of ale. "If he stays, I go. I'll not have that underhanded bastard fighting beside me, nor worry that he's armed and anxious for a chance at my back. You know as well as I he was behind my arrest, though I've yet to make him admit his guilt."

"Aye, you're right there," Hereward agreed. "He has certainly given you cause to hate the sight of him. Now, with his mother close at hand, he'll be even more of a nettle to chew." The Saxon rebel frowned. Esmond wasn't even present and the mention of his name was souring everyone's belly. He stabbed a tender chicken breast with his fork and offered it to his wife. "Take the time to relax and eat, darling. With all your extra tasks, you'll need the strength. Have you found room to quarter all our new arrivals yet?"

Frida accepted the chicken and took a delicate bite before explaining that the two recent widows and Morwena would share a room, and the fourth lady, the wife of the retainer who had been captured with Esmond, would share her husband's chamber. "Until they take their leave, his mother may share Esmond's room. That takes care of everyone unless you've someone else I have no knowledge of."

Busy with his food, Brand suddenly paused and looked across at Frida. "And Alysaun, m'lady. Where is she, that you have made no mention of her name?"

Frida looked at him askance, surprised that he should even question where his wife would sleep. "Why, in your quarters, sire. After she recovered from her faint, I took her directly there, to afford the poor child a chance to rest. She would eat nothing and, given her condition, I do not feel easy with her lack of appetite."

"You've tended to her wound, Frida," Hereward interrupted. "A bit of rest and the lady will be on her feet within the day. What 'condition' do you speak of? Clear the meaning of that phrase or you'll have Brand here choking on his victuals."

"I may be mistaken, but Lady Alysaun's faint, followed by her refusal to eat . . . well, time will tell if I am right but I do believe the lady is with child."

"She said nothing, though?" Brand had suddenly lost his appetite, the contentment of his reunion with Alysaun marred by Frida's suspicions. "I will ask her directly and lay your curiosity—and mine—to rest."

Brand rose from the bench and Frida, alarmed by his irritated expression, touched her husband's arm in appeal. "Tell him not to go to her, Hereward. Brand will listen to you. The girl is too exhausted to face a questioning. Oh, how I wish I'd held my tongue."

Hereward patted her hand, trying to calm her, but his sympathies lay with Brand. " 'Tis not for you or me to interfere, Frida. The annulment was falsely granted and Brand is the lady's husband, with all the rights granted him by church and law." He glanced up at Brand, brow furrowed in concern. "I've no right to stay you from seeking out your wife, Brand, but I like the lady well and in my opinion she's had more than her share of grief. Go easy on her, son."

Brand nodded, irritated not by the couple's concern for Alysaun but by the implication that he was somehow going to threaten her with harm. "As you said, friend, I've a husband's rights. Your worries are unreasoned, though, for Alysaun and I were reconciled ere we entered the gates of Ely. The inquiries I'll make will be couched in civility . . . no matter what the answers be."

Despite his assurances, Frida fretted as she watched Brand walk away, afraid his temper would overcome his intent to be courteous. A reconciliation so recently decided upon, no matter how much desired by both parties, was akin to crossing the fens—both requiring caution and keen senses to stay upon an even, firm path. If her guess was accurate, the birth of a child might serve as a mortar to strengthen the bonds of their marriage.

Brand climbed the stairs with a slow tread, his mind still assimilating the shocking news. It was possible that Frida had guessed wrongly in assuming Alysaun was carrying a child, but if it was true, why hadn't his wife told him? Why, indeed, unless she feared he would deny he had sired the baby? The thought that Alysaun might be burdened by Esmond's seed stopped Brand in his tracks, stunning him so he leaned against the stone wall of the stairwell for support, his legs as wobbly as a newborn foal's.

After several deep breaths to calm the racing of his heart, he shook off the doubts and revulsion aroused by that possibility and climbed the last steps that brought him to the landing of the upper hall. If Alysaun was a few months along, there could be no doubt whose baby it was. Outside the door to his room, Brand reached for the latch and paused, suddenly aware of how selfish his thoughts had been.

His concern had centered on the chance that his wife would bear Esmond's by-blow, and the grievous insult that such a birth would deal his pride and vanity. Yet in bearing a child she knew to be other than his own, Alysaun would suffer twice over any misery he would feel. No matter that a man she hated had left her burdened by his seed, the child would be hers as well, nurtured by her body and fiercely protected by a mother's instincts.

Loving her as he did, Brand could but pray that if she was pregnant, it was their union that had sparked the life she carried. Even if he never made mention of his doubts, the issue of the baby's paternity would divide and put asunder whatever chance they had for happiness.

He raised his hand to knock and glowered at the tight-clenched fist that made a mockery of all his gentle, caring thoughts, hating for a moment the man who would seek to awaken innocence and exact a painful blush, a trembling brow, the salty tears to balm his own aching heart. By force of will, his fingers relaxed, and he lifted the latch with studied patience.

The room was shadowed in gloom except for the single flickering glow of a rush lamp on the table that cast a soft halo of light upon the sleeping girl. For long moments—nay, minutes—Brand stared down at Alysaun, entranced by the peace that veiled her face, a serenity of spirit that elicited his envy. If only once he could claim that he had acted selflessly, prompted by another's needs to disregard his own gain, such tranquillity would be his.

Brand carefully picked up the chair, bringing it from the table to the side of the pallet, wary of the scrape of wood that might disturb his wife's sleep. Alysaun stirred, a whispered sigh escaping the parted curve of her lips. He held his breath, unwilling even to let the rush of air escaping his chest stir her from the rest she so well deserved.

Nestled against the pillow, slender white hands folded beneath a fair cheek whose flesh was as smooth as white silk, Alysaun slept on, unaware that Brand sat near, tormented by his brooding thoughts, guarding her against all and any who might mean her harm, including himself. Having thought himself above reproach and far from the judgment of any sins, Brand had taken this young, beleaguered girl and found pleasure in the sweet response of her willing body, in the offering of a timid love that had blossomed ripe and lovely, bold and so giving that she had unknowingly laced his heart with ties that would forever bind him.

Brand's shoulders slumped, his head falling heavily against his hands. Never a religious man, he now believed there was some greater power whose unseen hands moved people toward and away from each other, with a far-ranging wisdom mortals could only ponder. This omnipotent being had directed his path to cross Alysaun's. Surely, if he had learned humility in loving her, then God had taught him a harsh but needed lesson . . . and just as surely God must be aware of the remorse he felt. If His wisdom was tempered by mercy, He would not take from Brand the one person who had altered his character for the better.

And what of Alysaun? Had she been a mere pawn in effecting his transformation from a selfish, arrogant fool into a man humbled in the face of love? She had given him her love, humbled her own spirit in his behest, sacrificed her own towering pride to give him more than any man had a right to expect. Could it be that at the moment he recognized the depth of his feelings for her, Alysaun was to be taken from him, her strength and faith destined for some other man?

"How long have you been sitting there?"

271

Alysaun's voice, soft and low but fully awake, startled Brand out of his dark reverie. He raised his head slowly, wondering how much of his soul-searching she had witnessed before speaking. "Not long," he said, then, with a cynical quirk of his lips, added, "Forever and a day, it seemed. I . . . didn't want to disturb your rest. I have, anyway. Forgive me."

There was still a shadow beneath Alysaun's eyes and fine lines of weariness and anxiety radiating from their corners, but the tranquillity that had softened her features in sleep remained. She smiled, a faint, concerned smile, as she studied his face. "Even as worn and weary as you look, sire, the fineness of your features is a welcome sight upon waking." She reached out for his hand, requesting his assistance in rising to a sitting position, trying to hide the ripple of pain the movement dealt her wounded shoulder.

Reluctant to let loose her warm, soft hand, Brand stood and settled on the pallet to Alysaun's left. His gesture was hesitant but she made no protest as his arm slipped around her waist to draw her against the support of his chest. Alysaun turned her face up and smiled before she laid her head against his shoulder, content for the moment just to be held in his arms.

Brand, too, was content. There seemed to be nothing more natural in all the world than to have this gentle woman by his side. His purpose in seeking her out no longer seemed so consumingly important. At any rate, he could scarce think of a way to phrase the question of whether or not she was expecting. Too bluntly put, it would sound like an accusation.

"Brand?"

"Yes, love?" Even dusted with the ash of Havistock's fire, Alysaun's hair was silken soft against his chin. Brand's fingers brushed the tendrils of gold back from her forehead and bent to press a light kiss upon the same spot.

"I've something to tell you, a confession I meant to make when we stopped for rest in the clearing this afternoon. 'Tis not an easy thing to confide—"

"Then if its telling gives you distress, save your secret for another

272

time, sweet," Brand broke in, thinking that Alysaun meant to tell him of her relationship with the dead Norman, young Brian. Platonic as they may have been, the feelings Alysaun had evidenced for the man were still a sore point with Brand. "You're tired and most likely famished. Why don't I have Frida send up—"

Alysaun drew back a few inches and gazed up into her husband's face, somewhat impatient with his unwillingness to hear her out. "I am not so hungry that I cannot wait a while longer," she insisted, "and what I want to say distresses me not—only your reluctance to listen does."

A sigh rushed from Brand's mouth, followed by a shrug of his shoulders. "Confess, then," he said. "I will try my best to understand why he so quickly won your warm regard and—"

"Brand, are you referring to Brian?" Alysaun's eyes widened in surprise at the mildness of his words. Brand *had* changed, drastically. No jealous recriminations came forth at his assumption that she meant to speak of how she felt toward the Norman. His expression seemed resigned, a trifle uneasy but definitely set to hear her praise another man's character. "I'll speak of him another time, darling, when we can both feel easy with the mention of his name."

"Then what . . ." Alysaun displayed a most contented smile and a proud look that gave him pause.

"Brand, I am carrying your child." The statement needed no embellishment. "Though Morwena has as little experience with the subject as I, together we managed to agree that the babe would be born close to Candlemas." Her head was high, evidencing the pride of her accomplishment, then a slight blush crept over her complexion as she glanced at him and admitted, "She could only guess from the time that had passed since I ceased my monthly flow, but *I* know the exact moment I conceived." The admission was rather smug but endearing in the light of Alysaun's blushing contentment. " 'Twas on that day you first convinced me to . . . to shed my modesty and allow you your way with me. The sun warmed my skin—"

"And wrought a deeper rose than your embarrassment at such naked reveling," Brand recalled with a grin. "And the wildflowers bent their heads in shame, unable to compete with either your beauty or the rich fragrance of your bare flesh. I agree with you, my darling. If any moment of pleasure could breed a babe, 'twas that day you put aside your shyness that did create a life within you.''

She didn't need to ask if he was happy with the news. Brand had that preening-peacock look, that see-what-I-have-done countenance that mirrored her own pride. The moment was very special, drawing them closer together in the knowledge that the intimacy they had shared had flowered in a new life, a part of each of them joined forever in a child of their own.

''The babe is a boy,'' Alysaun stated confidently, proud that her son would be heir to his father's features and noble bearing.

''Ah, then he's spoken to you already?'' Brand teased, indulging her whimsical belief with a generosity born of his own paternal pride. ''And did he by any chance happen to tell you whether he will favor his mother's golden-haired fairness?''

''No, m'lord, I've not yet had the time to question his appearance. My assertion that the child I carry is a son stems from his strength and vigor. Already he moves with all the assurance of his sire.'' Even as she spoke the baby stirred, and with a look of wonder, Alysaun caught Brand's wrist and laid his fingers across the curve of her belly. For a second the firmness of her womb became taut in a small contraction, then the rounded flesh softened and a small, insistent fluttering moved against his fingertips. If possible, Brand's expression was more full of wonder than his wife's.

''You're right, Alys,'' Brand admitted, raising his hand to cup her chin and, in a tentative, searching kiss, communicate the love he felt for her, the strong emotions stirred by the feel of his child moving within her. ''Though the time for him to enter the world is not yet ripe, my son is eager to make an appearance.'' Again Brand's mouth touched Alysaun's, and as his hand curled around her nape, his lips evoked a passionate response from hers. A desire too long denied swept them both, leaving Alysaun shaken by the quickness of her arousal, by the ability of this one man to set her mind and body afire with yearning just at the touch of his hand. Now, as his lips nibbled at the sensitive skin of her throat in tiny, stirring kisses, his voice, hoarsened by longing, whispered against her ear, "My God, Alysaun . . . why would the little one want freedom when his prison is a paradise? 'Tis an onerous fate that traps him where his father would give an eyetooth to be welcomed."

"No such bounty is required, my lord," Alysaun answered softly, an alluring smile curving the corners of her mouth as she drew away from Brand and lay back on the pallet. "Only a request from his mother to proceed gently, with a care for the tenderness of her shoulder. Other than that one caution, sire, no restraints are placed upon your passion." The smile widened to an impish grin. "I'd be willing to wager the babe will find his own delight in being rocked to sleep. No doubt he will think us the most considerate of parents."

12

Several hours later, when Brand reappeared in the hall, Hereward was still present, seated in a comfortable chair drawn close to the hearth. With most of her duties finished for the night, Torfrida had settled contentedly in a chair next to his, merely happy to have him safe at home once more. Morwena sat on a bench close by, the firelight illuminating her handiwork as she altered a tunic Frida had found for Alysaun to use.

The majority of the raiders had retired early, their sleepiness enhanced by the flow of wine and ale that had welcomed them home. Their leader was more than a little in his cups, but his capacity for strong drink showed only in a certain mellowness of mood. At Brand's approach, Hereward cocked an eyebrow in curiosity over the length of time it had taken his friend to ascertain his wife's condition; he belched heartily and grinned an apology to the ladies present before raising his ale tankard in greeting. "Well, son, by the time it took you to ask the lady your questions, she could've had the bairn," he jested, ignoring his wife's frown.

"Don't be keeping us all in breathless anticipation, now . . . have we something to celebrate or 'twas it a mere fancy of Frida's?"

Brand grinned and winked at Frida. "By the look of you, my besotted friend, you've already celebrated aplenty. Poor Frida will be having to drag your overgrown carcass to the scullery to let you sleep it off amongst the garlic and onion sets." Frida started to giggle, then, as Hereward's brow furrowed in a glower, covered her smile with a hand, wisely returning to her own sewing.

"To answer you, though—there is a well-founded reason to drink a toast this night." Morwena glanced up, pausing in her work, and Brand smiled at her. "By general consensus, Alysaun will deliver my child—a son, she says, and I believe it—in early February." There was a flash of a smile from Morwena before she returned to stitching. Frida looked as pleased as if she were the proud mother-to-be and Hereward sat up, slapping his knee in delight and uttering a wickedly hearty oath that normally would have drawn his wife's silent rebuke.

"Christ's eyes, I knew 'twould work out all for the best. Mother, fetch us more ale—we've tankards to lift in honor of our Brand's virility. Ah, but a good man's aim ne'er fails to sink true." The look Frida gave him was half indulgent, half chiding of his brazen speech before a young lady like Morwena. And yet Morwena seemed not to mind. She bent to her work with a satisfied expression, pleased everything was finally going well for Brand and Alysaun.

"Before I forget, Frida, I'd be most appreciative if you'd have something warm and hearty sent up to my Alysaun," Brand requested. "She's wide awake now and claiming the babe is clamoring for something to grow on."

" 'Twill be my pleasure, Brand," Frida replied, stopping beside him to smile and touch his cheek. "With all my heart, I can truly say I've ne'er been happier to hear such fine news. Don't you be letting anything come between you and your Alysaun again."

"He *knows* you wish him best, Frida," Hereward interrupted, anxious to get on with celebrating. "Now, be about your tasks, good wife. Most likely Brand's tongue is curled wi' dryness."

"Not quite, Hereward," Brand said as Frida hurried off, "but I do feel an o'erpowering need to quaff a drink in honor of my good fortune. 'Tisn't every day a man can hear so proud a piece of news."

As Brand settled into the chair Frida had vacated, Hereward turned to him with a teasing expression in his blue eyes. "Truer words were ne'er spoken, son. Well do I remember the night Frida did confirm what we had hoped for. Took her right off to bed her, I did, just to make the babe's acquaintance." His deep, gruff laughter rolled forth as he gave Brand's ribs a hearty poke. "Did the same, now, didn't you, lad?" Brand's effort to maintain a certain amount of decorum in Morwena's presence failed as he nodded and then grinned.

"Ah, my friend," Hereward sputtered through his laughter, "a man after me own heart, you are." His chuckling lessened, leaving a good-humored trace of a grin on his rough-hewn features. "If Devon grows as tall and fine, I'll be well pleased. Tis but a shame that our celebrating is colored by sadness at your departing. I'll miss more than your good sword hand at me side, I will."

Brand's rust-colored eyebrows were raised as he puzzled over the statement and he straightened in the chair, canting his head to ask the obvious. "Do tell, before my own mind is fogged by drink, sire . . . what has fatherhood to do with taking my leave of Ely? Somehow I have missed the lean of your thoughts, for I'd no intention of going anywhere."

Hereward stared at him as if he had gone daft, and it was Morwena who, understanding the rebel leader's concern, interjected an explanation. "If I may speak, sire, I think what Lord Hereward means to say is that now you've a wife *and* a little one to care for, you cannot be so heedless of the risk involved in continuing to do battle with the enemy."

"Aye, 'twas exactly my thought, m'lady," Hereward said, acknowledging the girl's support with an appreciative glance. "Clearly you haven't had time to consider it, son, but you can't go off and fight with the same concentration you knew before. A child left behind can make all the difference in how you comport yourself in a fray.''

Brand still didn't understand what the fuss was about. "If anything, 'twill improve the caution I've always employed. You have a son, Hereward. The fact that Frida and young Devon wait upon your return from raids has no bearing on your efficiency.''

Frida returned then with a servant bearing a tray laden with tankards and a flagon of mead, as well as two silver goblets filled with a sweet, spiced apple wine for herself and Morwena. Other serving men carried mead to those few people scattered around tthe hall who had stayed for late companionship.

"What long and serious faces abound,'' Frida commented, retrieving the goblets to hand Morwena one while the servant offered the tankards to the men and filled them to the brim with the dark, honeyed ale. "Why so solemn, sweet?'' she asked her husband, soothing away the wrinkles that furrowed his brow. "I thought to find you all merry and full of jest.''

"Your husband, dear lady, was just telling me how unworthy a warrior I'll make now I've a wife and babe to worry over,'' Brand said dryly. "Though he is hard put to explain why that matters so greatly over his own worries for his family.''

"I'm not hard put to do anything, sir,'' Hereward growled and, remembering Brand had a reason to be testy this night, added, "And I forgive the implication of your words.'' He looked up at Frida, standing next to his chair, and smiled, taking her hand in his to kiss her fingertips. "There's a great difference betwixt the two of us, m'boy. If I should fall prey to a Norman blade and pass on to my reward of Heaven or, as some may have it, Hell, I leave a lad old enough to see to his mother's welfare. And because of that, I'm past the caution that would slow my instincts and be more likely to cause my death than the keenness of the enemy's battle skills. 'Tis that small edge of caution, that thought for the helpless wife and bairn, that might give you pause and lay you open to a fatal thrust.''

Brand frowned, thoughts turned inward as he considered the wisdom of his friend's concern. It was true enough. He had never been hampered before by any worries in a fight, only for his own survival. Now he was beginning to understand that the desire not to leave a young widow and child would make him overcautious and just as vulnerable as if he ventured forth indifferent to the dangers of combat. "Right again, Hereward," Brand admitted finally with a sigh. "It does seem this is my night for owning up to mistaken impressions. Still, I am more than loath to part company. I have taken you and your cause to heart. 'Twill be a bitter herb to chew upon—this idea of abandoning your fight to safeguard my own life."

"How bitter, when it means seeing your son grow tall and straight, having known his father's love and protection?" Hereward leaned forward and though his tongue was somewhat loosened by his imbibing, the impact of what he had to say was no less stirring. "You have fought well and for the freedom of those to whom you owed no debt of kinship. There is no dishonor in withdrawing from this cause of ours, for what you lent to it has added to its life. Mayhap the reason we struggle against the Norman oppression has escaped you, Brand. I see it all the more clearly in your newfound joy."

Hereward raised his tankard, clinking it against Brand's. "God grant that you be allowed to see your babe to manhood, a lad free to guide his own destiny, unhampered by the forced will of tyrants." Both men drank deeply at that hope. " 'Tis the most that Englishmen or any other breed can ask of our lives, the freedom to direct what we do and say, a cause beyond the issue of ejecting foreigners from this English soil."

"Peace be unto you and yours," Brand replied, and raised his tankard in a return of the toast. "If I leave Ely, I leave my home . . . if I leave you, Hereward of Lincoln, I leave a brother more dear than any ties of blood could make us. I would that such a happy event had not come between me and my loyalty to you."

"Even leagues parted, your loyalty goes unquestioned," Hereward answered. "Comes a time in every man's life when he must decide what's best for him and his own. Ofttimes have I pondered the stubbornness of my soul in choosing this bloody course of resistance that endangers my family.'' Hereward grinned, and the shrug of his wide shoulders seemed to be an effort to cast off the solemnity of his mood. ''Perhaps 'twas the course that chose me,'' he suggested with a mirthless chuckle, ''and not the other way round.''

A flush of embarrassment deepened the ruddiness of his fair-skin. ''Christ's blood,'' he swore, and gulped down several successive swallows of ale, which left a frost of foam upon his thick, wiry mustache. Hereward swiped at the froth and glanced up to wink at his wife. '' 'Tis either the late hour or the sogginess of my brains, but if we don't turn to serious merrymaking, these Saxon eyes of mine'll rheum with a womanish show of tears. Is there a man yet awake who can call up a song from lute or lyre and dispel this gloom? Tired as they be, my feet itch to dance a few steps in honor of my friend''—Hereward smiled at Brand—''my *brother's* good fortune.''

Brand returned his look with an expression of mock reproach. ''Sire, you wound me gravely,'' he jested. ''By your side sits the most skillful musician in all of England, and you would seek some other? If Frida would dispatch a servant for my lute, I'll strum a tune that will have you dancing like a great trained bear.''

Without waiting for Hereward's request, Torfrida hurried off to see to the task herself. She was bone-tired and heaven only knew what was keeping the battle-weary men awake, but on so special a night, there was no possibility of suggesting the wisdom of retiring. In the weeks that he had been with them, nothing had stirred Brand to play, not even her gently put suggestion that a touch of music might improve his dark moods. Now Frida retrieved the instrument from a storeroom near the kitchens and, cradling its pear-shaped bottom as carefully as she would a swaddled infant, brought it to the hall and delivered it to Brand.

One of the men who had gathered around to join the celebration produced a willow reed and started the entertainment while Brand tinkered with the tuning keys of the lute. Finally he joined in, easily catching the lively tune piped by the reed player, his artful strumming blending melodically with the thin, high-pitched whistling emitted by the reed.

Hereward had lumbered to his feet, unsteady for a moment before he found his footing, and drew his wife to dance in a circle of partners that included an at-first reluctant, then delighted Morwena and a Danish-Saxon raider named Swein, who had all the night been casting a sheep-eyed look her way. There were enough spectators to form another circle and the hall soon echoed with the lilt of feminine laughter above the relaxing lure of music. By skill alone, without thought, Brand's fingers plucked at the lute strings, his spirit only half awake when Alysaun was not present to hear him play.

In one of the ground-floor rooms off the hall, Esmond listened to the music, recognizing the player by his past performances and cursing his name aloud. His mother lay on a pallet across the room, a soft snoring issuing from her parted lips. It mattered not a whit to him that her arrogant form was clothed in an ill-fitting, borrowed gown or that her bed was a humble resting place for so high born a lady; better she grew used to such an ignoble fate, for Esmond meant to see her take the veil, and a lady without dower to offer the convent was of no more import than a penniless orphan brat.

Had not his downfall been greater? She, haughty dame that she was, had lost only land and the luxuries its profits could afford her, whereas he . . . *he* was bereft of everything that had made life worth living. And the lute player had won: Against all odds, Brand de Reynaud lived and thrived . . . and once more possessed Alysaun. Esmond struck a clenched fist against the arm of his chair, cursing whatever forces had kept de Reynaud alive, damning the devil's own luck the man possessed.

Esmond was now free of the bonds that had secured him almost constantly since his ignominious arrival across the saddle of his mount. Still, what was freedom to him? A mockery only, like an illusory glimmer of sunlight to a blind man, the pain of a severed limb to a man lamed by misfortune. For long hours he had sat slumped in this plain-hewn oaken chair, fit only for a peasant, and tasted the bitter gall of knowing he had lost.

Even if Hereward had not burned Havistock to the ground, the estate and its wealth were irretrievably lost to him. The death of the Normans who had claimed it gave him no satisfaction. Nothing sated his railing resentment against the abrupt altering of his life, against the meanest cut of all, the knowledge that Alysaun was here, within the fortified walls of Ely, so close and yet denied him as surely as if a thousand leagues lay between them.

Earlier, for several hours after her arrival, Elfleda had exasperated his filial patience with her weeping, with her nagging insinuations that he had somehow brought the curse of paupery down upon their heads. Overly long had she whined a harangue of sullen accusations into his ears, petulantly insisting that his unbridled lusting after Alysaun had stirred the wrath of God against their proud name, against their hearth and station in life.

That sudden streak of piety in an otherwise immoral nature had elicited Esmond's laughter, an unending stream of maddened mockery that brought tears to his eyes and left him clutching his belly. She had slapped him then, dared to strike his face as if he were a child in need of reprimand. The only satisfaction of the day had come in viewing the stupified look of shock that had graced his mother's features when the instinctive blow of his open palm across her cheek had sent her slamming backward to land against the solid foundation of the rush-strewn floor.

More than the pain of the reddened, swelling imprint his hand had left upon her jaw and cheekbone, the audacity of Esmond's act had made her features into a mask of horror. The mask had crumbled quickly, though, revealing a succession of raw, naked emotions. The loss of her power to sway him, to alter his moods with a look or gesture, was so deep a pain that it left her too stunned to even cry. For the first time in his life, the hauteur that had covered any doubts or indecision in his mother's character faded and revealed a woman aware of her own vulnerability.

As much as he attempted to ignore it, the faint sounds of reveling drifting to his room from the great hall seemed to thunder against his door, to drum against an ear tuned to listen, even though the laughter and merriment were torture to an already ravaged pride. Jealousy, heightened by a vision of Alysaun listening to Brand, her face alight with that soft radiance she reserved for him, finally brought Esmond to his feet. The chair, thrust back by his abrupt movement, slammed against the floor with a loud crash that startled Elfleda awake.

Seeing him at the door, she called out, asking groggily where he was bound. The only answer was a whoosh of air that entered the chamber as her son tugged open the door and the rattle of the metal latch against the doorjamb as he shut it firmly after himself.

Esmond's walk reflected his temper as he strode in long, jerky steps to the edge of the hall. There he paused, surveying the scene with heavy, sullen eyes, searching the length of the room for Alysaun. The fact that she was not present gave him some satisfaction; the sight of de Reynaud lounging in the midst of friends and well-wishers brought a sneer to his thin lisp.

No one seemed aware of his presence. When the music ceased, Hereward dropped his huge frame into a high-backed chair, wiping at his sweaty forehead before he made a loud, jocular comment to the effect that, though pleasurable, dancing was harder on a body than a day's raiding. The others around him moved to seek some refreshment to lessen the thirst of expended energy, and Brand laid his instrument aside to lean forward and speak with Hereward.

Although his approach was quiet, almost stealthy, the conversation grew hushed, the air chilly with a frost of disdain. Eyelids hooded, half concealing the hard, ice-blue color of his irises, Hereward was the first to acknowledge Esmond, his contemptuous gaze sweeping from the booted feet that paused near his chair to the pouting, willful set of the dispossessed lord's face.

"What, Rede—did the noise of our celebration disturb your night's rest?" Hereward drawled with a smirk. "Or have you merely decided to honor us with your presence?"

Brand tensed, with much the same feeling one has in the presence of a snake, a blend of revulsion and caution. He had seen little of Esmond since the day they had ridden to the clearing in Grouneswold, the rendezvous point for his exchange. Now that the lout was free to roam, it was just as well Hereward had suggested that Brand leave Ely. Though he had no conclusive proof that Esmond had set the trap for his seizure, Brand knew that intrigue and deceit were as natural to the spoiled and arrogant youth as taking a breath.

"I did find your joyous excesses somewhat repugnant in the light of your assault upon and destruction of my manor," Esmond complained, ignoring Brand as if he were invisible.

Hereward exchanged an amused look with Brand and settled back in his chair. "But you are mistaken on two counts, Rede," he answered with a mock-innocent expression. "The manor of Havistock was no longer yours. Hence you've lost nothing by our day's work. And though we did enjoy an earlier indulgence in drink to toast our success, our rejoicing at this later hour is in honor of the good fortune that has seen Lady Alysaun returned to her husband's care." Hereward grinned at Brand and winked. "Should I inform our 'guest' of your news, my friend, or would you care for that pleasure?"

Brand leaned back, taking a certain righteous spite in the apprehensive suspicion sharpening Rede's features, deliberately delaying an answer to enjoy the squirming of his enemy. "I'll take the pleasure, with the added responsibility," he replied at last, and looked up at Esmond, mouth curving in a pleasant smile that jarred against the triumphant gleam in his eyes. "Tonight we have laughed and danced and drunk to celebrate my wife's revelation that she is carrying my child."

The blood drained from Esmond's face and for a second his thoughts were open to view, pinching his long nose, flaring his nostrils in disbelief, then despair before he recovered his wits enough to hide what he felt. "Alysaun is no longer wife to you, de Reynaud," he insisted, and recklessly added, "Furthermore, you seem gullibly content to believe 'twas you who sired the babe."

The jibe was meant to spark his fury but in recognizing that fact, Brand refused his avowed enemy the satisfaction of an angry retort. "Our marriage vows stand as true as on the day they were said, sir. Your persistence in believing them severed reveals a strong inclination for self-delusion. Likewise, I find the implication that you are responsible for fathering Alysaun's baby utterly ridiculous."

"Why so, de Reynaud? I passed many a night in the girl's bed and lay with her often enough to leave you with a doubt."

"Nay, I've no doubts at all," Brand asserted with a confidence that salted Esmond's wounded vanity. Despite a desire to loose his fury at the callous pronouncement of the passion Esmond had spent on Alysaun's unwilling body, Brand was intent on cutting the youth down to size with words instead of a weapon. "I'm aware of your fumbling attempts to take what was mine, boy," he stated coolly, "but they could not have bred anything but Alysaun's pity. A child oft attempts to ape his elders but, lacking maturity, falls short of the mark."

The color came flooding back into Esmond's face, a bright flush of crimson that bespoke how deeply Brand's verbal knife had stabbed. "Only time will verify your claims or see them mocked by a child stamped with my features," Esmond replied with a trembling arrogance that was almost pitiable. "I'll discourse no longer on a subject so dependent upon the passage of time to evidence whose seed took root."

Ignoring Brand again, Esmond faced Hereward and demanded that the rebel deliver over the gold coins seized in the raid. "You cannot claim them as Norman pillage, for the money was mine, and I will not go forth penniless while you possess it."

"The money was lost to you ere the Norman, de Bourney, set foot upon your property, sir. Why should I return what was pledged to my cause and, further, which I had to risk *my* neck to take?" Sober, Hereward's rein on his temper was short; his hold on it now was just shy of blasting Rede's impudence with a Hell's-breath of sizzling oaths. "You try me too far, boy. Be glad I did not let your mother crisp in Havistock's flames, and take a measure of relief that you still possess your health. You've a knight's training, sir. Go and put it to use. I owe you nothing."

"You forget I risked my own neck to alert you of the sheriff's action against de Reynaud. Certainly the warning saved him as much as your mission to Cambridge—for that I claim his worth to you as the redemption of my pledge.''

Morwena, who had taken a stroll the length of the hall with her new admirer, returned in time to hear Esmond's statement and her knowledge of his deceit made the brazen comment twice as hypocritical to her as it must have seemed to the others. She knew how he had duped her into seeking the brooch that had sealed Brand's fate but, in her shame, had confessed it to no one, not even to the priest, who might absolve her sin. Hoping it would cleanse her soul of the guilt she carried, Morwena opened her mouth to tell the truth, but the words would not come.

''If you thought your journey so selfless, why did you agree to aid Hereward's cause?'' Brand asked, curious to hear the reasoning behind the pledge.

''For Alysaun's sake,'' Esmond insisted. ''She actually believes this rebellion has a chance to succeed.''

''And you don't?'' Hereward's voice cut in, dangerously low.

''Nay, I am too practical to believe so small a force can do more than sting William's flanks and nettle him. If he were not so busied with other uprisings, here and in Normandy, he'd have moved against you by now and crushed the token resistance here on Ely.''

The man's smugness was more than Hereward could bear. His face had reddened, a blue vein swelling at his temple, portending the stoppered violence of his temper. ''Then you gave your vow in bad faith?'' he asked, his head rising to pinion Esmond with a glare.

Too late Esmond realized the trap his vain opinions had set for him. There was no ally among those watching him. The sense of ill-will radiating toward him from their leader swelled with their support to wash over him in a threat that seemed minutes away from becoming physical. ''Nay, I merely gave new thought to the prudence of endangering myself for a cause that I felt doomed,'' he replied, his expression nervous, gaze shifting from face to face. ''Who can blame a man for lending a care to the needs of those who look to him for security?''

'' 'Tis the first decency to issue from your lips,'' Hereward said, "and for the same reason will I retain the cache of coins. These good people around me rest easier if I guard their welfare as diligently as you did Havistock's thralls. Say no more, or I'll not be held to account for the loosing of my wrath. Come morning, I want you gone from Ely. Blooded Saxon you may be, but God has never seen fit to mold an Englishman so utterly useless to his kind."

"How glibly does that condemnation flow forth—and from a man who would succor a foreigner and turn away his own countryman." The man was no more than a bewhiskered marsh rat. The idea that he should speak so contemptuously to one of his betters was galling, a sign of the times, perhaps, but no less annoying. Drawing himself up with a regal air, Esmond inquired, "Stripped of all I own, sir, exactly how do you propose I make my way? Surely you can't be suggesting that *I* . . . hire my sword arm out like some common retainer?" His offense at the idea was so great his aggrieved expression elicited a snickering laugh from a few of the men watching.

Hereward sighed heavily and rolled his eyes heavenward. "How else might you expect to earn your bread and keep, sir? I know 'tis a great shock to your august personage, but good, honest men like those you see about me *do* fill their bellies by exchanging a day's work for food and recompense. What bloody use is your knight's training if you'll not lift a sword to defend your country or support your needs? A foreigner Brand may be, but no charity he's asked or received, only recompense for his loyal efforts on our behalf." Scorn soured Hereward's mouth.

Too many Englishmen had witnessed the same losses Rede knew and picked up the threads of existence to make a new life. This man or callow youth was merely indolent, too embittered by his misfortunes to understand that he must stand on his own two feet. "There are lords aplenty, here and abroad, looking for skilled men-at-arms," he explained, and glanced over at Brand, to find him staring disgustedly down the length of hall. "For an example, Brand and I were discussing the chance he might go to Constantinople and join the Varangian Guards." At the mention of his name, Brand came out of his dark brooding and, puzzling over Hereward's sudden amiability, questioned him with a glance. His friend shrugged as if to say his mention of the mercenary guard was an attempt to rid himself of Esmond's obnoxious presence. "The duties are light, the pay rewarding. Many of our Saxons, Dane and Angle both, swell their ranks."

Watching Esmond's face closely, Morwena was horrified to see a glimmer of furtive hope light his thin, sharp features. It was quickly covered by a mask of congeniality, dispelling the stubborn sulking that had beset his expression for the past quarter hour. Her heart began to pace rapidly, bringing a dampness to her palms. She could almost hear the workings of his mind, the delight he felt at yet another opportunity to disrupt Alysaun and Brand's happiness, to scheme and lie in wait for the right moment, perhaps even to see personally that Alysaun was widowed and once again easy prey.

The rush of blood to her face renewed the aching of her bruised cheek and Morwena raised a hand to touch the swelling, listening carefully to Esmond's answer despite the preoccupied look in her eyes. "I owe you an apology, m'lord," he said most humbly, directing a brief, courteous bow to Hereward. "My losses this day have overwhelmed my senses, leaving my temper churlish. I find your suggestion intriguing and can see nothing demeaning to my pride in serving Byzantium." He bowed again to Hereward and included Brand in the obeisance, his thin-lipped smile as wicked as the bared fangs of a snake. "And you, sir. If we should meet again in the capital of New Rome, I've a hope 'twill be on more amiable terms."

Brand made no answer, disgusted by the thought. Though he had thought of turning homeward, the idea of serving in the elite corps of the Emperor's guard had held a certain appeal. Now, with the possibility of Rede joining the Varangians, Brand's interest turned sour. "Do as you please," he snapped. "I've seen the city. You will no doubt find it amenable and to your taste."

Esmond had started to turn away but paused at the possibility that Brand wouldn't be going to Constantinople . . . or taking Alysaun there. "You've decided against joining the guard...might I ask why?"

Morwena could no longer take the chance that Brand might be sucked into Esmond's scheming. "Because if Lord Brand was unwise enough to join, he would leave Alysaun a widow, his child fatherless," she said before Brand could speak. All eyes turned to her and though tears had sprung to her eyes, Morwena was resolute. "Do you think, Esmond, that he has not guessed at your duplicity?"

"You are *mad*," Esmond snarled, turning to the others with a bewildered expression and a shrug of his shoulders. "Clearly the blow the lady suffered has addled her wits. I care not—"

"My wits are sharper, sir, than when I allowed you to make of me an unwilling accomplice to this man's pain and sorrow." Her head held high in defiance, Morwena dared Esmond to deny she spoke the truth. She turned to Brand, who was staring at her in white-faced shock, and the tears spilled down her cheeks. "I beg your forgiveness, sire, for I have wronged you and Lady Alysaun by my own ambitious acts. Too long have I been loath to admit my guilt. Now that the threat arises anew, I must speak."

"How were you a part of Rede's plans, woman?" The stern query came from Hereward.

Morwena swallowed hard. Ashamed to look at either Hereward or Brand, she faced the man who had brought her to so low a state. "I...fell victim to Esmond's guile. He paid court to me, raising my hopes to become the mistress of Havistock, playing upon my weakness to make me his partner in the treachery he planned. 'Tis no excuse, I know. He asked me to take the circle brooch from your room. I did and saw it next the afternoon you were seized by the sheriff's men. Even then, when I was told to replace the jewelry, I did not question his motives. Only later, from Sir Edelbart's lips, did I learn how the brooch was used to condemn you."

"Lies...all *lies*," Esmond exclaimed, fixing Morwena with a menacing glare meant to silence her. "'Tis her word against mine. True, I dallied with her to pass the time, but she is exacting the vengeance of a woman cast aside."

"The night before, Alysaun worried over the sincerity of Rede's attention to you, girl," Brand said in a deadly calm tone, ignoring Esmond's flustering efforts to defame Morwena. "How soon afterward did he move to draw up the papers annulling my marriage to Alysaun?"

The smile that curved her tremulous lips was mirthless, a recognition only that her answer would decide the probity of her confession. "Lady Alysaun will tell you the same, sire. 'Twas but some three hours after the hunting party did return with the tale of your capture. I dare say you could not have yet reached Cambridge ere Esmond had moved to dissolve your wedding vows."

"And Alysaun, certainly she was not a willing party?" Brand knew the truth but he wanted to hear it affirmed.

"Nay, m'lord." Morwena's gaze softened with compassion. A good deal of the rancor between the couple had been her fault. Breathing seemed easier with her guilt admitted. "Esmond would offer his assistance in going to Hereward only if she promised to sign the papers. When she balked at such a price, he reminded the lady of the tortures used to extract information from prisoners."

He had known the deceit that trapped him was born of Esmond's selfish desires, but to hear the evidence of how coldly the plans were laid, to imagine Alysaun in a trap no less agonizing than his own, stunned Brand, leaving him senseless of his surroundings for a minute. Hereward, on the other hand, reacted to the revelation with a feral sharpening of his wits. His eyes caught the jerky, backward movement of Esmond's feet and even before his leonine, sandy-maned head had completely turned toward the retreating scoundrel, his men were obeying a growled command to seize Esmond.

The order stirred Brand's awareness and sent an icy shiver of fear down Esmond's backbone as Brand turned to look at him. Even in combat Esmond had never considered his own death, but in the glittering, steel-hard determination of that stare he saw a reflection of his demise. It was useless to struggle against the two men who had answered the rebel's call to secure him. Their hamlike hands held him at shoulder and forearm, banding his tensed, quivering muscles with unrelenting pressure.

"The dog's fate is yours to decide, Brand," Hereward said, resigned to carry out an immediate execution if that was what his friend desired. Rede had callously plotted to rid himself of Brand, breaking the holy commandment to refrain from coveting another's wife, and no court, ecclesiastical or civil, could deny he deserved death. "Shall I arm my men with bows or would you see him dispatched in a less merciless manner?"

"Nay, I will give the man the chance he denied me, to go down with a sword in hand, " Brand replied, and glanced around at those who had witnessed the disclosure of Esmond's culpability before he rose and stretched muscles knotted with tension. "If you'd do me the courtesy of sending a man to fetch my own sword and one for him . . ." Brand seemed dazed still and Hereward worried that the course chosen might see him fall, a loss too valuable to risk on Esmond's worthless hide. "And clear the hall, if you would. This work needs no witnesses."

"As you wish, son, but . . ." Hereward paused, fumbling for what he wanted to say, then swore a casual oath for his inability to frame his feelings in adequate words. "I just cannot see the need . . . well, yes, I can, but the son of a bitch doesn't deserve the chance you give him. I know well your skill of blade but a twist of fortune could see you bleeding your life upon the rushes and Alysaun a widow."

Brand grinned, recognizing the concern in Hereward's face. The hand he raised to squeeze his friend's shoulder was strong with purpose and confidence. "I swear the blood that stains the floor will not be mine and Alysaun will be no widow. Think you that I would let that quivering pile of jellied bones deprive me of the joy of seeing my son grow? Nay, put your worry to bed. Let me proceed before I am too tired to have done with it."

With that reassurance, Hereward moved quickly to follow through with Brand's requests. Esmond was dragged down the hall, kicking and protesting his innocence the entire time in a voice that squeaked with fear. Knowing she could do nothing to interfere with the chain of events set in motion by Morwena's confession, Frida took charge of herding the whispering, staring throng from the hall. Hereward, sobered now by concern, stayed by Brand's side until the servant he had dispatched returned with Brand's heavy, doubled-edged sword and a weapon borrowed for Esmond.

While Brand examined his blade, testing its edge and frowning over the fact he had not cleaned or tested it after the morning's raid, Hereward took the other weapon, one of a number of spare armaments stored in a wardroom off the entry. This one would do for Esmond's defense, thought Hereward, smiling to himself at the dull edge it possessed. Before Brand could see it and be disposed to claim a more equitable weapon, the thane sheathed it and traversed the length of hall to take a stand near the pale-visaged, weak-kneed captive and await Brand's leisure.

When he finally approached, Brand signaled Hereward to lay the weapon at Esmond's feet. He did so, ordering his men to release their hold and pausing long enough to assure Esmond in an acerbic tone that masses would be said for him, despite the fact that where he was bound, "shouted prayers to God could not be heard."

Esmond barely heard the condemnation. He stared after Hereward's retreating figure like a man plucked from Purgatory only to be deposited in Hell, in utter disbelief at his predicament and sure it was some fool's joke that would soon end in laughter and reprieve. But the sheathed sword lying parallel to his toes was nothing to laugh upon, nor, as his gaze rose from it to his opponent's grim expression, was the weapon Brand grasped. Its triangular tip was blunted, its edges fine-honed; it was a hacking weapon meant to dismember and maim.

"How can you be so very sure I am guilty?" he asked, stalling, postponing the time he must stoop to retrieve the sword and lift it on behalf of his own will to survive. "No one knows—"

"*I do*," Brand said, and indicated with a wave of his sword tip that Esmond should arm himself. "And beyond what your greed and spite have done to me and mine, I intend to see you cut down to the small shadow you cast in trespass against so many others." Esmond opened his mouth, but no plea, no bargaining for mercy, would change what was to be. "Save your air, Rede. If you've enough left before expiring, I promise you a priest will see you shriven . . . more than you did offer me."

"A kind offer and just but, then, you were ever the noble," Esmond commented dryly, scrabbling for the sword hilt despite the fact that Brand made no move to stop him. Rising with it, resigned now to fight rather than face the alternative of a defenseless, prickled death by arrows, he manipulated for time to size up his opponent's possible weaknesses. "You may keep your offer, sir, and save the priest's words for your own death." He laughed, a desperate, uneasy barking, drawing his weapon to toss the sheath away. "He may also give some comfort to Alysaun. 'Tis a shame only that her widow's weeds will be spoiled by the swelling of her belly."

Brand showed no reaction to the jibe other than a flaring of his nostrils, as if Esmond gave off an odor most foul. His right hand tightened around the pommel of his sword, all his fury centered in the taut, firm muscles of his upper arm. Esmond noted the action and, though his grip was lathered by sweat, reacted instinctively, hefting his weapon to ward off the heavy downward strike of Brand's blade. The blow reverberated, vibrating down the length of his sword to stir his hand with a buzzing sensation.

Lighter, more wiry of build, Esmond ducked and whirled to challenge Brand with a thrust to his left side. The broadsword parried, stopping the metal an inch away from Brand's ribs, and pushing the lighter, one-edged sword back with a powerful lunge that sent Esmond toppling backward. His foot caught against the raised dais, throwing him off balance to land on his buttocks. Winded and panting, with Brand closing in, Esmond scrambled, slithering across the rushes to roll on his knees and right himself.

From that moment it was a battle lost. Brand continued advancing on him, no matter what position he took, and, amazingly, the man showed no signs of wearing under the steady pursuit he maintained. A scurrying retreat across the breadth of the hall gave a moment's respite to catch his labored breath, but the sight of Hereward lounging against the vaulted entrance to the hall, grinning and confident of Brand's skill, further enervated Esmond.

Esmond waited for a charge from Brand, met it, and, with a thrust of his foot, kicked a stool in his opponent's path. It was easily avoided but the pause gave Esmond momentum for a vicious assault that slowed Brand's own offensive attack. One moment of triumph he knew, as the sword point sliced the blue silk tunic, the brief satisfaction of knowing his blade had met the flesh of Brand's shoulder . . . then an enraged bellow announced a fierce series of jabs and maneuvers that pushed Esmond back to the wall.

For one slow second Brand hesitated, and in that eon Esmond considered how futile were his efforts. Even if he won this combat, Hereward was at the ready to see him die. The time of death would only be delayed. His expression lost its fierce defensive look, replaced by a puzzled daze as he mused how all his efforts, his patient, perfectly executed plans, had come to nothing. A second later, as Brand's powerful forearm propelled his sharp blade forward, Esmond no longer puzzled. Every nerve in his body screamed as the sword slipped through flesh and muscle, organs and vessels, as easily as a knife in butter, to exit at the center of his back, severing his spine as it emerged dripping blood, smeared with gore.

When he saw the fatal thrust, Hereward loped toward Brand in a graceful panther's stride. The hall echoed with his footfalls, drawing Brand's attention from the ugly open show of guts the withdrawal of his sword had left, to meet the excitement of his friend's face with a look that was emotionless, neither pleased nor sorry, only relieved that the man's warped mind could no longer do his family any harm.

He dropped the sword across the crumpled, limp body and turned away, leaving the weapon behind without any care for its fine craftsmanship or tempered strength. Hereward questioned the deed, commenting, " 'Tis a waste of good weaponry to bury so worthy a man-slayer with the refuse of Rede's carcass."

Brand rubbed his forehead, suddenly aware of needed sleep, of muscles that ached from overuse. His shoulder was merely scratched; only a trickle of blood stained the pale blue tunic. It could wait upon the morning's light to be tended. "Let the sword go down in the earth with his body. It is poisoned by the rot that despoiled Rede's soul, and I would not care to handle it or even use it again upon any man."

Hereward still thought him crazed for wasting a costly weapon, but the matter was Brand's to decide. "So, our smith will forge you another, m'boy," he said, "an even greater sword than my own beloved Dragon's-breath. What say you to that?" He threw an arm around Brand's shoulder and, with the affectionate license of an older brother, ruffled his hair. He accompanied him to the vaulted archway that opened onto the rest of the living quarters. The others were gone but Frida waited, her worried expression vanishing at the sight of Brand, who was well and whole.

"Well, son . . . what's it to be?" Hereward probed. "You can scarce go about without a proper weapon at your disposal."

"Thank you, but I've a mind to wait upon the journey that sees Alysaun and me settled in Constantinople," Brand replied, surprising Hereward with the firmness of his decision to go there. Alysaun would love the city, for there was no other like it in all the world. A home there, far from the painful memories of England, would be a new beginning. Brand grinned at his friend. "The Byzantine armorers are famed for crafting a fine, tempered weapon of Damascus steel, not a man-slayer but one designed for dragon-slaying." Hereward gave him a doubtful look, then, as Brand added, "Even the most devilish fire-breathers," caught his meaning and joined in a laughter that was at first mild, then uncontrollably raucous, doubling them both with mirth. Frida, never having known the gut-twisting tension that coiled within a fighting man or the soaring of a spirit once more triumphant over possible death, could only smile and wonder at the cause of such abandoned merriment in the wake of violence.

PART II

Constantinople, June 1071

13

The soft summer breeze rising off the waters of the Bosporus was warm and slightly tangy. It stirred the bright golden tendrils that had escaped Alysaun's neatly coiffed braids and teased the pale lavender-blue veil that covered them. Early June in the temperate area surrounding Constantinople was one of the loveliest times of the year, and this day had been particularly beautiful.

Now, as the hour of dusk approached, she and Brand watched the city change to gold-pink as it reflected the setting sun. Their vantage point lay across the strait, on the opposite shore of the Pera District, a window on the top floor of the military Tower of Galata. Her back was against his chest, and Brand's arms circled her waist and held her close. For the moment, both were content to study the beauty of the view and revel in the rare day spent with each other.

The light was fading now to a purple haze. The approach of evening heralded an end to the day's shared intimacy, but an awareness that time was passing too rapidly shadowed Alysaun's happiness. She raised a hand to touch the corded strength of Brand's arm and ran her fingers across the scarlet silk sleeve of his dress uniform to cover his hand with her own. Brand looked so handsome and commanding in the bright, gold-trimmed tunic that marked him as a member of the elite Varangian Guards; it was the reason they had been allowed access to the tower, which was normally off limits to civilians.

Soon after their arrival in Constantinople, nearly twenty months ago, Brand had paid over seven pounds of gold to join the guards, whose primary duties were to serve as the Emperor's personal bodyguards. Then, with the newborn Matthieu to occupy her time, and since the empire was at peace, Alysaun had been proud and content to be the wife of a Varangian officer. Most of Brand's duties had been ceremonial, and he cut a most dashing figure as the captain of a *banda*, leading his cavalry unit on parade along the Mese, the broad boulevard that stretched from the city's golden gate to the imperial palace at its southern seawall.

Even with the rumblings of trouble on the empire's faraway eastern frontier some seven months before, Alysaun had remained relatively calm, sure that the vast Byzantine army of native *Themes* and hired mercenaries could easily put down any feeble attempts to encroach upon the vast territories of the empire. Three months later, when Emperor Romanus IV himself had gone into the field to drive back the Seljuk raiders, she had begun to worry that the minor frontier skirmishes were not so minor after all and would last long enough to see Brand's regiment called into action.

Now what she had dreaded had come to pass. Brand was leaving for the east, his unit called up to replace troops that had been with Romanus and had engaged the enemy for some time. Three more days—that was all the time they had left. Though she had been close to tears several times, Alysaun refused to yield to them. She wanted Brand to leave without remonstrances from her, no weeping and swollen eyes to mar their last days together.

Today they had left young Matt in the care of the older Greek servant who had been his nanny almost from the day he was born. Alysaun had packed a cold supper of smoked fowl and cheeses, bread and wine, and they had gone off for an afternoon of exploring spots in the city they had grown to love. At midday they had paused for a meal at a small inn on the Street of the Good Shepherd, not far from the huge, oval Hippodrome. Both of them had grown fond of the heavily spiced Greek delicacies, especially the rich, honeyed pastry called baklava.

A visit to the merchants' shops at the Augusteum—the open square bounded on the south by the palace, on the east by the towering, gilded dome of Hagia Sophia, and on the west by the immense arena of the Hippodrome—had followed the lunch. There they had parted briefly to "look for a surprise for Matt," but neither had much fooled the other with the excuse. When they met again at a bench across from the cathedral, each had purchased a small wooden toy for the boy and presents to give each other later in the day.

At a commercial quay not far from the imperial harbor, Brand had found an aged Greek fisherman who was willing to sail them across the Marmara to the southern tip of Pera. His asking price for the trip had seemed amazingly low, but during the half-hour voyage they soon realized they had to pay an additional price—listening to an unending recital of the man's many sea adventures. By the time the caïque had docked at the Pera wharves, Brand and Alysaun had been given a compact sketch of Marius Androthos's lifelong wanderings, including tales of the sea monsters he had encountered.

Now Brand bent his head, pressing a kiss upon the slim white fingers that covered his own, stirring Alysaun out of her musings with the suggestion that they should be on their way. " 'Twill be dark soon, love," he said. Even as he spoke, the lamplighters of the capital had begun their nightly rounds and, in the distance, the lamps along the streets began to twinkle.

There was just enough light left to pick out a path through the wooded stretch of grassy, sloping land that edged the southern shore of the peninsula. Arm in arm, they strolled beside the seawall, listening to the gentle lapping of the waves against the rock. It was a quiet, peaceful end of a perfect day and neither Brand nor Alysaun cared to break the comfortable silence.

Finally they stopped to rest beside a curve of shore very close to the spot where the strait met the Sea of Marmara. The metropolis glowed dimly across the waters, and the first evening stars seemed to shine only for them, two lovers who would all too soon be parted. The night air was cooler now, and Brand slipped his cloak over Alysaun's shoulders. Careful of the veil that covered her bright tresses, he tenderly adjusted the wrap about her throat, then, unable to resist, pulled her closer and bent his head to kiss her.

For several minutes they held each other and what had begun as a loving embrace soon warmed to a desire that gripped them both. It was Brand, remembering that Marius had promised to return to the wharf an hour after sunset to take them back to the city, who drew back and took a deep breath to calm his racing pulse. Alysaun knew the reason but pouted still, longing to have his arms back around her. Three nights left . . . so little time, and she wanted to spend it wrapped in his embrace. Too soon she would have only memories to warm the lonely nights without him. Now, while he was still with her, it was difficult to stay the need to indulge in the sensual.

To keep from reaching out and boldly enticing her love out of his caution, Alysaun walked to the seawall and stood listening to the soothing rush of the tide. Many times over the two weeks since they had learned of his impending departure she had considered the dangers Brand would face. Brand had assured her he would be cautious. He would be in the vanguard of the fighting, positioned near the Emperor to guard Romanus from assault; but, he insisted, it was the safest place of all. No emperor had ever been captured by the enemy.

Brand studied Alysaun's silhouette, the slender, patrician figure half turned to face the dark sea. He wondered what she was thinking and softly called her name. Perhaps he had wounded her pride by seeming to withdraw from her. "Alys?" he called again, and caught the reflection of troubled concern in her expression as she turned to him and stretched out a hand.

When he reached her side and caught her close, Alysaun was smiling, the hint of worry banished. She could not let him leave and carry along a concern for her that might affect his concentration in battle. "You're not to worry about us, m'lord," she insisted, reaching up to stroke his cheek with a light, loving touch. "We'll be fine, Matt and I. After all, I am no longer the young girl you wed."

Brand threw back his head and chuckled, then drew her closer in an affectionate hug. "What, has being a wife and mother aged you so, my sweet? You must be all of nineteen now, hardly a woman of years." Loosening his hold a bit, he tipped her chin high with his fingertips. "Alys, love—there's nothing matronly about you. I can assure you your features are untouched by time and, if anything, have grown more beautiful since we met. In fact"—he turned, looking for the basket that had held their supper, discovered it a few feet away near a rise of thick brush and bushes, then continued—"if you'll bear parting with me for a moment, I've a present I chose for you particularly because it reminded me of that day."

Despite the breeze, Brand's cloak was a trifle warm and Alysaun drew it from her shoulders. When he returned with the picnic basket, Brand accepted the cloak and spread it on the damp ground, then requested she be seated. With a courtly bow, he sank onto the cloak himself and held up his gift, dangling the dark velvet pouch before her by its golden drawstrings. "For you, m'lady . . . in fond memory of the day we chanced to meet."

The moon was just beginning to rise, its mellow gold reflecting across the waves. Alysaun managed to catch the strings from Brand's fingers and, even as she chided him gently for teasing her, pried open the pouch to withdraw the small glass figurine of a fawn. She held the cloudy, amber-brown animal up to catch the moonlight, marveling over its delicacy. Poised on thin, fragile legs, it seemed ready to flee from some danger its gentle, lifted nose had scented. Alysaun was so moved by its beauty that her "I thank you, m'lord," came out in a hushed, throaty whisper. "You . . . you said it reminded you of our first meeting. Tell me why, please."

"You remember that morning in the greenwood?" Brand asked,

and smiled. Alysaun nodded, suddenly embarrassed. She looked past him, eyes dreamy and distant with remembering.

"How could I forget? Even now I can see how fiercely you glowered over the loss of your provisions. And merely because of a borrowed apple—"

"*Stolen*, m'love," Brand corrected. "And 'twas a rabbit and *two* apples, if I'm not mistaken."

Alysaun's eyes met his, a full, lovely pouting of her lips rebuking the exactness of his recollection. "I was famished, sire, and did not pause to question the source of such bounty. Do you still begrudge the sharing?" Alysaun smiled and shook her head. "Nay, you are too gracious to hold the debt over me. I think you had forgiven me by the time we took to the road together."

"Sooner than that moment, my sweet. When I first spied you in the clearing, young and fragile, yet somehow haughty in that drab and ragged gown, you took away my breath and, with it, the thought of vengeance." Brand reached out to take the crystal fawn and balance it on the back of his left hand. "You were already facing danger and, like this young deer, alert to flee from your enemy."

"So . . . following on the heels of righteous anger, the next emotion you felt for me was pity." Alysaun's mouth quirked in dismay and she reached out to pet the fawn's delicate nose with a fingertip. How had love flowered from such an awkward beginning? "I'm most thankful, sire, that you made no mention of such feelings when I appeared at your camp. My pride would have made me turn away, though I needed your help."

" 'Twas not pity so much as sympathy, Alys. And, truthfully, I did make use of my growling belly to cover the deep wrench of unease you stirred in me. Put a fair distance between yourself and this girl, I remember thinking, for she will spell an end to your carefree days." Brand laid the figurine on the velvet pouch and took Alysaun's hand in his. "I am most grateful that I ignored that inner voice of warning, truly as it did prophesy."

"Was it so terrible, then . . . to lose your freedom to wander?"

"I will answer your question with another. Do I have the look of a discontented man, wife?" He smiled as she shook her head in answer, then his look sobered again. "And now," he said ruefully, "now I must leave you. If I had not pledged my word and sword to—"

"I know, Brand . . . nothing would take you away." Alysaun sighed. "But you would not be the man I love if your pledge were not so sacred. I cannot keep you from your duty. It is just that we have so little time to share." Alysaun lifted her head, parting her lips in an unspoken invitation. Brand smiled, the past forgotten as he lowered his mouth to accept the sweet offering.

For moments they held the kiss and the passion that had earlier flared flamed into a searing fire that could not be dampened. Alysaun slid her other hand around his neck and relaxed, her clinging embrace bringing him with her as she lay back upon the dark-wine mantle.

Everything, the softness of her mouth, the firmness of the full breasts pressed beneath his body, spoke of Alysaun's willing surrender to desire. Even as her boldness pleased him, Brand puzzled over the almost deliberate seduction. He had suppressed his desire earlier, remembering their appointed rendezvous with the boat that would be their only way home. Again, she seemed unconcerned with the hour, and it was he who withdrew from the embrace.

"How can you ignore the call of your senses, sire?" Alysaun inquired petulantly, clinging to his neck, her fingers interlocked at his nape. "If we are calling up memories this eve, Brand, I do recall quite vividly the delight you took in our honeymoon. Though you made me blush at the immodesty, *then* you did not hesitate to possess me. In fact, I think you reveled in the impropriety of making love with the sweet grasses of the meadow for our bed."

"'Tis not fear of discovery that makes me pause, Alys. Would you have us stranded here over the night and leave poor Sophia concerned over our fate?" Alysaun was smiling, a sweet gentle curving of her mouth as she toyed with the rust-brown curls at his nape. She looked not the least concerned with what Matt's nurse might think; in truth, with her lashes half lowered over a warm and sensual gaze, with her fingertips lightly massaging the tension from his neck, she seemed intent only upon having her way.

"We *have* time . . . especially if we waste no more of it discussing its passage," Alysaun insisted. "Give me one reason why we should not make love here, with the stars as silent witnesses, the rush of tide whispering around us?" Brand said nothing, but a slow grin spread across his mouth. It was an irresistible offer. "You see," she declared, "I'm right."

"I see only that marriage has given you an insatiable lust, my darling," Brand teased, his grin widening as she opened her mouth to protest. "And 'tis clear as crystal that I must sate them for the time being or risk being assaulted on board Marius's boat."

"True . . ." Alysaun fell in with the teasing banter. "You've chanced upon a most intriguing idea, sire. Now, wouldn't *that* add to his list of tall tales,"

Brand bent his head and pressed his mouth to the hollow beneath her throat. "Not another word out of you, m'lady." His fingers brushed aside the silk of her wimple, caressing her skin with a familiar, possessive touch that stirred shivers along the length of her body. "If Marius fails to wait for us, we'll be forced to spend the entire night thus." Brand emphasized the "penalty" by running a hand along her back, down the curve of hip and thigh to tug at her hem and expose one slim, alabaster leg to the moonlight. The hand that stole upward, to slide between the warmth of her thighs, was chilled by the night air, but more shocking to Alysaun was the jolt of desire its caressing fingers stirred. As Brand moved over her, an airy puff of cloud sailed across the moon, shadowing the two bodies that merged as one.

Two hours later Brand and Alysaun were safe at home, and Marius was spending the extra coins Brand had given him to compensate for their tardy arrival at the dock buying a round of drinks for his friends and grinning over the excuse given for being an hour late. He had been young once and in love enough times to make an allowance for the slight twist of truth that covered the lovers' trysting.

Oh, they'd become lost, sure enough, but only in each other's arms. Marius took a swig of the heavy, sweet wine and, recalling a pleasurable moment from his youth, raised it in a salute to the couple. They'd claimed to be wed, but he'd never seen a married couple so enamored of each other's company.

Still, as he had sailed the boat out into the open sea and set her course for the homeward voyage, Marius had overheard snatches of intimate conversation that hinted at domesticity. The young guardsman had promised to write often, and his lovely companion had given him a cross to wear about his neck to keep him safe in God's care. Really, if they weren't married, it would be a shame to spoil such bliss with vows. Marius settled back more comfortably in his seat and propped his legs up on a nearby chair. Wed or not, they were a nice couple and he wished them well. 'Twould be a shame should the nice captain not come home unharmed to his lovely lady . . . or, worse, not come home at all.

Even before his personal servant entered his tent to awaken him, Brand was up and alert, nearly dressed in his uniform. The same tension that had made sleep so difficult now set him to pacing the breadth of the tent, walking off the coiled energy that preceded an anticipated engagement with the enemy. Brand's expression was fierce as he mentally tallied the readiness of his armor and weaponry.

The rest of the huge fortified camp on the outskirts of Manzikert would not be moving about for another hour, but Brand, for the first time in the fifteen years or more he had been raising a sword with skill, was worried about the clash with the Seljuk forces camped not three miles away.

In his own prowess he had every confidence. He could stay mounted in the thick of battle and use his double-edged sword of imported Damascus steel to cut a swath through any field of combat, no matter how fierce the combatants. No, it was a warning born of many battles' experience that jangled his nerves and brought about this odd unease. No one could name him a coward—he had fought in his native Provence and for men he trusted, such as Hereward of

Lincoln; but although he had sworn an oath of loyalty to the empire and to Romanus as its leader, Brand could not claim that this day would be theirs.

There were too many factors that could result in a defeat, and if the scouting reports of fresh reinforcements for the Sultan's camp were correct, it would be a decisive one. The very size of the Byzantine force was a major hindrance. The actual number of fighting men available was only a third of the entire body. The rest were servants, engineers to manage the siege machines, cooks, camp followers. The list of nonmilitary personnel attached to the service of cavalry, infantry, and bowmen was endless, and aside from making its movements sluggish, the task of feeding so vast a force had become more of a problem than engaging the enemy. Indeed, some of the troops had been dispatched as far afield as Georgia simply to forage grain and foodstuffs from the land.

The native districts giving service to the empire numbered at least forty themes, but these had been vastly reduced by the Emperor's predecessors. Poorly equipped, irritable at being drawn far from home at harvest, they could scarce be counted as eager or battle-ready. The truest of the experienced warriors were the mercenary and auxiliary troops drawn from the farthest reaches of the empire's northern and eastern frontiers. Of the foreign regiments, the Franks could be balky, having in the past actually refused to fight in the midst of battle. The Armenians were excellent fighters, as were the Uz mercenaries, but their loyalty in this encounter was questionable. Indeed, not three days before, an Uz detachment had deserted to join the Seljuk ranks.

The rest of the mercenary troops were seasoned and loyal, but for one small factor—no one had been paid in almost two months, hardly the greatest inducement to men who had offered their lives in return for coin of the realm. Morale had never been lower, and yet Romanus, desirous of an end to the Turkish encroachment on Byzantine lands, could not turn away from the chance to see it finished here at Manzikert in one final confrontation.

Brand finished his third inspection of his equipment just as the young Saxon lad who was his personal servant entered the tent. John Brodby had left England with his brother and father in the wave of English escaping the reign of William. His brother was with a mercenary troop stationed in Bari, the last of the empire's territories in mainland Italy, now threatened by Normans under Richard Guiscard. His father had died on a foraging party, not a month ago. With all his heart the boy wanted to be a Varangian, but his lack of the gold needed to buy membership in the corps had made the dream an impossibility. He had bonded himself out as a servant, just to be close to the guards, and had wound up as Brand's aide.

"You're about early this morn, m'lord," John commented, and cast an apprehensive glance at the armor and mail his master had been inspecting. Even before Lord Brand had retired, the weapons had been polished and sharpened. The coif and hauberk gleamed from several hours of industrious cleaning. Had the captain found something amiss? His broad shoulders looked tense and, as he turned, he looked vaguely irritated. "You seem displeased, sire. Is my work not satisfactory?"

"Nay, John," Brand said. "I've no reason to question your efforts. 'Tis only . . . I have never been a patient man and 'twill be hours before we meet the enemy. I would that it were as simple a task as other combats I have known."

Young John breathed a sigh of relief, brushing a thick lock of white-blond hair from his eyes. He was eager to be in the battle himself and understood his lord's desire to have it done with. "Shall I fetch your meal, m'lord? Or perhaps food would not sit well with your temperament. Mayhap a draft of cool wine to ease the waiting?"

"Aye, that would do well, son. Go fetch it, then, and bring a cup for yourself as well." John looked shocked at the suggestion that he join the master, and Brand's face creased in an amused smile. "Were it not for the want of gold, you'd be riding with us, lad," he assured him. "And I care not to drink alone. Hurry off, now. My thirst is growing even as the sun climbs higher."

The servant, flushing a ruddy shade that contrasted with the fairness of his complexion, bobbed a quick bow and respectfully tugged his forelock. When he was gone, Brand sat down on his cot and pulled out a small slate mat to finish his letter to Alysaun. He hadn't written in four weeks and the sheet of vellum parchment he drew from his wicker chest had the beginnings of several letters written and scribbled out.

Undoubtedly he had had reason for the delay in corresponding, but he *had* given his word to write faithfully. Still, as he began anew and found himself straining for words, Brand realized that it was not lack of time that had kept him from it so much as his attitude. Alys knew him so well that even if he touched lightly on his duties and the everyday happenings of the camp, she would be able to sense his dissatisfaction. And at this distance, how could he explain the worry that nagged him without making her more afraid for his safety than she must already be?

Finally, because there was always the chance that he might not return from combat, Brand pushed aside his unsettled thoughts and wrote of how he missed her and Matt. It was a short note, renewing his vow of love for them both, touching more upon how happy she had made him than on army news. He had just finished sealing it with a waxen imprint of his ring when John returned with the wine.

Though the boy still seemed ill at ease with the idea of socializing with his superior, Brand insisted that he sit down and share a cup. "'Twill help me to relax, John, and I've some favors to ask of you."

Several hours later, by the time the roused encampment had been called to assembly, Brand was ready to do battle. He made a heroic figure, standing tall and straight-shouldered despite the weight of the gleaming suit of mail that protected his body to just above the knee. The golden hilt of his sword, set in a scabbard engraved with the same rampant lion found on his signet ring, glistened in the bright morning sun.

John stood at attention when Brand emerged from the tent, holding the reins of the huge, braid-tailed charger that would carry his lord into battle. Other officers passed, exchanging wishes of luck and fortune, but to John's misted blue eyes, none appeared so grand as Brand de Reynaud. John had good reason to be so emotional. Lord Brand had entrusted him with a note to be dispatched to his wife, and John had solemnly given his oath that should anything happen to Brand, it would be delivered to Lady Alysaun. Then, after de Reynaud had made sure his personal effects were neatly stored in the chest, he had turned to John and offered him a purse heavy with coins.

"To reward your loyalty, John," he had explained, brushing aside the stuttered words of gratitude from a stunned and pale John. " 'Tis enough, with what you have saved, to buy you a place in the guards." Now, as Lord Brand mounted and took the charger's reins from him, John stared up and swallowed hard.

"God bless you, sire. May He keep you safe from the heathen." He swallowed several times more and his prominent Adam's apple bobbed. "And, m'lord . . . again, I . . . I thank you for—"

" 'Tis nothing, John," Brand insisted, and drew his helmet on, adjusting the metal strip that protected his nose. Already his eyes looked distant; clearly his thoughts were on the coming battle. Despite the tension of his earlier misgivings, Brand de Reynaud was eager to ride forth, an almost arrogant confidence apparent in his carriage and expression. A tug on the reins brought the horse's head back, and horse and rider turned to merge into the tide of passing cavalrymen. John stared after them and caught the flash of a grin as Brand called back a reminder to say a prayer for victory.

John watched until he could no longer see the valiant figure in mail. Lord Brand would return safe, the day's victory would be theirs, surely the sun would set on a vanquished Turkish force, he assured himself. Yet the boy could not help but remember the afterthought that had followed on Brand's gracious gift. The money was enough to buy him into the Varangians, providing, the master had added, "that there *is* a guard to join, come nightfall."

An actual clash with the enemy was delayed until the sun was lowering in the west. By late morning the Byzantine forces had assembled in their customary two lines. Brand's unit was arrayed behind Emperor Romanus, other Varangian *bandion* protecting his

313

flanks and forming an intimidating vanguard of armored, ax-bearing warriors. To their right, the line consisted of a division of thematic troops and Uz mercenaries; to the left were the Western themes and Patzinak auxiliaries. The second line comprised reserves under the command of Andronikos Dukas.

Throughout the day, the Byzantine advance had been steady, and the retreat of the Seljuk mamluks had seemed to the less seasoned soldiers to be a sign of their eventual victory. Brand, who had joined the Emperor in time to see the Turks in action at Erzurum, some eighty miles from Manzikert, knew better. This was the manner in which they fought, their show of retreating only a ruse that frequently led the enemy into a trap. Still, the Greeks outnumbered them.

The heat of the sun burning down on the heavy coat of mail, the clouds of gritty dust that rose from the chargers' hooves, the delay of action—all combined to bring a return of Brand's irritation. The advance across the plain ringed by hills seemed more an exercise than a battle, and if not for the distant cries of minor skirmishes on their flanks, it would have seemed as if the endless ride were merely a part of the previous night's dreams.

By late afternoon the line had paused. Romanus called his commanders in with the news that his scouts had learned that some ten thousand fresh troops had joined Sultan Alp Arslan's force. With night fast approaching, Romanus was worried about the security of their camp, left entirely undefended in the rear.

When the order came back to Brand to return to camp, and the imperial standard was brought about, he ordered his own command to follow suit. Further along the ranks, the order was either muddled or contradicted. Suddenly confusion reigned in place of calm reason. To the left, the Armenians rapidly seized the chance to desert. The right flank held, but when rumors of the Emperor's death were whispered, even its commanders were at a loss as to how they should proceed.

Pandemonium took over, and waves of savagely shrieking Turkish horse and bowmen swept down from the hills to take advantage of the confusion. They easily cut into the nearly undefended left flank, partially severing the front line from the reserves under Dukas. There were more desertions, more wild rumors of defeat, and several officers in succession were sent back through the lines to call up the reserves.

The Varangians closed in a tight, protective circle around Romanus, fighting now against the Seljuks, who had broken through the ranks toward the standard and the imperial commander it represented. Brand had only a moment to look back, and that quick glance revealed the disheartening sight of the Emperor, still astride his mount but bowed over its neck, a Seljuk arrow protruding from his shoulder.

Now that the fighting was man-to-man, Brand had all he could manage just to stay mounted and defend his flanks from the lances and swords of the Turkish cavalrymen. Everywhere he looked, a sea of dark, almond-eyed warriors filled the plain. The circle surrounding the Emperor was breaking; he thrust with the full strength of his sword arm and managed to withdraw it from a Seljuk's chest only with a great effort, then wheeled the charger up and back, toward the floundering royal defenses.

Then his stallion screamed a shrill, agonized whinny and seemed to hang in the air, an arrow buried deep within its great ebony chest, and Brand's instinctive jump saved him from breaking a leg beneath the charger's falling weight. He landed hard on his left knee and felt something give, then tumbled off balance, a spray of bright scarlet blood spattering his armor as a comrade nearby decapitated one of the enemy.

The ground was slick with blood and spilled guts. Those still fighting, and most of them seemed to be Turks, were so covered by gore it was difficult to tell if they were wounded or not. Brand shoved aside a Seljuk who had fallen across his legs, firmed his grip on his golden sword hilt, and started to rise.

Those animals still unhurt by the slaughter were panicked in the melee. They lost their footing, slipping only to rise again and trample fallen bodies as they tried to escape the whiz of arrows and the slash of metal weaponry. A wildly rearing horse he never even saw crashed its back hooves into his helmet at the left temple and punched the metal inward. The blow sent Brand flying, and he landed on his back atop a heap of bodies. Before the darkness engulfed him, a sticky flow of blood pulsed from the links of chain mail pressing against his temple, and the world turned a rich, vibrant red. In the second before his fingers went limp and released the sword hilt, a rapid flash of emotions rippled through his brain—disbelief, regret, but most intense of all, sadness.

The Sultan's personal physician walked down the row of wounded soldiers, pausing at each pallet to check a pulse or reassure a patient that he was, indeed, mending. At the last pallet, he studied the profile of its occupant and smiled to himself at the pretense of sleep. The physician felt a natural concern for the officers and men who had been wounded in the great victory over the Greeks two weeks before, but this tall foreigner intrigued him. Professionally, Abak el'Suile found this patient a challenge. He had been brought in from the field with a concussion, still alive but breathing shallowly. At first sight, the doctor had nearly consigned the man to those whose wounds were mortal or too much of a shock to the body to survive. Whatever had prompted his change of mind, he was now grateful.

It had taken five able-bodied men to hold the man, for in the attempt to pry the bent helmet from his head, the pain had stirred him to consciousness and to a wild strength that hampered the attempt. Once the metal cap was off, el'Suile had shaken his head in wonder. Such a wound, with the helmet pressing the links of mail into it for the hours he had lain unattended on the field, should have killed him.

A draft of opiate had sedated the wild thrashing enough for a thorough examination and cleansing of the depression at the temple. Unless the pressure were relieved, he would die anyway. More sedatives were administered, and the patient was tied to the pallet as an added precaution. Using skills he had learned at the Fatimid court in Damascus, the royal physician had trepanned the wound, lifted the broken piece of skull that pressed on the brain, and sutured the wound partially closed to allow for drainage.

Now, after two weeks of recovery, the stranger seemed physically well. It was his loss of memory that fascinated the learned physician and brought him time and again to talk to his prize patient. He discovered that the man spoke the odd, guttural English tongue as well as the softer, mellifluous speech of a southern Frank; he also knew some Greek and Turkish.

His intelligence was obvious and unimpaired by the wound. He could think and reason, function as perfectly as he would have before the battle, but he could not remember who he was. Now that the Byzantine emperor had signed the terms of the treaty proposed by the Sultan, he and all of his officers had been freed, even given provisions to make their journey home easier. This nameless one had been kept hidden from the rest of his comrades, though, and was the last of the enemy to remain.

"How are we faring today, my son?" el'Suile now inquired in a patient, even tone. "The healthy color is returning to your face. You may walk today if it taxes your strength not overly."

"It taxes my strength just to *think*, sir," came the snappish reply. "I was resting. What do you want of me?"

The physician made allowance for the rude answer. It was not easy to lose all the familiar details of one's life, especially the name by which one was known. "As part of your recovery, you must make an effort to rise each day and walk about the camp. Now that the fighting is past, the countryside is quiet and most pleasant." Always affable, the doctor tilted his head and offered a smile. "You were ill, and now God has seen fit to mend you. Come now, Cuibhil Rustim, I will accompany you in a brief stroll." El'Suile had mentioned his patient's possible value as an interpreter to his majesty and even provoked a chuckle of amusement from his sovereign by suggesting they dub the stranger the Red Cub, a title that played upon the meaning of Alp Arslan, Mountain Lion.

"My name is *not* Cuibhil Rustim," the man insisted vehemently, stubborn defiance written across his strong, handsome features. It was clear even to himself that he was not of Turkish stock. His coloring was sun-darkened but naturally medium to fair. His eyes were a changeable hazel green, his hair a rust brown. "I am no Seljuk to carry such a title."

"Then tell me your name or at least where you were born," el'Suile insisted, knowing that he could not answer.

"I don't *know* my name, only that 'tis *not* Cuibhil Rustim." Having heard himself called it enough times to begin thinking of the title as his, he still found its foreign sound unsuited to the look of himself in a mirror. He glanced up now, wondering why this man, who had apparently saved his life, was so persistent in his questions. When he tried to puzzle out his identity or summon images from his blank past, the only result was an angry frustration that left his temples pounding.

"Then I will not press you further, my son. I do insist, though, that you walk with me. The change of view, the sunlight, will continue your mending. Come, I offer you my hand." The physician pushed back the full, draped sleeve of his long robe and held out a hand that was surprisingly smooth and firm for his age. Cuibhil thought of refusing, but he owed the man a measure of respect and courtesy for his care, and he wasn't sure he could manage without the assistance. In two weeks he had spent little time on his feet.

With a good deal of caution, he planted both feet upon the woven rug beside the pallet and, with el'Suile's hand firm beneath his elbow, came to a standing position. Not really weak but nowhere near his normal strength, Cuibhil chanced a few steps and found his legs obeying a silent order to advance. El'Suile took his hand away, walked toward the rear of the long, rectangular tent, and disappeared for a few moments behind a wooden screen.

He returned with a smile and, noting that his patient wore only a thin, shapeless shirt of muslin, he remarked, "Even in the warmth of a September morning, we must protect you better than this. This should fit you," he continued, and offered a rather garish peacock-blue robe that stretched to the ground as his own did. "It is meant to be loose but you are so tall. Let us try it anyway." He held the robe

318

up and helped Cuibhil slip his arms into the full sleeves, then tied the three sets of silk cord to the left, beneath his arm. Stepping back, he appraised the robe and pronounced it wearable, then stooped to produce a pair of open-backed slippers that were hidden behind the voluminous folds of his robe.

"Walk along with me, son. If you feel any weakness, I am here to assist." He stood back and allowed Cuibhil to precede him down the aisle between the two rows of pallets, observing approvingly the relatively strong strides his patient was able to take. Indeed Cuibhil forced his short, somewhat corpulent mentor to hurry just to stay apace.

Outside, the bright sunlight seemed to stun Cuibhil for a few seconds. He paused, shading his eyes from the glare until they adjusted to the increased light. The camp, though at peace now, was still a beehive of activity. Up a hill to his left, a unit of some twenty Seljuk horsemen were exercising their sturdy mountain ponies, racing them past a target on the ground to swoop low and catch up a strip of silk. Even as he watched, one young warrior missed catching the material and was forced to accept the jeering calls of his comrades.

He was about to turn back to el'Suile and ask some questions that had been bothering him when a shy giggle, echoed by three more women, drew his attention to a tent across the way. A young woman, veiled but clearly pretty in a dark, petite way, had been about to enter the tent, followed by her attendants. She paused only a moment more, silencing her still-giggling maids with one commanding glance from a pair of lovely almond eyes, then demurely stepped into the sanctuary.

In answer to the curiosity in Cuibhil's glance, el'Suile explained that while the Sultan's troops took a well-deserved rest, the camp would remain intact for at least another week or two. A few of the court nobles had allowed their wives and daughters to visit before the army moved on to an assault on Damascus, their original objective before the taking of Manzikert had drawn the Byzantine emperor out for a defensive battle. The maiden they had glimpsed was the youngest daughter of Alp Arslan's second-in-command, Soundaq the Turk.

The physician suggested that they walk through the encampment, insisting for his own sake that they set a leisurely pace. Everywhere young warriors were busily sharpening their weapons or honing their fighting strength in wrestling exercises that lured their companions into high-spirited gambling bets. Try as he might, Cuibhil could not find one face that looked familiar, nor did anyone hail him as a former comrade-in-arms.

At the top of another hill, east of the camp, the two paused for a rest beneath a stand of cool, lush olive trees. It was then that Cuibhil had an opportunity to ask for information about himself. If he was a mercenary who had fought for the Sultan, as el'Suile had told him he was, why had no one recognized him? Why were there no other Western mercenaries in a camp that was clearly populated by nothing but Muslim Turks? Where were his personal effects, his clothing, his armor?

Where, indeed, thought el'Suile in a sudden panic at so many rightly curious inquiries for which he had not prepared answers. It had been his idea to suggest that the young man be employed as an interpreter to the Sultan's military council and his suggestion as well that they claim he had been fighting on their side. Having become genuinely fond of the man, and sure that if he knew he had been found in a uniform of the Emperor's famous Varangian Guards he would seek to leave in a fruitless search for his forgotten past, el'Suile had concocted the story. Now what could he say that would sound plausible? He hadn't thought far enough ahead to prepare a soldier's pack of clothing and personal items, and since Cuibhil Rustim was so big, there was no one in camp whose tunic or boots would fit him properly.

"I'm gratified to see that your mind is still sharp and functioning as it did before the wound stripped you of your memories of us, my friend," el'Suile finally answered, refusing to meet Cuibhil's anxious gaze. The physician rose from the worn boulder where he had rested his bulk, stretched, and gave a weary sigh that suggested the walk had been too much exercise for him. "Your questions are very perceptive and in due time will all be answered." He turned and smiled down at Cuibhil with so innocent an expression it seemed childlike and out of place among the lines and wrinkles of advanced age.

"You were not with us long before our recent victory," he went on, "and we were most grateful for your pledge to fight under the Sultan's standard. In fact, his majesty is most concerned that you make a full recovery. Come, return with me now and rest. I would not care to suffer my lord's wrath if you should suffer a setback in health."

Before Cuibhil could reply or even pause to consider how smoothly his new friend had sidestepped answering with any detail, el'Suile was off, waddling down the hill with an energy that belied his age and girth. Cuibhil had to jog a few steps to catch up, and when he finally came abreast of the physician, he was, indeed, too worn to press his inquiries. Once the older man had escorted him safely back to his pallet in the cool dark of the hospital tent, he paused just a moment to assure him that time would both heal him and see the answers to his concerns revealed.

A week later, with so much of his strength returned that he was able to spend most of each day exercising in the sunlight and fresh air, Cuibhil found that the doctor's predictions had come true. He resided in his own private tent and had found within it an array of clothing that, if as new as the identity he had assumed, fit his measurements exactly. His personal servant, a boy of not more than twelve years, had welcomed him home with the enthusiasm of Joseph's brothers, assuring Lord Cuibhil that he had guarded his tent and possessions as if they were his own.

Cuibhil soon slipped into a daily ritual of rising early after only some five hours of sleep. His nights were troubled by dreams that often brought him suddenly awake, to find himself drenched in sweat. The images that peopled his dreams were vague and shadowed, tantalizingly elusive figures that dissolved when he reached out.

He had become a familiar figure in the camp, up at dawn for a run twice around its perimeter, followed by two hours of lifting heavy trunks and stretching. Sometimes his mentor would appear and sit in a nearby spot of shade, admiring the tireless efforts that such conditioning exacted, beaming with an almost paternal pride when a passing Seljuk warrior paused to envy Cuibhil's height or to admire his stamina.

On this morning he had been working for a longer period than usual. The disturbing flashes of a slender, faceless woman who haunted his dreams had been particularly unnerving in the early hours before dawn. It seemed as if he could almost discern her features, and then, like a door closing, the enticing figure would recede into the mists of the dream.

It was more a desire to exorcise than to exercise that prodded him to work until his well-muscled chest, bared to the waist, glistened with a film of perspiration that only emphasized the ripple of corded muscle and tendon. As Cuibhil paused to drink two dipperfuls from a bucket of cool water, before he splashed another across his neck and shoulders, he was unaware of the imposing figure he made, his forearms bulging with the swell of his exertions, his skin once more a deep, healthy tan. The single narrow strip of linen that banded his temples and secured the small pad of cloth over his healing wound made him look all the more dangerous.

He first heard the sounds of a commotion, then, on the heels of a feminine scream, as a petite young girl with tawny braids flying whirled desperately around the edge of his tent. She tumbled against him and would have fallen if Cuibhil had not stretched out his arms to catch her. Not much more than his servant's age, she was clearly terrified, and the sight of him, bare-chested and towering, did nothing to lessen her fears.

As two thickset, burly guards rushed around the corner with swords drawn, the girl gave a shriek and clutched at Cuibhil, losing her fear of him in the face of a greater threat. She was crying now, pleading for his help in what Cuibhil recognized as a Greek dialect.

322

The two men chasing her paused, frowning at the tall foreigner who stood between them and their quarry.

From behind them, an arrogant voice called out a command and the two men sheathed their weapons, coming to attention as their superior came into view. The girl's terror seemed renewed by his appearance, and Cuibhil shoved her behind him before he turned with deliberate leisure to survey the man. Apparently he was a noble of the court, for his embroidered coat of crimson silk was finely cut and fastened at the waist with gold plaques. There was some foreign blood in him; the shoulder-length hair and two side braids were not the usual Seljuk black but a rich, dark brown.

He, in turn, had paused with arms akimbo to take Cuibhil's measure with a sweep of dark blue eyes whose arrogance matched his voice. Obviously he considered the young girl his property and would have her back despite the tall stranger who had dared to interfere with her capture.

"Seize her," he ordered in his own tongue, and Cuibhil knew enough Turkish to understand the command directed to one of the guards. He smiled before he told the girl to back away and stay near the open flap of his tent. A gentle push sent her in that direction as she hesitated, and Cuibhil flexed his arms and readied himself to defend himself against his approaching opponent.

A crowd had begun to gather and were now in hushed conversation as a circle formed about the antagonists. At its edge, a horrified el'Suile looked on, his mouth opening and closing as he sized up the situation. Even as Prince Malik Shah's aide made a rushing lunge at Cuibhil, it was too late to warn the lad that he had interfered in the royal heir's business. Even if he won, he might well lose his head for such audacity.

For a man of his size, Cuibhil moved with the fluid grace of a lion. Mindful of his still-healing head wound, he crouched just moments before his attacker reached him, bringing his left shoulder up sharply into the guard's lower chest and using the force of the lunge to flip him over his head. The man landed in the dust with an audible whoof of escaping breath, began to rise, then fell back.

Cuibhil couldn't resist a brief grin, the sight of which, added to the humiliation of seeing his man handled as if he were a bothersome fly, sent Malik Shah's temper raging. He ordered his other aide in, hissing a tight-lipped warning of his fate should he fail. Caught midway between his fear of the prince's wrath and the obvious skill of his opponent, the aide hesitantly went forth, watching for the move that had downed his fellow guard.

Cuibhil sensed the man's apprehension and feinted to the left, then to the right; to the enjoyment of some members of the crowd, he threw back his head and laughed at the nervous jump the feint inspired. El'Suile, anxiously watching his prince's reaction, saw Malik flush with embarrassment and gnaw his bottom lip in worry. Beside him someone was taking wagers on the outcome, and most of the bets were in favor of Cuibhil.

Suddenly the assembly was hushed and the physician turned to see the royal guard make his attack. He charged Cuibhil Rustim's right side and for a brief second they were locked in combat. El'Suile flinched, raising a hand to his own right temple as if anticipating the pain of a blow against his patient's bandaged wound. With eyes tightly shut, he missed the lightning movement of Cuibhil s hands as one gripped the guard's right shoulder, the other his wrist. An easy twist of his right leg hooked behind the man's knees to send him tumbling gracelessly backward. The memory of a promised punishment for failure stirred him to attempt to rise, but the heel of a polished black boot pressing his neck against the ground discouraged the effort.

"If you *still* claim the girl is yours, m'lord," Cuibhil declared, "I most humbly challenge you to defend your property yourself." There was a deathly hush as all eyes turned to the prince. His mouth was stubbornly set in a hard line, his gaze never leaving Cuibhil's face even as his hands worked to loosen the bows that secured the diagonal flap of the *muqallab* under his shoulder.

A cheer went up from his father's gathered warriors, and excitement coursed through the crowd, now three rows deep and growing as word spread through the camp. Disturbed by the unusual noise, the Sultan himself had appeared at the entrance to his tent. Seeing Cuibhil Rustim at the center of the crowd, he smiled, then craned his neck to see who had challenged the mercenary. He approved of a good match, finding that in times of peace his men needed to vent the energy they usually channeled into battle.

He had fought many a wrestling match himself in his younger days and was interested in seeing how well the young man who reminded him of his heir in manner and build could acquit himself. The soldiers parted as Alp Arslan moved to the inner ring of spectators, where he discovered his own son, the heir apparent to the throne, entering the arena of combat, stripped of his coat and wearing only the thin muslin undershirt tucked into his leggings. The Sultan's eyebrows drew together in a frown, but even as he wondered what reason the two had for the fight, it had begun.

Having allowed the pinned guard to escape, Cuibhil moved back and poised in readiness to take on the man's superior. Above average height for a Turk, the man was still several inches shorter than himself. He looked to be in good condition, and the wary caution reflected in his narrowed eyes reminded Cuibhil that this was no mere lackey.

He waited for the man to make the first move and, when a sudden tensing of his muscles predicted an assault, easily sidestepped and whirled to face him again. This happened twice more, and each time a deeper frustration lined his opponent's face. Using the same feint that had been successful against his second attendant, the prince managed to butt Cuibhil's midsection with a sharp jab, knocking him off balance long enough to pin him.

The crowd went wild, and in their midst the Sultan couldn't resist a grin of pride. Moments later there was dismay as the royal heir was sent flying head over heels, propelled by a springlike action of Cuibhil's long legs. He landed, raising a cloud of dust and grit, and silence reigned as everyone waited to see if he was injured.

His pride was wounded more than anything else. It had seemed that victory was his, and now the stranger was up and crouched in that catlike style, waiting to continue the fight. Malik shrugged away the hands that offered assistance and came to his feet, clapping the dust from his crimson leggings. He was breathing hard, and yet the man who had fought twice already barely seemed troubled by the exertion. As Malik cautiously circled and prepared to engage him again, he could not help but admire the man's skill and wonder who he was.

Despite his calm demeanor, Cuibhil was tiring quickly. If he didn't best the nobleman soon, his waning strength would see him the loser. He wanted to win, not only because the outcome seemed likely to decide the girl's fate but also because the fellow needed his arrogance trimmed a notch or two. Finally the man made his move, swinging a blow with his closed fist that thudded against Cuibhil's right shoulder, knocking him back but not hard enough to fell him. The soldiers cheered, and his own lack of support firmed Cuibhil's determination to triumph over the favorite.

From the corner of his eye he saw Alp Arslan standing at the edge of the crowd. Cuibhil smiled to himself, making several false passes to lure the nobleman around the ring until his back was to the Sultan. Then, an arm's length away, he glanced past the man, stepped back, and executed a most courtly bow in honor of the royal presence. Malik stared at the sight, then turned to glance behind him and, for the first time, realized his father was watching.

The ruse had gained the advantage for Cuibhil, just long enough for him to charge and, again, use his shoulder to knock the prince backward. The crowd drew back and fell silent as their royal hero lay in the dust, with a worn and panting Cuibhil Rustim pinning him to the ground.

Malik raised his head, then let it fall back. He had gone down in defeat and, worse, before the Sultan. Malik's embarrassed flush was hidden by a layer of dust, but he admitted grudgingly, "The girl is yours, won by your victory."

Cuibhil struggled to his feet and took a moment to catch his breath before he bent and offered assistance to his defeated opponent. Clearly there was a struggle in the proud features, but as the prince accepted the offer of a hand up, the crowd cheered him as if he had won. For a few seconds the two stared at each other, each puzzling over the other's identity. It was the prince who voiced his curiosity, wondering aloud whom he had fought.

The answer came from the Sultan. Alp Arslan grinned, pleased that his son had fought well and conceded in an honorable way. "We call him the Red Cub, my son," he answered, clapping a hand on Malik's shoulder, "and for reasons you now must recognize."

Cuibhil paled slightly at the realization that he had fought the Sultan's son, wondering whether he would have acted differently if he had known. Beyond Alp Arslan, at the edge of the crowd, el'Suile stood, an ear-to-ear grin revealing his pleasure in the outcome of the combat. Cuibhil glowered at him for a second, transmitting a look that said he might have warned him.

The physician gave an expressive shrug in answer and came forward to pay his respects to the prince, offering a flowery but vague compliment to Malik. The Sultan suggested that Malik escort Cuibhil into the royal tent to share a drink in friendship. "And tell Kassim to bring water to wash the dust away. Go on, I will follow you shortly." Both he and his physician watched the two young men go off, accepting the plaudits of the parting crowd, who now seemed to accept Cuibhil as one of their own. Arslan noted how much alike they seemed and, remembering that el'Suile had brought the foreigner to his attention, mentioned that he would grant a suitable reward to him. "Already the fight is forgotten, el'Suile. I think my son has found a valued friend."

"I agree, your majesty. Indeed, it had been my fortune to observe that the best of enemies often become the best of friends."

14

Alysaun leaned against the casement of her bedroom window, watching the lowering mists of the thick gray stormclouds that had threatened Constantinople for the past two days. A damp breeze touched her face, caressing features that mirrored the melancholy weather. Like the clouds, pendulous with unshed moisture, her eyes glistened with dammed tears. Only a stubborn determination not to shed another, self-pitying tear kept the floodgates shut.

She knew well enough the reason for her brooding. In another week her son would turn four, and for the second year his father would not be present to see Matthieu's face light with the joy of that special occasion. Matt was too young to remember how great a pleasure Brand had taken in celebrating his day of birth. Although the small face framed by russet curls reflected more of his father's features with each passing year, Matt had only vague memories of the tall, handsome man who was his sire.

Perhaps Matt was fortunate to have been so young when Brand disappeared. He had Hereward to wrestle with and young Devon, now of an age to join his father in the elite Varangian Guards, to teach him all the many lessons that a woman could not. For Alysaun, though, two years of mourning had not lessened the empty ache within. There were times when she thought it impossible to go on, when, waking in the still of night, she had instinctively reached out for Brand and touched only the coldness of the sheets in place of his body's warmth. In those utterly lonely moments she mocked the reasoning of a God who had allowed her to drink the heady wine of love, only to snatch the cup away ere her thirst had been slaked.

In the light of day, when her misfortunes seemed less harsh and her spirits were buoyed by the warmth of Hereward and his family, Alysaun could not bring herself to blame heaven for her fate. There were other, far more earthly reasons for what had happened. It was not the first time in history, nor the last, that ambition and greed had made widows out of wives.

Word of the Turkish victory had trickled back slowly to a tense and anxious Constantinople. A treaty had been signed, ceding important territories to the Sultan. Some of the returning troops claimed that Emperor Romanus had been executed; others claimed he was merely a hostage until the treaty terms had been enforced.

Each day Alysaun stood watch along the Mese, one of many women who crowded the capital's broad, main boulevard hoping to see their husbands and lovers among the returning warriors. The days passed into weeks, the weeks into a month. Suddenly, without armed rebellion, Romanus was deposed, named a traitor. His young stepson, Michael, was proclaimed the new emperor, raised to power at the age of nine by his uncle, the Caesar John Ducas. The Caesar, the same ambitious man whose son had failed to bring his reserves to Romanus's aid, announced that he would rule as regent until his nephew attained his majority. The empress Anna, wife to two emperors, mother of yet another, was banished, exiled to a secluded island in the Aegean.

By December the Ducas faction was firmly entrenched. Word came from the south that Romanus, blinded at the order of the Caesar, had made his way to his wife's side. The first month of 1072 had arrived with an uncustomary blast of wintry northern winds, and with it came the report that Romanus had died of his infected wounds.

Very much alone in a city she had come to love, Alysaun had despaired more with each passing day. A few of the Varangians who were with Romanus until the Caesar's vengeance had caught up with him returned home to their families. None of them could say that Brand was dead; to a man, they were sure that he was not among those who had been captured with Romanus and then released.

Aside from the anguish of uncertainty over Brand's fate, Alysaun was close to impoverishment. The small cache of funds that had seemed limitless when Brand departed in July was now nearly gone. She had dismissed the servants one by one. The owner of the small house they had rented clamored daily for his overdue rent. Her position was ambiguous; Brand was missing and his monthly guard pay had been stopped, yet no official would declare him to be one of the honored dead of Manzikert. She did not qualify for a widow's pension . . . she qualified for nothing.

The strain of worry took its toll. Thin and nervous, aware that she must find some source of income or watch her child suffer, Alysaun prayed as she had never prayed in all the years of her young life. The only thought that saved her sanity was a hope that soon Brand would appear at their door. That he might be wounded may have kept him from coming home sooner, but she was sure he was alive and would come back to her.

One of Brand's fellow Varangians, moved to compassion by her plight, offered to take her into his home. He was an older man, a widowed Norwegian with six children, one of them close in age to her own Matthieu. Sven Esgarrdson meant the offer kindly. He was far too paternal a figure to worry her with the thought of an intended seduction. In return for what she might otherwise consider charity, he asked that she oversee the religious training of his brood and herd them all to mass at least once a week. He would provide shelter and necessities for Alysaun and Matt. The idea of handling seven children all at once was overwhelming to Alysaun, but she was in no position to refuse. Too clearly she remembered the lean, hungry days before her path had crossed Brand's. In her love for Matthieu, she could not let him suffer so.

Then, like an answer to her prayers, on the very day she was to send her answer to Sir Esgarrdson, Hereward had appeared at her door. She nearly fainted at the sight of his dear, familiar features. Despite the justness of his rebellion against King William's tryanny, Alysaun had left the island fortress of Ely with an unvoiced dread that Hereward would die in the cause of England's freedom.

Shocked by her obvious frailty, Hereward delayed telling about his escape from William's siege of Ely until he knew the reason for her condition. Repeating the few known details of Brand's disappearance to one who well loved him had released a long-suppressed torrent of bitter weeping. The sharing of her sorrow eased the pain and heartache; the relief of knowing she was no longer alone was a blessing in itself.

Hereward would not allow Alysaun to join Esgarrdson's household now that he and his Frida were in Constantinople and longing so for her company. "Ye wouldn't know Devon. Why, he's near as tall as I am," he had exclaimed; then, remembering that she was still carrying Brand's child on their departure from Ely, Hereward asked after the health of her son.

"How ever did you guess that 'twas a son?" Alysaun had asked in wonder, then laughed, for the first time in months, at his explanation. It seemed that Frida, deemed a witch by the superstitious Norman fools who feared her knowledge of ancient folk arts, had correctly predicted a son for Brand.

Then, taking Hereward by the arm, Alysaun led him into Matt's room to show him her pride and joy. Though it was Matthieu's nap time, they found him wide awake and sitting on the floor, playing with his puppy.

Now, two years later, the fawn-colored whelp was fully grown, still playful but nearly the size of a small pony. And the toddling Matt had lost both his baby fat and his awe of the towering Hereward, who spoiled him far more than he ever had his own

Devon. Matt and Hereward were nearly inseparable except for those times when the boy "allowed" Hereward to go off and tend to his duties as the captain of a *banda*, a unit of the Varangians assigned to protect the young emperor Michael at the imperial palace. Fortunately for Alysaun and Frida, with Devon and his father both serving in the guards, the empire was in the midst of an uneasy peace, broken only by brief incursions of the Seljuks upon the gradually shrinking Byzantine borderlands.

Hereward was a wonder. He was a father in Brand's place, a protective guardian angel to Alysaun, a strong, hearty man whose very presence inspired hope. Much of his free time had been spent questioning the veterans of Manzikert, though he learned little more than had Alysaun. He had made sure that Alysaun's petition for her widow's pension was filed. Through a combination of bluffing and badgering Hereward had extracted the handsome amount of ten pounds of gold from the imperial treasury as compensation for Brand's service.

In spite of the family's overwhelming kindness, Alysaun felt she could not go on forever as Hereward's pampered guest. She and Matthieu fit neatly into the family fold, but Devon would soon be old enough to consider taking a bride and his parents deserved a chance to live their lives in contented privacy.

A loud bark from the hall beyond the open door of her bedchamber startled Alysaun from her memories. She turned and found herself the object of an affectionate assault as Matt raced the hound, Bracken, across the slippery, tiled floor. Matt won, but as he pinned his mother's legs in a tight hug, the dog, sliding in for a howling, skittering second place, collided with Alysaun and Matt, and both of them went down in a jumble of tangled limbs.

Neither seemed hurt by the fall. Alysaun looked up and fixed Bracken with a stern frown. The huge dog was up in a flash, his head cocked to one side as he measured the extent of his mistress's irritation. A soft whimper sounded in an almost human apology; then, before she could raise a hand to stop him, Bracken came closer and roughly scraped Alysaun's cheek with a drooping, wet tongue.

Try as she might, Alysaun could not maintain her composure; she started to giggle, and Matt joined in, so puzzling Bracken that he settled back on his hind quarters to study the display of silliness.

A footstep sounded at the door, followed by an astonished curse. Devon knew a wealth of oaths, learned early at his father's knee, but his voice still lacked the older man's authority. Bracken picked himself up, tail wagging as he padded over to Devon's side and nuzzled his nose against the young man's fingers, eager to dissociate himself from the accident and its results.

"You great, lop-eared cur," Devon swore. "*Now* you've gone and done it." He ordered Bracken to sit and apologized to Alysaun as he started across the room to help her up. When she giggled anew and covered her mouth with both hands, he glanced back to see the dog stretching the muscles of his huge forepaws in a haughty show of unconcern. Bracken then gave a shake that rippled his shiny coat and trotted off. A *"Hold,* Bracken" was ignored as well as he went off in search of one of his many hidden bones.

Devon glared after him, then turned back to offer his hand to Alysaun. "That mongrel never obeys," he complained, and, when Alysaun was on her feet again, added, "And I think our master Matt here is fast learning Bracken's habits."

"Ah, but there was no harm done," Alysaun replied soothingly, though she fixed her young son with a look that questioned his lack of discipline with his pet. "Though there well might have been had I not been so nimble," she continued. "You must keep a better mastery of him, Matt. I'd not want to hear a tale of how he'd knocked over some poor stranger."

"Of course, *ma mère,*" Matt replied, his spirits only slightly dampened by the reprimand. "He's just got too great to hold back. I hope he don't grow more bigger till I catch up with him."

"You hope he does not grow bigger, dear," Alysaun corrected. "You cannot say *more* bigger, only bigger."

"Aye, 'tis my constant prayer, m'lady." Matt looked up, blushing at the laughter his answer had elicited from Devon and his mother. He loved Devon, almost as much as he cared for Bracken, but of late Hereward's son had taken to acting all too stiff and proper in Matt's mother's company. Now Dev was gazing at her all moon-eyed, hanging on her every word and trying to look especially manly.

Matt tugged at Devon's sleeve, eager for the day's promised outing. "I know I promised Matt," his mother was saying, "but I cannot rid myself of this headache." Matt tried again, poking Dev in the ribs. "I'm sure it must be the weather. Mayhap the rain will come to relieve the air." Alysaun glanced out the window. The clouds were darker now and rolling with an increased wind.

With no hope of gaining Devon's attention, Matt turned his efforts on his mother. She looked down and smiled at the anxious expression in his blue eyes. "Yes, darling, what is it? Have we ignored you? 'Tis difficult being small at times, isn't it?"

"I am not too little to go to the Forum with Devon," he protested, afraid his mother's vague malady would keep him from the excitement. "You promised we could go . . . can't your head wait to ache some other day?"

Devon frowned. "You're heartless, Matt—and behaving like a baby. Have you no feeling for your poor mother in her misery?"

"Oh, I'll survive, Dev. I am not in so much pain that I would make you and Matt suffer with me," Alysaun insisted, giving Devon a smile for his concern. The young man so openly doted on her that Hereward had apologized for his son's behavior. She did not mind so very much, and, as she had told Hereward, Devon's attentions were thoroughly innocent and harmless. Alysaun ruffled Matt's unruly thatch of red-gold curls. "Devon, dear, I would not ask you to abide this rascal's company if he were not so set on seeing the Forum's sights. Truly I would join you but for the press of the crowds . . ."

"I understand, m'lady," he replied quickly, eager to accommodate her slightest wish. "I only . . . I had hoped . . ." His voice trailed off in embarrassment. Lady Alysaun knew how dearly he would have loved her to accompany them. Though Devon didn't doubt her claim of an aching head, he fancied that he knew her well enough to guess what lay behind the excuse.

Often, in the first year that she and Matt had spent with them, he had observed her adoringly from afar and witnessed brief moods of melancholy. They came less often as time moved forward with no word of Brand's whereabouts. He suspected that today something had stirred her memory to dwell again on her lost love. Devon thought her the embodiment of an angel. If only there were some way for him to comfort her or offer some heartening news that would dispel the dark solitude of her reveries.

To hide the rush of compassion he felt, Devon took Matt's hand in his and smiled. "We shall go and bring your lady mother a surprise, some trinket from a tradesman's stall, eh, Matt?" The boy was nearly jumping with anticipation and Devon had to remind him to plant a kiss on Alysaun's cheek.

"All right, then. Off with you, and mind you stay by Dev's side and obey him," Alysaun cautioned. "Matthieu?" He was already halfway across the room but his mother's tone brought him up short. "I'd not care to hear you've led Dev a chase about the Forum," she said. "*Please, let him* enjoy the outing, as well."

"Oh, aye, m'lady." Matt grinned and winked at her. For a moment Alysaun's eyes misted over, for the gesture was so like his father's it was like seeing Brand once more. One could not miss whose son Matt was.

In the street Matt raced ahead of his companion, then, remembering his mother's admonition, slowed his pace to wait for Devon. They were bound for Constantine's Forum, the largest of the capital's six public squares and, to a boy Matt's age, the most fascinating.

Matt slipped his hand into Dev's and made an effort to calm himself. Though Hereward's tall son was at an age when decorum mattered above all else, the young boy's enthusiasm was catching, and Devon found himself anticipating the scene that would greet their arrival.

This particular forum was the city's social confluence, *the* place to see and be seen by Constantinople's most influential citizens. Still, an amazing mix of people filled the large, tiled square situated on the Mese. Beneath the shade of its surrounding, double-tiered arcades, the noble ladies of the town gathered to take in the day's sights in their sedan chairs. The square was an ever-shifting scene of entertainment and provided some gossip before they moved on to enjoy the luxury of the Baths of Zeuxippus.

Here color provided a key to reveal the occupations of the passersby. The solemn, withdrawn ascetics wore scarlet robes to denote piety. Across the way, two gentlemen in gray pondered a weighty problem of philosophy. At the center of the square a gathering of physicians robed in blue listened to a visiting colleague lecture on the necessity for a united protest against the state practice requiring doctors to devote service to the capital's many free hospitals.

"My friends, my fellow healers," the learned visitor concluded now with a dramatic flourish of his arms, "can you accept this bureaucratic meddling in our profession and meekly turn the other cheek? *No.* I say it is our Lord's desire that men of learning be adequately compensated for such labors in behalf of the common man."

The clouds parted for a moment and sunlight struck the gleaming golden cross that topped the shaft of porphyry rising from the center of the Forum. The lecturer took this as a sign of heavenly approval for his message and gestured, but before he could make his claim, a priest in the heavy black robes of his office raised his voice and addressed the gathered doctors.

"Our Savior decreed that we should render unto Caesar that which is Caesar's," he intoned. "And did not the Christ also say that our reward will be found in Heaven?"

The holy man did not stay to see what effect his words had had. He walked on and, with his passing, the clouds closed once more, leaving the impression that his words of mild rebuke were spoken with some divine authority.

Devon waited a few moments to watch the foreign physician's crestfallen expression as his audience dispersed. Then, with Matt pulling him across the square, the two headed for the row of stalls crowded by the hungry and the curious.

The canopied stalls were temporary affairs rigged by merchants eager to reap an afternoon's profit from the city's idle rich. Their more substantial shops lined the Mese from the Forum south to the imperial palace. In a long-established tradition, the closer one came to the palace, the more rare or expensive were the items sold.

Devon slowed his pace, searching the stalls for something suitable for Alysaun. They passed a seller of icons, a merchant who dealt in fine linens, and another who sold imported silks. Across the way a tradesman displayed jewels to dazzle a favorite lady; another offered exotic blends of perfume to appeal to her senses. A sigh escaped Dev. His funds were limited and what he could afford had looked cheap. He bought a paper cone of sugared dates and divided them. Even those came at a dear price.

For a few minutes he considered a multicolored array of silken veils, and Matt, forgetting his promise, rushed off to study something that looked more interesting. When Dev finally looked up and noted his charge's absence, he was both angry and alarmed that he might have lost Matt. The crowds passing by the stalls shifted, and he finally caught sight of Matt. The boy's expression was rapt as he watched one of the Forum's many fortune-tellers read a customer's palm.

The fingers that fastened on Matt's small wrist were firm but in no way punishing. He found himself looking up into Devon's annoyed gray eyes and immediately flushed with guilt, hearing again his mother's warning. "I'm sorry, Dev, and I swear I'll not leave your side again," he chattered on, trying to keep an eye on the fortune-teller and still make an apology that sounded sincere.

"Well, see that you don't, scamp," Dev replied, and let Matt return his attention to the palm-reading process. Too mature himself to give much credence to such superstitious nonsense, he stayed to watch for Matt's sake, listening carefully to the seer's predictions.

This particular scoundrel was a Russian, a dark, full-faced man whose heavy, hooded eyes made him seem mysterious and, therefore, believable. The majority of Constantinople's populace were devoutly Christian, and yet public sentiment strongly favored the mystical. In an area where East and West melded, the Orthodox Byzantine Church tolerated the patronage of these mystics only so long as there was no organized effort to lure people away from the true faith.

A few feet in front of the stall, the man's assistant, whose features unmistakably marked him a son or close relative, called out a well-polished litany designed to tempt the passing crowd to sample his father's talents. Clearly the business was a competitive one, for down the row, several others were bidding against the young man for the interest of the more gullible.

In most cases the men who practiced the art merely had a discerning eye and an ear for gossip that allowed them to flavor a generalized fortune with a sprinkling of details that might impress the customer. The young man who had just had his palm read seemed to fancy himself a ladies' man. Though his attire seemed a trifle worn, he had ambitions to better his lot in life.

The fortune-teller, known only by his professional name of Gnosticus, the knowing one, had played to the man's vanity and predicted that a raven-haired young noblewoman would soon grant him her favors. Since there were several who fit the general description and one in particular who might greatly advance his prospects for wealth, the man was happy to pay his money. Before he left, he leaned forward to whisper something to the seer.

Devon heard only a young woman's name mentioned and saw Gnosticus smile and nod agreement. Apparently the young man was taking no chances with his future; he wanted his name mentioned if the lady in question should stop to inquire of her own destiny.

When he had strolled off, whistling happily to himself, Gnosticus turned his attention to Devon and Matt. Both were dressed in simple tunics and breeches but the fineness and condition of the linen revealed a well-to-do status. In general he disliked youth but Gnosticus was not one to ignore a potential patron, no matter what his age.

"You, young man," he said, addressing Devon. "I sense you are troubled by some problem not easily resolved. Lay your palm down and see what answer I can find written upon your flesh.''

Devon grinned at the attempt to draw him in. "I've no problems time won't solve," he replied, "and, I predict, giving up a hard-earned coin to you will make a fool of me." Matt was bored by now, his attention wandering. He spied a lady with a tray of sweets and tapped Devon's arm.

He glanced at the sweets-seller and frowned. "Your mother will have my hide if I bring you home all sticky-faced and too full to eat a proper supper," he chided, but was about to give in when Gnosticus, seeing his chance about to slip away, called to his son and asked that Devon wait one moment.

"Andreyas, my son, take a well-earned pause from your task and treat yourself and this young boy to a pick from the lady's sweets. And mind you keep an eye on him for a bit." Andreyas was suspicious of the unaccustomed generosity until he realized his father meant to isolate and pluck another pigeon. The day's pickings had been slim. His father smiled encouragement to the young boy and added, "Go with him, son. Go on, he's got a sweet tooth himself, does my Andreyas." His voice lowered as he said, "Take your time choosing and bring back something for your brother here."

"He's not my brother," Matt explained, wide-eyed at the offer. "Devon's m'friend." He looked up suddenly at Dev, wondering if he were going to be denied this treat because they did not know the man well. "I'll stay put, I swear. You can see me from here and I'll not wander."

Devon mistrusted the offer, but there seemed to be no harm in letting Matt accept. "As long as I can see you clear, Matt," he warned. "If you start off . . ."

"I promise I won't," Matt answered, fairly jumping to impress Devon that he meant it. To show good faith, he took Andreyas's hand and walked sedately at his side until they reached the pretty, buxom girl selling the candy.

Matt studied the proffered tray with so serious a mien it brought a smile to Devon's face. Noting that his success lay more in courting the youth's affections for the boy and his mother, Gnosticus channeled his efforts in that direction, clearing his throat to again mention a troublesome problem.

"As I said, sir, I've no desire to part with my money in such a foolish manner," Dev replied, and frowned. "If you thought to change my mind by bribing—"

"*Please*," the fortune-teller protested in a wounded tone. "You insult my good intentions and shadow them with talk of personal gain. He is a dear boy...I *am* a father as well as a businessman. Besides, 'tis not your fortune that needs telling. You must understand, there are ways other then palmistry to learn what fate has planned. Knowing our future, we own the right to challenge what is written."

"I am my father's son, old man. We come of a long line of truth seekers but find it not in the imaginings of those who would profit from the fears and hopes of their fellowmen." Devon sat down, only partially facing the fortune-teller as he alertly kept an eye on Matt. The wind had come up suddenly, stirring the awnings to flap and waft a none-too-pleasant odor of spicy food and stale flesh from the heavily robed and sweating Gnosticus. The man could use a day away from his trade to attend the public baths, Devon thought.

"And when the veil is lifted for a short span, 'tis a mean and close-coined friend who would deny some solace to a lady in despair," Gnosticus rejoined, knowing that he had struck a nerve when the lad gave his full attention to him. Suppressing a desire to grin at the gullibility of youth, he kept his features set in a serious demeanor. So easy was it to be a reader of faces and minds, it was almost a sin to make a living at the vocation. "A fair and light-eyed young woman did my mind's eye glimpse, too young to be left alone with a little son to raise." He sighed heavily, then touched his temple in a weary gesture. "Still, I think...no, it just isn't clear, not at all."

Devon eyed him suspiciously. The description sounded very like Lady Alysaun, but there were many fair-complexioned, light-eyed

341

ladies in a city the size of Constantinople. He had the vague feeling he was being duped, that some trap lay in giving voice to his curiosity. "You speak in riddles, mystic," he snapped, and began to rise.

A hand shot out quickly and closed up Devon's sleeve. "Riddles is my business, son. Be not so hasty to decide I talk of falsehoods. My arts are old as time and sometimes, I admit, puzzle even me. One must have the 'sight,' of course, but there's secrets to clear away the fog that shrouds the future." He released Devon's arm and shrugged. "She, whom I did mention, is someone dear to thee. The name is not clear, only her anguish. If you do not wish to help her . . . pass on. I will not force the truth on one who loves money over friendship."

"Her name alone would give you access to her future?" Dev was interested now but still uncertain. "How so, when she is not present to have her hand read?"

"There are other ways, lad. Why, just last week, a newlywedded man did come begging for my help on testing the fidelity of his spouse. I used the crystal to see how she did spend the hours not in his company."

"And?"

"The young wife was as faithful as the bells that call to mass. In fact, those times spent away from her home were passed in the care of her mother-in-law. I was able to tell the relieved husband some news the lady had not yet revealed . . . that seven months hence he would be a father."

"Truly? And were you able to tell him whether 'twould be a son or daughter?" Devon's voice was tinged with skepticism.

"Some things, my doubting Thomas," Gnosticus retorted, "are better left for time to reveal." He crossed himself in a show of piety. "God allows us a glimpse of what lies in store, not each and every detail."

"Surely to increase your repute you color your predictions with only glad tidings."

"Nay, I tell only what I see," protested the seer, his face

becoming melancholy. "Yesterday past, another sought my aid in concern over his sister's illness. I was distressed to say she would not recover. Now, if you do not wish to use my talents, there are others who need assistance."

"What is the truest method if the person is not present?"

Gnosticus glanced down to avoid smiling. He almost had the lad. "Pray do not ask if you are a doubter, young sir. The cards are most accurate but their revelations are clouded by the closeness of a suspicious mind. Ask sincerely, pay my small fee of one nomismata, and I believe your lady will have reason to bless your solicitude."

The cost was high, near a fortnight's wages of his pay. 'Twould seem more a blessing on the fortune-teller, Dev thought, but reached for his purse and withdrew the coin, He laid it on the man's open palm with the caution of a man who worked hard for his money. "Read the cards, then, and be quick. My young charge and I must be home soon."

Now Gnosticus gave into the relief of loosing his smile, pocketing the coin before he reached for a worn deck of tarot cards. It seemed the little boy lived with this tall, blond fellow and if his mother did as well, she would be a widow. "The lady in question is not of this land. Though I cannot quite grasp her name, she is fair . . . russet or golden blond . . . and has eyes the color of a clear dawn sky."

Devon watched as the cards were laid out in a pattern, surprised at how the description fit Alysaun. There seemed to be no harm in mentioning her name, especially if it would make the forecast more accurate. "She is called Alysaun . . . more I will not say."

He had guessed as much. The lad was Saxon and this Alysaun as well. They would be one of the many who had fled England's shores because of that Norman, William. The Varangian Guards were fast becoming English. If this Devon was one, then Alysaun's husband may have been, too. "Alysaun . . . hmm, yes, I thought the name began with the letter A. I can see more clearly now." He turned over a card and frowned.

"What is it?" Suddenly alert to trouble for Alysaun, Devon sat up straight in the chair and stared at the picture card showing a knight. "Tell me, *please*."

"This card only shows the reason for the lady's grief. 'Tis her husband, a member of . . . of a cavalry guard, perhaps . . . yes, it is the Varangians." He looked up to see a verification of his guess in the lad's startled gray eyes. "He is missing, is he not, presumed killed in a battle?" At Devon's nod, he turned another card and a dismayed sound rattled in his throat.

"Be not alarmed, son," Gnosticus said soothingly, holding up a hand to request patience. "This row of cards reveals the past and this second, the present. The last card, here, tells me the poor woman—a girl, more likely—cannot accept the idea that her beloved is dead. There is pressure to remarry."

"True, sir," Devon admitted. "Lady Alysaun has many suitors, yet . . ."

The fortune-teller dealt out another row of ten cards. He turned the first card over, starting from the left. "She cares for none of them, does your lady. I see each suitor failing. No one stands so tall and straight as he who is a memory." He turned the second card over and looked surprised, then in rapid succession revealed the remaining cards. For a few seconds there was a tense silence as he studied their meaning.

"Pray do not tell me there is more misfortune awaiting her," Devon insisted anxiously, "for she has suffered unduly for one so fair and innocent."

"I have the best of news to reveal, tidings that will soon see an end to her uncertainty. There is travel in Alysaun's future and . . ."

Devon poised on the edge of the chair, so tense and nervous his palms were sweated. "Go on, tell me everything."

"Even now, a man . . . I see only a dark, hooded face . . . is coming to Constantinople. He will bring proof that the lady's husband is alive. A joyful reunion will follow on the heels of this revelation."

Gnosticus sighed wearily as if the reading had worn at his strength, then glanced up to find Devon staring at him, his fair skin

344

pale, expression stunned. That he wanted to believe the prediction there was no doubt; that he found it difficult to accept was as obvious.

"At times it is difficult to extract the exact meanings shown in the cards but this much is certain: Her husband is alive and she will see him again," he said, tipping the scales in favor of his prediction.

"W-when . . . how soon?" Devon managed to stutter. "When will this messenger come? From where?"

"The cards show only that he is a man and that the event is even now maturing. I cannot say for sure. Perhaps a week, more or less, will pass before he arrives. Longer until the reunion is a fact."

"Oh, would God that it comes true." Devon breathed the words in an emotion-filled whisper. He was thrilled to have such news for Alysaun and yet afraid to believe it could be so. Anxious to rush home and tell her, he imagined the brightening of her lovely features, the joy that would replace her sadness. "Thank you, sir, a thousand times have you my gratitude and . . . oh, sir, are you *sure* this will come to pass?"

The seer looked preoccupied, thoughtful in the face of such enthusiastic appreciation. "I am, as sure as I sit before you, moved by the joy my prophecies have wrought. 'Tis times such as these that make a pleasure out of what has often been a heavy burden." Gnosticus grinned at Devon, then leaned across the counter to pat his shoulder. "You owe me nothing, son. In fact, I would venture that your visit has given me as much satisfaction, or near as much, as it has to you."

Still in a daze, Devon glanced around to find Matt nowhere in sight. His heart skipped a beat or two before Andreyas came around the corner of the stall, Matt trailing slightly behind him and frowning with concentration as he tried to work a string puzzle.

"For a moment, Matthieu, I thought I'd lost you," Devon greeted him in relief. "Were you with Andreyas the whole time?" The boy nodded, too frustrated by his inability to follow the pattern of lacing shown him by Gnosticus's son. Andreyas knelt down next to him, amazingly patient as he again worked the weaving of the string.

345

Matt tried it once more and a brilliant, ear-to-ear grin of accomplishment lit his freckled face.

"My thanks for watching him," Devon said, and held out his hand to take Matt's. "We'd best be off now or risk worrying your mother."

Gnosticus waited until the two were well away from his booth, then crooked a finger at his son, motioning him to come close. "Follow them," he said, and to emphasize the import of the order, caught a lock of Andreyas's lank, black hair and pulled his head down until his ear was close enough to hear the harshly whispered, "And stay *well* back so our friend don't see you."

Andreyas whined in protest and winced as his father gave his hair another pull before he freed him. "You never tell me anything. What reason have I got to be followin' them two? I did my part. 'Twasn't easy to keep the brat happy."

Gnosticus glowered, wishing that this issue of his loins had more of his father's wits and less his mother's cow-eyed stupidity. "I'll give no reasons to an idiot," he roared in an exasperated growl. His palm just missed the boy's face as Andreyas anticipated it and sidestepped the swat. "Go now, fool . . . before you lose them. I would know the street *and* the house wherein they enter. A mistake will cost you dearly."

As the only son and heir, it sorely grieved Andreyas that his father treated him as no more than hired help. One day this words-and-air business would be his, and the great Gnosticus had shown him none of the tricks that made the lies seem so believable. Still, he obeyed, nearly stumbling over his own feet in his eagerness to comply. The old man had a heavy hand when displeased and he was a shrewd one, no man's fool. There would be some sly means of profit in the information for which he had been sent, and *that* could only make Andreyas the richer for his efforts.

15

Devon had been bursting to tell Alysaun the good fortune that was to be hers, but as he made his way back through the crowd, it occurred to him that Gnosticus's predictions might prove less than accurate. If Alysaun's hopes were raised and the expected messenger failed to appear, her disappointment would be too keen to bear. In place of revealing the prophecy as his gift, Devon stopped at one of the last booths on the square and bought her a white silk veil with a fringe of lovely, pale violet.

Alysaun was pleased by the present, a little embarrassed that Devon had remembered to bring her something and had not done as much for his mother. He seemed in such high spirits that she questioned his mood, but Devon insisted that he had just enjoyed the afternoon. The good humor lasted the week, as if he cherished some secret that gave him a great deal of pleasure. Finally, from Matt's review of the sights they had seen, she learned that Devon had stopped to have his fortune told.

It was not her place to ask him, especially if Devon didn't care to confide in her, but Alysaun guessed that he had been given a hint of a romance in his future. Nothing else could account for the ebullience that he exuded as the days passed. He was waiting for some fresh-faced lass to cross his path, looking forward to wooing her, perhaps with predicted success. The idea enchanted Alysaun; and in remembering her own love, she could only wish that Hereward's son might find the same joy that had been all too briefly hers.

Now that he was gone, Alysaun could not remember one fault Brand had possessed. She remembered, instead, the splendor of lying in his arms, recalled and cherished that particular gentleness of his and the poet's compassion too often masked by a cynical mien. He had loved her, and only for her had the mask dropped to reveal how sensitive he was to the world around them. All she had now were memories—days of loneliness and nights of longing.

Tonight she was alone and full of regret that she had not surrendered to Frida's pleas that she join the family at the Hippodrome. The regent, John Ducas, was in attendance for the command performance of games and entertainments honoring young Emperor Michael's saint's day.

For two years she had lived with the dwindling hope that Brand was still alive. Reason said he was dead or else someone would have heard news of him. On the surface she had accepted his death. Even Hereward had lost hope. Only deep within her soul did she cling to an angry, tenacious refusal to believe Brand had passed from her life forever.

Alysaun paced her room, fighting depression. She *should* have gone; she could not seclude herself from life forever. With a frustrated sigh, she sank onto the bed, fighting the tension that knotted her throat, the tears that threatened to spill over yet another time. If she had been left childless, it would have been a natural course to seek the quiet retreat of a cloistered life . . . but she was not alone. She had her son to consider. Matt was growing so fast, the time appeared to fly as he matured from a toddler to a strong and sturdy young boy.

No, she could no longer abandon life because she hugged her loss close in comforting self-pity. If she had died in place of Brand, she would have wanted him to go on. *It was just... how could she accept the thought of her Brand, so full of love and courage, lying forgotten in some unmarked plot of land?*

An abrupt knock at her door so startled Alysaun that she jumped, heart pounding rapidly in surprise. "Yes? What is it?" she called, trying to compose her voice as she wiped away the tears. Hereward's house steward, Dismus, answered that she had a caller. Should he admit the man?

Her fair, arched brows raised in puzzlement. Of late there had been a few gentlemen pressing for her attentions but none so ardent he would risk her anger by calling at so late an hour. "Let him in," she replied, "and have him await me in the entry hall." Whoever it was, he did not deserve the courtesy of being received in the comfortable hall reserved for invited guests.

A few minutes later, her face freshly washed of tearstains and her manner once more serene, Alysaun made her way to the narrow, dimly lighted entry. A cloaked man of medium height and frame waited there his face half shadowed by the cowl drawn forward. He seemed to be daydreaming and failed to hear her approach, so that when she at last spoke, the sound of her voice brought his head up sharply in surprise.

Alysaun saw little of his features, just a hint of a young, full face cut by a narrow mouth. She didn't know him and said so, adding, "What reason have you for calling at so odd an hour?" His eyes remained hooded, gaze shifting about the hall, adding to Alysaun's impression that he was nervous.

"I was sent with a message for a Lady Alysaun. Be you she?"

His voice was muffled, increasing her impatience with his manner. "Of course I am. Speak up and say who it was who sent you and your message or I will call the steward and have him see you out."

"Ain't any need to be so testy, m'lady," the youth whined, shuffling his feet several times before continuing. "The merchant Sharak al'Deina hired me to fetch you to his ship. He said to tell you that, for a price, he . . . he has proof to show you that you ain't a widow."

It took several seconds for her to realize the import of his words. Alysaun was torn between a dawning hope and the feeling that someone was playing some cruel sort of joke upon her. "What proof could he possess? I don't believe you . . . you've made up this lie for your own profit—"

"I never have seen you, have I? I don't care if you believe me or not—I done my part." Andreyas turned away, acting out the part just as his father had told him to. And just as Gnosticus had predicted, the lady did not let him leave; she couldn't afford to lose the only contact that might reunite her with her husband.

Alysaun reached out and caught his sleeve, her voice shaking with emotion as she asked him to wait. The young man tugged his sleeve free but turned back. "If this merchant has evidence that my husband is alive, why can he not come here? I will pay him whatever price he asks if he does, indeed, know that Brand is well."

She was falling neatly into the trap. His father had promised him a reward, and he was eager to collect it. Within the hour the lady would be aboard the slaver's galley, and when his father saw how lovely she was, perhaps he would increase Andreyas's share of the commission al'Deina would pay. "He didn't say nothing about coming here—that's betwixt you and him. I was to repeat his message and bring you or your answer back to his cabin."

Alysaun bit her lip, wary of an evil purpose in the simple message. "I will pay you to return and bid him come, then," she said cautiously.

"I know his answer, lady, and 'tis too long a walk back and forth to bother. I'll be leavin' now and tell him you wasn't interested."

"I will come in the light of morning," Alysaun insisted. "The waterfront is no place for me to be in the dark of night."

She had some sense, the woman did. He would earn his money from this one. "He leaves on the morning tide. 'Tis your choice, but he won't be back for another three months."

Alysaun was torn by indecision. She could not risk the chance of losing even so thin a lead as this one, and yet her instincts warned that she was a fool to go off with a stranger. If only Hereward were here. "Will you wait here until I send for a friend to accompany us? He is not far, only minutes away at the Hippodrome."

"Nay. I have business of mine own that awaits. If you want to come, let us go now. If not . . ."

She almost stamped her foot in exasperation. "Then our steward will join us," she replied, clutching at straws because she was still so afraid to go alone. "Surely you can have no objection to that?"

"I only know al'Deina said to bring *you*. It makes sense to me that if he's up to sellin' information, he don't need any extra ears to overhear the sale. It's you I take, or word that you ain't interested."

"Oh . . . all right. Give me a moment to think." Dismus would raise every objection she had if he knew the truth. His loyalty to Hereward would not allow him to see her go off to the wharf district so unprotected. "Wait here . . . no, wait outside—upon the steps. I must leave an excuse for my absence."

Andreyas smiled and reached up to draw his cowl closer about his face to hide his satisfaction. For a moment he watched her, noting the flush of color that stained her cheeks. The lady's emotions were all a storm of hope and doubt; her guard was down, leaving her vulnerable, easy prey. "I'll wait, but not overlong," he allowed, making a brief, jerky bow.

Both nervous and excited, Alysaun found it difficult to contrive a plausible excuse to give Dismus. She was free, of course, to come and go, but a troubled Dismus would only delay her, and she could not chance making her guide wait.

Finally she called out for him, and when Dismus stood before her with an expectant look, Alysaun took a deep breath and told him she was going out. "Lord Hereward sent this lad to fetch me to the games. It seems he chanced upon a friend from our days in Ely." She paused, hoping that she sounded convincing. "'Twill be a pleasure to see him again," she added, and wondered if she had gone too far with her explanation.

The story Lady Alysaun had given him seemed unlikely but it was beyond Dismus's province to question her. Still, since the master was so particular of the lady's welfare, it did seem odd that he would send a common hireling to escort her. As well, there was something feverish about the lady's expression that increased his misgivings. "If I may, m'lady . . . might I suggest that one of our own housemen accompany you to join Lord Hereward? It is a precaution, for one cannot be too—"

"Oh, the streets are well lighted and safe, Dismus," Alysaun insisted, anxious to be off. "Hereward is a cautious man. He would not have sent just anyone. I'm sure he's employed this fellow before. Now, if you would fetch my cloak, please. I'm eager to join the family."

Dismus sensed her nervousness but his expression remained blandly courteous. "Of course, as you wish, m'lady. I thought only to take an extra measure of concern for your safety." He signaled a servant girl waiting in the atrium hall and had her bring Alysaun's woolen cloak. When Alysaun had donned it and given him a grateful, preoccupied smile, Dismus made one last attempt to ease the worry troubling his conscience. "I am free to escort you myself, Lady Alysaun. 'Tis but a short distance and the walk will benefit my night's rest."

"Nay, Dismus, I would not so impose upon your time. Your workday is long and busy enough to make sleep come easily." Alysaun twisted the ribboned ties of her pale blue cloak, unaware of the nervous gesture, then glanced back toward the family wing of the villa. "Do favor me with a few minutes of your time, though, and look in on Matt. An hour ago, he was sleeping like an angel."

"Aye, m'lady, I will," the steward promised, then gestured to the portal. "As soon as I see you—"

"Do it *now*, please."

Alysaun's voice was sharp and impatient, unusual for one so even-tempered. "Yes, m'lady," he replied with a bow, hesitating before he started off for Matt's room. He glanced back, beginning to wish her God's grace, but she was already at the door. His voice trailed off as she lifted the latch and slipped out into the night.

Dismus frowned, for once at a loss as to what he should do. It occurred to him that the lady might have an assignation but, no, Lady Alysaun still mourned her husband's loss. She might allow a caller in the afternoon hours, but she was too much a young woman of quality to sneak off for a lovers' tryst in the dark.

He could just be mistaken. The matter might be as simple as stated. If so, he risked the lady's indignation and the master's as well by doubting her word. He turned back and proceeded to young Matthieu's room, next to the lady's own. He was, despite his standing and responsibilities, only a servant.

Alysaun meanwhile was following the young man with some apprehensions of her own. She was risking everything, and yet the danger was nothing if it led her to news of Brand. She didn't want to believe it, on the chance that this merchant was mistaken, but he had mentioned proof.

Her guide moved quickly and Alysaun had to hurry to keep pace with him. He took her through the narrow, cobbled streets, twisting right or left at each junction until she was no longer sure which direction would take her back to the villa.

The houses grew less well kept as the neighborhood changed from that of the wealthy to a less fortunate class of citizen. The streets themselves seemed to reflect the poorness of the district, and, unlike the clean, brightly lighted thoroughfares off the Mese, were neglected and littered by refuse.

The people here were as shabby. Barefoot children played among the rubbish, dressed in threadbare clothing. The adults seemed attired in newer wear but for the most part looked dirty and unkempt. Here and there a group of women were gathered, openly drinking from a shared bottle of drink, yelling an occasional threat to a child who strayed too far. Toward the end of the street several women in loosely clad gowns lounged at the door of a tavern, apparently awaiting the night's prospects.

Alysaun shivered and made an extra effort to stay close to her escort. He seemed perfectly at ease in passing through the area and quite used to the jostling of an occasional drunk. Past the tavern, he made a turn to the left, and most of the crowd was left behind. Alysaun breathed a sigh of relief and in a whisper asked if they could not stop a few minutes so she might catch her breath.

"Aye, but not for long, mistress," Andreyas replied. Having run the gauntlet of the slum district, the lady thought the danger past. The next few streets that would lead them down to the docks were secluded and dark, however, and many a man had lost his purse to a skulking thief. A decent woman had no business venturing there, and deserved whatever fate befell her. He was nervous himself, for she was his to protect until he had her aboard the ship. "Mind you stay close through here. There's drunks and beggars would slit your throat for no more reason than they wanted to see was your blood red or blue."

The warning left an already shaken Alysaun in the grip of terror. She held her hood close about her face, apprehensively gazing about for any sign of a suspicious character. Before she knew it, he had started off again and she raced after him, calling for him to wait. "Please . . . I cannot keep up if you move so fast, ' Alysaun pleaded. He slowed for a minute until she was next to him. Just then, several drunken sailors lurched out of a nearby tavern, and Alysaun moved to his right, putting her guide between herself and the men.

Though she still suspected he might be leading her into a trap of some kind, the alternative of being left to fend for herself on these dark streets was more frightening. They were near the end of one street when she caught his sleeve and tugged. "*Stop*." The tone of authority in the command apparently penetrated his careless attitude, and he paused to ask her what she wanted. "I'll go no farther with you unless I know more of this merchant . . . what was his name?"

"Al'Deina, Sharak al'Deina, m'lady," Andreyas replied. "I know little of him but that he deals in lots of trade goods. You must hold your curiosity, for even I do not care to keep to these passageways longer than need be. The wharf is not far and is better lighted than here. Ask me there what you will, though I know little enough. Now, come or be left behind."

354

Alysaun hesitated. "If you be thinkin' I has lied, why, I will go about my business and let you return home."

"No . . . *wait*. I didn't say . . ." Alysaun glanced around. The street onto which they had turned was little more than an alley, and the overhanging balconies of its dilapidated houses further shadowed the passage. She could smell the waterfront, a pungent odor of saltwater and garbage. Alysaun sighed. She had come this far. It would take more courage to wend her way back through the unfamiliar slums than to follow this rude hireling to her goal. "All right, lead on. But stay while I speak to al'Deina and I'll reward your patience with coins equal to those he paid you."

"Aye, Lady Alysaun, I will wait. 'Tisn't often I can earn so much in one night." He made another jerky bow and gestured to her to walk at his side. "Come, then. The sooner I see you safe to the ship, the sooner I can be off to spend my newfound wealth."

Though she didn't fully trust him, he seemed the least of her worries. Alysaun took a deep breath and again drew her cloak close, little protection that it was. "Lead on, then, but pray not at a run, or I shall be too winded to make my inquiries."

Andreyas did as she asked, keeping a wary eye on the wells of shadow on either side of them as they made their way down the alley. Alysaun was grateful for his company when a figure suddenly loomed out of a darkened doorway to her right. The man was tall and strongly built, but his gait was unsteady as he lurched forward, fumbling with the rope belt that secured his breeches. After they passed him, Alysaun heard a lewd giggle and glanced back to see a tipsy bawd appear at the man's side, her loose gown still disarranged from a tryst with him.

A shiver passed down her spine. If Hereward found out she had followed a complete stranger to such a sordid area of the city, she would never hear the end of his raging. With any luck, she might be able to talk with al'Deina and yet be home before he and Frida returned from the games.

Finally they reached the wharves, deserted but for a few harlots who strolled the docks looking for customers. A variety of ships were moored at the six docks jutting at parallel angles to the main wharf, mostly galleys, though here and there a large dromond or small felucca was tethered to a piling. This harbor was one of four that served Constantinople and was reserved primarily for visiting merchantmen. She had seen only one other, the neatly maintained basin adjacent to the palace, where the imperial fleet rode at anchor.

The youth continued down the wharf, more solicitous now that he had been promised money. They passed a brazen and openly curious whore who leaned against a timber piling. At the third dock, he paused and pointed down the line of four ships. "That last one is al'Deina's, the one with a torn tops'l."

Alysaun wasn't sure what a tops'l was, and the ships all looked the same to her inexperienced eyes. "Tell him to come and meet me here," she insisted, hesitant to leave the "safety" of the dock for the unknown, perhaps more dangerous domain of a private galley. "If he wants to sell his information, he'll come. There's naught that cannot be said here as well as in his cabin."

That was not a part of the plan. Andreyas tried to think as his father did, but he was not as wily nor as quick on his feet. He glanced around, looking for the guard who patrolled the wharves. If the lady did not come aboard quietly, the trap would not spring as easily as Gnosticus had planned. Al'Deina was a shrewd trader; he wanted no trouble from the authorities, though for the most part, his activities were overlooked by the generously paid watchmen.

Two sailors came strolling down the wharf, singing in loud, drunken voices. One stopped at a call from the whore, listening as she displayed herself and named a price. His companion poked him and doubled over in laughter at the offer, then pulled him along. She cursed the men and called a few disgusted epithets after them, then returned to lounging at her corner.

Andreyas took advantage of the scene to frighten Alysaun. "Would you risk being left alone, even for a short while, m'lady?" he whispered. "Those two are looking for someone more comely than the old tart. They want—"

"I know what they want," Alysaun snapped, warily drawing her hood close about her until the men were past. "They are gone. I'll be—" Just then a door of one of the taverns along the wharf opened, emitting a dull, yellow light and the sound of raucous laughter. A man lurched unsteadily onto the wharf, stumbling over to one of the docks to empty his gut of too much cheap wine.

"Take me to al'Deina, then," Alysaun said, shuddering at the retching sounds that accompanied the drunk's heaving. "Now, before I am too faint to be able to think."

Andreyas smiled to himself. Clearly fortune favored his task this night. He must remember to embellish the difficulties for his father. "A wise decision. Come, follow me, and take some care on the boarding plank. 'Tis a short but wobbly path to the safety of the galley's deck."

Alysaun cautiously followed his advice, gripping the guidelines with white-knuckled intensity. She had been aboard a ship a few years before, for the journey from Marseilles to Constantinople. By then the early sickness of her pregnancy had passed, but she had weathered the voyage badly. Now, as a queasy feeling seized her nervous stomach, she had a suspicion that she was just not meant to leave the solidity of dry land.

She failed to notice that Andreyas was familiar with the ship's lay or, with her face growing pale at the rise and fall of the groaning ship, that he led her directly to the large cabin in the stern. She noted only the dipping shadows cast on the narrow walls of the passageway as the oil lamps swayed in their brackets.

A slight film of perspiration dampened her forehead as Andreyas paused before the last door. She pushed back her hood and pressed the top of one hand against her cheeks. Unlike her temples, they were hot and dry, flushed from nervous excitement.

Andreyas gave his name in answer to the thin, reedy voice that replied to his knock. He opened the door and gestured for Alysaun to enter. "Al'Deina awaits within, m'lady. He is, I think, even more anxious than you are for this meeting."

It seemed a strange statement, but Alysaun was eager to finish the business with the merchant and return home. She opened her mouth to remind him of his promise to wait for her, but he rudely cut her off, his thin fingers grasping her arm to propel her into the cabin's interior.

Alysaun glared at him and tugged her arm free. His manner had abruptly altered. No longer did he seem the disinterested hireling. He shoved back his cowl, revealing an expression that seemed both impudent and mocking, then used his foot to kick the door shut.

"You took your own sweet time coming," a hoarse, raspy voice complained, and Alysaun turned, peering across the shadowed cabin to try to discern who had spoken. "I trust it went as planned?" The same voice made the inquiry and Alysaun saw it belonged to a man whose features closely matched those of her guide. He sat slumped in a chair drawn up to the only table; another man was seated opposite him.

"Aye, well enough," Andreyas replied, "but the lady was shy of coming at first. It took all my wits to convince her the need was urgent."

"All your wits, eh?" Gnosticus laughed at the conceit and turned to his companion. "I could've sent a chicken in his place, Sharak, for all the wits my boy possesses."

"Well, I done your dirty work and the proof stands here. If I be so witless, then hire the chicken to hawk your bloody customers in for a fortune."

Alysaun listened to the nasty exchange with a dazed feeling of disbelief. "I came not to hear your squabbling but for promised news of my husband. I can pay well if you've proof he is well and hearty." Behind her Andreyas snickered and Alysaun felt a cold dread settle over her heart. She ignored his idiot's laugh and directed her gaze to the man addressed as Sharak.

"You are the merchant, al'Deina? The one who sent this . . . fool to fetch me here?"

Sharak al'Deina hadn't taken his eyes off her from the moment she stepped into his cabin. Now he rose and came toward her, considering her with a practiced eye, taking in the flushed and lovely features, the seeming slenderness that matched her fine-boned face.

"I *am* al'Deina," he admitted, continuing his survey as he spoke. "And some may *think* of me as a merchant." In the background Gnosticus's laughter mocked the claim. "I buy and sell, do I not, Master Gnosticus?"

"That he does, Lady Alysaun, though in some quarters his trade is frowned upon," Gnosticus commented, still chuckling.

"Is this pretty golden shade natural, my dear?" Sharak asked, ignoring his old friend's humor as he raised a hand and tested a stray wisp of Alysaun's hair with his fingertips. "Some women aid nature's gift with artif—"

Alysaun batted his hand away, angry at herself for having fallen for some trickery these men had planned. "Keep your hands from my person," she damanded, and took a step back, only to find Andreyas blocking her way. "You never *did* have information to sell me." She was frightened now, alone with these three unscrupulous men and far from the safety of Hereward's home.

She would waste no more time playing their game. Alysaun had started for the door when, at a sudden, hard-voiced command from al'Deina, she found herself caught by Andreyas. She struggled for moments, then turned her head and glared at the merchant, even more alarmed at the oily grin splitting his mouth.

"I had no information to sell, my girl, but through the kind offices of my friend and his son, I *will* make a purchase this eve. Hold her tightly, lad," he added to Andreyas, and as the hands closed more firmly on her shoulders, al'Deina pulled at the ribbon securing her cloak, pushing it away to reveal the form that had been hidden by its voluminous folds. "You did well this time round, Gnosticus. With her fair coloring and youth, she'll bring a handsome price. I know just the man to appreciate so comely a face. Though he has a preference for red-haired bitches, he may snap this one up."

Alysaun heard what he was saying but could not comprehend through the shocked daze that had settled upon her. "You won't auction her, then?" Gnosticus asked, rising to his feet to come closer and study her himself. "Her looks are rare enough. Just by displaying her on the block, you'd drive the bidders wild. Still, what you fetch is your business, once I've had my fee. Who is this man with a taste for light meat?"

That callous phrase brought Alysaun to a terrified awareness of her fate. She thought to scream, but what would a woman's scream matter, coming from a slaver's ship? She turned to look at al'Deina, who had purposely delayed his answer until he had her complete attention.

"Who is he, you ask, eh? The only man I know who is wealthy enough to indulge his fondness for female flesh and virile enough to keep all of his slaves contented. He is none other than the sultan of the Turks, his highness, Malik Shah."

Alysaun heard Gnosticus complain that his fee had been too small in light of what she would bring. His voice trailed off to a dull buzz, a distant drone of protest and she felt her knees give way, her muscles going slack as a dark cloud rolled across her mind, thankfully shutting out the sounds of the two men bartering, arguing over the price her body would bring, silencing even that finally when she slumped unconscious in Andreyas's arms.

Across the city, Dismus had just opened the door to admit Hereward and his family to the entry hall. He waited until all three had come in, then glanced hopefully outside, looking for some sign that Lady Alysaun was, indeed, with them.

Hereward took his wife's cloak and looked about, frowning at his steward's strange behavior. "By Christ, it's a chilly night, man. Why you dawdle at the open door escapes my comprehension."

Dismus reluctantly shut the door and latched it, then turned to gather the family's outerwear with a worried frown. It had been hard enough to spend the past hour worrying alone; now he faced the task of how to tell the master what had happened. "Sire, I . . . is it possible that Lady Alysaun stayed behind to return home in your friend's company?"

"What friend?" Dismus paled at the question, and Hereward glowered. "Except I know you despise the stuff, I'd be thinking, Dismus, that you had tippled a bit too much this eve. You know full well we left the lady safe at home. What is this nonsense of meeting a friend?"

Usually nothing ruffled the steward's tranquil nature, but now he quaked at the duty that lay before him. "You sent no hired man to escort the lady to the Hippodrome, m'lord?" Even as he asked, Dismus knew the answer and cringed in anticipation of Hereward's roared denial.

"I did nothing of the kind. Why do you persist in this puzzle? I am far too tired to—"

"I think you'd best listen close, m'lord," Frida interrupted, "for Dismus is not a jesting man." For weeks Frida had felt a vague sense of distress concerning Alysaun. She had dismissed it time and again. Both she and Hereward thought of the girl as the daughter they had never had, and Frida especially had grown very close to her. Now, with the steward's unusual air of confusion, her fears had taken a more solid shape.

Hereward was an impatient man, all bluster and action, but his wife's disquietude combined with Dismus's strange behavior to penetrate his weariness. "All right," he sighed. "Frida, go and find us something hot to drink, and I'll try to sort out what has happened." Devon looked as apprehensive as his mother and Hereward nearly ordered him to keep her company. He waited until his wife had left the room, then turned on the pale, sweating servant and asked his explanation of why he had thought Alysaun had joined them. "She was safe at home when we left and had no intention of going out."

Dismus swallowed several times before gathering up his courage. "I know, m'lord, but then you sent . . . oh, I *knew* something was amiss. A young man—I didn't like his looks from the first— came and said he had a message for the lady. She spoke with him and—"

"And *what*, man? This tale sounds more dark and twisted by the minute."

"Well, sire, after she'd talked to him, she called me and and said that she was going out, that the young man was waiting to escort her to the Hippodrome." Dismus patted his damp brow with a hand that

shook. "Oh, I should have *known* better. Lady Alysaun had an od
look, all excited and yet . . . worried."

"What else was said?" Hereward snapped. Trying to pull th
details from Dismus was as frustrating as plucking a goose.

"She said, the lady claimed, you'd happened on an old frien
from England, sir, and she could not wait to see him. I offered t
send one of our own men along, but she wouldn't hear of it."

"So *you* let her go off with this stranger?"

"Sire, I . . . 'twas not my place to deny her leave to go. She woul
not even let *me* accompany her."

Hereward had begun to pace, his brow furrowed in fierce concen
tration. "Is that everything?"

"Aye. Well, she did ask me to look in on Master Matthieu. 'Twa
odd how she insisted I do so immediately. I went as ordered, bu
stopped to look back."

"And?"

"The lady was already half out the doorway, so great seemed he
haste to be away."

Devon watched his father resume his energetic pacing. From th
moment he heard that a message had arrived for her, he was sur
that it was the seer's prediction for Alysaun, come true. Hi
excitement had faded to worry, though, as Dismus's tale unfolded
Alysaun had lied in telling the steward the messenger had come fron
his father—she *must* have. Just as Dismus had doubted the wisdon
of her leaving the house with a total stranger, so, too, woul
Alysaun.

There was only one explanation for her incaution, one thing tha
would be important enough to take her out into the dark of night
news of Brand. But why the need to cover her purpose with a lie
And why not take the steward's offer to see her safe to he
destination? Devon was suddenly afraid that his visit to the fortune
teller had ended as a trap for Alysaun. Because the lure was Brand
she had let her emotions overrule her good sense. He had to know i
he was responsible. "What did this fellow look like?"

Hereward paused in mid-stride, glancing curiously at his son, the turning his attention to Dismus. "Aye, can you at least describe the lackey?"

Dismus concentrated and frowned at his own lack of attentiveness. "He was nothing out of the ordinary, master. A medium-to-slight stature, a hint of a ruddy coloring . . . I'm sorry, sire, but he was one of the sort you couldn't pick out in a crowd. He was all bundled and, you see, his cowl was drawn up, covering his features. I recall a thin mouth. And he spoke in English."

"But it was not his native language?" Devon asked, though he already suspected the stranger was none other than the fortune-teller's son, Andreyas.

Dismus considered this and nodded. "Now I think of it, his speech was not the true English tongue, young master. But he mumbled so, 'twas difficult to make out his words."

"Devon, what are you pursuing?" Hereward inquired. His son looked pale as a ghost, even a little gray, as if he were about to be sick. "If you know something, for God's sake, spit it out. We've already wasted a precious lot of time in talk."

Frida returned carrying a tray with several steaming mugs of mulled ale. One look at her son's face made her turn the tray over to Dismus and go to Devon's side. She touched his forehead and found his brow damp and cold, then felt him start as Hereward bellowed a command.

"Boy, if you do not speak what you know, I'll—"

"Hereward, I won't have you threatening him," Frida warned, scowling at her husband's brusque manner before stroking the hair from Devon's temple. "If you know something that will help, my love, tell your father. That bruin's roar of his only covers a concern for Alysaun."

Devon gulped hard, swallowing the flow of saliva that threatened to choke him. How could he begin? Unable to face his father, he looked into his mother's sympathetic eyes. "Last week, when I took Matt to the Forum . . . you remember, Mother, Alysaun pleaded an aching head and stayed home. Well, she was just in one of her sad moods and I . . . I thought . . . you know how I adore her, I wanted with all my heart to cheer her.''

Frida ignored her husband's exasperated growl and smiled encouragement. Though Devon was grown, he was close to tears and his father's impatience was only making him more flustered. "Go on, dear. How did you think to lift her spirits?''

"Well, I happened on a fortune-teller. His son watched over Matt while I . . . I paid the seer to read the cards for Alysaun.''

Hereward held his breath. He was beginning to grasp what worried Devon. "What did he predict . . . and what was his name?''

"Gnosticus was his name, sire. He seemed to know things about Alysaun that I had not told him. He knew she was widowed and described her fair enough.''

"And I suppose as he made his guesses you confirmed them, eh? Ah, son, I've *told* you not to trust so easy. He only turned about what he learned from you.''

Devon looked up, his face burning with shame. "But how could he guess so close to true?''

"A hundred ways there are, depending upon how easy a mark the scoundrel finds. These soothsayers are nothing but cheats.''

"Hereward, let him be,'' Frida insisted. "He has not your vast experience on which to draw. Continue, Dev—what did this Gnosticus predict for our Alysaun?''

"That she was grieving overlong for her husband and that . . . there was no need to sorrow. He was alive, and soon, in about a week or so, a message would come confirming it.''

"Did this false prophet mention Brand by name?''

Devon looked up at his father and nodded. "Yes. Wait, now that I remember, he didn't. He simply said her *husband* was alive.''

"What makes you so positive he is behind this business tonight?''

"Because, m'lord, the stranger who came to fetch Alysaun seems to fit . . . his description sounds very like the seer's own son, Andreyas.''

Hereward let loose a string of oaths that reverberated in the marble hall and made his wife, who was used to his cursing, cover her ears to shut out his anger. For minutes more he raged on and left no one but Frida unscathed by recriminations. Finally when his fury had sputtered out and reason replaced it, he came to stand before his son. "You'll come with me, son. We've our work cut out for us this night and, as usual, the Devil's henchmen have a good head start. We must search out the quarters of this Gnosticus and his son."

Now, in addition to her fears for Alysaun's safety, Frida had to worry over Hereward and Devon. "Where will you look at this late hour, m'lord?" she asked, twisting her hands nervously.

"Where else would one seek a rat but in its hole, wife? This scum is not the sort to spend his profits on decent lodgings. Someone in the slums will know of him."

Frida came to him and, as his arms went around her, pressed her hands upon his chest and appealed to him. "Even armed, you risk your lives by searching there. Oh, Hereward, I am so frightened."

Hereward lifted her chin with his fingertips and, when their eyes met, asked, "Frida, you love me, do you not?"

"You know well the answer, m'lord. With all my heart I do."

"Then have the courage to believe I would not risk losing that love for anything but such a cause. Alysaun had only me to protect her, and I failed her. As you pass the hours in prayer, pray that I find this bastard before dawn lights the city, before he sees his wicked ends accomplished."

"What are they, Father?" Devon's voice was low and shaky. "What will he do with her?"

"How else would such a man profit from the capture of a lovely woman, son? Unless I . . . we . . . find her, Alysaun will be sold."

His wife and steward knew what Hereward meant, but Devon was yet too green and untried to understand. "Sold? How can he . . . a free woman cannot be bartered."

Hereward felt a tug at his collar and found Frida silently beseeching him to be patient. "On such a matter, a slaver has even less scruples, lad. If we do not find the seer and soon, Alysaun will be a slave, and Gnosticus will be counting his evil gains."

Devon paled a deathly white before he bowed his head. His mother was torn by compassion for his suffering but restrained a desire to go to him and offer comfort. His innocent blunder had endangered Alysaun's life and left her child alone, now bereft of both parents. She pulled away from Hereward and went to her son, reaching out to squeeze his hand. "Up, Dev, and be an aid to your father. Two searching will make the task easier. Go—you'll find Alysaun. I . . . I am sure of it."

Frida had been sure, but by the first rays of morning light, Hereward and Devon had searched every tavern, hostel, and brothel in the old section of Constantinople and failed to find their quarry. No one remembered seeing Alysaun, and though Hereward had blustered and threatened, even bribed, no one who belonged to the fraternity of poor inhabiting the slums would admit as much as where Gnosticus had his lodgings.

By the time the sun was fully risen and too cheerfully bright for the despairing temperament of father and son, they had been to see the prefect consul of the city and alerted the civil authorities of the kidnapping. Hereward hired a conveyance to carry them home, then insisted Devon sleep while he shared a meal with Frida, refusing to let rest interfere with his vow to continue the quest.

"You'll be too tired to think, even if you find some trace," Frida protested. Then, knowing his concern would fuel him in place of sleep, she let him be and asked what he would do next.

Hereward stretched and pushed his plate away. "There are slave traders to talk with, though if she's already been sold, whoever bought Alysaun will remove himself quickly." He rubbed his puffed, bloodshot eyes and gave a helpless shrug. "I fear for her, Frida. By Christ, how I wish we had not attended the games. She'd be home safe and sound now, Alys would, and not in the hands of God knows what manner of human refuse. A girl with her beauty cannot just disappear without someone taking notice."

"She may yet be held somewhere in the city, love. And her captors might even seek a ransom for her. Only some eight hours have passed. 'Tis not enough time to arrange a sale and transport out of Constantinople." Frida came around the table and bent to hug

366

Hereward's neck and press her cheek close to his. "Take heart, husband. You have only tried and not yet failed in her behalf."

For the second time, Frida's desire to encourage her menfolk had overcome her natural instincts. Even as she voiced the reassurance, a galley bound for the seaport of Ephesus cleared the harbor breakwater and set a southerly course that would skirt the shoreline of Anatolia. The ship was seaworthy and fast, despite the need for paint and repairs. As the ship passed the great barrier chain that guarded the Golden Horn, her sails filled with a strong south wind and billowed. Above the top spar it whistled eerily through an open flap of torn canvas topsail, keening mournfully and setting the crew on edge.

16 ·

As Abbar Ben-Mustapha paced the yard that stretched between the slaves' quarters and the villa, an anxious, overeager Sharak al'Deina followed closely on his heels. The royal escort that had seen them as far as the estate had departed for Iconium, their duty done in having seen the Sultan's gift safely delivered to his kinsman's home.

Ben-Mustapha's broad, jowly face was set in a frown as he surveyed the slaver's latest offering. Ordinarily the expression was merely part of the bargaining, a thoroughly understood and expected measure to lower al'Deina's asking price to the actual worth of his stock. Today, though, the overseer's irritation was as real as the biting winter chill that had swept down from the north over the usually temperate plains surrounding Derbe.

"How long have you been coming to this place, al'Deina?" Ben-Mustapha asked in a tightly controlled tone. "By my reckoning, I have seen you three, perhaps four times in the year and a half that Lord Cuibhil has owned the estate, at least as often in the days when it belonged to his father-in-law. After so many visits, should you not remember and respect your buyer's needs?''

Al'Deina nodded, but as no answer was really expected, Ben-Mustapha continued. ''Seven months ago I asked you for field workers, for women strong enough to clean and cook, for a skilled weaver, for a man who could keep records. Three months ago you came...with children, with a sick old man, with everything but what I need.''

The eunuch turned on al'Deina abruptly. ''There is *nothing* in this ragged lot I would buy, son of a she-goat,'' he stormed. ''You waste my time and insult my lord by offering such refuse. Now, be gone—and do not show your face again unless you bring slaves worthy of my master's gold.''

''But surely, your worship, there is a place for one or two of these,'' al'Deina whined, silently cursing the eunuch. True enough, the slaves were the last of the forty or so he had brought to the capital, and the nobles of the court had taken the best. Still, so that his trip would not be wasted, he grumbled and lowered his prices.

''This boy has worth...I paid dearly for him.'' The slaver grasped the shoulder of a young blond boy and pulled him out of the line. ''See how fresh-faced he is...and he sings with a voice as sweet as heaven. I will take ten dinars...half as much as I was offered by a captain of the royal guard.''

''You should have taken the offer, fool,'' Ben-Mustapha sneered. ''My master's tastes do not run to young boys, as well you know. Though you likely extracted too dear a price for the woman, the Sultan's gift will please Lord Cuibhil well enough.'' He walked down the line of shivering, lightly clothed slaves and studied a dark-haired woman, firmly grasping her jaw to pry open her mouth and examine her teeth.

''How much for this one? And *think* before you answer, scum, or take your wares elsewhere.''

The slaver shoved the boy back in line and scuttled to Ben-Mustapha's side, considering how far he could stretch the price. ''She's a good worker, fit for the fields or tending your cookfires, sire. I could not take less than...seven dinars. Even at that, I lose—''

"Spare me your whining—you have a sale," Ben-Mustapha said, and signaled for a servant to take the woman while he paid out each coin with a look of disgust for the trader's greed. "Remember—do *not* come again unless you bring more able-bodied slaves," he warned. "I do not buy the leavings of Iconium's nobles, al'Deina."

A witness to the transaction, Alysaun stood near the covered cart that had brought them here. She shivered and turned her head away. The creamy, fur-edged woolen cape that draped her shoulders was warm enough. The disgust of watching while yet another helpless being was sold, haggled over like some used and valueless piece of goods, brought a bitter taste to her mouth.

She was luckier. Had the others not told her so during their journey? They resented her, with the dull, sullen resentment of the oppressed and hopeless. And truly, she could not blame them. Their clothing was threadbare, hers new and luxurious, if simple. Their fate was to find some new master, kind or harsh, who would extract whatever effort they had to give until there was nothing left to give. She would be pampered, well fed, waited upon...as long as she pleased the man who owned her.

To Alysaun, her fate was no less degrading than theirs. She still belonged to someone, a stranger who might be as cruel as he wished, with no one to curb whatever his appetite might dictate. Whatever worth her beauty held, she had to obey him or suffer. If she attempted to escape...Al'Deina had beaten slaves for as little as daring to look him full in the face. He had warned her, delighted at frightening her with the idea that escape would be punished by flogging, perhaps marring her beauty, her worth. Still, to live as someone's property—no more than a coveted belonging until use required its replacement—such was not life to Alysaun.

Who was Cuibhil Rustim? The slave trader would not enlighten her, preferring to let her imagination dwell fearfully on the little she knew. He was a kinsman of Malik Shah's by marriage to the

Sultan's cousin, and a wealthy man. She knew nothing more, only that she hated him already.

Abbar Ben-Mustapha ignored the thanks and effusive praises heaped upon him by the satisfied trader and turned to consider the Sultan's gift. The foreign woman stared off across the yard, her gaze directed at the slaves' quarters, but he had the impression that she looked without seeing, that her thoughts were turned inward. The slave trader had claimed the woman had known but one master, but al'Deina was a wily cur, a born liar who could not be trusted to speak the truth, even to God.

He would soon find out her background. It would be several days before Cuibhil Rustim returned from a visit to his house near the seaport of Tarsus, enough time to test her willingness to serve, her suitability for the station assigned her.

The slaves were loaded into the cart, and al'Deina, eager to be on his way and perhaps make another sale before the day ended, brushed past the woman. His wide grin was one last mockery, the hard glint of his dark eyes jeering at the sudden apprehension that tightened her fine features.

Alysaun hated the man with more passion than love had ever inspired, but he was leaving her behind. A cold chill that had nothing to do with the weather snaked along her spine. She knew the extent of his cruelty, knew it had been restrained only because he was more greedy than lecherous. Given a choice, she would have gone with him, for her unknown fate—the finality of being left behind to await the absent Cuibhil Rustim's return—could be worse than anything she had already endured.

A hand, firm yet gentle, grasped her arm. Alysaun startled, panic widening her eyes as she looked up at the massive figure of the overseer. Ben-Mustapha was as large a man as Hereward, but the loss of his masculinity had made his body corpulent. "I see why you were given the name Safirah, woman. Your eyes—they are the color of the sky before dawn. My master will be pleased with the Sultan's choice of a gift." He realized how frightened she was, and though a certain amount of fright commanded respect, there was no need for her to be so terrified.

"Come with me into the house," he ordered. She stared at him, immobilized by fear. The eunuch caught her hand, realizing the fact hidden by her cape; she'd been kept bound. Thin rawhide strips were wrapped several times about each slender white wrist, binding them together and chafing the delicate flesh. He frowned, silently cursing the departed trader for the needless measure.

"Did you try to escape al'Deina, little one?" he questioned, suspicious of the possibility that the woman possessed a rebellious nature.

Alysaun shook her head, a glimmer of irony lighting her eyes as she replied, "Nay, sir. I am amongst strangers in a strange land. Where would I go?"

At least she was realistic. This would help her to settle in. "There was no need for such a restraint," he said, and glanced back in the direction the cart had taken. "Would that I had known . . . but it is no matter now. Once inside, we will see these cut away and burned. Praise be to Allah that our master will not return for a while. I would not want to present a gift that showed signs of mistreatment."

Though Alysaun grimaced at the reference to herself as a gift, she thought it hopeful that Cuibhil Rustim frowned upon punishment. She was less afraid now and followed the overseer, hurrying to catch up with his long strides.

Inside, the villa was more lovely than she had imagined. Many of these villas had been built by the Greeks; some, even older, by the Romans. Now almost the entire Anatolian peninsula, excluding Constantinople, was a Seljuk province; the lands and homes left by the fleeing Byzantines had been taken over by the Turks. Civilization was slowly entrenching the hitherto nomad Seljuks, another sign of hope for Alysaun's despairing heart.

The house was, in many ways, similar to the villa Hereward had rented, so that Alysaun felt almost at home. Rich silks draped the arched portals; finely carved furnishings and sculpted statues lined its halls. Though much of its interior must have looked as it had in the days of its former proprietors, there were clear signs of added luxuries that spoke of Bey Cuibhil Rustim's wealth.

Ben-Mustapha led her to the women's quarters, a full wing on the west side of the house. Servants scurried by, and she received more than one curious glance. Embarrassed by the speculations that would inevitably circulate about her, Alysaun felt her face flush and kept her eyes averted, meekly following until she found herself in a small, comfortably appointed room. There was a window, its shutters open to admit the afternoon light. Alysaun crossed the room to see the view, a lovely pastoral scene marred by the heavy wrought-iron bars across the window. She sighed and turned to survey what to her was a prison cell. A metal-lined stone brazier sat in the far corner, the smoke from its burning coals vented through a tiled opening in the ceiling.

She crossed to the brazier, stretching her chilled hands before its warmth. Suddenly Ben-Mustapha was beside her, a sharp, wickedly curved knife in his hands.

He saw the raised eyebrow that questioned him. Though she had forgotten his promise to free her, she no longer seemed afraid. "Hold forth your hands, Safirah. I would not care to risk my master's wrath by leaving even a scratch upon—"

"His property?" Alysaun finished, and was immediately sorry for having indulged in sarcasm. She held her arms forth, wrists apart as much as the tight bindings would allow. The knife sliced the knot in a second; Ben-Mustapha's fingers, as gentle and agile as a woman's, pried the rawhide loose from her wrists.

The bindings dropped into the fire and as the eunuch massaged the tender skin, their eyes met. "Yes, property. Not what I was about to say, but fitting. The sooner you accept that, the easier life will be. And, of all of us who belong to Lord Cuibhil, you will have the lightest duties."

"And what do they entail, sir?" Alysaun's voice was haughty. She could not help but feel humiliated.

"When the master does not call for you, or when, as now, he is absent, your time must be spent improving upon the natural beauty

374

that Allah has granted you. There will be women to serve you, trained in every artifice that might heighten your appeal. You must remember your place, Safirah, and never forget that you must be prepared to attend our master at a moment's call." Ben-Mustapha studied her features. The slave would have to learn humility, else she would bring suffering upon herself and others. "What arts were you taught in the house of your former master?"

Alysaun frowned and pulled her hands away, an audacious action that made Ben-Mustapha glower fiercely. "I have never *had* a master," she snapped, then took a deep breath in wonder at her own daring. Not long past she had been quivering with fright; now the storm of anger that furrowed Ben-Mustapha's brow brought home her helplessness and she said, "I . . . I'm sorry. I spoke without thinking. But 'tis true. By al'Deina's trickery alone did I become a slave. I know not what arts you speak of."

Ben-Mustapha cursed and turned away, less angered by her attitude than by the revelation that the slaver had cunningly enhanced the girl's value by claiming she was an accomplished *houri*, that her master had auctioned her on the block only because he had fallen on hard times. He turned back to her. The hauteur was gone, vanished before his anger. She was not cowed but neither was she as bold as before. "Then time must be spent teaching you," he said, "and every moment must be spent making you as desirable as possible. Oh, that all of Hell's demons might rise up and run that cheating cur to the ground."

The eunuch turned and strode to the doorway, shouting for two servants by name, his voice thundering in an echo down the marble halls. They appeared so quickly it was as if they had anticipated his call. For a moment he spoke to the two women. Alysaun could not understand his words but she thought he was speaking Greek.

The women—one of indeterminate age, the other a girl close to Alysaun's—followed Ben-Mustapha into the room. The girl hung back, her gaze lowered while the woman chattered to him, her hands waving as she walked around Alysaun, taking her measure. They seemed to be arguing about her and Alysaun felt embarrassed as well as puzzled by the woman's attitude. Finally Ben-Mustapha nodded and looked at her. "Lilah is charged with overseeing the female slaves. Once, further in the past than she will admit, she was one of the old Sultan's *houris*. She will see to your care. We start now."

Ben-Mustapha walked to the door and turned and leaned against the frame, crossing his arms over his broad chest. At a nod from him, Lilah came forward and pulled at the woolen cape, carelessly tossing what was once a luxury on the bed.

There was an intensely speculative look on the woman's face, her head wagging this way and that as she commented on Alysaun's figure. Alysaun stared past her at Ben-Mustapha, brushing the older woman's hand aside as she moved to further unveil her figure. "Can this not wait until the morrow?" she asked him sincerely. "We traveled far today. I am hungry and I ache in every bone." Again Lilah pulled at the corner of the veil covering Alysaun's hair and Alysaun made to move past her, her voice beseeching now. "*Please,* stop her."

Lilah crowed over the color of the new slave's hair, lifting one heavy braid to test the texture against her fingers, tossing a comment over her shoulder that made the overseer grin. "You are to stand perfectly still while Lilah does as she has been commanded. She must judge your size and coloring if a proper wardrobe is to be assembled."

"But—"

"Speak again and I will see you gagged, woman. You will be fed." Ben-Mustapha clapped his hands and called the girl to his side, followed by an order that sent her scurrying out of the room.

Alysaun stood perfectly still, infuriated but sure that Ben-Mustapha would follow through on his threat if she said anything. Lilah started to lift the hem of her kirtle and Alysaun's cheeks burned.

"Neither slave speaks your tongue," the eunuch said, almost as if he had read her thoughts. "The sight of your nakedness will not disturb me. I am able to judge flesh without feeling desire."

Nonetheless, Alysaun could not bear the thought he might see her unclothed. She turned her back, lifting her arms grudgingly as Lilah

ugged the cotton up and over her head. The woman came around to
ace her, fingers nimbly untying the laces that tied the bodice of the
unna across Alysaun's breasts. Again a wash of humiliation flooded
Alysaun, but she dutifully let the woman take the last layer of
lothing. Though she felt like cringing, her head was lifted, her
arriage straight and proud.

Lilah circled her, running her fingertips from Alysaun's throat to
he curve of her breasts, prodding and testing the firmness of her
lesh and occasionally making a comment to her superior. When the
nspection was complete, she circled once more, standing back
efore pronouncing her judgment.

"You have had a child." It was more a statement of fact than a
question. Alysaun turned only her head, glaring at him, remembering
.is threat to gag her. She nodded, hoping that the fact somehow
nade her unacceptable. "Turn and face me," Ben-Mustapha or-
lered, and though she dared not disobey, she turned with obvious
eluctance. He crossed to stand before her, studying her figure for a
ew moments before he said, "Only another woman would have
quessed. I see nothing that would displease my lord. I deem you
cceptable."

Alysaun, incensed by her position as much as by the detached,
old survey, tilted her head up and cast a sullen glance his way.
Vhat, she wondered, would they have done if she had not been
'acceptable''? And did it matter, anyway? She was tired and
ungry, suddenly very cold and aware of a breeze from the open
vindow.

The girl came back with a tray of soup that smelled heavenly.
'lacing it on a low table near the silk-cushioned bed, she stepped
ack and awaited further instructions. Alysaun swallowed hard. It
vas difficult to maintain a haughty attitude with a growling belly.
'Eat now, there will be more later, after you've been bathed,"
3en-Mustapha ordered, then spoke a command to the girl, who
lisappeared and was back in minutes with a loose silken robe to
varm Alysaun's shivering body.

Afterward, with the thick broth of lentils consumed, Alysaun's

strength returned. She was escorted to the bath, a heated room muc
like the Baths of Zeuxippus at home. Ben-Mustapha left her then i
Lilah's care and reappeared only when she was back in her chamber

There was another inspection, but this time the room was warmer
The window had been shuttered, the fire stirred in the brazier; an
perhaps because the warm, scented bath water and massage tha
followed had calmed her, she found herself less embarrassed.

While she had been luxuriating in the bath, material had bee
brought to her room, bolts of every texture available, sheer laces
silks, and soft, woven woolens. There were subtle shades of ever
rainbow hue as well as deep purples and scarlets; there were eve
colors that had a multishaded sheen, like the feathers of the lovel
peacocks that paraded in the gardens of Constantinople's roya
palace.

Tirelessly, Lilah unwrapped each bolt and held the materia
against Alysaun's body, employing a trained eye to test the suitabili
ty of each color to her fair complexion and hair. Hour after hou
passed, the time wearing heavily on the drowsy Alysaun, and whe
dusk came she was more than ready for rest.

Still, the trials went on, Lilah calling for more lamps as th
darkness encroached. Alysaun protested she could stand no longer
and finally was allowed to sit. Ben-Mustapha was gone for a while
the house quiet.

When he returned from his supper, the overseer found Lilah stil
at work, though her charge lay curled beneath the fur-lined coverlet
Despite his protest that the slave would not be ready for thei
master's return, Ben-Mustapha had to agree with Lilah's assertio
that the woman needed rest as well as the proper attire to appea
pleasing.

"And you, woman," he said to Lilah, "I have seldom seen yo
so wide awake at this hour." There was a flush of color in he
cheeks, a hint of the prettiness that had once brought her royal favor
She admitted an excitement in once more being called upon to use
her skills, an excitement that banished weariness.

"He will be content with this gift, will our lord," she commented ooking at the sleeping Alysaun, thinking that perhaps, through this woman, she would gain for her efforts to make Cuibhil Rustim happy. "Truly, even without accomplishments, I think she will find favor in his eyes." Lilah had come to the estate as part of Princess Farazha's retinue and stayed on with little to do but supervise the care of the daughter the young woman had left at her death. The master was a good man, a foreigner by birth, but he was lonely. And, she thought, feeling somewhat guilty, he had seemed so even when the lovely Farazha had been alive. Always his expression had a subtle look of longing, as if he wished for someone or something denied him. If anyone could give the handsome widower a respite from his solitary reflections, it was this young woman, who spoke his own tongue. Especially when Lilah had finished enhancing the beauty nature had bestowed upon Alysaun.

The next three days were a blur for Alysaun. She was still unused to the Turkish name the Sultan had given her and often, at first, failed to answer when addressed by it. Each day began early and, broken by afternoon naps, ended late. The entire household seemed marshaled to the effort of transforming her into a gift that would delight their lord. Far into the night, the women most skilled in fine sewing worked on her attire; each day there were hours of alterations, then fittings for new robes and gowns.

Alysaun could not imagine so extensive a wardrobe for the slave of a noble foreigner. She doubted that even Matilda, wife of the Bastard William, was clothed in such finery.

She had no time to dwell on the admiration of those around her, little time to consider the wicked enjoyment of being treated like a princess when she was no more than a piece of property that could be sold. She had no time to herself at all and at night was too worn to do more than fall asleep.

Finally that awful morning came when Lord Cuibhil Rustim was due to return. She had been bathed, fussed over, and dressed twenty times until finally Lilah announced that perfection was not to be tampered with and insisted she sit still in her room until *his* arrival was announced. And so she sat, the shadows of the day lengthening before a disappointed Lilah had come to tell her a message had been received. Cuibhil Rustim would not be home for another week.

The tension of waiting, the long hours of endless preparation, the expectation, and the anger at being treated like a rare delicacy that would be served up to his lordship left her breathless and irritable. She lashed out at Lilah, venting her feelings in a torrent of words the woman could not understand, pacing the floor of her room, even screaming at the top of her voice. No doubt the household heard the commotion and thought her mad. Surely Lilah, at last tired from the endless hours of activity, thought her possessed. She ran from the room, calling for Ben-Mustapha as if Judgment Day had come.

The worst of the thunder had stopped, the lightning flashes of temperament fading as the eunuch arrived with a babbling Lilah in tow. Alysaun was lying on the plush, thick pillows that formed her bed, weeping as furiously as she had screamed, pounding the cushions with tight, balled fists. She glanced up at the sound of hushed voices, further outraged by the awe her temper had inspired as well as by the understanding she saw reflected in Ben-Mustapha's eyes. She started to yell at him, then gave up trying to explain what she herself could not understand, and simply buried her head in her arms and sobbed.

Ben-Mustapha wisely left her alone, knowing there was no solace he could offer. When she had at last quieted, emotions spent, the servant girl, Anika, appeared, bringing a tray, which she placed on the table. Ben-Mustapha ran the house as if it were a part of him; he knew of every event almost before it happened. The crystal goblet of wine he ordered for her contained a small draft of opiate, enough to soothe Alysaun and bring on much needed rest. She lay there, her thoughts drifting aimlessly like the currents of a river, while Anika bathed her puffed eyes with cool, rose-scented compresses.

With more time to prepare before Lord Cuibhil arrived, the tension at the villa eased. More elaborate attire was designed and the weather warmed to its usual balminess. The days grew long and quiet, uncluttered by any duties more arduous than fitting her new clothing.

Ben-Mustapha seemed convinced that she would make no attempt to escape, for she had spoken truly when she said there was no place for her to go. She was allowed to explore the villa and often found the tranquillity of the gardens pleasant. It was there, late one afternoon, that she heard the child for the first time. At first she thought she was imagining the sound, the faint, tremulous wail that pricked at her experienced maternal ear.

Alysaun closed her eyes, afraid that in her longing to be with Matthieu again, she was going mad. The crying ceased, then sounded with renewed vigor, and she rose to follow it to its source. She found the room, darkened against the daylight by heavy draperies, and entered. Ignoring the protests of the baby's nurse, who had dozed off in a comfortably cushioned chair near the silk-draped cradle, she went to the baby and drew back a layer of swaddling that had wrapped itself across the infant's mouth in its struggles.

The nurse knew who she was, of course; but this chamber was her domain, and she was highly offended at any interference. She chattered in a foreign tongue, then gave a horrified shriek of protest when Alysaun calmly ignored her and bent to scoop the child into her arms. In a whirl of dark veils, the woman stomped from the room, eager to find Ben-Mustapha and report the trespasser.

The baby was lovely, a delicate little girl with tiny wisps of auburn curls framing a sweet, distressed face. She quieted instantly as she was held in Alysaun's arms, her tiny fingers reaching out to grasp the thin gossamer veil covering Alysaun's hair. Alysaun was enchanted with the child; she had not known of her existence and wondered now, as she whispered to her and stroked the soft, downy cheeks, why she had not heard her cries before.

When Ben-Mustapha appeared at the door, Alysaun was seated in the nurse's chair, the baby cradled in her arms and fast asleep. The nurse stood behind him, arms folded across her ample chest in a righteous posture, waiting for the overseer to chastise the intruder. He turned around and gave the woman an order, silencing her outraged protests with a look that warned of retribution if she failed to obey him. The woman glared at Alysaun before she flounced away, no doubt to spread word of her treatment.

Ben-Mustapha crossed the room, moving quietly for one so large, stopped to look down at the child, and lifted his eyes slightly to question Alysaun. "The woman was sleeping while the baby cried on and on," Alysaun said, defending her actions. "I could not bear to listen . . . you see, all she needed was to be picked up and held."

The child did seem content, downy lashes resting on her rose-blush cheeks. Taris stirred for just a moment but, as Alysaun tightened her hold, slumbered once more in peace.

Ben-Mustapha's first thought was to reprimand her for disturbing the tranquillity of his well-run establishment, for she was, after all, just another of the slaves under his command. Something in the way she held the child, however, protective and maternal, stirred his curiosity. "You were separated from your own child," he guessed, and she did not have to nod to admit it; for a moment she stared past him, her features soft and vulnerable, eyes glazed with a sheen of tears. "Your duties in this house are clear," he continued. "They are more important than caring for the little one."

Alysaun looked up, fighting the tears that threatened to overspill her eyes. She did not want to cry in front of Ben-Mustapha. She had once, and the weakness had embarrassed her. For some reason it was important for her to have contact with this small, helpless infant, second only to her longing to return home again and see her own child. She was willing to risk anything to get her way. "Nothing is more important than caring for a helpless babe," she insisted. "The woman ignored her when all—"

"Taris is not to be coddled every time she whimpers," the eunuch explained. "The nurse attends to her needs, and the child is fed and well clothed. She lacks for nothing."

"Nothing but affection, a gentle voice and touch," Alysaun retorted. "Babies thrive on love as much as on mother's milk, Ben-Mustapha. Is there no one here who cares to let her wriggle in the garden sunlight or to laugh a moment at her antics? Does Cuibhil Rustim care so little for his—"

"He loves her well, but a man—"

"Cannot show tenderness, I know," Alysaun said impatiently. "Well, you are wrong. My own father, important as his duties were, never took the time to show us affection. And my . . ." She was about to speak of Brand but the thought of him was too painful, especially with this child, who reminded her of Matthieu, held close in the crook of her arm. "Anyway, I *do* know it to be true. I want time to spend with the child. You called her . . . Taris?"

"Yes, but I cannot grant you this wish. When he is home again, his lordship will expect you to be fully attendant to his wishes. I would not test his wrath with an excuse that you are otherwise occupied."

"You need not, sir," Alysaun said, releasing the breath she had held; half her battle was won. "The nurse can care for the babe, see her fed and washed and dry. I ask for only a short time, each day, to spend with Taris. He need not even know."

"He will find out." Mustapha shook his head. "No, I will not allow it.

"You must."

"Why? You have forgotten—"

"I haven't forgotten that I have no rights, Ben-Mustapha," Alysaun interrupted. "But if you were not to allow me this small favor, I might be so disconsolate my appetite would completely fail me. Were I to begin to look unappealingly frail, I think your master would notice it far more than he would miss an hour of my time when he does not require my presence."

Ben-Mustapha opened his mouth, then shut it and frowned. This woman's insolence knew no bounds, yet if he meted out the punishment such behavior merited, he would have to explain the reason to Lord Cuibhil. The simplest solution seemed to be to allow her what she asked, yet it did not sit well with him that a mere slave should gain her way so easily. "You may see her when *I* say, for as long as *I* say. If you disobey, I promise you, you will not be allowed to see her again, and we will test how long you can go without eating."

A small victory, perhaps, but at that moment it meant the world to

Alysaun. "Thank you, Abbar Ben-Mustapha," she said. The brilliance of the grateful look she gave him assured him more than words that she would not break their pact. "May I stay for yet a short while?" He seemed about to say no just because it was in his power to deny or grant the request. "*Please* . . . I'll leave at your command."

"Until I find Erinia and explain this odd new arrangement," he allowed munificently, "you may stay."

17

Cuibhil Rustim and his party of guards and attendants arrived at the estate close to midnight on the expected day. The men were happy to see the familiar torchlit facade of the house loom before their tired eyes, more than pleased that the journey was at an end. Lord Cuibhil's mood was irritable, his temper having been roused by a chance encounter with a much-disliked neighbor, Omar Ben-Assanil.

The ever alert Ben-Mustapha greeted his master at the portal with a low bow. Taking Lord Cuibhil's dusty cloak, he clapped his hands to summon the servant who waited nearby with a basin of warm water scented with oil of musk rose. Washing the grime of travel from his face and hands improved Cuibhil's mood somewhat, but as he settled into a comfortable chair in the common room, the memory of his meeting with Lord Omar renewed his anger.

Ben-Mustapha, who often served his master as a sounding board, stood nearby, waiting patiently as Cuibhil wet his parched throat with a draft of wine from a bejeweled, damascene-worked goblet. "There was trouble on the road, my lord?" Ben-Mustapha asked finally after a period of long silence. "Surely you were not attacked by—"

"Thieves?" Cuibhil finished the question, then flashed a grin that deepened a dimple on one side of his tanned face. "Nay, not the common sort, anyway. This one goes about in disguise, but Omar Ben-Assanil's fine clothes cannot hide his nature."

"What business saw him on the road at so late an hour, master?" Mustapha was not merely curious. Anything that troubled Cuibhil Rustim troubled his overseer.

"The devil lost another of his female slaves. He had the impertinence to ask my assistance in a search for her." It was common knowledge that Assanil treated his property poorly. No one wondered that he spent much of his time retrieving the slaves who tried to escape his cruelty. "I, for one, hope the poor girl finds someplace to hide." He looked up at Ben-Mustapha and asked, "Has anyone reported seeing her?"

"No one, sire. In their loyalty to you, none would keep such knowledge a secret."

"I doubt no one's loyalty, certainly not yours, Ben-Mustapha. Enough of the matter . . . how goes everything here? Briefly, please. My temper will much improve with a night's rest in my own bed. Any problems that cannot await the morning light?"

"No, sire. If you wish, a bath might help to make your sleep more tranquil. The new slave, Safirah, will attend you and perhaps ease the strain of a long journey."

Ben-Mustapha had sent him word of Malik Shah's gift. The Sultan was a generous man, one who often took more delight in presenting gifts than in receiving them. Even before Cuibhil had married Malik's cousin, the two had been close friends, more kindred in nature than the young prince's true brothers. Though he had assumed his father's crown, Malik had not changed.

"I am too worn to do justice to such a gift this night, my friend. A bath will work wonders, but I'll save the surprise of meeting this Safirah for tomorrow. Is she aptly named?"

"Yes, m'lord, and worthy of belonging to you. I think your

surprise will be a pleasant one. She is a foreigner and speaks your own tongue, and in a voice as sweet as an angel's. Are you sure you would not care to meet her now?"

"Nay, better to dream upon imaginings and wake with a longing for reality. Have the bath prepared. I'll be in my chamber when it is ready." Cuibhil sighed and slowly swung his long legs to the floor. He was saddle-weary, almost willing to slip into bed without the bath, but aware a cleansing was warranted. "I'll see the girl after my morning meal. Have her wait in the garden."

Ben-Mustapha nodded and respectfully touched his forehead in obeisance as Cuibhil rose and stretched tall, then walked past him toward the open hall that led to the perimeter of the garden courtyard. The overseer moved to escort his master but Cuibhil waved him off. "See to the bath, Ben-Mustapha, or I'll be asleep before it's drawn."

"As you wish, master." The eunuch waited until Lord Cuibhil was out of range before he called to an attendant and ordered the bath prepared. "Be hasty, but forget not that his lordship will be displeased if the water is too cool."

Hidden in the deep shadows of the courtyard, Alysaun was about to cross the hall and return to her chamber when the sound of footsteps made her dart back to the safety of the shadows. Already nervous and tense from a stealth that was uncommon to her nature, she held her breath and stiffened, her body molded to one of the columns between two rose trees.

The footsteps came closer; she dared not look, but as a small, apprehensive face appeared, to peek around the edge of her door, Alysaun risked disclosure to wave a warning. She did not know the girl's name, nor could she understand her speech, but the weeping that had brought her to her window not fifteen minutes before had crossed the boundaries of language in its distress.

It had been dangerous to try to slip outside. The household was alert despite the late hour, and servants scurried along the halls. Once she was outside, the light of a full moon had shown her the reason for the girl's whimpering cries. Her back was lacerated, the tender flesh torn by whip lashes. Alysaun knew immediately she was not from the villa. Slaves were punished here, but in a less harsh manner.

Even if she were caught helping the girl—and the poor thing was no more than a child—Alysaun felt she could count upon the same privilege that had aided her in the matter of Taris. Still, it was best if the matter escaped Ben-Mustapha's attention altogether. The girl had slipped back into her room. Alysaun tried to merge with the darkness but found her efforts impeded by the rose tree's thick branches. One of its many thorns had caught her veils; she dared not move for fear the approaching servant would discover her and raise a cry.

Suddenly, with hardly a pause in the footfall, Alysaun's arm was seized. She found herself dragged from her hiding place, and minus the veil caught upon the thorns, into the softly lit hallway. Instinctively swatting at the firm hold upon her wrist, she decided her best defense would be indignation, a claim of injured innocence. "How *dare* you handle me thusly," Alysaun hissed, keeping her voice low, still hoping she might intimidate the manservant into freeing her without alarming the entire house. "Let go," she insisted, struggling with her free hand to pry his fingers loose. "Free me, fool, or Ben-Mustapha will . . . will *flog* you."

Cuibhil didn't recognize the young woman he had captured, but her imperious tone brought a grin to his tired face. He easily caught her other hand, pulling her into the pool of flickering light cast by the oil tapers to inspect his catch. "He will now, will he?" he replied, his amusement turning to admiration when he caught sight of her face and unveiled hair, cascading in a froth of burnished curls around features flushed with anger. "If the punishment is set, then perhaps I should take a kiss in reward ere you call out alarm. Why have you not screamed, fair one . . . is it that you have been caught in some clandestine act?"

At the sound of his voice Alysaun froze. The timbre was so close to Brand's that she thought she must be dreaming. She closed her eyes, opened them, and took a long, hard look at her captor. The man had her husband's build, his height, even his manner, but though his eyes were warmly appraising her, it was not, it *could not* be Brand. This man, who she realized now could not be a mere servant, was dressed in a richly embroidered, if somewhat dusty, tunic of the finest silk.

His captive had gone pale and ceased her struggling. Indeed, as he held her with both hands, she seemed ready to fall. Her eyes were fixed upon his face as if in horror. Cuibhil could only surmise that she had realized his identity and feared he would exact some punishment for her audacity. "Where are you quartered?" he asked. Still she only stared, seemingly struck speechless with apprehension. "Speak *up*, woman. Which room has Ben-Mustapha given you?"

Alysaun could not answer; she could barely think. Undoubtedly it was Cuibhil Rustim who stood before her demanding a reply, but his resemblance to Brand was so close it was uncanny. He frowned, turning his head slightly to survey the row of doors lining the inner hall. Only one was open, he noted as a spill of yellow candlelight washed over the marble floor.

Even as she denied the face could be Brand's, Alysaun saw his profile. His nose had the same slight crook as Brand's, the result of his harsh treatment at the hands of Sheriff Fitz Walther. It could only be Brand and yet... there was no recognition in his eyes, only a slight impatience at her lack of response.

Now that she believed it was, somehow, Brand, she was too stunned to protest as he started for her room, pulling her along in his wake. All thought of the injured slave girl vanished from a mind dulled by shock and reeling with the import of this odd reunion-of-sorts.

Once within, she was deposited in a chair. Cuibhil took a stance before her, his expression half puzzled, half irritated. The woman, who could be none other than his new slave, Safirah, had not taken her eyes from his face. They were lovely eyes, twin pools of azure, but filled with some emotion he could not discern.

"Now, if you would be so kind," he said, trying to look

threatening though he was but curious, "explain what you were doing in the coutyyard. I know your identity. You have guessed mine. I am weary from travel and eager for my bath." She looked down, her fingers clenched so tightly together that her knuckles whitened with the strain. "Perhaps I make you too nervous to reply?" He sighed impatiently and turned to pace toward the window. Pausing there, hands behind his back, he rocked slightly on his heels. "I am waiting, Safirah."

"My name is not Safirah, m'lord." Alysaun half believed this was some pretense on Brand's part, but she could not comprehend what advantage such a ruse would give him. And Brand was never deliberately cruel. She watched him carefully for a reaction as she said, "I have lived too long by my christening name, Alysaun, to answer to any other."

Cuibhil Rustim turned his head, showing only heightened curiosity at her bold assertion. The questioning, arched eyebrow was so typical of Brand that Alysaun's heart skipped a beat. Her face was not familiar to him; her name had elicited no more recognition than if she had claimed it was Mary. Suddenly she tensed, a blush of color shading her cheekbones. Two small, dirty feet poked out from beneath the heavy brocade draperies, a startling reminder of the runaway slave hidden not two feet behind the spot where Cuibhil Rustim stood.

"I . . . I owe your lordship an apology," Alysaun said, her attitude so abruptly altered that Cuibhil's eyes narrowed in suspicion. At first rebellious, then puzzling, her mood was now soft with kittenish appeal. He watched her warily as she rose and approached him, silently measuring the sincerity of her actions.

"I was rude when . . . when you happened to catch me coming in from the garden." She paused before him, thoroughly contrite and seemingly eager to make amends. The impact of her gaze, when she lifted her head to look directly at him, was unnerving. He saw nothing but two wide blue eyes, framed by thick golden lashes, silently appealing for his understanding. "Truely, m'lord, I spent but a few minutes strolling through the courtyard." Alysaun knew he believed her and felt strangely guilty for the lie. "Perhaps"—she glanced down, lacing her fingers together to still their fluttering—"I could not rest tonight. When your arrival appeared delayed once more, I felt..."

"Disappointed?" Cuibhil smiled, thoroughly enchanted by the girl's fair, blond beauty and quite ready to accept an explanation that appealed to his vanity. As if by magic, he no longer ached from his long and tedious ride. His gaze swept over her figure, her slenderness veiled by layers of pale green silk, a complexion as fresh and fair as a child's, and hair... He reached out to feel the texture of a wave that looked as light as spun gold thread, then found himself lost to, and deeply disturbed by, the startled glance she gave him.

Cuibhil wanted her; his body acknowledged the desire before he had even organized his thoughts. "You have no reason to fear me, Safir..." He remembered her given name and said it in a hushed voice. "Alysaun... yes, it suits you well. I like the sound."

Hearing him say her name was too much for her. Alysaun paled once more, her eyes shut tightly for a moment to hide the pain. This *was* Brand, yet the hand that lightly traced the outline of her shoulder, to sweep confidently along her throat and lift her chin, this belonged to the stranger, to the man who owned her and seemed eager now to exercise his dominion. She could not look at him. When his fingertips followed the curve of her cheek, she could not help but raise a hand to cover his and make him cease his maddening exploration. She was not brave enough to risk speaking. In place of a spoken appeal, she let the trembling of her hand communicate her feelings.

His need for her growing stronger with the closeness of their two bodies, Cuibhil mistook the trembling for an alluring naiveté. Their eyes met. For a fleeting moment he felt a tug of some emotion deeper than physical need, then instinct swept all reason from his mind. His arms were around her, his head bending to capture lips that had parted in protest, a mouth that was vulnerably open to the trespass of his tongue.

Alysaun stiffened, battling her mixed emotions toward this confident male animal who was, and yet was not, Brand. All too briefly she fought the familiar rise of longing, her resistance ebbing as his hands roamed possessively across the contours of her body. To fight against what she had longed for on many a sleepless and lonely night was like railing at the heavens for allowing the sun to rise anew. Neither her passion nor the sun would fail to rise for all the protests ever uttered.

Cuibhil Rustim felt her resistance die and slowed his passionate assault as Alysaun's body signaled a surrender of will to the senses. She was his to possess, a flower too fragile to crush in the hasty embrace of a man not yet cleaned of the sweat and dust of the road. Now that she was aroused, a brief—he pressed his lips against the white column of her throat and felt a pulse beat throb—yes, a *brief* spell in the heated pool would make his conquest all the more pleasurable for the slight cessation of desires.

She was in his arms, lifted effortlessly, abandoned and breathless, a rose flush of desire staining the soft, high curve of her cheeks. Forgetting everything but the reward of vanquished desire, she lay curled against his chest, listening to the strong and steady drumming of his heart.

He carried her across the room, pausing near the cushioned bed. Cuibhil glanced down at it, almost giving in to the urge to lay her pliant form upon it and sate the drawing need to release his aroused passions. One look at her face, flushed as with a fever and more lovely for its sensual abandon, firmed his intentions to spend hours, not mere minutes, in a leisurely exploration of his newfound treasure.

Turning toward the door, Cuibhil was surprised to find Ben-Mustapha standing there looking, for the first time he could remember, awkward and ill at ease. A dull-red flush suffused the eunuch's full, jowly face. He had taken in the romantic proceedings and he was at a loss as to how to handle the very difficult matter of the disembodied set of toes protruding from beneath Safirah's window draperies. Should he mention the fact to his master or deal with it himself?

The choice was no longer his. Cuibhil Rustim had turned and

lanced back at the window. His gaze settled on the toes, which
nmediately wriggled as if aware of being observed. In his arms, a
nguid Alysaun opened her eyes, their dreamy expression vanishing
: the heavy-lidded, threatening look Cuibhil gave her.

Before she knew it, Alysaun was flung toward the cushions,
nding in a startled tangle of limbs. Cuibhil stalked across the
om, expecting perhaps to uncover a hidden lover, when his arms
ntrapped the trespasser and drapes. He whirled the slight figure,
urprised by its light weight as well as by the distinctly feminine
:ream that was only slightly muffled by the brocade.

Of master and overseer, Cuibhil was the most stunned. Ben-
Iustapha had guessed from an earlier report by one of the servants
tat the runaway was hiding somewhere in the villa. Alysaun, who
ad gathered her disarrayed clothing and was sitting up, merely
ghed, knowing there was nothing more she could do. The girl
abbled in some Turkish dialect, pleading pitifully for mercy as she
owered at the feet of a discomforted Cuibhil.

Cuibhil spoke a reassuring phrase that transformed the frightened
·ailings to cries of gratitude, muffled as the girl clutched at his
ooted feet and sobbed in relief. The clotted blood that streaked the
ack of her torn gown elicited a fierce scowl, and, speaking in
urkish, he gave Ben-Mustapha an order to take the girl and see that
er back was tended, to feed her and find a place for her to rest. He
ad no intention of returning her to Omar; she was too frail and
oung to live through another brutal whipping.

Ben-Mustapha came forward and helped the girl to stand. Her
:arstained, dirty face was so transfigured by the relief of deliver-
nce, it was almost painful to see. She called blessings down upon
is master's head, and when she passed the bed where Alysaun sat,
ue bent to kiss the fair white hand of the woman responsible for her
afety.

Finally Cuibhil and Alysaun were alone once more. Alysaun's
nees were drawn up, her hands clasped together atop them. Her
ice was solemn but unafraid. She refused to acknowledge him,
iough a second sense alerted her to his penetrating stare. Cuibhil's

393

emotions were an odd mix of relief, anger, and admiration for th
risk Alysaun had taken. He wasn't sure what punishment he wou
have allotted if it had been a lover hiding within her room. Thoug
his household consisted of slaves, none were ever beaten for mi
deeds. Indeed, they were treated with the consideration given fre
men and women, and for this reason they were loyal and obedien

It was her guile that angered him, and the memory of how she ha
suddenly turned into an enchantress that pricked at his male prid
Alysaun had used her woman's wiles in an artful attempt to dra
him away from discovering the hidden slave girl. And he, like
fool, like a gullible, inexperienced boy, had neatly played into h
hands. Deprived of a pleasure he had highly anticipated, Cuibh
Rustim was determined to make her pay a price for his disappointmen

He approached the bed, and even when two black boots in a
angry stance appeared beside her, Alysaun refused to acknowledg
him. "You seem to feel no shame for your misdeeds, woman. Wh
have you to say in defense of your actions?"

"Compassion needs no defense, m'lord," Alysaun asserted, rai
ing her head in defiance. "The girl was but a child. She needed hel
and I—"

"You took it upon yourself to lie for her and would have stolen a
well, had you not been discovered," Cuibhil interrupted. "Surely
was food from my pantries that you would have given her."

"I would have shared my own portion with her."

"The food you're fed belongs to me—everything in this villa
mine, including you. I forgive what you did for the girl's sake, but
will not have a slave lie to me."

In truth, Alysaun had forgotten she had claimed to be out for
walk to cover his discovery of her near the garden. It seeme
excusable to her in the light of her reasons. "One lie to aid a
unfortunate child I count no sin, sire."

"*One* lie? Even now you continue the deceit." Cuibhil was fa
more angry than the situation warranted, his bruised pride requirin
recompense. "Did you not claim disappointment that I had n
arrived, so distressing you that a walk in the night air was necessa

ease your restlessness? You not only speak in falsehoods, woman,
ou use your body as a lure to abet them. No doubt your former
master found this trait as distasteful as I."

"No man has ever been my master, Lord Cuibhil," Alysaun
snapped, matching his indignation. "I was kidnapped, trapped by
my own desires to..." She could not finish and admit it was her
longing to be reunited with him that had led her into the humiliation
of becoming a slave.

"That may be true. Certainly you do not act as a slave should,"
Cuibhil admitted.

Fury made her forget she was already in trouble, and brought her
to her feet with an angry jerk. "And how *does* a slave act, Lord
Cuibhil? Tell me exactly what you expect. Should I grovel at your
feet and pretend I admire your every deed? Regardless of what *you*
think, sire, I am no man's property. My respect cannot be purchased
in any coin—even a whip cannot exact that intangible from my
heart. Do as you please with me but you may rue the day I was
'given' to you. I may give you more trouble than I am worth."

Cuibhil studied her, still angry but intrigued by her courage.
"We will see just how much you're worth in the weeks to come,"
he promised, his mouth quirked in amusement as he made a bold,
leisurely survey of her face and figure. "You may not have known
a master ere now, *but*, my fine rebel, you will know before I am
through with you how to show respect for the man who controls
your life."

The threat was not an idle one. Whether it was her fault or some
new dimension of his character, this man who was once her husband
was determined to have her docile. Alysaun suddenly considered the
many ways in which she could be made subject to his will, none of
them pleasant, and found she regretted her open defiance. "I'll not
disobey your commands, m'lord," she said in a hushed tone. "But
if your methods reduce my life to such misery that it seems not
worth the effort to continue, your victory will be an empty one."

"I think that before we reach that point I will have won more than
a slave, fair one. Do not resist me only out of pride, and think not

395

that I would make you suffer the whip upon your tender flesh. Ther
are other ways to bend the will that resists. I will have yours bent t
mine without breaking what I find reason to admire.''

With that, Cuibhil smiled, an arrogant smile that left Alysau
suddenly frightened and, as he turned abruptly and left her, ver
much alone. More than the real apprehension a beating migh
inspire, the hint of emotional duress stirred her imagination. She la
down upon her bed, trying to think what he had meant by ''other'
methods, and finally gave up. She would have to await his move
and that uncertainty was the beginning of her punishment. Sh
barely slept, and was troubled by dreams of shadowed menace.

She did not see him the next day. When she inquired of Ben
Mustapha how his master's mood was, he replied noncommittall
that Lord Cuibhil's temper seemed vastly improved over the previ
ous night. The day passed in preparation for a call that never came
She felt oddly depressed for the uselessness of hours broken only b
bathing, dressing, and staring out the barred window of her room.

Late in the afternoon, she began to realize the subtlety of Cuibhi
Rustim's plan. Ben-Mustapha came to her, shortly before the hou
she was due to spend with Taris, to tell her that she was to be denie
that pleasure. She was unprepared for such a decision and speechles
for minutes until rage set in. She argued with Ben-Mustapha
reminding him of the threat that had first secured her the privilege
When he answered that she was free to deprive herself of nourish
ment if it was her desire, she whirled and furiously paced her room

He had additional orders. She was to eat her meals in her room
She was to use the bath each day, but she was denied the use of th
gardens and was confined to her room. ''Go back to your master an
tell him . . . tell him I . . .'' Alysaun paused in front of the placid
faced eunuch and crossed her arms under her breasts. ''You may tel
him his methods are exceedingly petty and—'' She stopped i
mid-sentence, realizing it was exactly what he wanted to hear
''No . . . tell him I understand his reasoning and find his judgmen
most merciful.''

Ben-Mustapha canted his head, puzzled by the sudden change o

hrase, then nodded. He had orders to recall everything the slave
aid and did and to report them to Lord Cuibhil. He was just about
» leave when Alysaun touched his arm.

"When he summons me tonight, I will tell him this myself. Say
othing, for I would like the chance to apologize myself."

"The master will not be home this evening, Lady Alysaun."

Alysaun stared at him, surprised to hear him use her given name.
pparently she had been the topic of discussion between Cuibhil and
is overseer. "And is it impertinent for me to ask what business
kes him away from his home?"

"The master does not discuss his plans with those who serve
im." She looked crestfallen, and Ben-Mustapha's stern expression
oftened for a second. "Lord Cuibhil plans a visit to an old
cquaintance who lives nearby."

"How long has he been friends with her?"

"Since—" Ben-Mustapha's expression was suddenly shuttered.
'I have said too much. Do you wish me to give Lord Cuibhil any
essage?"

"*No.*" The temptation to further berate Cuibhil was almost too
reat to resist. If this was his game, she would play it and win.
lysaun smiled, then dismissed the eunuch by turning to stroll to the
vindow. She waited a few moments before glancing over her
houlder. Ben-Mustapha had vanished.

By evening, when her meal arrived, Alysaun was no longer so
omposed. The rectangular room with its high ceilings and pleasant
urnishings had seemed a delightful private haven, but now that she
vas confined to it, she felt like a bird in a cage. There was nothing
o break the monotony, nothing to occupy the hours that dragged,
nd staring out the window, with its sturdy bars only reminded her
he was not free.

Despite her hunger, when the servant left the tray of tempting
past duck and herbed rice, Alysaun promptly took the tray and
laced it outside her door. There was no guard set to watch her, but
he suspected an attempt to sneak into the gardens would be

397

immediately discovered. Later, when she gave in to the ravenous demands of her stomach and went to retrieve the tray, it was gone.

With all her bold threats to starve herself, Alysaun had not counted on the very real pain of going hungry. How could she ignore her punishment if her own body would not cooperate? The hunger was more acute as the evening dragged on, with nothing to keep her from dwelling on the memory of how succulent the duck had appeared, how delicious had been its odor.

Retiring early, she had ample time to dream, and this night the shadowed imaginings took on a more terrifying aspect. She saw herself wasting away, a gaunt creature with sunken cheeks, all bones and dull, lusterless hair.

In the morning, prompted by real hunger as well as by the nightmare images of starvation. Alysaun ate every crumb on her plate and was tempted to request another tray. Only the idea that her hunger would be reported to Cuibhil and taken as a weakness kept her from giving in.

The day was a long repetition of the previous one; her boredom was broken only by brief activity in the orchard some forty yards from her window. Normally, the idea of watching men trimming trees would not have struck Alysaun as interesting, but the men sang a work chant as they progressed. She felt so isolated now that the sound of human voices joined in song was a balm to her loneliness. When they at last finished, she was loath to see them depart. The silence that followed reinforced her feeling of imprisonment, but there was no one in whom to confide, no human contact save the serving girl who brought the midday repast.

She was truly beginning to chafe under this sentence of punishment Cuibhil Rustim had decreed. Yet in her darkest moments of brooding, she realized it was his way to bend her will to his, and that knowledge reaffirmed her determination to come through the ordeal unbowed. Though she was eating with a hearty appetite, the third day of her punishment had a decided effect on her spirit. The brief time spent in the luxury of the baths was almost taunting, serving to emphasize the many idle hours that filled her day.

Late in the afternoon of that third day, Ben-Mustapha appeared with an excited Lilah in tow. Servants carried her new wardrobe in, filling the room with neatly folded piles of colorful gowns and robes. Thrilled by the company and attention, Alysaun's mood lifted. Apparently her punishment was at an end.

All Ben-Mustapha would admit was that she was expected to serve her master at a banquet to be held that night. Lord Cuibhil's friends would be there and she must look exquisite. Alysaun was completely docile, contentedly allowing herself to be pulled through a complex ritual of preparation that included a two-hour soak in the steamy, fragrant waters of the bath chamber and an hour's massage with a variety of rich, soothing unguents and creams.

Wrapped in a loose silk robe, her freshly washed hair bound in a soft towel, she returned to her room to sit patiently while Lilah's skilled hands applied perfume and various lotions and powders from her tray of pots and jars.

Alysaun had given little thought to the banquet. Indeed, as she relaxed in the chair with eyes closed, she could think of nothing but the luxury of being pampered. The chatter of the slave girls as they came and went was music, though she understood none of the foreign phrases.

Only when Lilah was finished and the room had quieted did she think of the summons to appear at Cuibhil's side. He obviously thought she had been punished enough; he wanted to show off his new acquisition. It never entered her mind that the night was to be the final part of his plan to see her humbled.

Lilah now held up a large, oval mirror. The face reflected was Alysaun's, and yet, with the artful highlights enhancing the high curve of her cheekbones and the rose cream applied at temple, cheeks, and throat, she looked . . . exotic and very foreign. Her eyebrows had been plucked and their full, graceful arch was enhanced by a creamy, honey-blond stick. A powder the same shade, brushed upon her long eyelashes and applied a second time, made both upper and lower lashes a thick fan that framed her eyes. A light line of kohl added depth close to the lash line, and a dot of blue cream just at the corners of her eyes made the color of her irises more brilliant.

She was not quite comfortable with the transformation, finding it too bold for her tastes. Expecting to be dressed next, Alysaun was startled to see Lilah bring forth a long, wicked sharp razor. She tensed, ready to shriek for Ben-Mustapha if the woman attempted to use it on her hair. As if her apprehension had silently appealed to him, he appeared at the door.

"Ben-Mustapha, what does she intend to do with that blade?" Alysaun asked, and, as the eunuch questioned the woman, watched him for some sign of support.

"She knows what is best for you. The master expects your beauty to shine tonight. Make no move while she trims your waves. Their weight and length drag upon the natural curl. Be still or your movement will make her hand slip."

There was little she could do to protest. Her hair had not been trimmed since she was a child; its length hung sleekly down her back to reach her hips. She closed her eyes, wincing as Lilah applied the sharp blade to her still-damp tresses. Only when a pleased grunt escaped the woman's lips did she open her eyes again and the hand she raised to touch her hair trembled. Almost before she called for the mirror, Lilah produced it, proudly surveying her handiwork and calling for Ben-Mustapha's opinion..

Lilah had lightened the weight of the thick, luxurious mass by cutting layers that began some six inches below the crown and continued through a total length that now reached only below her breasts. Alysaun wasn't sure whether to be horrified or enchanted by the effect. Nearly dry now, her hair was a light halo of golden curls, very full and soft. She touched the tendrils, turned her head, then shook it as she decided she liked the light, airy feel.

There were still more preparations to come. Lilah took away her robe and made her stand still as a frosted gold cream was applied to the edges of her shoulders, to the rounded curves of her breasts. She scarcely needed the artificial highlight. The fact that she was totally naked in a room with three women and Ben-Mustapha had suffused her skin with an embarrassed blush.

The first layer of clothing was an undergarment of creamy white silk, a tissue-thin sheath that ended in a wide hem of gold embroidery just above her ankles. It was not until she had struggled into the close-fitting garment that Alysaun realized how little it concealed. Thin ribbons of a pale gold shade trimmed the deep, V-shaped bodice, and the same ribbons closed the gown with five ties, the last just below her breasts.

Once the sheath was adjusted, its sheer material clung to every line of her figure, more like a second skin than an article of clothing. Alysaun did not need to see her reflection in a mirror to realize the effect, and she began to grow angrier by the minute. The edges of her breasts were barely covered by the costume, her nipples clearly defined and more accented than if she wore nothing.

There was an icy frost to her eyes as she turned to stare at Ben-Mustapha. "*He* chose this . . . this bit of nothing, didn't he?" The eunuch hesitated, then, with a shrug of his immense shoulders, nodded. "I will not attend. If he thinks I will allow him to humiliate me—"

"You have no choice, Alysaun. Lord Cuibhil wishes you to be there . . . and you will be."

"*No!*" Even as she refused, Alusaun knew her protests were useless. Still, the idea of being paraded nearly naked before his guests was too much of a blow to her dignity. Tears stung her eyes and only through a great effort did she quell a desire to cry. Tears and weeping were a useless weapon. That was what he wanted from her, and she would not give it. "I'll embarrass him before his friends," she threatened. "Go and tell your master that I will never acknowledge his authority over me. *He* will look the fool this night when his latest acquisition pretends he does not exist."

Ben-Mustapha bowed his head and, without another word, left her with the women. Because she had no way of making Lilah understand her, Alysaun allowed the woman to continue her work. Sandals with golden laces were slipped on her feet; a lovely necklace of fine gold links studded with sapphires was fastened about her throat; heavy, banded bracelets were fixed about her wrists. Finally a voluminous caftan of sheer black silk was hung about her shoulders, the full circle of its hem weighted by gold thread embroidery to a depth of six inches.

Lilah stood back to admire her efforts, brows furrowed as she searched for any small detail that might ruin the total effect. The two servants assisting her stood to one side, looking awed and somewhat excited. One of them exclaimed and whispered to Lilah, reminding her of a forgotten item. She frowned, apparently at her own lack of thought, and turned to the bed to search among the garments strewn across it.

Alysaun had tried to maintain an air of indifference, but even she gasped at the sight of the intricately worked circlet in Lilah's hands. A narrow band of beaten gold secured a delicate circle of carved flowers and leaves so finely wrought they appeared real.

Lilah carefully combed the bright curls forward, smoothing Alysaun's crown before she placed the circlet upon her head. She stood back, a pleased smile announcing her satisfaction. The girls chattered, complimenting Lilah on her artistry, until even Alysaun was curious.

She reached for the mirror and held it before her. The woman who stared back from the mirror's polished surface was not herself. She smiled and the reflection imitated the curve of her lips, but the alluring, sensual female was surely only an illusion painted on the polished silver.

There was a sound at the door. Ben-Mustapha stood there, and at his signal, the women retreated from the room. Alysaun lifted her head, tossing the mirror on the bed as she came forward to address him. "Well? Did you tell him I refused? I hope he was able to accept his disappointment."

"He had no reason to be disappointed." At the answer from his master, Ben-Mustapha bowed and backed away. Cuibhil Rustim stood there, a tunic of fine russet silk covering his broad, straight shoulders. He had prepared himself for this moment, but Alysaun looked so incredibly lovely he could not help but stare. For a

402

moment he considered calling off his plans to test her in this public display of submission. It had taken much willpower to deny himself the pleasure of bedding her these past three days; now he wanted his reward in an acknowledgment that she belonged to him.

"My guests will be enchanted," he said, reaching out to capture her fingers and lift them to his lips. "Surely none of them can claim to own a more beautiful slave."

Alysaun struggled to retrieve her hand but Cuibhil's grasp was too firm. "You do not *own* me, m'lord," she insisted. "My body may be captive. I have no one to deny you what pleasures you would take or to keep you from displaying my form as if I were your whore. But my heart you cannot take from me—'tis given to another—and what you desire, to hear me acclaim you my master, that I will not give."

Cuibhil Rustim smiled, his expression reserved but courteous. "You may yet before the evening ends, my sweet. We will discuss your obstinacy after the banquet. Now my guests are due . . . let us not keep them waiting."

18

Alysaun maintained the submissive posture that had seen her through the humiliating ordeal of the banquet, her head bowed, hands clasped upon her lap. Cuibhil Rustim stood a short distance away, bidding his last remaining guest good night. Inwardly she seethed with fury and a desire for revenge. She had played the role of the respectful slave and her "master" seemed pleased by her efforts, but Alysaun had plans for the rest of the evening that would take the fine edge from his supposed triumph.

Of all the boisterous males who had passed the hours drinking and leering at the serving girls, calling out lusty encouragement to the plump, partially clad dancing girl, this man in particular had disgusted Alysaun.

Though he was attired in the finest of silken robes, his appearance was slovenly. A scraggly black beard, shot through with a yellowed gray, gave him the look of a randy old goat. The deep-set eyes that had never left her face, even when the dancer had whirled suggestively before him, added to her impression that he was a lecherous satyr.

Now a belch of ugly laughter bubbled from his fleshy throat. Despite a shiver of revulsion, Alysaun risked a glance toward the two men to find his hot, lusting gaze fixed upon her. Cuibhil's expression was polite but tinged with impatience. Obviously he wished the man gone, but his duties as host required a measure of courtesy.

Finally Alysaun heard a rustle of clothing and the tread of receding footsteps. A relieved sigh whispered from her. The tension that had gripped her all evening had left her exhausted, but the goblet of spiced wine she had shared with Cuibhil had helped to ease the stiff, taut muscles, and only a small ache remained in her lower back.

But for a cool breeze that stirred the trees to a soft sighing, the courtyard was silent. Sure that she was alone, Alysaun stretched and rubbed at her back, then looked up and froze. Cuibhil lounged against one of the marble pillars, arms tucked across his broad chest as he studied her.

The expression in her eyes was a blend of startled wariness and muted irritation. She had done as he commanded and endured the lascivious appraisal of his guests, played the meek and obedient slave to soothe his masculine pride. What else could he have planned?

"You have a legion of admirers," Cuibhil said. "Just now I was offered a most impressive sum from Ali Barak'ji. He will scarce sleep this night for the desire you stirred within him." His mouth curled up at the corners, his amusement evident.

"And what was your reply, m'lord?" The thought of being sold to the potbellied old lecher alarmed Alysaun, but she was sure Cuibhil would not give her up . . . not at any price.

"I told him you were not for sale. A gift from his highness, Malik Shah, cannot be treated lightly." His smile widened to a grin that showed a flash of even white teeth beneath his curved mustache. Cuibhil straightened to unfold his long arms and stretch them high with the grace of a large cat, then strolled forward in an easy stride that brought him before her kneeling figure.

406

In a fluid movement, he hunkered down on his heels, staring deep into her eyes until it was Alysaun who dropped her gaze. "I found reason to admire your attitude tonight, rebel. I half expected your temper to overcome your sense. If you had not..."

Alysaun's face flushed an angry rose, her chin lifting high at the unfinished threat. "If I had not, m'lord? What would you have done? You do not beat your slaves...this I know to be true." She smiled, confident that there would have been no way for him to chastise her without embarrassing himself before the assembled guests.

"Look there, Alysaun...to your left, behind you." Cuibhil motioned with a tilt of his head and Alysaun slowly turned. On one of the slim columns that lined the courtyard a narrow chain had been secured at a height of some six feet. She stared, puzzled, until she felt Cuibhil's warm fingers slide between her throat and the necklace of gold and jewels that formed a loose collar about her neck.

With the comprehension of the threat came a cold, icy fear coupled with an unreasoning rage. Her fingers closed over his, the sharpness of her nails digging into his skin. "You've never beaten a slave, certainly not at a gathering of your friends. I don't believe—"

"But you are not sure, eh, little one?" He scarcely felt the cut of her nails, which were pressing hard enough to break his skin and draw blood. Cuibhil closed his fingers on the necklace and pulled, ignoring the slim hand that resisted by pushing at his shoulder.

His free hand swept beneath her arm, supporting her as he rose to stand, bringing her to her feet with him. Alysaun struggled indignantly, now pulling at the firm grasp of his fingers with both hands. "I *am* sure," she insisted. "Such mistreatment would mock the Sultan's generosity." She paused, a little frightened of the hard, unyielding look in Cuibhil's eyes. Her mouth went dry, her breathing becoming ragged. *Was* she so sure he would not follow through with his threat?

Cuibhil sighed, as if her confidence had pushed him a touch too far. He tugged on the necklace, his fingers cushioning the bite of the gold links as it grew taut around her slender, white throat. "You still have much to learn, Alysaun," he said regretfully. She had no

407

choice but to follow as he led her the few steps toward the column. Once there, he pressed her back against its hard, fluted surface.

Releasing his hold on the necklace, Cuibhil used his body to pin her against the column. Alysaun sputtered, more infuriated than frightened. Her fingers curled like the claws of an angry lioness, and she raised them to scratch the half-shadowed arrogance from his face.

Cuibhil laughed, enjoying the struggle that had transformed Alysaun into a spitting, cursing wildcat. Somewhere beneath his amusement, there was a stir of desire for the soft, veiled flesh pinioned beneath him. Catching her wrists with one hand was child's play. He drew them up, stretching her arms high as his head bent to seek her mouth. The force of the kiss cut off a string of hissed epithets.

Alysaun tensed in impotent fury, unable to free herself of his hold or the plundering rape of her bruised mouth. She tried to raise her knee but Cuibhil anticipated the move and shifted, pressing his hip against her belly. An infuriated, muffled whimper broke from her throat and suddenly her mouth was free.

She took several deep breaths, her eyes misted over with a film of hot, angry tears. Before she could raise her head to scream at him, she heard a metallic click and found her wrists firmly manacled to the chain. She tugged once and the action made the bracelets bite into her wrists, then she glared at her captor and tried a savage kick aimed at his shins.

Cuibhil easily evaded the kick and stepped back a few feet to survey her helplessness. His expression was serious, almost contemplative. With a nod of satisfaction, he moved to her right, and, catching the length of chain hanging from the one encircling the column, he attached it to a clasp on her necklace.

Alysaun was now beyond fury. A cold fire of spite burned within her. She refused to struggle any longer. If he found pleasure in seeing her trussed in this degrading position, she would not add to his delight. "You have forgotten your whip, Lord Cuibhil." She had meant to sound haughty but a betraying splash of tears coursed down her cheeks, adding to her displayed vulnerability. "If . . . if you must prove your manhood by striking a bound woman, God help you."

"This has naught to do with my manhood, sweet," he replied calmly. "You seem to enjoy a confidence in your immunity from the whip . . . justly so, for I would never apply a lash to skin so fair and silken. You did ask, though, what measure I would have employed to suppress a rebellion, and I am only answering your query." Cuibhil walked around her in a semicircle, studying how well she was secured. "I told you there were other ways to make defiance a misery."

Though Alysaun stubbornly willed them to stop, her tears continued to flow. She managed to shrug, a graceful gesture of disdain despite her ignoble position. "So . . . you thought an hour of such a display before the dogs you call friends the means to see me humbled? Not *I*, sir," Alysaun insisted, and even managed a mocking smile through her tears. "I would have simply closed my eyes, *thus*"—she shut her eyes tightly before continuing—"and seen not a glimpse of their leering gazes."

Cuibhil shook his head, his lips quirked in admiration. She looked the brave martyr, Alysaun did, and 'twas almost a shame to take the dignity of defiance from her. "You are but half tamed, woman. This was only a portion of the trial I would have put upon you."

That brought her eyes open; they were wide and curious, two orbs of azure framed by thick, tear-spiked lashes. "I am not half tamed at all, m'lord. This punishment of yours is but a brief discomfort."

Cuibhil stepped forward to stand before Alysaun. Even with her body stretched taut, he towered over her. His fingers were surprisingly gentle as they brushed away her tears. "I would that you had learned from it," he said softly, "but your continued disrespect leaves me no choice."

Alysaun watched him cautiously, determined to resist whatever means of domination he meant to impose. There was no anger in his expression. Indeed, his gaze was warm and his suntanned complexion darkened by a hint of passion. He moved closer, leaning a hand on each of her shoulders, eyes fixed upon her lips as he lowered his

409

mouth to hers. Alysaun turned her head aside in rejection, but Cuibhil seemed unperturbed.

His breath was warm on her throat, his lips tender as they nibbled at the soft, perfumed flesh beneath her ear. Alysaun stirred, still anticipating some punishment other than this gentle assault upon her senses. As his kisses trailed lower, she strained away as far as her bonds would allow, only to find his arm tightly banding her waist, his body pressing her against the marble.

She had expected him to take her to his bedchamber tonight. A part of her had even anticipated a surrender to this stranger, who was in reality her husband. Now, as his fingers stroked her body in bold, possessive caresses, calling up memories of those long nights of frustrated desires, her mind rebelled against the slow, deliberate seduction.

"This was your chastisement, then . . . to make a spectacle of fondling me before your guests?" Alysaun marveled at the refinement of the method. It would have worked, too. Even now, without anyone present to watch, she felt vulnerable and exposed, a victim of her own rising passion.

Cuibhil's voice betrayed his own arousal. His answer, when at last he raised his head from the soft, sweet curves of her breasts, came in a low, hoarse timbre. "As I said, Alysaun, there are many ways to elicit cooperation. I would rather you bend to my—"

"*No.*" The word slipped out before Alysaun thought, and she caught her bottom lip between her teeth at the fierce anger that flared in his eyes. He moved back, then tugged at the sheer material of the black caftan. Alysaun stiffened at the tearing sound, then looked away as he pushed the remnants of the lovely robe out of his way.

For minutes there was silence between them. Suddenly something as cold as ice touched her skin. Alysaun looked down and gasped. The sharp, polished blade of an ornate dagger was pressing flat against the curve of her breast. She tried to still any movement and as she held her breath for long, torturous moments, the blade coldly kissed her trembling flesh.

Cuibhil stared at Alysaun's face. She was deathly pale, her eyes fixed on the dagger and wide with fright. He hadn't meant to terrify her so; his grip was such that the blade would not scratch her tender skin. Suddenly he was tired of this prolonged battle. It would end in only one way—she was his whether he could make her admit it aloud or not. "I would not take you in front of other eyes . . . not you, Alysaun," he whispered as the knife moved, its edge easily slicing the first of the ribbons laced across her bodice. "Nay, I meant only to show them a hint of what I owned." She gasped as the remaining laces were cut. The thin silk, stretched taut by the ribbons and now loosed, edged farther apart with every shallow breath, exposing the tempting fullness of her breasts.

"You would not . . ." Even as she tried to say the incredible, Alysaun knew she had misjudged him. She closed her eyes, envisioning herself stripped naked and helpless before that rutting crowd of males. The flat of the blade touched her belly and she let out an involuntary whimper before the edge turned away from her skin and sliced down the length of the sheath to its hem.

Cuibhil stood up, staring at the beauty of her unveiled figure for minutes before he looked up and met her own stare. The dagger dropped from his hand, its steel blade ringing as it clanked against the tiles, a sound neither heard.

"You would have, wouldn't you?" Alysaun was both awed and angered by the lengths to which he would have gone to see her subdued. If he had no feelings for her, why was it so important to him that she admit his domination? "I . . . I believe you now. What is it that you want from me? Shall I call you master and tremble at the sound of your voice? And when you take your pleasure from this body you claim to own, shall I cry praises for your prowess?"

He was ashamed of himself now. Alysaun was physically his captive, but her words cut as deeply as if it were she who wielded the blade. Cuibhil reached out, unable to contain a desire to brush away the clinging silk and bare the firm perfection of a full and rounded breast.

"I want you, Alysaun. That I will soon have you we both accept, but I would that your pride and mine might find some truce in the

411

pursuit of pleasure." The night air was growing colder, and the slightest breeze stirred the ragged edges of the sheath. Cuibhil stared as the smooth circles of tawny flesh surrounding her nipples contracted and blushed a deeper rose with the caress of the breeze. Swallowing hard, he strove to control his passion, to rein in the lustful urge to take her here. He tore his gaze away from the curves and hollows of her figure to look into her eyes. "You will need to utter no false claims of ecstasy to flatter my vanity," he insisted.

For that moment it seemed almost as if their positions were reversed. His eyes, hooded with desire, were the same that had often looked at Alysaun with love. Except that he answered to another name, and but for a domineering streak that absolute power had brought to the surface, he was Brand. Any rapturous cries that might escape her in his embrace would be well won, but she would not tell him that. "I am in no position to refuse you anything, sire," she answered, and a movement of her chained wrists spoke an eloquent, clinking reminder of his hold over her.

Cuibhil flushed at the sound, embarrassed now that he had used restraints as a show of strength. "I would not have so exposed you," he said, hoping she would believe him. His fingers fumbled at the clasp of the necklace, then reached higher to free the bracelets. "Rare beauty should be treasured in privacy."

The moment she was free was an awkward one. The ruined gown hung open, seeming to reveal more than if she were naked. Cuibhil stepped back, then alertly moved to catch Alysaun as her knees buckled.

Safe in his arms and afforded some modesty by the position, she pretended to swoon, burying her head against his tunic. He was hesitant, full of remorse, and not at all sure where to carry her. Alysaun solved the dilemma by her shivering. "I am quite chilled, m'lord," she said softly. "Might I perhaps seek the warmth of a bath before you . . . before we . . ."

"Of course. Yes, of course," Cuibhil muttered, eager to make amends for his harsh treatment, "the bath." He paused, then gathered his wits and headed in the direction of the large, heated ath situated near his own apartments. He had imbibed a good deal of wine during the evening, but the actuality of subjecting Alysaun to near-naked bondage had sobered him, leaving him too aware of the limits to which he had allowed her to push him. He would have a cup or two to ease his conscience and pass the time.

Alysaun had other ideas, though. By the time Cuibhil had set her carefully on her feet in the warm, steamy room, he had been persuaded to remain because she was feeling "light-headed." Believing himself to be the source of her distress, Cuibhil was relieved to find himself cast in the role of her protector and acceded to her wish.

She took advantage of the few minutes spent in a hushed conversation with Ben-Mustapha to slip out of her ruined gown and descend the wide, oval steps of the bath. The former owners of the villa must have enjoyed exercising in the bath, for the pool was long enough and deep enough to swim in. Off the steps, the water reached to the top of her breasts. Alysaun moved her hand, delighting in the warm swirls that swept her skin as gently as a lover's caress.

When Cuibhil dismissed the overseer, he turned back to tell Alysaun that he had ordered wine and a light meal of bread and fruits. Catching sight of her discarded gown, he crossed to the spot where it lay and bent to retrieve it. The ripped material reminded him of the beauty the knife's cut had revealed and he glanced up, searching the shifting mists that curled across the pool.

Two marble couches, skillfully carved at the head in the shape of a huge seashell, with comfortably padded benches extending some six feet, sat parallel to the pool. Cuibhil settled on one, watching the water and trying to discern the girl through the drifts of steam. Hearing a splash, followed by a soft, relaxed sigh, he lay back and waited for the slave to bring the wine.

"Alysaun?" His voice echoed slightly against the marble walls. For a few seconds Cuibhil was tense until at last her answer came in a soft call from across the pool. Leaning back, one arm resting over his eyes, he smiled contentedly. "What are you thinking?"

"How very delightful the water feels, m'lord," Alysaun replied, and then fell silent again, wondering what had prompted his curiosity to know the thoughts of a slave. The steam had tightened her natural curl and she gave up an effort to keep the light, feathery waves around her crown dry. Slipping beneath the water, she swam across the pool toward the steps, rising for air only when her fingers touched the side.

Cuibhil rolled onto his side at the sound of a splash close to the couch. Alysaun emerged, shaking off the water that weighted her mane of golden curls, smiling at Cuibhil until she realized the direction of his stare and demurely slipped lower. Finally she leaned forward, placing both arms on the edge of the pool and tilting her head to gaze up at him.

"Who taught you to swim so well?" he asked. "You move through the water like a nymph, as though born to the element."

"My husband, sire," said Alysaun, shaking her hair to dry it. The action sent a light spray of droplets flying from her damp curls and some of them landed on his leather boots. "At least remove your footwear for comfort's sake, sire. You needn't be so formal on my account. This *is* your bath."

"I am *well aware* whose bath it is," Cuibhil snapped, puzzled why his answer seemed defensive. "Where is he, anyway?"

"Where is who, m'lord?" Alysaun replied in wide-eyed innocence, knowing full well he had finally broached the subject of her husband.

"This husband of yours." To cover his interest, Cuibhil sat at the pool's edge and began to work his boots off. "He is careless of his possessions, else you would not now be my property."

Alysaun took a deep draft of wine to conceal her amusement. She could hardly be offended by the statement when it was her own husband insulting himself. "When he was still with me, never was a man so full of care." The thick fan of golden lashes hid her gaze as Alysaun lowered her head to rest it upon her arm. "He . . . he fought with Emperor Romanus at Manzikert."

Cuibhil hoped his relief was not evident. With a tug his second

414

oot came free and he tossed it carelessly aside. "You are widowed, ıen . . . a sad fate for one so young."

"Nay, I cannot truly claim I am, m'lord," Alysaun replied with a olorous sigh. "Brand never came home, but his . . . his body was ot recovered from the field."

"By the mercy of Alp Arslan, all Byzantine captives were eleased. If he lived, I vow no one could keep him from returning to o lovely a wife. I was there . . . at the same battle," he said, and, hen she glanced up with a curious look, explained, "One of your killed Byzantine bowmen downed my mount and sent me tumbling eneath the clash of hooves. I remember nothing of the weeks that ollowed . . . even the description of my fall was told me. 'Twas a ng while after the battle was won before I came to my senses."

"*Lost*, you mean." Cuibhil's eyebrows drew together in puzzle-ıent at the word, and he sensed the bitterness within Alysaun. "The attle was lost because Romanus was betrayed. Ambition and not a ıck of tactics or valor saw his forces meet with disaster."

He understood her viewpoint and did not care to challenge it. "A voman left alone by fate's decree has reason to feel cheated." He eaned toward the table to pluck a few amber grapes from the platter nd offer them to her. "Two years have passed. Now, a peace ffering—from one who is not your enemy, m'lady."

Alysaun studied his features for a moment before accepting the rapes. The talk of Brand had not stirred the flicker of memory she ad hoped to see. If her face and name, *his* name, made no npression, then perhaps she was widowed. If his memory was gone ompletely, Brand no longer existed. "May I ask you something, ord Cuibhil?"

"You may, my beauty," he said in response to the formal address. It is my fondest desire to gratify any wish of yours."

"How is it, sire, that your coloring is akin to that of one born on ıe European continent, that your command of both English and rench is so fluent, yet you bear a Turkish name and owe fealty to a eathen sultan?"

The inquiry was audacious, but Cuibhil had promised her an

answer. He didn't care to dwell on his life before he had become
Cuibhil Rustim, if only because it physically pained him to try t
recall details. "The old sultan, Alp Arslan, named me. He wa
called the Mountain Lion and, I think, found it amusing to play upo
the title by dubbing me the Red Cub. I cannot say where I was bor
or lived, only that my life dates from the Sultan's generous treatmen
of a homeless foreigner."

"But surely you must wonder if you haven't family grieving ove
your disappearance. If so, I feel for them, for we are kindred i
knowing less than the true fate of our loved ones."

Cuibhil pressed his fingers to his temples, trying to still thei
sudden throbbing. The subject was not one he cared to discuss. "N
more, if you've any mercy, Alysaun. To tax my mind with vagu
rememberings was furthest from my intentions this evening."

Much as she would have cared to wring some spark of recognitio
from Cuibhil, Alysaun saw only Brand's suffering at her pursui
"Perhaps, m'lord, if you would be so gallant?" She held out he
hand and smiled. "I'll come forth and join you in a toast to th
present."

The image of Alysaun emerging from the waters like a Venus,
clothed in nothing but a veil of crystal droplets, turned Cuibhil fron
his brooding. He returned her smile, offering her both hands i
assistance. Too late, when he felt her arms tense and caught the flasl
of a wicked grin, did he realize the trap she had laid. Beneath th
water, Alysaun had braced her feet firmly against the side of th
pool, giving her enough leverage to pull and send him flying past he
into the water.

Cuibhil landed close to the middle of the pool and came u
sputtering, at first furious over her guile. Shaking his hair free of th
water that plastered it to his head, and rubbing his eyes, he swore
string of oaths that elicited only a peal of silvery laughter fron
Alysaun, who had taken refuge in the clouds of steam. He turned i
the direction of the sounds, then heard a splash from a different area
"You'll rue the second I find you, minx," he threatened, though he
was beginning to see that she was merely playing a game.

"You must *catch* me first, m'lord," Alysaun replied with another nkle of amusement. "And *I've* the advantage." Cuibhil hadn't loved, and with the weight of his sodden clothing impeding his rogress, he would tire before he managed to catch her. Still, she did ot want him *too* worn. He hadn't answered her challenge, and Alysaun listened warily for any sound of movement. "I shall keep ou at bay, Lord Cuibhil. I can, you know."

Cuibhil smiled. Two could play at this game. Already Alysaun ounded less confident of her claims. Slowly, and as quietly as he ould, he tugged the weighted breeches off, letting them float to the urface and away. Then, his task made easier by submerging, he ulled the silk tunic over his head and stripped himself of the ncumbrance. Now *he* had the advantage. As skilled a swimmer as he was, his greater strength would allow him easily to outdistance er.

"Alysaun?" There was no answer. "I offer you the chance to urrender, *now*. Show yourself or suffer from your obstinacy."

From the direction of his voice, Alysaun knew he still hadn't moved. She tried to peer through the heavy mist, but it was his ally ow as well as hers. "Your bluff will not work, sire," she replied. "You must work for—" Suddenly she realized she was giving her osition away and fell silent. Dipping under the surface, she swam long the length of the pool opposite the steps and came up some ten eet away.

Alysaun clung to the edge, listening. A few moments later the ound of a splash at the end of the pool startled her, but brought a mile to her lips. Just in time had she escaped discovery and capture. A chance to surrender . . . *indeed*. It would be *he* who finally gave up he chase.

Using the cover provided by his tossed shirt, Cuibhil dived earching the water with open eyes. It was clouded by the oil used to cent it, but he managed to discern a vague silhouette some nine feet way that assumed the most enchanting form as he swam forward.

Alysaun was preparing to issue another teasing challenge when a air of strong hands seized her legs and pulled. Her mouth opened in a startled shriek as she was dragged beneath the surface, arms flailing as she struggled to free herself. With consummate ease Cuibhil caught her by the waist, turning her around and pinning her against his chest and belly before a powerful kick of his legs brought them both to the surface.

Choking and coughing from the water she had swallowed, Alysaun was as much infuriated by the sly ruse that resulted in her capture as by the embarrassing position in which she was held. Cuibhil swam the few strokes to the poolside and pinned her against it, waiting patiently until she had ceased sputtering before he said anything.

Alysaun was stiff with anger, more put out by the ease of her capture than by the dousing. Cuibhil took a second to catch his own breath, delighting in the firm, rounded globes of flesh cushioned against his groin. He leaned close to whisper against her ear, seeking an acknowledgment of his victory; but in answer, Alysaun only tilted her head high and ignored him. She wasn't to be allowed that hauteur long. A few seconds later, one of his hands grasped a breast, the other sliding down her belly to insinuate itself between her thighs.

Uttering an indignant, feline growl from between clenched teeth, Alysaun struggled to free herself of the leisurely, exploring hands. "Let go, loose me at *once*," she hissed. It was ridiculous to claim he had no right to hold her so or to deny he had won the game she had initiated, but her pride would not allow an admission of defeat. She wriggled and pulled at his hold, to no avail. Only when she heard a low chuckle and felt the results of her thrashing nestle firmly against the curves of her derriere did she cease any movement he might take as additional encouragement.

"I admit your victory," she whispered in so soft a tone that Cuibhil made her repeat the words aloud. "I *said*, sire, that I admit you have won. I . . . I surrender. Now, can you not be generous in your triumph? Or is this . . . fondling to be my punishment?" She turned her head, eyes misted with an appeal.

Cuibhil grinned, then his expression turned more serious as he pressed a kiss upon the tender flesh behind her earlobe. "'Tis no

unishment, sweet," he insisted. "I only seek to exercise the
victor's rights to a reward. 'Tis possible for us both to share in the
winning. Turn to me, Alysaun. Offer willingly what I desire."

A momentary resistance showed itself in a stubborn pout, but
then he freed her, Alysaun turned to face him. She refused to raise
her head, though she offered no resistance when his fingers gently
raised her chin.

"You want me, though your body is not formed to show desire as
easily as mine," Cuibhil claimed. "There is no defeat in admitting
that you feel."

Alysaun gave up her pouting with a sigh, then slid her fingers
through the crisp mat of curls covering his chest. "Nay, m'lord."
She put her arms around his neck and stretched on her toes to press
her body against his. "In place of words, I shall show you my
feelings."

Modesty was a vain conceit of new brides and virgins. It was not
Cuibhil Rustim who held her close in a lover's embrace; it was
Brand. As if all the lonely nights had gathered substance to form this
dream, she was his again and nothing else mattered. A pair of
half-closed eyes, thickly fringed in gold, spoke more of her desire
than any phrases could transmit, and her parted lips curved in the
barest hint of a siren's smile.

The water lapping at their bodies was warm and soothing, but as
Cuibhil slid his arms around her, pressing the length of his swollen
organ against her belly, Alysaun could not help the shiver that
coursed over her skin. Her eyes closed and she abandoned herself to
the delight of anticipating what would come.

The softly parted offering of her lips seemed to plead for tenderness,
and Cuibhil restrained the wild tug of passion inspired by the feel of
her silken curves naked against his own flesh. But, too long had he
denied the fires kindled at their first meeting. His fingers slid
upward along the column of her slender back to tangle in the thick
mane of golden curls. The pliant softness of her body spoke
surrender, but such was the overwhelming sense of power he

experienced that he grasped a handful of burnished waves an
arched her head back.

Alysaun winced at the sharp tug, her eyes flying open to find hi
gazing at her with something akin to reverence. Her eyes close
again and a moment later the caress of his fingertips at her nap
begged her forgiveness. In the depths of her own yearning, Alysau
knew the reason for the unexpected roughness and forgave him. Th
kiss that followed was tender and stirring, a quiet moment before th
storm that would follow.

Shaken by the wash of desire that radiated through her limb
Alysaun clung to him. Cuibhil lifted her body with one arm an
placed the other beneath her knees, carrying her across the pool i
powerful strides that easily overcame the water's drag. He could n
take his gaze from the curves and hollows of the beauty cradle
against his chest, and by instinct and memory, he found the couc
and gently settled her on its pillows.

He stood there, drinking in the splendor of her naked form, th
beaded film of moisture clinging to flesh that blushed a ros
reflection of the heat that burned within. Her hair was a mass of go
ringlets, a halo that enhanced the unmasked sensuality of feature
too delicate to belong to a flesh-and-blood woman.

Cuibhil stroked the curve of her thigh and Alysaun instinctivel
tensed before the teasing brush of his fingertips relaxed her. Sh
moved restlessly, eager to have him close again, the muscles of he
thighs trembling as Cuibhil gently prodded them apart and kne
before the exposed crescent of pink flesh wreathed over in fine
tawny curls.

With a heavy-lidded gaze, she watched him crouch over her,
male animal whose corded muscles rippled with every move. He
skin tingled as his hand followed the contours of her figure, tracin
the flare of hips to the curve of a slender, narrow waist. To Alysau
the slow, teasing exploration was a kind of torture; she knew h
body well and longed to move on to the rapture that came of hi
possession.

Because he had no memory of having known her, Cuibhil wa

roughly entranced by Alysaun. She was a fresh, new territory to nquer, and he meant to leave his imprint in a slow, deliberate duction. His fingers brushed the taut peaks of her nipples, eliciting igh. She moaned when his lips parted and his tongue swept circles und the sensitive peaks, whimpered when he drew the deep-pink d within his mouth and rolled the firm mound in massaging cles.

Unaware of anything save the pleasure of his mouth, Alysaun isted with a building fever. Her knees drew up, and the soft flesh tween her thighs pulsed and flowered in a crimson blush.

"My lord, I . . . ahh . . . oh, *God*," she gasped as his fingers found d gently probed her aching flesh. Cuibhil moved forward, lightly ting his body on hers, seeking and capturing her lips in a crushing s. His tongue stabbed within, matching the invading stroke of his gers. Alysaun's hips rose instinctively, meeting each thrust, the der skin of her breasts roughly teased by the wiry curls covering hard, muscled chest.

The hard, pulsing length of his erection lay against her flat belly, pped between their damp bodies. Alysaun drew her fingernails htly along his back and traced the familiar leanness of his narrow s, the taut muscles of his buttocks, then boldly caressed his spare, scled belly.

The touch of her fingers, tentative at first but more confident as y touched and curled around his rampant organ, dragged a hoarse an from Cuibhil. All innocent and fair as an angel, the woman neath him stirred the rise of lust as no other ever had. His breath me harsh and ragged as Alysaun's slender fingers moved along the sitive shaft, drawing his pleasure to an unbearable peak.

He parted from the bruised softness of her mouth to balance on an n and stare down at the shadowed space between them. The sight her fingers wrapped around the width of his engorged member ightened the intense feelings of power surging through his loins.

He drew his hand away from the silky curls at her thighs, covering hand that held him and stilling the liquid stroking that had nearly en him over the edge. Denied a pleasure she clearly enjoyed,

Alysaun seemed to pout. Cuibhil grinned, settling back on his knee He brought his hands up against the back of her thighs and push them high and apart.

Alysaun caught her bottom lip between her teeth, twisting h head to the side, aching with anticipation as the air teased h exposed flesh. She was wildly eager to feel him within her. Nev before had her sensitive, yearning flesh seemed to await his ent with such longing.

At the first contact, Alysaun cried out, something throaty a unintelligible, a whispered encouragement, a plea. For what seem like an eternity, Cuibhil penetrated no farther than to part the burni valley of flesh with the thick head of his organ. Alysaun tried move her hips and draw him deeper within but Cuibhil's han firmly controlled her body.

Angry and frustrated, dry-mouthed and close to tears, Alysa had the look of a leashed lioness, her fury barely checked.

Cuibhil continued the teasing intrusions but he was rapid approaching the point when his love play might lose both of the the pleasure they craved. With a slight shift of position he plung forward, sinking into the sheath of liquid fire that grasped and he the pulsing shaft with far more strength than had Alysaun's finger

Alys screamed, a ragged sound that tore from her throat as h yearning flesh received the thick, hard organ that would ease t building torment of passion. Cuibhil paused, afraid he had hurt he but the welcoming ripple of tiny muscles that tensed and untens against his member and the hips that twisted to encourage t movement assured him she knew no pain. He drew back slowly, th slammed forward, repeating the movement again and again . . . a again.

Tears flowed unheeded from her eyes. Alysaun stole sobbi breaths between the surges of passion that left her helpless, ca afloat in the wake of a warmth that melted liquidly throughout h being. The hard, driving assault was a blessed relief from the tensi of long-checked desires.

Cuibhil slid forward, his body stretched taut between her thigh

hips moved of their own accord, a separate part of his body,
ich was haunted by the need to possess every inch of this
man-angel, this creature who moved in ecstasy and drew from
a more than he had known he possessed.

Suddenly a rush of feeling made him oblivious of everything save
desire to release the power that burned in his loins. The melted
e of passion flowed from him, erupting from his organ in spasms
intense that he felt immortal, a man made a god by the passion of
oddess. For longer than he knew, his hips plunged rapidly against
softness, delving deeply to bring soft, mindless whimpers from
throat.

Finally he collapsed, every ounce of energy drained in pursuit of
rare rapture they had shared. He rolled and Alysaun moved to
ke room beside her, then turned to cuddle against his chest. It was
a while before her panting breaths came easier, before she was
are enough of reality to try to form words. "I was . . . oh, dear
d . . . I never thought such . . ." Alysaun lifted her face and slid
 hand up to touch his cheek, smiling through a mist of tears.
ou see how you have left me, sire," she whispered, "a woman
eft of her senses. I cannot even say how—"

Cuibhil caught her hand and pressed a kiss on her palm, then
ed so he was covering part of her body with his. She had a
cial glow, the translucent ivory of her complexion tinged with the
eding heat of a lover's flush. "If I remember well, you promised
r body would speak your desires. I need no confirmation of what
old me. Wordless cries and whispers and, yes, even tears"—he
t his head to kiss away a crystal drop that had tarried on her
ek—"say more than can any flattery imagined or writ. I have
y one regret."

Alysaun's eyes widened in alarm. "What is that, m'lord?"

"That I denied us both this journey through heaven for the three
s past. If I had but known—"

Her finger pressed his lips to silence the thought of what was past.
here is always tomorrow, m'lord. And each tomorrow breeds yet
ther."

19

Returning unaccompanied from Tarsus, Cuibhil Rustim spurred his mount forward at a rapid canter, eager to be home as soon as possible. He had been absent from the estate for a week, and though his duties were still unfinished, he had postponed further negotiations for the outpost Malik Shah wished to establish on the eastern Mediterranean and left for his estates.

He thought of Alysaun, most likely fast asleep at this late hour, and smiled. After that first wild night of lovemaking following the banquet, he had been like a man bewitched. Alysaun was an enchantress, intriguing him with her seeming rejection, winning him with the surprising passion of her surrender.

Attending the negotiations had been a mistake from the first. His mind wandered from the boring details of bickering with the town's officials. Each time he had tried to concentrate on the fort plans or argue over the size of the proposed garrison, a vision of Alysaun's face floated before him, her wide blue eyes framed by the lush length of golden lashes.

He almost distrusted how easily she had become part of his life. The importance of having her close by had become as necessary as breathing or sleeping, a need that had nearly eluded him the past seven nights. He had even, in an attempt to make himself independent of desiring her so, taken a young and buxom tavern girl to his rooms, only to send her away in tears when his conscience had balked at the seeming infidelity.

Who was *she*, to have so strong an influence over his mind and body? A slave only, one of many he owned, and yet in the face of his longing, it was more as if *he* were the bondman. His need for Alysaun extended beyond the physical. They had passed hour upon hour talking, and he enjoyed those lively, challenging discussions nearly as much as making love. Even in the quiet times when he would sit in the courtyard and watch her play with Taris, just the sound of her laughter was enough to bring him pleasure.

The child's mother had never elicited so strong a devotion from him. Indeed, if Taris were not tangible proof of their brief marriage, Farazha might have completely vanished from his memory. Certainly Malik's dark, frail little cousin had possessed nothing to compare with Alysaun's bright, fair beauty. She had been as shy and nervous as a bird, forever tense and anxious in his presence.

In those times when the sight of his daughter raised thoughts of the dead girl, he pitied her. Farazha's life had ended too early, her marriage but a brief respite from her parents' domination. Cuibhil chose to believe that he had given her some moments of pleasure, especially when she had revealed the news that she was carrying his child. Now all that was left of her were the dowry monies and estates that she had brought as her marriage portion, and her daughter, Taris.

Though he and Malik had been friends before the marriage made them cousins, Cuibhil was now firmly entrenched as one of the new Sultan's inner circle. As a favorite, he had received the monetary benefits the status granted him, along with the envy of those courtiers who held him suspect because he was not a Seljuk. Their

islike could in no way touch him, though, for he had Malik's
complete trust and protection.

Cuibhil had promised Alysaun that upon his return he would take
her to the capital and introduce her to the splendors of the Turkish
royal court. Though she seemed content with him, there were times
when a fleeting sadness touched her face. In answer to his concern,
she would only smile and shrug off the mood by explaining that she
missed her small son. That might well be true, for with Taris,
Alysaun was the vision of maternal devotion. Still, the sense of loss
that haunted her went deeper, and in those moments when her gaze
and thoughts seemed distant, Cuibhil suspected that she stubbornly
held to her love for the husband who must surely be long dead.

He found himself increasingly jealous of that bond, but how could
he fight for her and win against a bodiless memory? Resenting her
hold on his heart and the strength of her commitment to the past, he
had several times answered her cautious inquiries about Farazha with
embellishments of his dead wife's virtues. Farazha had been a royal
beauty, raised to please a man; she had been gentle and demure, a
woman whose loss he mourned.

Only a brief pleasure came of those false claims, followed by
remorse at the wounded expression Alysaun tried to cover with a
light smile. Oh, he had acted the heartless bastard, too often by his
own reckoning. He could only think that his sullen attempts to
outstrip her own spouse's memory were engendered by the depth of
his feelings. He loved her. Yes, it was true, he did. And admitting to
himself so strong a tie, Cuibhil wanted her to return his love
absolutely, as if her Brand had never existed.

Though he had said nothing to her yet, Cuibhil intended to marry
her when they reached Iconium. Malik would be delighted by the
match, especially because the romance had come about through his
generosity. Such a marriage would solve another problem, one he
suspected but had not been able to make Alysaun admit. She was
proud, certainly as proud as he, and though he had demonstrated his
affection openly, her position as his property had reduced her dignity.
With the marriage, she would no longer feel the invisible collar of

bondage. Alysaun would have the honor of his vows to love and hold her safe.

Pausing at a roadside trough to water and rest his mount before continuing, Cuibhil slid down from the saddle and stretched muscles that had grown stiff during the long ride. He could hardly wait to reach the villa and surprise her with the decision. Above him the clear, deep azure sky, studded with thousands of twinkling stars, seemed to shine all the more brightly for a lover eager to return to his beloved's side.

To exercise his legs before he resumed the journey, Cuibhil paced back and forth behind the trough. A smile curved his lips as he envisioned waking Alysaun. Her eyes, those lovely orbs that mirrored the blue of heaven, would lose the haze of sleep and widen in surprise and . . . what, delight?

Like a cloud suddenly shadowing the horizon of his expectations, it occurred to Cuibhil that she might not view the offer with the same happiness he felt. She might even balk, and with that thought, his features froze in an expression of wounded hauteur. Nay, she would not dare insult him by refusing so obvious an honor . . . or would she? With an irate curse, Cuibhil retrieved the gelding's reins and mounted, wheeling the horse back to the road with so sharp a tug that the alarmed animal whinnied and snorted in protest.

With emotion ruling his temper, Cuibhil set the steed to a gallop, racing him homeward at an ever-increasing speed. Torn between his desires and the nagging suspicion that Alysaun might reject, even mock, the decision, he spurred the panting animal to such an effort that they seemed to fly down the path. He *would* know, before the morning star rose to announce the dawn, the true extent of her affections.

What would he do if she refused him? He had no way of forcing her to love him.

Though Cuibhil had no way of knowing it, the matter was out of his hands. Even as he raced the gelding toward the villa at a breakneck speed, two shadowy figures crouched in the heavy brush

at hedged his orchards, continuing their watch on the darkened
ouse as they had since nightfall.

Hereward glanced up at the evening sky and frowned. The lack of
oud cover did not favor their mission, but at least the moon, full
nd bright the past three days, was on the wane. They had arrived
our days before, delayed by the necessity of keeping off the main
oads.

Eleven long weeks had passed since he and Dismus had departed
om Constantinople. The steward had volunteered his aid to Hereward
ecause he felt responsible for having let Alysaun slip away unprotected
at night. When his master balked at the request and insisted he
ould go alone, Dismus had reminded him that his knowledge of the
urkish language would see the task of finding Lady Alysaun done
ore quickly and with less danger.

While a thorough, persistent questioning of the slavers present in
e city revealed no leads, the authorities had checked the harbor
aster's records and discovered that an unscrupulous trader named
'Deina had sailed the morning after Alysaun's disappearance.
hough Hereward had concurred with their belief that Alysaun had
een aboard, he did not immediately set out to follow the slaver's
ourse. He wasn't about to take the chance of chasing the slaver's
alley only to find the lead a false, delaying one.

No, he had reined in his impatience to be gone and used the time
o search out, with the help of several of his comrades, the
ortune-teller's lodgings. Gnosticus had not made an appearance at
is stall for five days, but a rival, seeing his chance to reduce the
ompetition, had offered the information that he and his son kept a
oom above the Taverna Nos Patrios, a rundown hovel at the edge of
e waterfront district, known for its dicing games and bad wines.

The sight of the five, ax-wielding Varangians who burst into his
oom that evening so terrified Gnosticus that he turned a deathly
ay-white shade and lost control of his bladder. The guardsmen
rcled the cowering man, keeping him intimidated by their long,
icked axes until Hereward stepped forward to demand knowledge
f Alysaun's whereabouts.

When one of the guards laid the ax blade against his neck Gnosticus left off his protestations of innocence. The stench of fear emanating from him was far more odorous than the urine he had loosed as, quivering and sweating, he admitted his part in her disappearance. Andreyas returned to the loft in time to hear his father lay the blame fully upon his shoulders and, as one of the Varangians moved to catch him, he bolted, abandoning his cowardly sire to whatever punishment was to be meted out.

In minutes he had given them the entire story and named al'Deina as his accomplice, then he slumped to his knees and begged for mercy he neither deserved nor would find. One of the guards shoved him to the floor and held him there with a boot upon his chest, then asked Hereward what form of justice he thought worthy.

"Death is too merciful a fate for this cur," Hereward had replied. He suggested that since Gnosticus, with his false predictions, had greedily laid a snare for an innocent woman, he should be deprived of the chance to harm anyone else with his prophecies. Hereward had turned away then, ignoring the desperate, squealing pleas for mercy from a man who had shown none to Alysaun. His companions had closed in, pinning the wildly struggling seer, and as Hereward reached the door, there came a strangled scream and choking sound that ended in a bubbling gurgle.

The next morning he and Dismus had taken passage on a felucca bound for Ephesus. They were six days behind the slaver, but Hereward knew al'Deina's planned stops. From his experiences as a former slave, Dismus predicted that Alysaun would not be shown at the public auctions. She was enough of a prize to keep hidden until the trader reached the Turkish capital and produced her for the bidding of some wealthy nobleman.

He had been right, too. In Ephesus they learned that al'Deina had been there and gone on, and no one recalled a girl of Alysaun's description. It was the same tale as they journeyed inland. In every large town al'Deina had shown his slaves, sold some and purchased others, but had displayed no fair, blond beauty for sale.

By traveling night and day, the two of them had made up lost time

430

t still arrived in Iconium to find the slaver three days gone. Again, quiries brought them no word of Alysaun.

Dismus was sure she would have been offered in the capital. The rks were a dark people, and a slave with a fair complexion and lden hair was sure to bring an exorbitant price. Still, if the owing had been private, there was little possibility of discovering ho might have purchased her.

Al'Deina was expected to pass through the city again on his return urney to the western coast. Hereward and Dismus took rooms at an n near the capital's public auction blocks, waiting impatiently for ws of his return. Each day they wandered through the bazaars and ctions, hoping to find some clue to lead them to the vanished lysaun.

One morning Dismus chanced to overhear a conversation between o courtiers watching one of the auctions. The discussion had ntered on the attributes of a golden-haired slave girl being shown, d one of the men had commented on the Sultan's acquisition of o young girls for his growing harem. The other had replied that ly one girl was joining Malik Shah's personal attendants. The her, a light-skinned blonde who far outshone the beauty on the ction block, had been bought for presentation to his majesty's usin, Bey Cuibhil Rustim.

Even with that lucky piece of information they had been forced to de their time and wait for al'Deina. This cousin of Malik Shah's d several estates in far-flung provinces. Alysaun, if it was indeed e, could have been sent to any one of them.

Finally the day had arrived when they heard the gossip that the ver had come back to Iconium. Hereward had spent the day dying the man identified as al'Deina, watching with restrained ry the cruel and harsh way the man treated his slaves. Later that ght, after Dismus had lured the trader to an isolated spot outside e city's patrolled gates on the pretext that he had several stolen ves to sell him, Hereward was able to exercise a long-awaited ngeance.

Al'Deina was complaining about the long walk from his lodgings

when a large hand swept from behind him and covered his mouth
cutting off a garbled scream as a long, finely honed knife blade
pressed his throat. Hereward had freed the man's mouth after the
slave trader had nodded agreement not to raise a cry. At first he
denied knowledge of Alysaun, but a nick of his flesh with the sharp
blade stirred a total recollection of the girl and what he had done
with her.

The Sultan had indeed bought her, and as part of the purchase
price, had insisted that al'Deina deliver her in the escort of a royal
guard to his cousin's estate near the town of Derbe, situated about
midway on the trade route between Iconium and Tarsus. After
describing the access to Cuibhil Rustim's estate and how well
guarded it was, al'Deina was bold enough to ask who had betrayed
him. He enjoyed a brief moment of callous laughter over the
fortune-teller's fate before it dawned upon him that he was in the
hold of the same man who had ordered Gnosticus silenced.

Al'Deina pleaded for his life with far more command of his senses
than had the trembling, shaken fortune-teller. Whereas Gnosticus
had merely begged for mercy, his cohort offered money and jewels
in exchange for his freedom. Hereward listened for only a few
seconds before his fingers tightened on the knife hilt and pressed the
blade into the slaver's flaccid skin. A hand muffled the scream of
protest. Hereward had slowly, with infinite pleasure, silenced the
sounds as the blade sliced through a taut tendon and opened the
jugular. His hand had come away as the mouth of the dying al'Deina
filled with his life's blood, then fell open to emit a red stream that
joined the river of blood pulsing from his gaping throat.

Hereward had carefully wiped his knife on the crumpled body,
then ordered a white-faced Dismus to help him strip the rings and
jewelry from what would appear to be the hapless victim of
robbery. When a search of the slaver's robes had turned up, among
other stolen items, an emerald cross that belonged to Alysaun,
Hereward had known a fury so fierce he wished he owned the power
to resurrect al'Deina, just to have the enjoyment of killing him more
slowly.

They had left the body lying there, then washed at a nearby stream, where Hereward had changed his blood-spattered caftan for a fresh robe, burying the other in a thicket. The next morning, when they left the city through the south gate, the talk among their fellow travelers was full of worry over the safety of the road that led south to Lystra and then west to Derbe and Tarsus. It seemed another poor soul had been set upon and murdered for his purse and jewels. Hereward drew his hood close and shook his head in apparent dismay.

Now Hereward squatted next to his companion, his fingers opening and closing on the cross. The house had been quiet for close to three hours, the servants long asleep. Fortune had smiled on them in the form of a young goatherder from a village not far away. Dismus had bought several of his cheeses and helped to catch a stray kid that had wandered from its mother's side. In gratitude, the boy, whose daily duties allowed him little chance for company, had been a fount of information about the local landowners.

Lord Cuibhil, for instance, was away from his estate on business for the Sultan. Oh, yes, he was a most important man, a kinsman of the Sultan and trusted with representing his majesty on matters of importance to the realm. He was gone to Tarsus this time, young Achmal had confided. On his weekly stop to sell his cheeses, he had heard it with his own ears. The bey had seemed most sad to part with his mistress, though she was only one of his slaves. Achmal had been close enough to hear the lord tell her that the ten days would pass quickly and remind her she had a journey to the capital to look forward to upon his return.

With the master gone, the men assigned to patrol the grounds and stand watch each night were reduced to a guard of some ten trusted slaves. Three days of studying the timing of patrols and watch changes had left Hereward confident that he could leave Dismus waiting in the orchard and approach the house without notice between the hour after the midnight watch took charge and the hour before the first light.

That time was now, or they would have yet another day's wait

433

along with the added chance of discovery. "I'm off," Hereward
whispered, and exchanged a tense look with his steward before he
hefted the cross and chain in his cupped palm and made his
expression more confident. "With God's grace, the lady will be back
with me and *this* will hang in its rightful place." He twisted the
chain several times around his belt, then dismissed it from his mind
as he again thanked Dismus for his loyalty.

"You know what the plan is if I am discovered. Don't think you'll
be saving my hide by blundering in to be seized yourself." Hereward
squeezed the man's shoulder and rose in a slight crouch to take a
look at the house.

"M'lord, I . . . would feel like a coward—"

"*Nonsense*, man. What good would it do to be captured as well?
If I don't come back, I won't need company. And someone must tell
Frida. Now, keep an ear cocked. I'm off." And he was, moving
forward into the open in a dash to cover nearer to the rear of the
villa; the keen survivor's instincts that had seen him through three
years of hit-and-run battles against his hated Norman foe rose to
transform Hereward from an aging mercenary into a sharp-witted
agile warrior in search of his objective.

On the previous night he had scouted the building and decided
was close enough to the typical Roman villa, indeed to his own
home, to allow him reasonable confidence as to the layout. The
south-wing rooms were grated with heavy wrought-iron bars. The
majority of these rooms were the sleeping quarters of the more
important house slaves. The north wing was similar; but its windows
were unbarred, the guest rooms, no doubt. The west end of the
house had a low-walled private courtyard in addition to the central
atrium. An awning, now rolled and secured to the house, was an
additional luxury that proclaimed the master's private apartments.

The promised trip to Iconium, which the goatherder had mentioned
suggested that Cuibhil Rustim appreciated his gift from the Sultan
No doubt he had moved her out of slaves' quarters to a room where
she would be close by—his own bedchamber, if he were as enchanted
as Achmal had claimed.

Hereward started out of the thick brush and froze at the sound of a boot scraping gravel. He had barely made it back to his cover of dried, tangled vines before a tall, skinny fellow carrying a closed pot at arm's length appeared around the corner, hurrying toward the waste-settling pool some thirty yards north of the house.

Hereward let out a sigh when the slave disappeared, deciding to wait until the man had returned to the house before making a sprint for the wall. If he had been a few feet closer to the servant, the man might have seen him, though he had been grumbling over the unexpected late call for such an unpleasant duty.

Finally the slave passed again, and when the house seemed quiet and settled, Hereward moved. The wall was low enough for him to vault, but he wasn't sure what lay on the other side and couldn't take the chance of crashing into a clay flower pot or a piece of furniture. With more skill than grace, he caught the top of the marble wall and hauled his weight over, peering down into the dark, shadowed length of a small garden. Some six feet of mosaic-tiled veranda extended to a pair of heavily carved doors. There were four windows, two on either side of the double doors, each of them a foot short of the roof and ground.

Hereward frowned. His task would have been easier if some light spilled out through the shutter slats, but at this hour no one was up. Finally, on close inspection, he found the first window on his right was slightly open, to admit the evening air. With a deep breath held, he pried the shutter open wider and listened. Not a sound, at least no snoring to alert him to a man asleep within.

Bolder now, with time passing too fast for indecision, he pulled the shutter as wide as it would open, parted the drapes, and peered in. It was the master bedroom, all right, and one far more luxuriously appointed than his own. Whoever he was, this Rustim was a man who appreciated beauty and had the funds to surround himself with it. A candle burned low across the wide room, letting off a dull glow as it sputtered, near to flickering out.

The silk-draped canopy bed was immense. It rested on a raised platform, and the mattress of thick, soft cushions was on the

platform surface. As Hereward stared at the bed he could just mak
out a shape beneath the tumble of a silk coverlet. 'Twas Alysaun'
size, sure enough. *Think long, think wrong,* he remembered hi
nurse telling him when he was a child.

With a careful tread, he climbed the three wide steps and stare
down. 'Twas so *damned* dark. In his effort to discern the face mor
closely, Hereward leaned over, resting one knee ever so lightly at th
edge of the bed. Seconds later, as the overhanging coverlet sli
beneath his boot, Hereward was falling forward, unable to keep
himself from landing on the half-curled figure.

Whoever it was, she was a female and, frightened as she was, a
indignant one. She took action before resorting to speech and shove
away one of his huge hands, which had accidentally landed on he
breast. She wriggled out from under him and turned to strike hi
shoulder with a balled fist. " *Out*—get out or my screams—"

Hereward was rubbing his shoulder, but at the sound of her voic
he stopped and whispered, "Alysaun? Alys, by Jesus, 'tis you."

Alysaun sat bolt upright, unable to believe she was hearin
Hereward's voice. "Hereward?" Tears of joy stung her eyes as sh
flung herself forward and into his arms. "Oh, Hereward, where di
you come from? 'Tis like God dropped you upon my bed from
thousand miles away." She was crying now, sobbing happily agains
his shoulder for the sheer joy of having his familiar strength s
close. "How did you . . . are you alone? Oh, I've a hundred ques
tions to ask."

"And no time to hear any answers now. Get up, lass. We must b
gone."

He dragged her out of the bed. In freeing her of the clinging fold
of the cover, the chain and cross unwound and dropped noiselessl
to the floor. Suddenly Alysaun tugged on his hand. "*Wait*, I'm no
dressed, at least not decent. Oh, stop pulling for a moment an
listen."

"Alysaun, I have maimed one man and killed another, bot
deserving, and traveled across a thousand miles or more to save ye
Now you balk and risk both our heads as well as poor Dismus

waiting in the orchard. *I* say you hold your tongue till we're clear or will . . . ah, Christ, a woman is ever for arguing." Surprising her, he bent and hefted Alysaun high like a sack of barley. She called his name again, but Hereward ignored her, muttering curses under his breath as he retraced his path to the open window and climbed out.

At the wall he lifted her to the top, then climbed up, jumped over, and reached up to catch her. She seemed to be hesitant still, but finally, as he tugged impatiently on one ankle, she slid down and was caught in his arms. A glance around showed him he was clear to run.

A few minutes later he dropped her none too gently next to Dismus, huffed a few times to catch his breath, then hunkered down beside her and glared. "Now, if you please, what was so goddamned important it couldn't wait?"

Alysaun stared back at the house, her lip caught between her teeth. Finally, she looked up at him. "Whom did you rescue me from, Hereward?"

"*What*?" What in Christ's creation has *that* got to do with anything? You know as well as I—a Seljuk bey named Cuibhil Rustim."

"Hereward, Cuibhil Rustim is Brand—*my* Brand." He looked at her as if captivity had taken away her wits. "It's *true*, and when he finds me gone—"

"Look, lassie, I can't make sense of what you're talking about, but all I know is that you've been gone three months from Matt and he *still* don't know why. Now decide—do I take ye back to that fancy bed or home, where ye belong?"

Alysaun again stared back at the house. She was crying, thinking of her boy, of how she missed him so. There was no choice. Matt needed her, she needed him. Brand was a proven survivor. "Let's go. *Now*, before an alarm is raised. I want to go home."

EPILOGUE

rand stood in the entry hall of Hereward's villa, waiting while the
eward went to announce his presence. Not much past an hour ago
e had arrived in Constantinople. Soon after he had settled Taris and
er nurse, Erinia, in a comfortable inn near the cathedral of Hagia
ophia, leaving them in the cautious Ben-Mustapha's care, he had
one in search of Hereward's house.

When, six weeks before, he had stooped to retrieve Alysaun's
loss from the floor of his bedchamber, the world had seemed to
ash down about him. A blinding pain had come with the return of
s memory, and a thundering drumming at his temples that no
mount of drink could silence. For days he had nursed the wound
lysaun's loss had dealt him, taking a perverse kind of pleasure in
pening it anew each time he found himself excusing the way he had
eated her. Alysaun had not been kidnapped; she had been rescued.
he difference made of him something difficult to accept—he was
e villain and, if not responsible for her captivity, at least a partner
degrading the woman he loved.

His moods had alternated between self-pity and self-hatred. He would send no one after Alysaun, and yet each passing moment he had longed desperately for her company. Once he had recalled his identity, he remembered a flood of details that had colored their lives before that afternoon at Manzikert. Between that fateful day and Alysaun's arrival at the estate, everything else that occurred in those two years was a desert of emotion, a wasted effort of sleeping and breathing.

His son would be nearly four now. Brand had decided it was impossible to go back, to return and take up his role of husband, especially after the callous way he had bruised Alysaun's pride. It was his desire to see Matt again, that and the hope that Alysaun might still love him, that finally bestirred him to make the journey.

Whatever happened, there would be no return to a life as Cuibhn Rustim. Brand felt as if the man who had borne that name was dead; he could think of no one who would greatly mourn his passing. Taking only his personal funds, ceding the slaves and the villa to the Sultan, he wrote a missive to him that explained why he had to go, why he could not continue to live a lie.

Still, it had taken every ounce of courage to come here and present himself. Finding Hereward's villa had been the easiest part of the task; at the door he had nearly turned away. Whatever bitterness Alysaun retained toward his memory needed this chance to be set free. He would make his excuses for his behavior, allow her to vent her anger and ... who knew? Perhaps there might yet be enough love within her heart to effect a reconciliation.

What would be Hereward's reaction to his arrival? Even as Brand wondered, he heard a bellow from the direction the servant had taken. The words were indistinguishable, but the loud roar brought a wave of nostalgia crashing over Brand. No, Hereward hadn't changed. In fact, after Brand had taken time to consider the bold audacity of the rescue attempt, he had realized that only one man could have masterminded such a successful strike deep in foreign territory. He had no idea when Hereward had arrived in Constantinople, but for Alysaun's sake, and his own, Brand thanked God that he had come.

The slight, limping gait that carried Hereward of Lincoln across e antechamber no longer matched the strident, commanding voice. and reflected for only a second upon the changes time had ought, then looked directly into his old friend's eyes. He said thing, but his tense, wary expression bespoke an uncertainty of w warm his welcome would be.

To give Hereward his due, he paused only a few moments before ntinuing across the room with an ever-widening grin. His voice oclaimed his surprise. A few well-chosen epithets rolled off his ngue as naturally as a priest intoning blessings. The shaggy mane ash-gold waves was streaked with white, but age had not dimmed e brightness of eyes that crinkled to match his booming laughter. 3y Christ, I never counted this day would come, lad. These tired es witness the impossible—a Lazarus returned.''

The easy banter relaxed Brand, dissolving the last traces of ncern, and he grinned slowly as Hereward reached his side. epared to grasp hands in friendship, Brand issued a relieved sigh ly a second before a huge fist suddenly loomed before him. reward was still grinning as his right hand connected in a werful, smashing blow to the left side of Brand's mouth, sending m spinning backward to land in an ungainly sprawl.

His vision was blurred by waves of pain. The overwhelming armth of Hereward's greeting had left him totally unprepared for ch stealth. Brand shook his head to clear the fog of surprise, his ind and body alert to defense. Working his jaw to test its condi-on, he raised a hand to wipe at the blood pulsing from a split and pidly swelling lip. Slowly, his gaze rose to take in the two large ots planted before him, poised in a fighter's stance, then rose gher to find Hereward calmly surveying him.

''Well, old friend,'' Brand finally said, wincing at the pain of rming words with his bruised and bleeding mouth, ''I *knew* rchance we'd be meeting, but had I guessed 'twould be in a heated counter, I'd have planned my call to miss you. What elicited your expected wrath . . . or have I not the right to inquire?''

Hereward stared down at him with arms akimbo, a slight smile

curling a corner of his mustached mouth. "I'm thinking you kno
or should know, the reason without asking, son." He stuck ou
hand to help Brand rise. The gesture was met with suspicion, th
grudgingly accepted. "I'll not strike ye again—"

With Hereward's hand caught firmly in his own, Brand threw
punch with his left fist, a retaliatory blow that landed in an upwa
thrust against the Saxon's middle. The force of the strike, tende
with all of Brand's strength, would have doubled a normal man w.
pain. Hereward was bent only a bit as the air whooshed out of hi
He shoved Brand's hand away, straightening with a grin anticipate
of combat.

Brand was ready this time. The hamlike fist that swung towa
him missed as he ducked and rolled to the left, to land on his fe
and crouch. He was no more anxious to do battle than Hereward b
still they warily circled each other, neither willing to be the first
call for a truce.

"I want only to see my wife, you great lummox," Brand insiste
dipping agilely out of harm's way as Hereward made a lunge at hi
His breath came hard as he watched Hereward's expression, cautio
of the tensing of facial muscles that would betray another mov
"You've no right to stand between us," he added, easily sidesteppi
another blow and tapping Hereward's grizzled chin with a rigl
"Age and one too many ales have slowed you, friend. Why, thr
years ago, you—"

Brand most likely would have won from sheer endurance, keepi
the older, heavier man at bay until he tired, if he had not taken
moment to glance past his opponent. A young boy stood watchi
the fight, half hidden by a fluted column, his blue eyes wide as
worried the side of a small thumb. Rusty curls topped a face th
was anxious and troubled. A woman's skirts appeared behind t
lad, and Brand looked up to see Torfrida's pale, shocked face. Tho
few seconds of inattention cost Brand dearly.

Hereward's fist drove into his belly and doubled Brand over. F
slumped to his knees, gasping for a breath that would not come, h
eyes shut tight against the pain. His pride was wounded worse tha

s body. He knelt there, sweat beading his forehead, embarrassed, nely, an outsider who no longer belonged to these good people.

When finally he raised his head and opened his eyes, his young n stood beside him, gazing accusingly with eyes that mirrored lysaun's. "You're bad," Matt stated unequivocally. "You were ying to hurt Lord Hereward and . . . and I *hate* you." He swore an ath, one of Hereward's choicest, and his small fingers curled in a st. Before he could strike, a large, muscular arm circled his waist, aising the boy high in the air.

"By God's breath, son, who was't that taught you such lan-uage?" Hereward held the wriggling boy aloft and beamed at him ith paternal pride before gently settling him down on his feet.

Brand cocked a damp eyebrow. "Is *this* what you've taught him, lereward, to curse and defame his own father? Damn your eyes, an—he's but three and speaks a seasoned forty."

A storm of sullen resentment ruffled Matt's red-gold eyebrows. or all his proud stance, his small chin trembled. "I am *four*, you evil's spawn, and . . . my father . . . *my* father was a hero." He niffled, then angrily wiped his eyes. "He's dead, Father is, and if ou dare to speak his name, I will . . . I'll—"

"I have only the fondest regard for your father, Matt. In truth, I m—"

"An old friend of the family," Hereward finished, afraid an nexpected revelation of Brand's kinship would send the boy into ysterics. "Frida, love, would it not be a grand time for Matt to take nap?" he asked pointedly, then ruffled the lad's curls and smiled. 'After you've had a good sleep, m'boy, mayhap I could be persuad-d to take ye out to the Forum."

The stranger forgotten, Matthieu smiled, an angel's smile, and bediently slipped his fingers into Frida's hand. "I am too old, you now, for a nap, sire. Only for you will I do so."

Hereward nodded with a pleased look that faded as he glanced at Brand. The younger man, bruised from the fight, gazed at his son ith so bitter an anguish that Hereward's compassion went out to im.

"*Dismus.*" The steward appeared immediately, as if he had bee
waiting for Hereward's call. He cast one disparaging look at the
unwelcome visitor before directing his full attention to Herewar
"Dismus, have a ewer of fresh water sent to the solar, and clea
linens. Our visitor has come a far way and is in need of son
repair."

It took an admirable effort for Brand to rise to his feet without
grimace of pain. He stood somewhat unsteadily and glanced
Hereward, more dazed by his turbulent emotions than by th
physical effects of the fight. "You think to patch me up and send n
on my way without allowing me even a glimpse of Alysaun," I
guessed, and nothing in Hereward's expression denied the intentio
Dismus had vanished as unobtrusively as he had appeared. The
were alone, two old friends who felt uncomfortable with each othe
"For the sake of the past, you must let me talk to her." The fig
had gone out of him, but Brand was desperate enough to plea
"Can you take this decision from her?"

"Aye, Brand, though you do tear at my heart with the calling u
of fond memories. Think of Alysaun, son—has she not suffere
enough from your absence? By what she endured at your vei
hands? She mustn't be torn anew by your sudden appearance. N
matter your remorse, Brand, 'tis over 'twixt you and her." Hereward
countenance was stubbornly set, though he had to force the hars
words from his lips. "And the boy . . . think ye that he will unde
stand your resurrection? You heard him. His father died a hero
Manzikert."

While they spoke other observers had happened on the scene
Alysaun had come from the atrium, disturbed by the sound
strident voices. She paused on the top step leading to the garde
courtyard, her face drained of color. A companion joined her,
well-dressed young man in his middle twenties, curious as well ove
the disturbance in the usually tranquil household.

Hereward failed to notice the pair, his attention concentrated c
weighing Brand's requests against a desire to protect Alysaun fror
further distress. "Come along, lad," he insisted, gesturing towar

e solar. "Alysaun is presently occupied. Whilst ye rest awhile and
are a cup for old times' sake, we'll talk."

"My pardon, Lord Hereward, for interrupting." Alysaun immedi-
ely had the attention of all three men. The first shock of seeing
rand had dissipated. Her heart was fluttering like a bird's wings,
ut she was composed and her color was returning to normal. For
ne brief moment, when Brand's eyes met hers, there was an old,
miliar jolt of emotion, as if lightning had crackled between them.

Having noted the blood streaking his swollen lip, she looked
uestioningly at Hereward. He seemed discomforted, sheepishly
uilty, and Alysaun realized at once the reception that had been
ccorded Brand. "I would have a few minutes of privacy to speak
ith . . . our visitor. Would you be so kind, Hereward, as to keep Sir
lichael company?"

Hereward nodded, relieved that the burden of decision had been
fted from his shoulders. Brand had taken his eyes from Alysaun for
nly a moment, to measure the young man who stood so close, *too*
lose, to his wife. His youth was a shock. He was an untried
tripling who had just come of age to scrape the fuzz from his chin.

As Alysaun turned to face the youth and cast a beseeching glance
pward, jealousy colored Brand's complexion a dull red. Her voice
as hushed and solicitous as she apparently made an excuse for the
nterruption. She lightly touched his arm, winning his compliance
ith a dazzling bright smile. Alysaun's decision to grant the stranger
n audience did not sit well with Michael. The frown he turned upon
rand was met with a bemused, victorious smile.

Finally Michael bowed over her hand, pressing a light kiss on her
xtended fingers before he reluctantly strode across the room to
 lereward's side. Dismus reappeared, herding two servants before
im, and at a further command sent the cooled wine, water, and the
nens to the courtyard.

Brand crossed the room, ignoring the soreness from the punch to
is belly. As he reached Alysaun he steeled himself against a sudden
ush of boyish nerves, brought on no doubt by her calm, contempla-
ve glance. He was as self-possessed as a man could be with the

447

evidence of a losing fight swelling his bottom lip half again i
normal size.

Alysaun led the way into the gardens, knowing full well th
Michael's curious, brooding gaze followed them until they were o
of sight. She had no intention of losing her hard-won composure.
Brand intended to threaten or bully her, Hereward was only a ca
away. The servants had placed the trays on a low table of lacquere
cedar close to the fountain. Dismus cleared his throat, asking if the
was anything more he could do. "No, thank you, no," she replie
absently. Then, aware of the effect such a courtesy would have c
her husband, she summoned the steward back to ask that he sen
refreshments to the solar.

Dismus bowed and backed away, a slight arching of one thick gra
eyebrow acknowledging Brand's success as he passed him. At la
they were alone. Alysaun heard Brand approach her and inhale
deeply. Whatever had brought back his memory, it was he who ha
returned and must explain. She would be a fool to make his task an
easier.

Turning slightly, Alysaun glanced up at his face and felt a twing
of compassion, not only for his bruised, blood-streaked mouth b
for the forlorn expression on the face that had grown too lean. H
raised a hand, combing his fingers through his hair, awkward an
unable to think of a way to begin now that he was finally alone wi
her. "You . . . you're looking well, madame," he offered lamely.

"Would that I could say the same of you, m'lord," Alysau
answered with a hint of amusement. "Am I mistaken in noting th
imprint of Hereward's knuckles upon your mouth, or did yo
perchance meet with brigands on the road?"

"Brigands I could take on all the day, Alys . . . 'twas indee
Hereward's wrath as he struck a blow I had no reason to expect. 'Ti
good to know you've had so stalwart a champion." The split lowe
lip was beginning to throb. When he tried a careless smile, it dea
him a sharp jolt of pain.

"I'll not claim it was undeserved, sire. Hereward risked makin
Frida a widow when he came for me." Brand had the grace to flush

and Alysaun was immediately sorry. She swept past him, a little unnerved by his closeness and determined to maintain control of her emotions. At the table, she took one of the clean linen squares and dipped it in the water, then looked up and motioned for him to come to her. "If you would allow me . . . the cut should be washed clean."

Heartened by her seeming concern, Brand came to stand before her, bending his head slightly to accommodate her as she gently swabbed the broken skin. He found it a pleasure just to study her face. Tiny lines of concentration creased her fair brow. "I'd forgotten how tender your touch could be, my love," he ventured. Alysaun, annoyed by the soft, wooing words as well as by the movement that made her task harder to complete, finished with a harsh jab that rubbed away the last traces of dark, dried blood.

"Aye, but then there are volumes you have forgotten about me, sir," she replied righteously. Dropping the cloth upon the table, she handed Brand a goblet of wine. "Our cups mayn't be as fine as you are used to, Brand, but the wine will serve to soothe both wounds and injured pride."

Brand bowed his head, then lifted the cup in a salute. "To your sweet compassion, Alys. I hope it is generous enough to allow you to hear me out."

"If you say your peace without coloring the past too rosily, I will listen. Otherwise, I'd not have put aside my courtesy to Michael."

"Michael . . . so that is the whelp's name," Brand commented acidly, with a grimace that hurt his chances as well as his sore lip. "By God, Alys, even if he's about your age, he's hardly dry behind the ears. How can you entertain—nay, *encourage*—his hopes when you're a woman wedded?" .

His indignation was galling. "Had you recovered your wits a full month later, m'lord, I'd have been delivered of that state and legally free."

Brand glowered, his injuries forgotten. "How so, m'lady? Kindly explain to one who is justifiably puzzled how such a dispensation would be granted. A wife, unless she be widowed, is allowed but one mate."

"But a wife deserted two years, left to fend for self and child, ha every right to seek relief from unhonored vows. If Hereward had n arrived, your son and I would have starved, sir." In truth, Alysau had applied to the church court for a decree of dissolution but ha withdrawn the suit a week past. Let him think he had lost her . . . th agonizing would do him a world of good.

"And did you falsely swear before a priest that you knew nothin of my whereabouts? I know you well enough to believe you woul not lie before a man of God."

"What *should* I have said, then?" Alysaun was as indignant a Brand now, and was losing her temper, which she had vowed t restrain. "Could I ask them to believe that my husband had suffere a loss of memory but retained the wits to carve out a full an able-bodied life amongst our sworn enemies? You cannot even clai to have wandered penniless and destitute these past years. You forgo wife, son, and loyalty but not the charm to court and wed a wealth Seljuk maiden and sire her child. More would be my pity, m'lord, your lack of recollection had included the portion of your senses th lies *below* your waist."

"You sound as if you'd rather I'd been gelded than merel knocked about the head, Alysaun. I find it impossible to believe th you would wish me so disabled. If memory serves me right, yo were less vindictive in the throes of passion."

Alysaun blushed and sighed. "I wish . . . I wish only that yo had regained your memory *before* you took another wife. Thi sudden miracle of remembering comes too late."

"Aye . . . well, it might have come much sooner had you bothere to tell me who you . . . what our relationship had been," Bran retorted. "'Twas *I* who did not recognize you. You could have sai who I was, given some hint of what we'd shared."

"And how would you have replied?" Alysaun asked, steadil meeting his accusations without flinching.

The corners of his mouth quirked at the irony of her question "That you were mad to lay such a claim upon my head," h answered truthfully. "That so audacious a lie deserved only m corn and my contempt. At least that would have been my stance in the beginning. Later . . ." Brand faltered, for even later he would have been dubious.

He had had time enough to dwell on her treatment at his hands. In his arrogance he had taken advantage of her helplessness. Guilt deepened his frown as he reflected bitterly, "You've not only grown more lovely, Alys, but more temperate of manner in my long absence. You've the right to condemn me, yet your speech is soft and nearly devoid of accusation."

They were standing but a few feet apart, and yet the distance yawned between them like a great chasm that seemed impossible to bridge. Alysaun felt his frustration deeply, and yet her own resentment held sway, refusing to allow her the words that might ease the strain. His eyes were those of a condemned man who could not plea for mercy in words eloquent enough to convince. Brand's inner agitation revealed itself in numerous ways, the stiff, angry working of his jaw, the tense fingers that splayed to brush the auburn waves back from his temples. This last gesture was too familiar, calling up memories of other times she had seen Brand under duress. Alysaun glanced down.

"I no longer have the right to call you mine," he continued, his voice ripe with emotion, its appeal heightened by the hoarseness of tensed throat muscles. "God moves in ways I fail to comprehend. He gave me you to cherish and I . . . I have broken my vows to keep you safe from want and pain. I know not what sin of mine stirred so wrathful a judgment, but He can do no worse to me than deny my heart's desire. Hell is suddenly most attractive. Certainly it can be no more harsh than life without reason."

Brand studied Alysaun's features, shadowed by the play of sunlight passing through the branches of the tall cypress trees lining the courtyard. The urge to pull her into his arms and use his mouth and hands to stir a remembrance of sweeter days was so strong he had to clench his fingers to resist. If he could not convince her of his love with words, then an embrace would be empty of all that had once made it so enchanting.

"Say to me that you feel nothing for me, my love, and mean it
he asked finally. His arms raised, fists unfolding only to fall away
a dispirited gesture. "Convinced of this, I could go, knowing th
my acts no longer had the power to cause you distress. If I shou
pass from your life while yet you care, the remnants of your lo
would turn to hate. Hating will be no more satisfying than lovi
me, for both turn back upon your tender heart and wound it
Alysaun lifted her head and the thick sweep of golden lashes fram
eyes that had turned a stormy, turbulent blue-gray, the color of t
sea on a winter's day. To Brand her countenance seemed stubborn
rejecting. A deep, rumbling sigh broke from him before he turn
away, shoulders slumped in defeat. In reality, Alysaun was so mov
by his plea she had to steel herself against the overwhelming desi
to reach out and touch his beloved face. She longed to know th
security of his strong arms once again. Tensing to still the trembli
of her muscles, she stared after him and took a breath. There w
more, much more that needed to be aired before the past could
laid to rest. Brand's long strides had carried him halfway to th
portal before Alysaun's voice, sharpened by an effort to hide th
whirl of her emotions, brought him to an abrupt halt. "Pray te
sire . . . wherefore are you bound?"

The query raised Brand's hopes, then sent them plummeting
deep despair. She was curious only, not concerned. "Away,"
answered, and with another heavy sigh turned back to face h
"Somewhere . . . perhaps Tarsus. My thoughts are on myself, Alysau
'Twould tax my heart beyond its strength to dwell so near to what
want and am to be denied."

Alysaun's mouth turned down in a pout, her silk slipper, whi
matched her azure kirtle, tapping the mosaic tiles of the garden pat
"Will you never lose your arrogance, Brand de Reynaud?" sh
asked, and, refusing to approach, tucked her arms across her breas
and sat on the wide marble bench surrounding the spraying fountai
He stared at her with a puzzled air, drawing a further rebuke for h
assumptions. "Why must you ever decide *my* fate without allowi
me some choice in the matter? You claim to love me. Can a ma

452

ho truly loves a woman turn upon his heels and not tarry long
ough to await her answer? Never in combat were you a coward,
rand. Why now do you retreat?''

Challenged by the suggestion that his departure was less than
lorous, Brand slowly closed the distance between them until he
ood before her. He *had* been rather peremptory in taking the
cision from her. It occurred to him that she had been given reason
lenty to harbor resentment of his ways, but that beneath the
lcano that seemed ready to erupt, the love she once bore him
ight still smolder. ''You've not had your say, Alys. Feel free to
end whatever anger lies within, but say not that I 'claim' to love
u. I *do* love, and no number of sharp rebukes can change my
art.''

''Love does not turn away, Brand. Can you leave and truly believe
u do me a kindness? You say you have lost the right to keep me.
ave I then foreited my right to be your wife?'' Alysaun found it
npossible to think clearly with those ever-changing hazel eyes of
s staring down into hers, and she turned her head aside to gaze
wn into the water. ''More than the passing of time has come
tween us, Brand,'' she continued. ''You have a child, her mother
as your...'' Alysaun found it difficult to call Farazha his wife.
Did you love her?''

''No.'' The answer came so sure and quick it startled Alysaun,
awing her gaze back to his. ''The marriage was arranged,'' he
plained. ''Farazha had no more say in it than I.'' He shrugged and
shed a grin, ignoring the stab of pain in his bruised jaw. ''I did
press a certain reluctance, but the alternative was less attractive.''

''But you managed to overcome your reluctance?''

Brand noted the stiffness of her back, the feigned lack of concern
at masked her wounded female pride. She was jealous, Alysaun
as, and rightly so, but just the thought of her heart in the grip of
at possessive emotion sent Brand's spirits soaring. Alysaun could
arce feel such envy if she no longer cared.

'''Twas not your husband who entered into a union with Farazha,
ve, but a man stripped of all that had been familiar. Cuibhil

Rustim is now as dead as she. I feel no sense of loss in his demise. He reached out, gently lifting her chin. "That life is behind me nov I have shed it like a set of breeches that fit me ill. I am no one b the man you chanced to meet in a greenwood vale, half the world distance from this place. You took my heart then, Alys . . . 'twas n in my possession to give to any other woman."

Alysaun stared back at him, lost in the tender warmth of his eye Merely the sound of her name, spoken so lovingly by this man, ha the power to make her feel as though she were the only woman c earth. She said nothing in reply. She could not trust herself to speal

"You love me still. This I know now, and I curse the foolishne that did make me relinquish my beseeching so easily," Brand sai his confidence returning. He allowed himself the faintest smile triumph, then, recalling how possessive young Michael had been Alysaun's company, he mentioned him. "Your suitor . . . now that know how your true heart lies, he must be told his attentions a unwelcome. The lad languishes in Hereward's keep. Shall I not er his hapless waiting and reveal who it was that interrupted h courtship?"

"Be not so eager to send him away, m'lord. We've not yet settle our estrangement to my satisfaction. Your daughter, is she to li with us? You must have brought her. I cannot think that you wou abandon Taris to relatives."

Brand's expression was slightly sheepish. "Nay, I would nc Well knowing your generous spirit, I brought Taris with me. She ar the nurse are left in Ben-Mustapha's care. Just as our son nee renew my acquaintance, so the motherless Taris will need yo gentle ways to see her grow to a woman." Alysaun said nothing fc several moments and then nodded. She could not deny Brand h daughter, nor would she even if it were in her power. The baby wa young enough to accept her, and already they had a bond of affectic between them.

"Matt will balk," she said anxiously. "You cannot expect s young a boy to love you on demand. Unless you show him patienc he will think that he is mine and Taris yours." Alysaun sighe

reseeing a great many problems in the future. "Be prepared for his
sentment, Brand. If you cannot weather it, he will never believe
u love him."

"The lad will know my love. I swear, he'll have no cause to
ubt it, Alys." Brand's answer was so confident that Alysaun's
ars were eased. '"Tis his mother I may have trouble convincing.
an you still doubt I love only you, Alysaun? How can I prove it?
k upon me some trial—ask anything—and let me reveal the depths
my devotion."

Alysaun took a deep breath and held it a moment. They would be
amily again and soon, but still she had reservations. "I think time
ust be your trial, Brand. Most gladly will I accept Taris as mine.
e will know nothing less than my full heart's love. Indeed, though
thought that her mother lay in your arms leaves me wounded,
tle Taris is innocent." Alysaun gazed down into the pool and
udied Brand's strong, even features reflected in the shimmering,
n-gilded water, at once determined to test him, yet regretful that
ch a trial was necessary.

"I wonder, though," she went on, then paused to look up at
n. "Pray have patience with me, Brand, and indulge my curiosity,
t what shape would your feelings take if, after this long separa-
n, 'twas *I* who presented you with a stranger's child? Would
u . . . *could you* . . . accept someone else's baby without nurturing
entment?"

The import of such a hypothesis left Brand too rattled to reply. It
d never entered his mind to question his wife's fidelity. Why
uld Alysaun even suggest . . . *unless* . . . but no, she had spent
e time in Hereward's protection. His eyes narrowed as he puzzled
er the odd question. There was a hint of worry in his eyes.

"You have set me back with your question, love, but the indul-
nce you seek is but a small thing. Loving you, I could do naught
t love something that is a part of you. Of a verity, would I accept
d raise the child as my own." Brand smiled and reached out to
oke Alysaun's cheek with a light caress. "Still, I cannot believe

you could ever be less than chaste. I know you well, my heart. (all your many virtues, faith to your vows stands high."

The innocent suggestion had baited the trap that closed wi Brand's assurances. Alysaun would have him back but not before l learned a lesson and marked it well. Every morning for the pa week when she arose, her stomach had turned with a telling nause She was carrying his child, but that would be her secret for a whil Now she smiled at her husband, slipping her hand in his. "Yo answer heartens my spirits, m'lord. I ... I feared you would reje such a love child and act out the wounded and betrayed spouse."

"Alysaun—'tis no time to tease me," Brand protested. "Th journey was long and wearing, and I ache from the overzealo pummeling of your protector's fists." Her eyes, wide and blu gazed steadily, unnervingly into his. The slender, alabaster finge that lay within his own sun-darkened hand rested serenely. "Car this jest no further, madame. Why would you unsettle me with a intimation I have been betrayed? There is no child to make me dou your constancy."

"Oh ... but there *is*, sire," Alysaun protested, still smiling. "A your promise to love and honor its innocence has reassured me of a untroubled future."

Brand dropped her hand and scowled. "You still harbor reser ment toward me, though you have claimed otherwise, m'lady. I w not knowingly unfaithful. If this pretense is meant as a punishment—

" 'Tis no pretense, sire," Alysaun insisted, managing a wound look at his accusation. "There will be three to round out o family." Seeming to puzzle over his reaction, she canted her hea and studied his flushed expression. "You did *mean* what yo promised, Brand? I know't must be a shock—"

"*Shock*?" Brand's voice was both righteous and indignant. "M lady, your confession leaves me *speechless*." Brand stared at he incredulous at how diffidently Alysaun had offered the revelation. " vowed I would not put resentment upon an innocent babe, but yo would welcome me back with proof of adultery and expect ... wha a docile and forgiving husband?" With his thinking clouded by

rkening jealousy, Brand silently cursed the man who had dared to
duce his wife. The bastard had somehow taken advantage of
ysaun and left his seed planted to make his trespass more intolera-
e. Alysaun's face was expressionless, neither ashamed nor
barrassed.

Brand stalked away some twenty paces before turning abruptly on
s heels to glower at her. It did not help his temper that she sat
ere, hands folded in her lap, returning his dark glare with a patient
durance. The very *least* she could do was appear contrite. "I
ver said I would withhold my rage from the knave responsible for
ch a . . . a sacrilege. Name him, Alys. He'll not live out the day."

Suddenly Brand glanced over his shoulder and thought of her
itor. When he faced her again, his eyes were hard and menacing.
'Twas that mooning calf who gazed at you in such open adoration,
sn't it?" Again Brand looked incredulous. He had been cuckolded —
d by a mere *boy*. His mouth curled in scorn. "How well good
end Hereward stood guard. He grows blind or worse in his
tage."

"Hereward knows nothing of this," Alysaun insisted firmly, her
in lifted in a challenge. "And Michael is innocent. Come, Brand,
u said yourself he was just a boy."

Brand clasped his hands behind his back and strode forward to
use before her and demand that she reveal the culprit's identity. "I
ll know who dared this . . . this outrage against what is mine, and
ne alone. 'Tis to avenge your sullied honor as well, Alysaun," he
imed. "I will and cannot believe you played the faithless whore.
was rape and must be answered for. Now, describe him or—"

"Or *what*, m'lord? Surely you do not threaten violence to my
rson?" Alysaun's fine, fair eyebrows drew together in rebuke.
Can this be the selfsame man who only moments ago spoke of his
dying love? The same who, with excuse of clouded memory,
ported with slaves and took another woman as his wife?"

For a moment Brand appeared dazed, unsteady. *Where was his sweet
d loving Alysaun?* This strongly independent woman who mocked
n with is own words could not be she. "The horns of a cuckold rest

uncomfortably upon my brow, Alysaun. Further, you have no excu
of a lapsed memory to whitewash this infidelity.''

Alysaun sighed with forbearance. '' 'Tis painful to be accused of
misdeed of which I am blameless. As you guessed, sire, the m
took me against my will. But you must suffer with your injur
pride. He, who did this, can no longer be held accountable. Ev
then, one might say his mind was not his own.''

How could she speak with such calm resignation, as if she were
cloistered nun, a pawn buffeted by divine will? "It strikes me o
that this witless devil left you carrying his spawn from one incide
of rape.''

Alysaun shrugged a shoulder. "God decides such matters, Bran
And . . . 'twas not''—Alysaun hesitated, the fullness of her lip caug
between two pearly teeth—"the one time only." She stared at h
lap, afraid the ruse would be spoiled by a temptation to smil
Brand's face was transfused with an angry red flush, his air
injured dignity almost comical. "Ask no more, I beg you,'' s
continued. "Neither of us can gain by hearing the details voiced.''

"You seem inordinately fond of this mystery lover,'' Bra
growled, wrestling with tormenting images that were all too vivi
"Just how did it come to pass that there was more than o
occurrence? Was your lover's manner so forceful? Or mayhap 'tw
you who found *him* irresistible.''

"I say again, m'lord, I am innocent of wrongdoing and w
elucidate no further except to add, 'tis in the past and better le
there.''

"Put aside such retiring modesty, Alys,'' Brand ordered with
darkly threatening scowl. "It comes late on the heels of discover
Answer me and I may be able to forgive. Deny me my justice an
'twill never be forgotten.''

Alysaun looked up, relishing the fact that her pretense was a twi
of truth that, when revealed, would teach her righteous, waywa
spouse a lesson he badly needed. For all the tears she had she
during the long years of uncertainty and worry, Brand deserved the
minutes of frustration. "He had pleasing ways about him, sire, and

tain arrogance that reminded me of you. My protests were as
thing, easily silenced by a mouth sure of its power to subdue.''
How dare she taunt him with a description of her lover's prowess?
nd you obviously found this blackguard so charming, so adroit at
luction, that you could scarce call a *defense*.'' Again his answer
s an infuriatingly careless shrug of shoulders that stung his
sculine pride.

'' 'Twas two years you were gone, two lonely and empty years,
and. I had every reason to assume you were dead.'' With one
ebrow arched, Alysaun defended her ''infidelity.'' ''Had you not
en so determined to teach me *all* the delights of wedded bliss...Oh,
y do not judge me so harshly, Brand. You pressed for my reasons.
was not as if I were an aged *widow*.''

''Aye, you were not, and I did ask,'' Brand grumbled, sorry now
it he had pressed her. ''You are *still* not a widow, m'lady,'' he
minded her, silently cursing the twist of fate that had separated
em and now made this deed hang between them like a dangling
ord. He could not help but ask one last question. ''Were you...in
e with him?''

Brand had suffered enough. He had passed beyond indignation
d was utterly miserable. ''No, my darling,'' Alysaun assured him.
le could not have my love...I think he did not care to have it.
ly he had my pity more than affection. A part of him ever seemed
sent, as if he'd lost a portion of his soul.''

It was a feeling Brand could understand. At least Alysaun hadn't
ed him; the admission was some balm to his bruised pride. ''Alys,
. I spoke an assurance to you earlier that I might find difficult to
nor. Each time I see his child in your arms, I fear I will know an
reasoning jealousy. 'Tis not just, I know, but God help me...I
e you so.''

Alysaun rose in a graceful swirl of silks. Catching his hands, she
ged them and, in a soft, gentle voice, and in the same reasoning
ie she might employ with Matt, she admitted the truth. ''Brand,
a you not pause long enough to guess who sired the child I carry?
I speak of a man who took me against my own will, would that

459

not be Cuibhil Rustim? And if I claim he was a skilled a
accomplished lover, will you deny my judgment? He did not ha
my love. I have loved only one man, and if I cannot have *him*, I w
have no other."

"It seems God's will that you will have him," Brand whispere
"fool that he has been. Alysaun . . . how can you forgive what I'
done, the things I've said?" Brand shook his head in self-disgu
His gaze swept over her face, tracing each perfect feature as
marveled that she still belonged to him. "Aye, a fool unknowing
and an idiot whose thoughts have been too full of himself. How c
you love a man who has caused you such grievous suffering?"

Alysaun smiled. Her heart was too full at this intimate moment
dwell on what was passed. She stretched on tiptoe to kiss the bruis
corner of his mouth, as she might to ease the hurt of a child. "Ti
washes forgetfulness over yesterday's troubles, m'lord, but it m
have our consent to work. You are home. We are together, as
should be." Alysaun gave that little shrug that had become a hab
"Is there anything else that matters?"

Brand couldn't think of a thing. His arms went around Alysau
pulling her close. For a long time he held her against him, stroki
her head. Desire was only a small part of his feelings. The great
part consisted of respect for this young woman who knew him bett
than he knew himself. Without Alysaun he was only half a ma
with her by his side, he was what fate had meant him to be—a po
in love with his inspiration. Theirs was a love that had been trie
Above the wind and fire of passion, it would endure as did the star

ROMANCE...ADVENTURE ...DANGER...
by Best-selling author,
Aola Vandergriff

DAUGHTERS OF THE SOUTHWIND
by *Aola Vandergriff*   *(D30-561, $3.50)*
The three McCleod sisters were beautiful, virtuous and bound to a dream—the dream of finding a new life in the untamed promise of the West. Their adventures in search of that dream provide the dimensions for this action-packed romantic bestseller.

DAUGHTERS OF THE WILD COUNTRY
by *Aola Vandergriff*   *(D30-562, $3.50)*
High in the North Country, three beautiful women begin new lives in a world where nature is raw, men are rough...and love, when it comes, shines like a gold nugget. Tamsen, Arab and Em McCleod now find themselves in Russian Alaska, where power, money and human life are the playthings of a displaced, decadent aristocracy in this lusty novel ripe with love, passion, spirit and adventure.

DAUGHTERS OF THE FAR ISLANDS
by *Aola Vandergriff*   *(D30-563, $3.50)*
Hawaii seems like Paradise to Tamsen and Arab—but it is not. Beneath the beauty, like the hot lava bubbling in the volcano's crater, trouble seethes in Paradise. The daughters are destined to be caught in the turmoil between Americans who want to keep their country. And in their own family, danger looms...and threatens to erupt and engulf them all.

DAUGHTERS OF THE OPAL SKIES
by *Aola Vandergriff*   *(D30-564, $3.50)*
Tamsen Tallant, most beautiful of the McCleod sisters, is alone in the Australian outback. Alone with a ranch to run, two rebellious teenage nieces to care for, and Opan Station's new head stockman to reckon with—a man whose very look holds a challenge. But Tamsen is prepared for danger—for she has seen the face of the Devil and he looks like a man.

DAUGHTER OF THE MISTY ISLES
        (D30-974, $3.50, U.S.A.)
by *Aola Vandergriff*   *(D30-975, $4.50, Canada)*
Settled in at Nell's Wotherspoon Manor, the McCleod sisters must carve new futures for their children and their men. Arab has her marriage and her courage put on the line. Tam learns to live without her lover. And even Nell will have to relinquish a dream. But the greatest challenge by far will be to secure the happiness of Luka whose romance threatens to tear the family apart.

Don't Miss These Exciting Romances by VALERIE SHERWOOD

___**WILD WILLFUL LOVE**

by Valerie Sherwood   *(D30-368, $3.)*

This is the fiery sequel to RASH RECKLESS LOVE. S
was once THE BUCCANEER'S LADY...but when bea
ful, willful Imogene was tricked aboard ship bound
England, she vowed to forget Captain van Ryker, the da
haired pirate who had filled her life and heart—only
banish her so cruelly. Somehow he would come to
again, and together they would soar to the heights of p
sion they first knew on the golden sands of a distant isl

___**BOLD BREATHLESS LOVE**   *(D30-849, $3.*

by Valerie Sherwood   *(In Canada 30-838, $4.*

The surging saga of Imogene, a goddess of grace with r
ous golden curls—and Verholst Van Rappard, her eleg
idolator. They marry and he carries her off to America—
knowing that Imogene pines for a copper-hai
Englishman who made her his on a distant isle and pro
ised to return to her on the wings of love.

___**RASH RECKLESS LOVE**   *(D30-701, $3.*

by Valerie Sherwood   *(In Canada 30-839, $4.*

Valerie Sherwood's latest, the thrilling sequel to
million-copy bestseller BOLD BREATHLESS LOVE. Ge
gianna, the only daughter of Imogene, whom no man co
gaze upon without yearning, was Fate's plaything
scorned when people thought her only a bondswoma
niece, courted as if she was a princess when Fortune m.
her a potential heiress.

You'll also want to read these thrilling bestsellers by *Jennifer Wilde*...